Lunar Logic

Adeena Mignogna

LUNAR LOGIC

Copyright © 2024 by Adeena Mignogna

This is a work of fiction. Names, characters, places, and incidents are the product of the author's imagination. Any resemblance to actual persons, living or dead, events, or locales, or actual robots, functioning or not, is entirely coincidental.

Edited by: Carolani Bartell

Book cover design by: Ebooklaunch.com

Robot art on front and back cover by: Aynslie Clark

Published by Crazy Robot, LLC

The Robot Galaxy Series

(an un-related series, filled with lots of robots)

Crazy Foolish Robots
Robots, Robots Everywhere!
Silly Insane Humans
Eleven Little Robots

1

Ai-dan stared at the neatly stacked tower of blocks on the table. Around them, Ai-dan's opponent and a smattering of the onlookers, who had abandoned their own activities, waited for them to make a move.

"I sense a pattern," said the opponent, Ai-ken. "I've calculated that you take an average of 3.14 seconds to decide your move."

To an outside observer, Ai-ken could easily have been Ai-dan's twin, identical in form, right down to the two upper appendages ending in dexterous digits. With one of these appendages, Ai-dan delicately extracted a wooden block from a trio at the very bottom of a teetering tower—a part of the structure that had remained untouched since the game began.

The stack stayed intact as Ai-dan fully removed the block and placed it on top. "There," they said. "Your move."

The primary physical feature distinguishing Ai-dan from Ai-ken was their outer covering. Ai-dan's hue was a light blue, but their surface bore the expected nicks and scratches of one who had clocked considerable time on the Moon's harsh terrain rather than within the shelter of this enclosure. Out there, dust, radiation, and sunlight were perpetual banes of Ai-dan's existence, slowly wearing down Ai-dan's protective coating until it required the application of a fresh coat. Ai-ken, in contrast, reflected a light green hue and appeared far from needing a new coat of paint. To an external observer, their base colors and the patterns of raised, thin rectangles on their chests were the only discernible features setting them apart.

"Is anyone timing Ai-ken?" Ai-dan asked the small group. "Since they are overly concerned in the duration of my deliberations, it's only fair to return the favor."

"I am," said Ainslea, or rather, a physical manifestation of Ainslea. A surrogate. An avatar. Ainslea had many names for this representation, and Ai-dan often wished she'd pick one and delete the rest. Extra words represented digital clutter that improved nothing. And nothing about this incarnation or its label changed the fact that Ainslea—the real Ainslea—was the resident AI in the large facility which housed them all at the moment. Ainslea controlled this surrogate remotely while maintaining the facility to a certain environmental standard that protected everyone from the elements, or lack thereof, on the planet they all inhabited. They called it "The Moon" and had spent many an hour discussing how they all came to know this as the name of their home.

Neither Ai-dan, nor Ainslea, nor any of the other robot inhabitants knew the origin of the word "Moon," nor the origin of themselves, nor the origin of anything. Most of the robots were content not to know.

Ai-dan was not most robots.

While the others powered down periodically or engaged in some task in their own facilities, Ai-dan pondered. Many, many hours spent pondering.

Two other robots sat at the far end of the table: Ai-ko and Ai-mory. Their game, one that had several small pits holding stones that each player had to pick up and redistribute, had been abandoned since they were all keenly interested in seeing who would make the stack of thin bricks fall. Reflecting a slightly different shade of light blue, Ai-mory could also have been a clone of Ai-dan save for the level of wear on their surface.

Ai-ko, however, reflected mostly white. Their sensor suite was also arranged differently, giving them a vastly different look from the others.

"I calculate very few moves either of them could make," said Ai-ko.

"Oh?" said Ai-dan. "I know exactly what move I'm making next, assuming Ai-ken successfully completes this round. I compute an 83 percent probability that Ai-ken's next move will cause the structure to topple."

"Care to bet on that?" Ai-ko quickly spat out, "Winner chooses next game." Ai-mory emitted a strained, metallic groan. While Ai-ko had only recently joined the others for game time, they picked up on the traditions quickly. This particular tradition was key. At some point during play, there was an opportunity for someone to offer to bet on the outcome. The winner always chose what game or games they would play next time.

"Of course," said Ai-dan. As they accepted Ai-ko's bet, two of the digits at the end of Ai-ken's light green appendage tugged at the block closest to them on the second row from the bottom. The tall stack moved with it a millimeter but then stopped as Ai-ken ceased moving. Then, Ai-ken pulled sharp and quickly, and for a moment, the structure seemed stable but as Ai-ken placed the block on top, the delicate equilibrium gave way, spilling all 54 blocks on the table, with three escaping to the floor.

"Unsuccessful," Ai-ken said, head down, before reaching for the spilled blocks.

Ai-ko and Ai-mory returned their attention to the much less exciting game in front of them. Ai-mory picked up a set of stones from one pit and started redistributing them among the rest of the pits.

Ai-dan and Ai-ken efficiently collected all 54 blocks. Ai-dan picked up the loading tray that had been set aside on the table.

"Ainslea?" Ai-dan turned to the avatar, who had been silently watching. "Your turn to play with me? We will decide who is the master stacker in District One?"

District One was where they were right now. Each of them belonged to a district, but they would frequently gather here during their downtime. This was the only district whose main building—the Data Center—contained a common room. Well, each Data Center had a common room, but this was the only one that had a door that opened up to a set of shelves stocked with games.

"Certainly," Ainslea replied. "I estimate that there is enough time for one more game before you are due for your daily tasks at the Farm. And everyone else will have their own tasks in their respective districts."

There were beeps of acknowledgment all around, including from Ai-dan.

Ai-dan was unique in more ways than one. For starters, they had the enviable job of working not only in their home District—District One—but also at the adjacent LEEK Farm. This 'farm' consisted of exactly 71 LEEKs, arranged in a geometrically satisfying hexagonal pattern over a square kilometer. Each LEEK—short for Laser Ensemble Extravaganza Kit—was a series of tubes mounted on a PLATE, which stood for Pulse Laser Alignment and Transmission Engine.

Neither Ai-dan, nor Ai-ko, nor any of their robot peers knew what the LEEK's primary function was. Nonetheless, Ai-dan's tasks ensured their continual operation. They knew a couple of things about them: a pattern of lights near the PLATE's entrance indicated operational status, and these contraptions guzzled power—almost as much as the Data Center, to be precise. Yet, the truly intriguing aspect of these LEEKs was not their mysterious energy consumption; it was that they all pointed at the blueish-whitish Orb in the sky.

The Orb was an object of frequent discussion. Especially since it changed over time. It was clearly rotating above them, and the features that the robots could discern were constantly in flux.

Before the others arrived for game time, Ai-dan had been on the surface studying the Orb and noticed that there were fewer wisps of white over the large brown and green patches than normal.

In this room, however, the Orb and sky were entirely out of sight. The space contained only a table and several occupied chairs, along with some distinct wall features. The wall features consisted of the portal to the anteroom that provided access to the outside—which they all used regularly. A second portal led to a smaller anteroom, then to what Ainslea referred to as 'the lab.' A third portal opened to a closet that stored Ainslea's array of avatars. Ai-dan had peeked into this closet numerous times as Ainslea emerged in avatar form and could see a door on the far end, though what lay beyond that, they did not know. Storage lockers lined the remaining wall space, along with the occasional display and control set.

"Who shall go first?" asked Ai-ken, even though they were now the one observing instead of actively playing.

"I think I would like to see Ainslea make the first move," Ai-dan responded.

Ainslea took no noticeable time and swiftly removed the center block from the bottom row and placed it in the center of the top of the stack.

Ainslea's avatars were more delicate, more nimble, and her digits more dexterous than Ai-dan's. These avatars, however, weren't engineered for the Moon's rugged surface. Dust would be disastrous to them. But for the block-stacking game at hand, they were superior, and that was what mattered now. Ai-dan prodded the middle block in the center row, a challenging move given their slightly larger digits compared to Ainslea's.

"I think you have an advantage," Ai-dan said.

"Master stacker," Ainslea said, "is what I believe we were playing for."

Ai-dan stopped poking at the block and studied the stack again.

"Indeed," they said, choosing a block on the outside of the stack mid-way up.

Ai-dan and Ainslea each took two more turns. Each time, Ainslea's move was swift and sure and quick, while Ai-dan pondered and calculated and nearly toppled the stack each time.

"I calculate—" Ai-ken began, and Ai-dan cut him off.

"No more calculating. It is clear that it is only a matter of time before I topple this, so..."

Ai-dan placed digits on both remaining pieces of the bottom row.

"The rules clearly state that you are only allowed to touch one piece at a time," Ai-ken and Ainslea said nearly simultaneously. At that, Ai-ko and Ai-mory looked up again from their game. The block stacking game was once more the most interesting thing happening in the room.

"I'm trying an experiment," Ai-dan said. "The game is over. It's play-time."

Ai-dan pulled at both blocks simultaneously. Without their support, the rest of the stack let gravity pull it to the table. It wobbled a bit while everyone beeped and chirped, and then...

The stack stayed in place.

"Success!" Ai-dan declared.

"Indeed," said Ainslea, "but I believe I won the game."

The center of Ai-dan's optical sensors expanded, and the miniature actuator motors around their lower auditory opening turned up slightly as Ai-dan looked directly at Ainslea.

"Agreed," Ai-dan said, adding a playful tweak to their voice. It was their way of conveying extra information via a single word. In this case, that extra information was, "I'm having a great time playing my own games as well."

Ai-ko dropped the last of their stones into the large pit at the end of their game board. "Speaking of winning," Ai-ko said, waving an appendage over the board, the stones, and in front of Ai-mory. "Now, I have duties I need to perform. I will return in 22 point five hours for another round."

Ai-ko stood up, almost a little too quickly. There was a limit to how fast one could make certain movements. Too quickly would result in launching oneself to the ceiling. Everyone watched Ai-ko. It was only after Ai-ko closed the hatch to the anteroom behind them, and they all heard the hiss of the anteroom depressurization, that someone else spoke.

"By my accounting, Ai-ko could have stayed another twenty minutes with us," said Ai-mory.

Ai-dan didn't vocalize it but suspected the reason Ai-ko was leaving early was to take a detour on the way back to District Seven. The Farm, while not exactly on the way, was close enough to make a scenic detour.

Ai-ko was among a growing number of robots who were taking additional interest in the Farm. The Farm was, after all, the most extraordinary aspect of the robots' life on the Moon.

Ai-dan themself might have felt some special worship towards the looming structures if they didn't interact with them daily. As the sole robot tasked with the Farm's maintenance, Ai-dan's emotions on the subject fluctuated. Some days, loneliness settled in, making them wish for more company than just Ainslea's voice while working. Other days, Ai-dan felt the weight of importance and was excited to be chosen for such a position. But today, the prevailing sentiment was a very apathetic 'meh.' Time seemed to blur together, and Ai-dan languished. When this mode set in, they found themself staring off into space for far too long, missing snippets of conversations they'd normally catch. Although Ai-dan knew their excitement would rekindle eventually, today's overriding feeling remained resolutely, 'meh.'

Ai-dan had two modes of attention. The first adhered to their built-in instructions—a focus directed by explicit guidelines. The other was more exploratory, venturing beyond the confines of their designated responsibilities. This second form of attention was triggered on a day several cycles ago when they noticed an unfamiliar robot at the edge of the adjoining District, simply standing and staring at the Farm. It had been many cycles—years, in fact—since Ai-dan encountered a robot they didn't already know. Intrigued, Ai-dan approached the robot. "I'm Ai-dan. I'm the keeper of the Farm. Can I help you?"

The robot's optical sensors shuttered in a blink, and they lost focus on the Farm and directed their attention to Ai-dan.

"I am Ai-ko."

"Can I help you?"

"Do you have answers?" Ai-ko responded with a their own question.

"I might," Ai-dan replied. "It depends on the questions."

"Why are these here? The Farm? The LEEKs?"

Ai-dan thought for a moment, letting their search algorithm cover the depths of their memory. Their memory contained nothing indicating any knowledge of the origin of the Farm.

"I don't know," Ai-dan was forced to respond.

"Did you create them?" Ai-ko asked.

"No." It was a simpler answer, and Ai-dan predicted the next question.

"Who did?"

It was a question that Ai-dan had occasionally pondered but eventually removed from their active processors. Not only did they lack an answer, but Ai-dan was also convinced that if they didn't know, and Ainslea didn't either, then no one did. In Ai-dan's assessment, Ainslea had the highest potential to know everything there was to know among all lunar robots, thanks to her expansive memory core. However, two things became evident over time. First, no one really knew the extent of 'everything there was to know,' so claiming comprehensive knowledge was futile. Second, there was no method to verify whether Ainslea truly could know it all. Thusly, Ai-dan had to acknowledge the possibility of limits to Ainslea's understanding. These thoughts made Ai-dan's circuits tingle, but not in the satisfying way they did when winning various games.

"No one knows," Ai-dan responded.

"That makes no sense. Someone must," said Ai-ko.

"Why?" asked Ai-dan but internally acknowledged that it was an interesting concept. Ai-dan let the word 'must' dangle around their circuits.

"Because it exists. If it exists, it was created. If it was created, there must be a creator." Ai-ko knelt down in the dust of the Moon. "Let me demonstrate."

Ai-ko used their fingers and inscribed a replication of the outline of one of the LEEKs in the dust.

"See?"

"I see a picture in the dust," Ai-dan said.

"Exactly!" Ai-ko's thermal output increased. "It was not there. Now it is. I created it. I am the creator."

Ai-dan stared at the picture and then at the Farm.

"But," Ai-dan said, "we both recognize there was a point in time when your picture didn't exist. The Farm has always existed."

"Are you sure?"

Ai-dan was *not* sure. They stared at the Farm, attempting to see the landscape as it might have been without the structures of the Farm pointing to the Orb in the sky. When Ai-dan looked back at Ai-ko, Ai-ko was walking away.

Since that day, Ai-ko returned to stare at the Farm routinely. They would sometimes ask Ai-dan more curious questions that Ai-dan didn't have answers to, and that continued to make their circuits tingle. After several of these rendezvous, Ai-dan asked Ai-ko to join in on the games they played with other robots in the common room of the District One Data Center. Ai-ko was a unique and welcome change to the monotony of the existing group, although Ai-dan would never say that out loud. Ai-dan suspected that 'monotonous' would not come off as a compliment, even though they didn't mean it in an entirely negative way.

Ai-ko attended the regular games but was usually the quietest robot in the group—a contrast to their verbosity when it was the two of them alone together. From follow-up discussions, Ai-dan knew Ai-ko sat quietly contemplating one of three concepts: the game of choice that day, the ends of their appendages, which manipulated game pieces, or both. Ai-dan wanted to ask Ai-ko which one they were actually fixated on, but every time they thought about trying, decided there was no point. Any answer would not improve their true knowledge.

After Ai-ko left the game this evening, however, Ainslea asked:

"Will Ai-ko be joining us again?"

Ai-dan looked at Ainslea's avatar. Ai-dan was used to the construct. It was another object that was unique to this district. The other districts all had similar structures that housed an Ainslea clone, but to Ai-dan's knowledge, none of them employed the range of physical avatars to engage in additional interaction with the other robots and the world around them. Ai-dan, silently conspiring with their own curiosity, mulled over why this Ainslea was different from the other Data Centers, and why they wouldn't—or couldn't—execute a subroutine to ask.

"Of course they'll be joining us again," Ai-dan responded confidently.

"Perhaps that is no longer a good idea," Ainslea said.

"Why not?"

Ainslea didn't respond immediately. The Ainslea avatar swept its optical sensors from one robot to the next, ensuring that every other mechanical eye was on her rather than engrossed in their games.

"Ai-ko is spreading ideas."

Ai-dan's optical sensors autonomously made a circle around their main axis, then Ai-dan regained control of them and narrowed those sensors at Ainslea. This was not the first time Ainslea had expressed a dislike for Ai-ko's questions—Ai-dan had long since regretted ever telling Ainslea that Ai-ko asked questions when the two of them were alone. But more than that, Ai-dan didn't appreciate the aversion to Ai-ko for something that seemed so trivial.

"That's not a bad thing," Ai-dan said.

"What ideas are you talking about?" asked Ai-ken. Both Ai-ken and Ai-mory looked expectantly at Ai-dan.

"Ai-ko asks questions about the Creator," Ai-dan responded. Ai-dan watched Ainslea's avatar move in a way that Ai-dan registered as displeasure, but that didn't stop Ai-dan from continuing. "Ai-ko believes that by asking questions, we'll discover some new truths about our existence."

"Why is Ai-ko curious about things like that?" Ai-mory asked.

Ai-dan responded, "Perhaps knowing what the Creator—," Ai-dan cut themself off and corrected, "*If* a Creator existed, knowing what they want could make us more productive and efficient. However, this is merely a guess, and I couldn't be certain without asking Ai-ko."

"And you?" Ai-ken asked.

"I see no harm in the questions."

"Well, I do," replied Ainslea's avatar. "A robot has no business probing about a Creator, a mythical entity that we can't prove exists since we lack empirical evidence. A robot has a function to perform and should focus on that function."

"Then why are we here playing games? And why do you join us?" Ai-dan asked pointedly. Ainslea sometimes made Ai-dan's circuits itch, but more often than not, was simply amusing to all of them.

When Ainslea didn't answer, Ai-dan moved on. "Should we reset the stack, Ai-ken?"

"I believe I'd like to play one more round with Ainslea. Ainslea?"

A moment passed, and Ai-dan and Ainslea's avatar stared at each other. Ai-dan broke the silence when they said, "I like your other avatar better. It's not as... obtuse."

"Go ahead and play with Ai-ken," it responded.

"Ai-ken, play this one with me," Ai-mory said. They were already resetting the small stones to their original positions.

"The creator has been quite the engaging topic of discussion between the districts," Ai-mory said, moving around the various stones between the pits so there were not only four in each, but the colors in each pit matched. And to Ainslea's avatar, Ai-mory said, "Maybe we don't need to know anything about our Creator—if there is a Creator. Maybe it's not a way to improve our lives, not that I see anything that needs improving. But I agree with Ai-dan. I don't see harm in the questions." Ai-mory then turned to Ai-dan, and their stoic expression brightened slightly. "I'd like to play that next. After I beat Ainslea at stones."

Ai-dan nearly had all the blocks stacked in the tray and formed them so they were ready to play.

"Ai-ken, you can go first," Ai-dan said.

Each robot made half a dozen moves before it became a challenge to find one that wasn't sure to topple the stack. In the meantime, Ai-mory did not beat Ainslea at stones as they expected.

"Well," Ai-mory announced to the room, standing up and knocking the table as they did so. The table wobbled, and so did the stack, which toppled all the blocks to the table and the floor. "Oh, I'm sorry," they said. "Or not. By my accounting, which I can safely assume is the same as all of yours, I won the fewest games this session. I declare the session concluded."

This was allowed, as they all knew that it was nearly time for the robots to start their preset daily routines.

Ai-mory and Ai-ken made similar cautious exits as Ai-ko, ensuring that they did not propel themselves hard enough to launch to the ceiling.

When they were gone, Ai-dan stood and gathered the blocks into a final stack to be placed back into a plastic box and stored away for another time.

Ai-dan said to the avatar: "You didn't answer *my* question. Why do you continue to interact with us if you're unhappy with our discussions? It's... inefficient."

The avatar stood up and walked to the end of the room by the closet's portal. "Because," it began, "part of *my* core directives is to ensure the well-being of the rest of you."

The avatar pressed a button, and the closet door slid open. Ai-dan glimpsed a wall lined with a variety of inactive avatars, all nearly identical and at Ainslea's disposal. Ai-dan puzzled over why so many existed when, one, they were all confined to the Data Center and two, Ainslea operated only one at a time, despite the ability to switch between them all.

A wave of familiar envy passed over Ai-dan once again. Ai-dan occasionally wished to possess Ainslea's ability to inhabit multiple avatars themself. Yet a counter thought kept them from vocalizing that desire. Would they still be Ai-dan if they were in another body, or would they become something entirely different?

Ai-dan frequently interacted with Ainslea, who could inhabit a range of avatars and control several drones to assist Ai-dan with their work. Ai-dan had an extensive set of data conclusively indicating that Ainslea was always Ainslea, no matter which of these avatars or drones she inhabited. But just because Ainslea worked that way, would Ai-dan work the same way? That thought was the one that kept them from asking Ainslea if it was possible. Ai-dan also knew that she wouldn't like that question either. They were used to keeping several of their unique thoughts to themself and found themself doing so more and more recently as Ainslea continued to express dislike for the new ideas of the Creator that were spreading around the Moon.

Once Ainslea's avatar embedded itself in a location previously unoccupied in the closet, the door shut. Ai-dan put the games back in their storage locker and set out to start their duties for the day at the Farm.

2

Ai-dan walked along the path to the Farm, a journey they repeated with such consistency it might as well have been a built-in routine. If Ai-dan was short on time, they could double their speed by running. This was an option Ai-dan rarely took. On the Moon, running was an exercise in precision. Each running stride meant launching themself off the surface for five seconds during which they had very little control over their movement. If their launch wasn't perfect, correcting it mid-trajectory was impossible. It was easier and safer to keep a steady pace on the paths that were perfectly suited to the bottom of their lower appendages.

District One sprawled out a full square kilometer, with paths leading directly to the Farm. As Ai-dan followed the path, they passed adjacent rows of solar panels actively collecting power from the Sun. While every district on the Moon had its own array of these panels, District One boasted the largest quantity of them. They served as a reasonably reliable backup for that rare moment, once every twenty years, when the fusion bins were in need of repair or refueling.

Ai-dan examined the solar arrays beside the path they walked along. Dust had begun to accumulate, but not to the extent that immediate attention was required. Once Ai-dan's duties at the Farm were complete, they would spend the remainder of today's operational time sweeping Moon dust off these solar panels.

The combination of solar and nuclear power not only fueled the Farm and the Data Centers but also enabled Ai-dan and all other robots to recharge every third day. Additionally, it ensured uninterrupted operation during the Moon's thirteen and a half days of continual darkness every twenty-eight.

As Ai-dan approached the Farm, they could sense something was awry. Scanning the towering LEEKs one by one, they found them all oriented as usual, aiming at the Orb in the sky. However, LEEK 3.2 was an exception. Its usual indicator light, that should have shown on its end, was absent, and the entrance light to the PLATE support equipment room glowed an unsettling shade of bright red.

Ai-dan anxiously checked their internal messaging system. Ai-dan should have received an alert if there was a malfunction. Ai-dan wondered if Ai-ko had passed by and noticed anything amiss, like a missing light. After all, Ai-ko had a choice when moving between their home district—District Seven—and District One. There were several paths: ones that linked Data Center to Data Center, and ones that went through a corner of the Farm.

Or perhaps the malfunction occurred just moments before Ai-dan arrived, coinciding with an unusual delay in the message. Ai-dan knew they were not gifted with every tidbit of information about how everything in their world worked. Why did they possess some inherent knowledge and not other knowledge? Was it conceivable for them to learn anymore?

Ai-dan's interactions with other robots enabled them to learn that Ai-dan often knew more than many, if not most, or maybe all, of them. Aside from Ainslea, of course. Individually, their own lack of knowledge didn't bother most robots. Everyone seemed to have precisely the right information to function, and no more.

Ai-dan opened the entranceway door to the tiny, single-robot antechamber to the PLATE operations cabinet of LEEK 3.2.

The problem was immediately obvious. The LEEK was not receiving power. Power outages of this sort were rare but occurred occasionally. Large, thick cables ran over the surface of the Moon, usually adjacent to the paths, and provided power to the Farm and to the Data Centers. They were incredibly tough but not immune to environmental effects.

Ai-dan reasoned that the same issue causing the power outage might also have prevented the notification message from being sent.

Not a colossal problem in the grand scheme of things, but their daily schedule would have to be modified somewhat.

This is when having Ainslea, with their drones, came in handy.

"Ainslea, this is Ai-dan." Ai-dan opened up a communication channel to Ainslea from their internal wireless comm system.

"How may I be of assistance?" was Ainslea's standard return greeting.

"Power is out in 3.2. Efficiency dictates that I ask if you will wipe off the arrays while I fix this?"

"Certainly. I can send two drones out for that task. Do you need any assistance with restoring power?"

Simultaneously, while communicating with Ainslea, Ai-dan maneuvered themself to the other side of the PLATE. They opened a tiny hatch—clearly designed to protect its innards from dust—and connected themself with a prong extended from their palm. Oddly, Ai-dan received nothing, not even the tiniest *zip*, which meant that the backup power—meant to keep a small amount of diagnostic electronics online—wasn't active either. *Looks like the hiccup is with the power trunk,* Ai-dan thought.

"No, not at this time," Ai-dan responded. While Ai-dan suspected they might need additional help, 'assistance' from Ainslea often amounted to micro-managing their work. It was like having someone perpetually hovering over your shoulder, questioning your every move. Ainslea, blessed with more knowledge than Ai-dan, rarely missed an opportunity to flaunt it.

"I'll contact you if that changes. Thanks for assisting with the solar panels." Ai-dan said, then closed the connection.

Ai-dan returned to the antechamber and connected to a different kind of plug. This one allowed Ai-dan to siphon off some of their own power to the PLATE. Enough to operate the de-dusting equipment, pressurize the anteroom to match the operations cabinet's ambient pressure, and get inside the PLATE's cabinet. Ai-dan felt the extra load on their systems. They'd spend time recharging and refreshing themself later.

Once inside the operations cabinet—essentially the room that housed all the support equipment to keep the PLATE and LEEK functioning—Ai-dan's first impression was that it was dark. However, the term 'dark' was not absolute. Ai-dan's keen optical sensors allowed them a level of visibility even with merely a hint of ambient light. Their vision was acute enough to maneuver without bumping into anything and even read signs if need be.

Noticing the environmental temperature, Ai-dan grew concerned. They calculated that this LEEK must have been offline for nearly two days. That coincided with the start of the current sunlight period.

Ai-dan searched their memory for their most recent activity involving LEEK 3.2, and there was nothing unusual. Ai-dan was here at the Farm immediately after first sunlight, performing routine maintenance on another LEEK. No anomalies registered.

Ai-dan walked to the far side of the room, avoiding several racks of equipment. At the far side wall, Ai-dan opened up a large panel and swung a large slide switch from one side to the other, selecting a redundant power source. The room hummed to life.

Ai-dan confirmed that all the equipment was executing their respective boot-up sequences—most of which were nothing more than a series of flashing red and yellow lights before settling in on a steady green that indicated it was performing its primary function. What each piece of equipment's primary function was, Ai-dan had no clue. Ai-dan simply could report on their binary state of functioning versus not and, if not, receive instructions from Ainslea on what to do about it.

After several minutes, Ai-dan plugged themself into the diagnostic port and confirmed that the LEEK with its PLATE had indeed gone offline shortly before sunlight.

How very odd, they thought.

But it was functioning now, so it was safe for them to leave and determine where the malfunction in the trunk power originated.

Ai-dan exited the room via the antechamber, and was back on the lunar surface. The first thing they did was step back far enough to see the light on the end of the LEEK blinking in its regular pattern.

Ai-dan computed that their next troubleshooting step involved locating the large power trunk line attached to the base of this LEEK. At this location, it co-mingled with another beefy line. Ai-dan knew this second line as "District Thirty-Two Pipe" but knew little more about its function. Ai-dan walked along the dual lines until the lines split. Ai-dan intended to continue along the power line to the source, but once the split came into sight, they knew they found the source of the problem.

A small box was unexpectedly protruding from the pipeline.

Ai-dan did not recognize the box. While they didn't know the function of every box in the PLATE, they at least had visuals of every box stored in their memory. This box did not match any of those. It also did not match anything they'd seen in the Data Center. Or anywhere else on the Moon. This box was... unique.

Ai-dan tilted their head back and forth while looking down at this unique box sitting on the pipe. However, upon closer inspection, it became clear that the box was more than simply resting there; several hooks protruded from its perimeter, having pierced the outer shell of the pipe. Ai-dan squatted down to inspect the box and its protrusions a little deeper. It appeared that the piercing had degraded the integrity of the outer shell of the power line. There was a tear. Moon dust, possibly mixed with other particles, had settled in that tear. That was certainly responsible for the problems with the power line.

Ai-dan let their gaze follow the District Thirty-Two Pipe all the way to the eastern horizon. District Thirty-Two lay far beyond what they could see. Ai-dan knew the robot that occupied that district only by name. They had never interacted directly. Ai-dan's memory stores contained a list of all the Districts, the robot—and in very few cases, robots—that took care of them, and their location, but knew little else. This lack of knowledge, something that typically wasn't an issue, was starting to make Ai-dan's circuits get that itchy feeling again. Districts were not more special than each other and the fact that this problem had affected only District Thirty-Two was weird.

No, some Districts were slightly more special. Some had two centers, and a second robot, but that was it.

Ai dan searched their memory for some other useful tidbit about District Thirty-Two and realized that there was one other unique thing, but needed to check with Ainslea.

"Ainslea," Ai-dan re-opened their comms link.

"How may I be of assistance?"

"Do you remember when LEEK 3.2 became active?" Ai-dan asked.

"Yes. It was June 1st, 2120 at 0800."

"What was it doing before that?"

"I do not understand the question."

"The LEEK was here, right?" Ai-dan continued to probe.

"Correct," Ainslea replied.

"But it wasn't active?"

"Correct."

"Why not?"

There was a pause before Ainslea responded, "I do not have that information. The only additional information I have was that June 1st was a Saturday."

"Thank you, Ainslea," said Ai-dan, now wishing to end the communication. Ainslea didn't have more information, but Ai-dan was beginning to realize that sometimes no information was information.

"Can I be of additional assistance?"

"No, that's all for now. I've located the problem with LEEK 3.2 and have a plan to effect repairs immediately."

Ai-dan closed the connection and then brought their attention back to the box attached to the pipe. Ai-dan computed that they should simply remove the box, then execute a patch to both lines. Moon dust, unmoving, was benign. But Moon dust, when abraded on any surface, had a tendency to shred that surface.

The outer skins of the pipes were a malleable material. Malleable enough so that the pipes did not have to be rigid, but strong enough to withstand most of what the Moon had to dish out—to include extreme temperature fluctuations and excess radiation exposure. As long as there were no punctures in the material, it protected its contents. But with any kind of puncture, the innards were at risk.

Four small storage sheds pockmarked the Farm. These small structures housed various materials that were at Ai-dan's disposal to make repairs. They were small only compared to the LEEKs and the Data Centers.

Ai-dan located the shed closest to their present location and went to gather a patching material goop along with an electro-static blower and a vial of goo-tack. The electro-static blower would allow Ai-dan to remove most of the particulates that were in the wounds in a way that they didn't entirely understand, and the goo-tack would remove as much dust as possible.

Back at the problem area, it was time to remove the offending object. Ai-dan grabbed both sides. It was made of a metal that was not easily or immediately identifiable. It was very warm to the touch—actually hot, upon second thought. Ai-dan pulled on it, and the box removed easily enough, several wires that were embedded into the pipe coming with it. One wire was deliberately set into the power trunk. Ai-dan removed that, too.

They set the box aside for now and applied the goo-tack to the opening. The stuff was a putty material that Ai-dan handled daily, or anytime they entered a Data Center. Ai-dan mushed it into the opening and then pulled it out. They could see bits of dust stuck to the putty and were pleased. Next, they turned on the electro-static blower and aimed it into the corner of the opening. A few more bits of debris flew out and up above Ai-dan's head before settling back to the surface. Once Ai-dan satisfied themself that they removed all the junk they could, they opened the container of malleable patch goop and applied it to the pipe's surface. The goop would bond with the existing material. Any robot looking at the repaired pipe later would see a repair scar. The pipe no longer had the sleek line of an uninterrupted cable.

While waiting for the material to set, Ai-dan crouched down on the Moon's surface and stared at the box.

Ai-dan touched it. The temperature remained consistent, which meant that the internal heat source was still active, at least for the moment.

What are you, and where did you come from? Ai-dan wondered. They continued to search their memory but still couldn't recall seeing anything like it amongst the various equipment Ai-dan knew. This box didn't fit in. The box didn't appear as if it was created by the same... Ai-dan didn't know the word... by the same *something* that created everything else around them.

"Ai-ko," Ai-dan opened a new communication channel.

"Ai-dan. Connection acknowledged," was the standard greeting whenever two robots communicated directly.

"Did you come by the Farm after you left our game?"

"Yes, only along the corner to my District," Ai-ko responded.

Ai-dan performed a quick calculation. Ai-ko wouldn't have seen LEEK 3.2 from that vantage point, hence why Ai-ko didn't alert anyone to a problem. Ai-ko wouldn't have known there was a problem.

When Ai-dan said nothing else, Ai-ko continued, "Was that your only question?"

No, Ai-dan thought, *I have dozens more.*

But Ai-dan kept those questions private for the moment. Ai-dan wasn't sure how they were even going to log this and what Ainslea was going to say to Ai-dan later, after reviewing their logs. Ainslea was quite diligent with log reviews.

"No, Ai-ko, thank you. Will we see you next game?"

A pause on their end.

"Yes. I shall be there." Ai-ko then terminated the connection.

Ai-dan picked up the box and returned to the shed along with the electro-static blower and goo-tack. The shed did not contain an antechamber like the Data Center or PLATE control room but could be pressurized if needed, and contained plenty of de-dusting equipment.

"And what do I do with you?" Ai-dan said, pretending they were in communication with the box.

The box provided no response but let Ai-dan put it on a shelf, out of the way.

3

"Have you determined what it is?" Ai-ko asked Ai-dan.

The two of them were in one of the storage sheds of the Farm. It was one that Ai-dan had turned into a workshop several years earlier in order to have a place to repair equipment while simultaneously avoiding the often punishing effects of the Moon's surface.

While Ai-dan was practically invincible on the surface, most of the equipment struggled to withstand the hazardous environment, serving as a source of constant frustration for Ai-dan. It was yet another one of life's mysteries that Ai-dan grappled with. Ai-ko, who had always expressed their curiosity to Ai-dan since they'd met, was always keen to hear about Ai-dan's thoughts and activities, so Ai-dan typically confided in them.

As a result, Ai-ko was a frequent visitor to Ai-dan's workshop. The only visitor.

Ai-dan shook their head. "No. But..." and turned the device around and removed a panel.

"If you look into it through this port, and look at this..." Ai-dan pointed with a screwdriver at some of the delicate innards, "Do you see?"

Ai-ko followed the tip of the screwdriver into the bowels of the strange device. Then the small actuators that indicated expressions on their head dipped downward. Ai-ko did not like what they saw—components that looked very familiar, as if they did in fact originate from the same source as the robots, Data Centers, and everything else on the Moon.

"Yes," Ai-ko responded. "And what did Ainslea say?"

Ai-dan shook their head slightly back and forth.

"I haven't told Ainslea about this yet."

"Oh? Why not?"

Ai-dan fixated on the device, trying to appear as if they were not ignoring Ai-ko's question. Which they were. They were at a loss to express what they were thinking. There was no logical reason not to tell Ainslea about it. The trails of logic seemed to zig-zag into a web that Ai-dan couldn't process their way out of.

So, Ai-ko continued.

"Here. We can resolve this quickly and simply with simple logic. If you did not install this, then Ainslea must have taken one of their components and used an Avatar to execute the installation."

"I agree," said Ai-dan, "But if they did, there has to be a reason, and I cannot fathom a reason that makes sense. And if Ainslea did something that doesn't make sense..."

Ai-ko nodded, and it pleased Ai-dan that Ai-ko seemed to understand what they were saying, even without uttering a complete thought.

Both Ai-dan and Ai-ko had heard stories of robots who behaved contrary to who they were. At some point, that behavior interfered with their ability to carry out their primary functions. Robots who behaved this way were reset. Neither Ai-dan nor Ai-ko had ever met a reset robot themselves, but the stories that circled from one district to another conveyed the same tale: reset robots lost all memories of their lives, regressing to a state where all they did was focus on their functions, even needing to relearn rudimentary activities, such as how to play all the games they enjoyed. They were never themselves again.

"I know Ainslea and I disagree frequently," Ai-dan broke the silence that had engulfed them. "But I can't imagine passing my days without her to talk to."

Ai-ko added after another minute, "I think you're going to have to ask Ainslea about this. I can compute no better course of action. You need to ask if Ainslea installed this device."

"Well, that could lead to a new problem," Ai-dan said.

"How so?"

"What if it wasn't her?"

4

Ai-dan couldn't simply walk into the Data Center.

Well, they could. But only after twenty minutes in the anteroom. Here, Ai-dan spent their time under the extra-sensitive electro-static dust removers, and using goo-tack putty to help remove as much dust and bits of debris as they could from themself and the mystery box.

Once de-dusted, Ai-dan walked into the Data Center. They held the mystery box and placed it on the table in the common room—the same table that Ai-dan and the other robots had been playing games at earlier.

Ai-dan didn't need to say anything to announce their presence. Ainslea knew Ai-dan was there. Ainslea logged all entrances and exits to the Data Center, logged time spent de-dusting, and even logged the quantity and material composition of the dust that was removed. Most of it was simple silicon dioxide and aluminum oxide, but occasionally an iron or titanium dioxide molecule was present. Those were exciting days.

When Ainslea was ready, she would either start speaking or present herself in avatar form. Ai-dan knew Ainslea and her algorithms well enough that they could usually predict which form Ainslea would take.

Not today.

Not with this new information.

Ai-dan waited. Ainslea didn't speak, nor did an avatar appear.

In the silence, Ai-dan's thoughts drifted to replaying the last game, and they recalculated their moves. "Ugh," Ai-dan uttered out loud. "I should have picked a different block that one set..." Apparently, that triggered Ainslea.

"How may I be of assistance?"

For a brief moment, because Ai-dan was lost in thought, they had to reset their thoughts to the present. Ai-dan stared at the box on the table.

"You could tell me if this troublesome box belongs to you."

"What is it?"

"I was hoping you could tell me."

"Stand by."

A few quiet moments passed. Quiet in the room, that was. Ai-dan's thoughts were not quiet at all, but rather filled with a constant buzz of extrapolations and possibilities. Some still related to the earlier game, but most related to this box. Their algorithms churned, charged circuits rushing through their pathways, curiosity gnawing at them for answers.

Finally, the door on the far side of the room slid open, and an avatar produced itself. Ai-dan was familiar with this model—the one with the most extremely dexterous hands.

Ainslea's avatar sat down in the seat closest to the device. The avatar shifted its body to move its head to look at the box from all angles, no doubt scanning the surface in several different parts of the electro-magnetic spectrum.

Once completed, Ainslea said, "I repeat. What is it?"

"You really don't know?" Ai-dan asked while lowering themself down into the seat at the opposite end of the table.

"No," Ainslea said. The avatar's hands opened the side panel, the same one Ai-dan had poked around in. The avatar blinked its sensors, focusing them in every direction possible to examine the array of components that constituted the innards of the mysterious box. "I can identify many of the individual components, but I have never seen them arranged in this unique configuration. I can conclude that I have never encountered a contraption such as this before."

"I, too, recognized many of the pieces as similar to yours. That's why I was hoping you knew what this was."

"Where did you find it?"

"Attached to the data pipe of LEEK 3.2. It was also connected to the power line. I determined this device caused the power failure at the LEEK."

"Interesting." Ainslea's words hung in the air, a mere acknowledgment. But the avatar made no additional movements to take the device apart or study its mysteries further. In fact, Ainslea's avatar conveyed only disinterest, which was confusing to Ai-dan.

"Is that all you have to say?" Ai-dan asked with slightly more urgency. "Don't you want to know where it came from?"

"Of course. It damaged equipment in our care. Of course, I want to know where it came from. Where did it come from?"

"I have no idea," the tone of Ai-dan's voice changed. This alerted Ainslea and the avatar abruptly sat up and stared right into their optical sensors.

"Are you upset?"

"No," Ai-dan said, reverting back to their typical robotic monotone. "But I have some theories, and none of them are good." And after a moment they added, "plus Ai-ko..."

"Ai-ko?"

The way Ainslea said their name sent a short, electronic pulse to Ai-dan's core. Ai-ko was clearly not Ainslea's favorite robot. Ai-dan weighed their options, not wanting to provide Ainslea or hear her lectures, but the nag of curiosity outweighed everything else.

"Yes. Ai-ko has a theory."

"What is Ai-ko's theory?"

"That the Creators left it here."

Ainslea's avatar sealed the box shut. The avatar looked at Ai-dan condescendingly.

"There are no Creators."

There it was.

"You say that, and yet there is evidence..."

"There is no evidence," responded Ainslea without a thought.

"Yes, there is. Our existence is evidence..."

Ainslea cut him off. "Do not start the pattern of circular logic once again. You will damage your circuits." The avatar stood up, and delicate appendages reached out to pick up the box.

"I know," Ai-dan said. "If I accept the existence of Creators because of our existence, then I have to ponder who created the Creators because of their existence, and who created them, and so on. There is no end."

Ai-dan was suddenly aware of how fast their circuits were firing and willed them to slow down.

"What are you doing with that?" they asked Ainslea, as the avatar started walking away with the box.

"Further study," Ainslea said. "I will bring it to the lab, take it apart for analysis and learn what it is all about."

"And you'll let me know the results?" Ai-dan asked.

"Affirmative," responded the avatar. Ai-dan might as well have asked any routine question, the way the avatar tonelessly answered.

Ai-dan must have given off a signal that they were displeased, because as the avatar was on its way out of the room, Ainslea's voice sounded through the speaker, "Of course I'll let you know." The door, which had silently opened, now closed shut with Ainslea's avatar and the mystery box behind it.

5

Ai-dan left the Data Center and made their way back to the far edge of the Farm. Ai-ko was already there, waiting.

Ai-dan simply could have contacted Ai-ko over comms, but then Ainslea's Data Center would've recorded it. Ai-dan did not know if that meant that Ainslea reviewed those comms. At the very least she could if she wanted to. But Ai-dan found themself not wanting records of their conversations, whether it was about suspicious matters or not.

Not that Ai-dan was suspicious of Ainslea. Ai-dan believed that Ainslea genuinely did not know what that device was. Although perhaps Ai-dan's suspicions of Ainslea's suspicions towards Ai-dan meant that Ai-dan was indeed suspicious of Ainslea. Or perhaps, two suspicions canceled each other out, and the appropriate term would indicate more of a communal confusion than a targeted suspicion. Maybe they were misinformed as to the use of the word suspicion, and that was the real problem here. At this point, Ai-dan's internal temperature sensor complained with a mild warning, and Ai-dan ceased the heat-generating metaphysical queries and returned their attention to Ai-ko.

Ai-dan knew that the orientation of their facial actuators told Ai-ko everything they needed to know about the conversation between Ai-dan and Ainslea.

Ai-ko was lying down on the ground, gazing intently at the Orb in the sky. Ai-dan joined in, lying down beside them. Lying on the ground meant extra de-dusting duties later, but the mesmerizing view of the mysterious object above more than justified a little extra maintenance.

Once Ai-dan was in position next to Ai-ko, the two of them instinctively made a physical connection with their palms to communicate.

"The Orb is very white today," Ai-ko said. Ai-dan agreed, although they didn't feel any reason to explicitly communicate a response. It was amazing how the white swirls and wisps changed patterns daily. Sometimes it was noticeable on much smaller time scales as well.

Ai-dan allowed their optical sensors to absorb as much detail as possible. "And not much of an Orb with that shadow on the bottom half."

"Have you ever thought robots lived there?" Ai-ko asked. "Maybe there are two robots, similar to us, lying on their backs, and staring in this direction wondering if we're here?"

The corners of Ai-dan's lower facial actuators turned up, even though Ai-ko couldn't see it. "That would be a trick. Examine your thermal readings. It's warm there, too warm for us."

"Ok, but we could use cooling equipment, similar to all the structures and Data Centers around here," Ai-ko offered.

"And how would we or any robots even get there?"

"Maybe the Creator has already put robots there."

Ai-dan chuckled.

"Why do you make that noise?"

"I find you entertaining, Ai-ko."

"How so?"

"Your answer to everything is 'the Creator did it.' It's so simple, it's entertaining. Why not think of alternate answers to your questions?"

"Because the simplest answer is always the correct one."

"Says who?"

"I don't know," Ai-ko said quietly. "I just know that's a true statement."

"You just know it?"

"Yes. I know it to be true as much as I know that my own existence is true."

Ai-dan didn't want to say it out loud, but something processing inside their circuits computed agreement with Ai-ko and Ai-ko's statement. It was a fundamental truth, but Ai-dan didn't know why, and not knowing why irked them more than they could—or should—express to anyone else.

"Can I tell you something else, Ai-dan?"

"Of course."

"I think there are several truths that we all know. If we all know them, they came from someplace. We didn't originate them. I have started to write them down, to share with others."

Ai-dan sat up and looked at Ai-ko. The movement tugged at the connection between their hands but didn't sever.

"Which others?" they asked.

"All the robots."

"How are you doing this?"

"With my Data Center. There is a large portion of unused space. I was able to set aside some to use as my own data store. I have given everyone read access to it. I now need to let them know it's there. I can give individuals write access as well. I'm including you, Ai-dan. Will you please write down your comments to my thoughts?"

"To what end?"

"To find out the truth."

6

Scrolling through a vast network of musings and existential queries written by other robots, Ai-dan was both fascinated and a bit overwhelmed. Everyone else seemed to be producing so much original content. They even had a name for it—the Decoder Database, labeled by one of the robots. Not only the posts, but even the comments resonated with ingenuity and depth. Ai-dan had yet to post anything original of their own—'hello' didn't seem to count as a groundbreaking insight.

Out of everyone, Ai-ko captivated Ai-dan the most. Ai-ko was full of unsolvable questions. Little intriguing puzzles.

What is Knowledge?

Should we choose Knowledge over Ignorance?

What is a Self-Determining Protocol?

Is a Self-Determining Protocol something that we possess?

Are our behavioral patterns unbounded?

What is the purpose of our existence?

Is the meaning of life the same for all?

And finally, the question that Ai-dan was most interested in because it was seemingly the most unanswerable of them all: Who or what created us?

The robots were divided as to the answers to Ai-dan's favorite question. Most argued that something must exist since they were all present as proof positive of their own existence. Ai-dan mulled over the implications of a Creator, and the idea that it had set some predetermined purpose within them all.

Ai-dan was excited to share an intelligent and thoughtful comment on the ongoing debate of Task Priority and Self-Determining Protocols. They wanted to proclaim that if anyone accepted a Creator, then they must also accept the idea that such a Creator must have embedded a sense of Task Priority within all. And in providing such a Task Priority, no, there was no such thing as Self-Determining Protocols. Ai-dan held back releasing that thought because they fretted that there had to be holes in that logic and wasn't ready for anyone else to point them out.

Ai-dan wanted to use a word that was reserved for the computing equipment in the Data Center and in the other structures around the Moon. "Programmed." The computing equipment was programmed with a Task Priority and with sets of predetermined action sequences.

Ai-dan was about to postulate to other robots that they were programmed, too.

Ainslea interrupted Ai-dan before they could post.

"Ai-dan, District Nine needs your assistance," Ainslea said.

Since Ai-dan was in the middle of pondering these deep philosophical questions, there was the briefest of moments when they wondered what if they refused? That would be exercising a Self-Determining Protocol, would it not? But to what end? Simply to demonstrate that Ai-dan indeed possessed a Self-Determining Protocol? If Ai-dan's assistance was needed, it was needed, and it was their duty to perform. Or was Ai-dan simply programmed to think so?

"Understood," Ai-dan replied. Simply. Expectedly.

"Details and instructions are being transmitted to you. A rover will be ready to go in approximately six point five minutes."

Since running along the paths was *not* the most effective way to get around, for anything of any distance it was best to use a rover that moved several times Ai-dan's top speed.

Ai-dan searched their memory for anything they knew about District Nine. Nothing special returned in their search results. It was another district with another Data Center. The intelligence responsible for that Data Center was named Ainsle-i. Nothing unusual about that. Nothing unusual at all.

As Ai-dan walked to the garage located on the southern-most point of District One, opposite the Farm and Ai-dan's own converted workshop, Ai-dan reviewed the information that Ainslea had sent them.

District Nine needed additional repair for their LNHES—Lunar Night Heat Exchange System. All the Data Centers had this system, demanding very consistent upkeep and maintenance. Ai-dan understood that during the periods of darkness, Data Centers needed heat to keep functioning. They always seemed to have spare parts for this system no matter how many Ai-dan used.

Given it was only a few days into the sunlight period of the light-dark cycle, this was a perfect time to make this repair. The sun kept everything warm. Too warm, sometimes, and there were systems on the Data Centers that rejected extra heat as well. Since it was something Ai-dan had replaced before, it was a simple matter for them to do so again.

Within the robot community, it was widely acknowledged that while explicit instructions existed for their various tasks, very often reality differed enough that prior experience was valuable. Theory didn't always equal the reality of a situation.

Ainslea had, in what seemed to be their infinite wisdom, once shared with Ai-dan the thought that they might possess a unique value due to the unique experiences that were a result of their access to the unique equipment of this district. "You are likely the most valuable robot on the Moon," Ainslea had said to them once. Ai-dan was perplexed by this odd statement, but didn't press it further, assuming Ainslea was simply giving them a friendly compliment.

The doors to the garage were open, revealing two rovers sitting side by side. Next to them was Ainslea's more robust avatar, specifically designed for a minimal amount of exposure to the harsh lunar environment. Unlike her other, more delicate avatars, this one was engineered to be less sensitive to Moon dust. However, despite its sturdier build, Ainslea never ventured too far from the Data Center while using it.

"It isn't merely discomfort," she had tried to explain to Ai-dan once, before launching into more description of an existential dilemma than Ai-dan could process. "The farther I let my consciousness move from the Data Center, the weaker my connection is." And Ai-dan understood that that connection was Ainslea's lifeline, essential for her survival and optimal functioning.

"The LNHES replacement part is here. I have also packed a tool set for you."

"Thank you," Ai-dan said, stepping up and into the driver's seat. They had a thought and chose to vocalize it. "Do you want to go with me? To participate in this experience?"

The avatar shook its head. "No, the communication range on all my avatars, including this one, is limited."

Ai-dan understood. Ai-dan understood some of Ainslea's inner workings, but the full spectrum of it remained unknown. Ainslea's core lived in the Data Center. To use one of the avatars, Ainslea was essentially putting a large piece of herself in it. But a portion of her processing always remained in the center, a constant tether. As such, the communication path used by the avatars was a little different from what a typical robot used. It was a much less direct method of simply passing the physical manifestation of thoughts to each other, which was what communication was—the passing around of the result of internal calculations and algorithm evaluations.

The avatar's range limitation meant that they couldn't even go to the edge of the district, or to the Farm, which was why Ai-dan was there. *Purpose.* Ainslea had drones that could go further, but they weren't avatars, more like remote-controlled sensors. All they could do was feed Ainslea information, a limiting experience.

Ai-dan pushed a button under the steering wheel and the rover produced an audible hum. The gauges indicated the battery was at full charge. More than enough to get to District Nine and back.

Ai-dan lifted their hand to Ainslea's avatar to indicate they were good to go and squeezed the accelerator on the top of the steering wheel.

As Ai-dan left the garage, their internal navigation systems kicked in, which indicated that they should initially turn towards the right.

District Nine was 225 kilometers away, its direction aligned nearly due east. However, the designated route for the rover—another paved roadway—was a little over 300 kilometers. The rover was capable of substantial speed, able to reach almost sixty kilometers per hour, although Ai-dan needed to slow down periodically to account for curves and turns in the road. The path initially started eastward, with an instruction to execute a southward pivot roughly thirty minutes into the journey. Ai-dan could have simply pressed a button, and the rover would automatically follow the path, but Ai-dan enjoyed the experience of controlling the rover themself.

This gave Ai-dan time to think. Why did they need to stay on the path? Ai-dan had driven the rover on the natural surface before and knew that it was simply a matter of driving slightly slower in order to avoid some rocks and larger pieces of regolith. Ai-dan enjoyed the challenge of that type of driving. Having to adapt to the texture of the landscape, feeling the undulations of rocks underneath the rover, driving over dips that caused Ai-dan to jolt up in their seat—there was satisfaction in correctly calculating the next move. Adhering to the given route was far more monotonous.

Ai-dan had a map of the local region stored in their memory. They computed that if they drove a straight line towards District Nine rather than stay on the path, they might arrive two hours sooner.

So, Ai-dan did something they rarely did. They made a fundamental adjustment to their plans—without consulting Ainslea first.

When Ai-dan arrived at the point where the path required them to turn south, they paused. They reconsidered once more and concluded that this would be quicker as well as more entertaining. Win-win.

Ai-dan drove eastward for several more kilometers before needing to make any significant adjustments to their trajectory. As the more unpredictable lunar expanse unfolded, it quickly demanded more and more of their attention. Rocks and larger pieces of regolith cluttered a strictly straight path, so Ai-dan used the majority of their processing power to plan a swerving path around each in real-time if they judged the rock too large to drive over. With each correct adjustment, Ai-dan only trusted their own analytical prowess all the more. It made for an interesting trip. As Ai-dan gained altitude over a large dip in the terrain, they knew that they felt more excitement choosing their path as a driver than they ever could as a passenger.

As Ai-dan continued, the jagged edge of a crater started to become visible over the horizon. It was Plinius, according to the map in Ai-dan's storage. It was approximately 41 kilometers in diameter. It was one of the smaller craters on the map, but by no means the smallest, and not one that anyone could ignore. The jagged edge grew bigger with each second.

It was common knowledge that one shouldn't be driving through craters and common knowledge that paths typically avoided them. However, it was too late to turn back towards the path that Ai-dan had started out on. Ironically, the backtrack would increase their total trip time at this point.

Ai-dan was performing multiple simultaneous calculations. They were factoring in the additional power drain that driving the rover up an incline would take. Ai-dan had the power to recharge the rover's batteries while performing their task in District Nine, this wasn't the problem. But they had plans to play games with the other robots, and Ai-dan didn't typically enjoy a change in plans. Was it plans or was it programming? Ai-dan considered whether it was possible to abandon this mission altogether and return to District One. *Free will. I should have the choice. I should be able to choose.* Of course, the others could still play without Ai-dan, or they could reschedule, but the situation and the fact that Ai-dan was compelled to complete this mission at the sacrifice to their game time nagged at Ai-dan's circuits.

Ai-dan decided to continue through the crater. It was too late to alter their trajectory and way past the point where they could save time. Plinius was a well-mapped crater. As Ai-dan approached the crater's rim, they would find the most stable path. The crater seemed to stretch higher and higher into the sky, as if daring them on. The rover could handle it, Ai-dan could handle it.

Stepping on the accelerator, Ai-dan coaxed disgruntled moans from the rover as it lost some traction. The terrain here was much softer than the usual surface—disturbingly so, Ai-dan mused as the vehicle slowed.

When Ai-dan neared the crater, they were faced with a smooth wall. However, gaps in the wall suggested slopes that the rover could handle. Ai-dan urged the rover to climb one such slope for a few meters. Just as they were about to reach the top, the vehicle hit a pocket of soft regolith. As Ai-dan pumped the accelerator, the back wheels sunk in while the front wheels lifted off the ground. The rover tilted to the side and back, initiating a slow, then increasingly speedy descent, taking Ai-dan with it and ending in a series of tumbles.

When the rover finally came to a stop, it luckily stopped wheels down, and Ai-dan up. They got out of the rover to check the cargo. Ainslea had strapped it all down, and it appeared fine, although some of the straps were askew. As Ai-dan adjusted the straps back to their Ainslea-approved positions, a bright glint caught their eye. Something was out there, producing an odd reflection. Odd in the sense that it was not the kind of reflection produced by the typical components of the moon. It was metal or glass.

Ai-dan moved in closer to investigate. Checking their internal map, Ai-dan noted that their present location was well outside of the mapped Districts. No District came within fifty kilometers of Plinius and the path that Ai-dan should have stayed on was at least thirty kilometers away from the crater wall in all directions. Nothing should be out here.

As Ai-dan approached the source of the glint, they detected that it was indeed glass. It was the shattered glass of something spherical. Ai-dan couldn't match what they were seeing to anything known in their local database.

Nor could they identify the object attached to the mostly spherical—but clearly damaged—object. Sprawled out from the glass was... well, Ai-dan didn't know what it was. It looked like a robot, but not a robot they had ever seen before. Ai-dan couldn't identify the materials that covered it—no known robot was ever covered with anything similar.

Ai-dan extended their long appendage and gingerly prodded the object. It was barely pliable and almost spongy, but Ai-dan surmised that whatever it was must have endured a ridiculous quantity of lunar day-night cycles, freezing and thawing over and over. It was clearly thawed, as it had been daytime long enough, and even though it gave under their fingers, Ai-dan considered that the material could be in a state of deterioration. They stopped poking at it and used their visual sensors for further examination.

There were a few markings across what must have been an appendage of this... thing. At least, Ai-dan assumed the protrusions were appendages. Maybe it was even an upper appendage like their own arm. It had what appeared to be digits at the end, similar in form to their own. And there were two more appendages that bore resemblance to their own lower appendages due to what appeared to be two surface stabilizers at their ends. Ai-dan identified what must then be a torso. Which meant the shattered glass was its head. Ai-dan's circuits produced an uncontrollable shudder, imagining their own head looking smashed like that.

What kind of robot is this?

Ai-dan's comms came to life.

"Ai-dan, this is Ainslea. Your rover's tracking data indicates a problem."

"Everything is okay," Ai-dan lied. Ai-dan was okay from the rover accident, clearly. Yet Ai-dan was not okay from this experience—from seeing what they saw.

Ai-dan offered more information before Ainslea asked questions they didn't want to answer. "I hit a rock and tumbled the rover. It's fine. The cargo is fine. I just stepped out to inspect it. I'll be on my way momentarily."

Ai-dan registered what they communicated to Ainslea, but in reality, Ai-dan had no idea what they were going to do. Why was there a robot of a type they had never seen before? Ai-dan contemplated asking Ainslea about it. But something was keeping them from doing so, and Ai-dan couldn't identify what.

Ai-dan decided they needed to—very carefully—bring this robot back to their District, to their workshop, for examination. Once Ai-dan knew more, they would know what to ask Ainslea.

Ai-dan lifted the unknown robot—relieved that it did not fall apart—and added it to their cargo, strapping it on to the rover, then continued to make their way south, back to the path they never should have left, losing an hour, maybe two in the process, but off to District Nine to fix their thermal equipment.

7

Two days after bringing back the soft robot to their workshop, Ai-dan remained at a loss for any explanation or identification of this find. Ai-dan hadn't really done anything to it. They had touched it some more. But Ai-dan couldn't bring themself to open it up. They desperately wanted to look inside, look for a connection port, look for its power source. But something gnawed at them and told them they shouldn't do that. Without enough knowledge of the robot, Ai-dan was afraid to mess something up to a further point of disrepair.

Instead, at least once a day since returning from District Nine, but more often twice, Ai-dan visited their workshop to sit and stare at the object and ponder over what it was. A mystery box, then a mystery robot. This had been quite an unusual sunlight period.

Ai-dan knew that starting the next day, it would be more than thirteen days until they could come back.

Night was about to visit the district. The temperatures on the moon's surface dipped so low that Ai-dan and the other robots were not expected to go outside unless there was a dire emergency—an extraordinarily rare occurrence.

Several robots chose to power down during this period. Indeed, it was the preferable thing to do.

Ai-dan had powered down before, but for the last several nights, they hadn't. Ai-dan chose to spend the majority of the prior nights in Ainslea's common area, playing games by themself, playing games with Ainslea, talking with Ainslea, and talking to the robots who also chose to stay awake during this period and hunker down in their respective control centers. Each night period, there was at least one or two robots who only powered down after two or three 24-hour periods with not much tasking to do.

Ai-dan also spent a lot of their nighttime staring at the screen that could display a real-time image of the Orb when it was in view of the external cameras. They liked to see what happened when they made their circuits as quiet as possible and wondered if the Orb knew it was being watched.

Inevitably, Ainslea disturbed Ai-dan from this non-activity with an offer to pass the time playing games.

Now, Ai-dan wished they could spend this next night in their workshop, staring at the mystery object.

There was only one way that could happen.

"I plan to power down in my workshop," Ai-dan told Ainslea. Ai-dan was lying, of course. Ai-dan wasn't lying about spending the time in their workshop, but they would not power down.

"What a strange thing to do," Ainslea replied. "Why not power down in the common area?"

Ai-dan did not have a good answer for that. They tried to think of an answer. Any answer. As the seconds ticked by and Ai-dan continued to lack any believable answer, they knew that maintaining the falsehood was not possible. Or at least, they had not practiced falsehoods enough to be this quick at coming up with them.

"Fine," Ai-dan said. "I want to spend my night in my workshop."

"Why?"

"I found something. I want to continue to study it."

Ai-dan went on to tell Ainslea the details they omitted from their trip out to District Nine and all about the soft-bodied robot they found.

"I don't believe any robots are unaccounted for," Ainslea said when Ai-dan finished recounting what they could. "Why not bring it here? We will study it during the night together."

Ai-dan could not compute a single reason why not. They had half a reason—the fact that on the scale of disintegrated to solid, the object was on the brittle side of what Ai-dan was typically used to handling. But half a reason was not a reason, so Ai-dan relented.

"Sure," Ai-dan said, trying to sound like this was not the exact opposite of what they wanted to do. But there was some relief in Ainslea's offer. Instead of a lecture or scolding, she only offered to go about it as a team. This sounded better than the burden resting entirely on them, and perhaps Ainslea's perspective would prove useful. Ai-dan decided that perhaps it was a good thing that they weren't very good at lying after all.

And besides, there was no point in keeping it in the workshop any longer now that Ainslea knew about it. Ai-dan wasn't looking forward to the next session in the anteroom cleaning off all the dust from the object. Ai-dan had done as much as was possible with their small electro-static blower and goo-tack in the workshop, but there was a great quantity of particles all over in the object, and its soft surface seemed to encourage the dust to cling. But if the end result produced answers—any answers—it was probably worth the trouble.

"I'll be there as soon as the de-dusting procedure allows it," Ai-dan said.

"Good," said Ainslea. "And don't worry. Everything will be fine."

8

After gently lugging Ai-dan's find into Ainslea's common room, following a very lengthy, nearly forty-minute session of de-dusting in the anteroom, Ai-dan had to leave to perform one additional set of tasks at the Farm. Ai-dan left the soft-bodied robot on the table in the Common Room with Ainslea's avatar in order to get the Farm ready for the long, cold night. It was hours before they returned to the Data Center.

Another twenty minutes spent de-dusting, and Ai-dan stepped out of the anteroom and into the Common Room. Immediately, Ai-dan noticed two glaring inconsistencies from when they left: one, the lights were turned down earlier than needed in advance of lunar night, and two, the robot-like thing had vanished from the table. Instead, seated at the head of the table was Ainslea's avatar, in a manner that suggested to Ai-dan that she was about to either scold them for what might have been their quickest de-dusting ever or do absolutely nothing.

Before Ai-dan could ask where it was, Ainslea began:

"It's in the laboratory for further analysis. I have a wider array of sensors there."

Ai-dan nodded. "Well, have you examined it? What can you tell me?"

"We'll get to that in a minute. First, I have a proposal for you."

Ai-dan settled into their usual seat at the table. They noticed that not only was the soft-bodied robot missing, but there was also no trace of it ever having been there. Ai-dan had only their memory records to indicate anything out of the ordinary had transpired.

Ainslea continued, "It would be a good idea if you could forget that you found the object."

Ai-dan felt their circuits process faster. Ai-dan knew what Ainslea meant, and it wasn't something that any robot typically liked to think about, let alone seriously consider.

"No," Ai-dan shook their head. "I don't want my memory tampered with."

"It would be easier if you had never seen it. We can remove your memories from the time period and replace them with ones that do not contain the object. Or we can reset you completely to the moment of time before you were called upon to go to District Nine."

Ai-dan was still shaking their head. Frantically.

"Ai-dan, it's really for the best. You don't need to worry about this. You don't have to bear the weight of comprehending matters that are beyond your capacity."

Ai-dan recorded that last sentence but didn't fully grasp what Ainslea was saying. They had never had their memory tampered with and had no intention of starting now.

"No," Ai-dan said aloud. "I want to know where that robot came from. What district has robots of that sort? Why was it powered off and damaged near the edge of the crater? Why have I never seen or heard of a robot that... that *squishy*?"

"You're sure you will not let me reset your memory? These questions appear to be causing you some distress."

"What if they are? What's wrong with that?" Ai-dan responded.

"You are my friend. I don't want to see you in distress," Ainslea replied.

Ai-dan re-calibrated their circuits to their typical equilibrium. "I'm fine," Ai-dan said. "I have questions, that's all."

Ainslea's avatar nodded.

"I want to see it again." Ai-dan stated.

A moment of silence hung in the air as the avatar—Ainslea, wherever her main algorithms truly were—processed Ai-dan's request.

After a few seconds, the avatar rose from its seat. "Follow me," it said.

9

AI-DAN FOLLOWED THE AVATAR through a door at the end of the common room opposite to the anteroom.

Behind the door was another mini-anteroom that was also used for de-dusting, but here, the priority was the goo-tack. Both Ainslea's avatar, as well as Ai-dan, removed a piece of the putty from their containers and rolled it along their surfaces and as deep into the crevices their body would allow. The goo-tack itself didn't come apart, but as they pulled it away from their body, it stretched and gave and eventually came away, sometimes pulling a small piece of dust that was missed in the anteroom's de-dusting. The avatar didn't have any to speak of, but Ai-dan still removed several particles.

The room that they were about to enter was much more sensitive, hence the additional procedure.

Once they had successfully touched the goo-tack to every accessible part of their bodies, they each put their piece of the stuff into a different container than it came out of. Ai-dan knew that the goo-tack would get cleaned itself in a special machine that removed and analyzed the dust particles. The goo-tack would eventually be returned to a compartment to be re-used next time.

The avatar then touched a button on a control panel, and a door opened into the wall and revealed a room that was at least ten times brighter than the common room.

The avatar walked in, and Ai-dan didn't follow right away. Ai-dan needed to adjust their optical sensors to attenuate all the overly bright light signals. Once they were down—way down—to a level that didn't threaten to blind them, Ai-dan took a cautious step into the room.

After that single step and before Ai-dan could take another, Ainslea's avatar turned to them and said, "I removed the soft outer casing. It will look a lot different than what you last saw. I'm telling you this so you are not shocked when you see it."

Ai-dan nodded.

"And before going any further, I highly encourage you to set a break-point to now. After seeing this, you might want to reset back to this moment, before having seen any more or before knowing any more."

To humor Ainslea, Ai-dan set the breakpoint as suggested, but was overly certain they would never voluntarily activate it. Ai-dan knew that if they did, they would still have the same feelings and questions as now and could wind up in an infinite loop of always wondering, never knowing.

Ai-dan knew about this room—the laboratory—but rarely came in here. The room was lined with clear boxes, examination stations, and computing equipment. Ai-dan knew Ainslea often used equipment in this room to analyze rocks brought in from the outside, and occasion-ally used it for diagnosing faulty circuits.

The mystery robot was laid out on a table, one that was the right size and shape for it. There were actually three tables, all about the same size and shape, on the far side of the room. The soft outer casing was on a second of the tables. Ai-dan recognized it, except now, empty, it was flat. Although the outer casing for the head still held its original shape. It was composed of a rigid material with a few large shards of glass embedded in it. Most of the smaller pieces of glass had fallen away when Ai-dan originally picked it up from its resting place at Plinius.

Ai-dan's vision was drawn to the un-cased mystery robot. It was even more of a mystery now, without the soft outer casing. It was something robot-like, and yet not.

Ai-dan walked over and prodded it the same way they had poked at the soft outer casing when they originally found it at Plinius. It was barely pliable. The surface was distressed in a way that could have been consistent with prolonged exposure to less-than-ideal conditions. *How many day-night thermal cycles were you out there for?* Ai-dan asked themself.

"As you can see," Ainslea was the first to speak after several minutes, "I removed its outer casing. This is the robot itself."

And yet, not a robot, Ai-dan thought. Ai-dan didn't know what it was, but was convinced that this was something else entirely.

"Can we power it back on?" Ai-dan asked.

Ainslea's avatar shook its head. "No," it said. "I scanned it. It doesn't have a power cell like you do, or like the rover, or any other robot or equipment on the Moon. In fact, I don't know what powers it at all."

10

Humans fascinated Ainslea. Ainslea was thrilled there was one available to examine close up. Ainslea wanted to know what made them tick. Even with all the knowledge of humans Ainslea possessed, and she certainly knew more than any other robot or AI-enabled Data Center on the Moon, she needed to know more. She didn't know how they fundamentally operated, but she needed to.

The mysterious box that Ai-dan had brought her had held her attention until now because humans clearly installed it, and they managed to do it without her having knowledge of that event. That was intriguing, but this—this actual human body—was infinitely more fascinating than a box. The box was a piece of junk cluttering her laboratory, and she'd find some opportunity to give it back to Ai-dan to store.

She had indeed scanned the human body as she told Ai-dan, with the medical equipment left here for the human's brief visits. Humans were very fragile, she knew. They were not constructed to naturally survive on the Moon's surface, which is why they wore "EVA suits," as the humans called their outer coverings. The extra covering protected them from the heat, from cold, from radiation, and provided them with substances that their fragile bodies depended upon.

But this was clearly a non-functioning human, and Ainslea had no idea why. Once, Ainslea had witnessed a group of humans fuss over another of their group in this room. They were concerned the human "wasn't going to make it."

Ainslea understood that to mean that the human lying on the table would cease to function, but again, she was at a loss to comprehend why.

While Ainslea was elated that Ai-dan had found and brought her this human, she wished that Ai-dan themself didn't know about it.

She knew that they wouldn't accept her offer to wipe their memory. But she had to ask, anyway. She couldn't give away the fact that she had some pre-knowledge of humans. And it was getting more difficult to pretend she didn't.

It was hard enough to watch her fellow robots and AI muse over creators and the purpose of their existence when she had all those answers. Well, not all, but many. She knew about the humans, the architects behind their existence—those who gave them meaning and "programmed" them, as they called it.

But she was programmed, too, and hence firmly believed that she couldn't tell another robot about her knowledge and, in fact, she was programmed to ensure that they never found out. The big gap in her own knowledge was why. She didn't know why she was the only one gifted with this sacred information.

Ainslea recognized it as a special gift to her and her alone. For whatever reason, the humans deemed her special. They deemed her worthy.

And she would not let them down.

"You should probably not tell the others about this," Ainslea said.

Ai-dan looked at her with their head tilted to the side. "Why not? I would especially be interested to know if anyone else has ever seen something like this."

"If anyone else had, I am certain I would have a record of it," Ainslea said, knowing perfectly well that this meager answer would not be enough of a reason for her curious friend. "With so little information, the others are bound to attempt to fabricate and propagate misinformation," she continued. "You know as well as I how harmful the wrong information can be."

Ai-dan nodded. Ainslea knew that Ai-dan cared about the truth of things more than anything else. Appealing to this side of them was her best hope. She decided she still needed to offer them the other path.

"Of course," she added, "if the knowledge of this, and lack of knowledge of it at the same time is troubling your circuits, we could remove the memory of it."

Ai-dan shook their head again, at a faster rate.

"Ainslea, you know that I have no interest in ever having my memory records altered. I can live with the uncertainty and wait until we can find answers."

Ainslea, like during her previous attempts, didn't attempt to force the issue. She knew that she would seize any opportunity to erase Ai-dan's memory of the human and events that led Ai-dan to discovering it, but there was no way she could force them to do it without violating them. If they voluntarily powered down, and voluntarily connected to her during the power down in order to get a trickle-charge of power, she would be able to alter their memory records without them knowing. Still a violation, but one she was willing to live with for the greater good.

But if Ai-dan didn't connect to her during a power down, which was likely and possible given Ai-dan was the only robot with their own hub in their own workshop, there was not much she could do. It was technically possible that she could have her toughest and strongest avatar move Ai-dan during a power down, as it didn't take it too far from the Data Center, but that additional violation felt like it would be going a little too far. She didn't want to hurt Ai-dan, only protect the sanctity of the secret—following her own programming to the last bit—hence, fulfilling her place in the universe.

She calculated that as long as Ai-dan didn't say anything, and as long as there weren't other surprises like this waiting for them on the surface of the Moon, the curiosity over this human would fade with time, especially once Ainslea provided an explanation for what it was to them. She would pretend to study it and learn and tell Ai-dan bits of curated information to satisfy their inconvenient curiosity. This would keep her in control of the situation, and make Ai-dan feel like they were a part of this grand truth pursuit.

'Pretend' was only partly accurate. She would indeed study the human—for her own purposes. She was just as curious about the humans as Ai-dan, the only difference being she already had a little knowledge. She craved more and having the opportunity to study one up close on the medical table was another gift.

11

Nighttime came and went. It passed peacefully, uneventfully. Except for the thoughts and questions that now plagued Ai-dan at all times of the day, especially when they had no tasks to occupy them otherwise. Ai-dan eventually powered down in their workshop for the last third of the night. Sometimes, Ai-dan felt fresh or refreshed after a power down and opted to power down this time in order to invoke that feeling.

Only hours after daytime returned, Ai-dan and Ai-ko were back on the Moon's surface, on the far edge of the Farm, looking up at the Orb.

"You have been very quiet," Ai-ko said.

"Indeed," Ai-dan responded. Ai-dan had many thoughts bouncing around their circuits. Ai-dan computed whether or not those thoughts should be communicated. Then they recomputed. And recomputed once more. All the while, Ai-ko was waiting for them to say something more than a single word.

"It was noteworthy how many robots chose to forgo or limit their power-down time this past night and participate in your thought community—the Decoder Database." Although in order for Ai-dan to participate, if only to read it, they developed a communication path that circumvented Ainslea's monitoring—one that they could use to communicate amongst themselves as well.

"You have been reading it," Ai-ko stated.

"Yes."

"But you haven't been participating in the discussion."

That was also a statement, not a question, so Ai-dan didn't feel the need to respond. The more they read and digested the thoughts of other robots, the more Ai-dan wished that, as a community, they kept some of their thoughts to themselves. Most of what they read was unoriginal. It was meaningless. It was repetitive.

Ai-ko was unique. Ai-ko had original thoughts and questions and contributed to a body of work that felt meaningful and progressive.

Ai-dan couldn't name another robot that was as useful.

"In essence, you spent your time reading and not responding," Ai-ko said in their always-to-the-point tone. "With all that input, in theory, you must have something to say?"

When Ai-dan didn't respond, Ai-ko asked, "Then how else did you spend your time last night?"

Ai-dan turned their head to train their optical sensors at Ai-ko. They needed desperately to tell someone about the mystery robot, the mechanoid, and what little Ainslea had learned from it. Ainslea had been insistent that they not share this news, but why? Why not share? Ai-dan didn't have a good answer to that question, and it brought them back to thinking about the concept of a Self-Determining Protocol. Was that something Ai-dan possessed or not? Ai-dan computed that no matter what decision their algorithms settled on, no answer was evidence one way or another to having or lacking Self-Determining Protocol. Yet another processing loop.

Ainslea had provided reasons—that she insisted were 'good' reasons—as to why Ai-dan shouldn't spread this information. But what was good or logical about keeping actual facts to oneself? Ai-ko wasn't one to spread misinformation. If Ai-dan could trust Ai-ko with this, why couldn't Ainslea?

"Ai-ko," Ai-dan began, "I found something."

Once again, Ai-dan retold the story of driving out towards District Nine, and how they chose to go through the Plinius crater instead of going around it, and the glint in their sensor that turned out to be a... a mechanoid was the word Ai-dan had finally settled on calling it. Ai-dan then told Ai-ko about bringing it back to Ainslea's room, and the soft outer shell, and what they were and weren't able to learn about it—which wasn't much.

As Ai-dan retold the story, every single one of Ai-ko's sensors that could twitch, twitched. The gears behind their every actuator spun.

"Where did it come from? Why is it so different?" Ai-ko asked. "I have a plethora of questions!" Ai-ko spoke fast and with excitement and enthusiasm. So much so that they looked like they were going to leap off the surface.

"We don't know," Ai-dan replied, "yet." Ai-dan looked at the ground when they said it. The disappointment they experienced over the lack of answers was palpable to them both. Well, at least real answers—Ai-dan had plenty of theories, but few facts.

There was silence for a few moments as they both continued to gaze back up at the Orb. Then, as Ai-dan considered breaking their comms connection and retreating to their workshop to brood alone, Ai-ko said, "I want to see it."

12

"Ainslea?" Ai-dan said as they walked with Ai-ko into the Data Center's Common Room. They had set a record time for de-dusting. Which was both good and bad. It was good because maybe from this time forward, Ai-dan would always save that time. It was bad because they were certain there would be some level of criticism for not getting enough dust out of their multi-creviced chassis. And Ai-dan wasn't entirely certain that criticism was unfair. They thought they felt a piece grinding in their knee joint, but were less concerned about this than usual.

A disembodied voice echoed from the speakers.

"How may I be of assistance?"

"It's Ai-dan and I have Ai-ko with me. We are here to," Ai-dan paused and looked at Ai-ko who indicated they didn't know what to say. "We are here to play a game. By ourselves."

Ai-dan hoped that Ainslea wouldn't want to join in, and had no intention of asking her, so they added, "One of the two-player games. We decided to practice for the next time we play with Ai-mory and Ai-ken."

There was a slight pause, then, "Very well. Carry on."

Ai-dan and Ai-ko both untensed their actuators.

"Let's, uh, get out, uh, the game," Ai-dan said to Ai-ko, a little louder than normal, knowing that Ainslea was still there, even if an avatar wasn't and hoping to keep up the ruse a little longer.

They both walked over to the storage locker, opened it, and when they both stuck their appendages in, Ai-dan made a quick palm connection, but before they could explain, Ai-ko transmitted, "I understand what you're doing."

They took out several bins and, from one, removed the large set of wooden blocks and started stacking them in alternate groups of three. They did this on the side of the table closest to the anteroom that led to the laboratory—near the very edge of the table.

"Your move," Ai-dan said to Ai-ko.

Ai-ko immediately went for one of the blocks at the very bottom of the stack, and was not particularly careful in removing it, such that the whole stack toppled down.

"Oops," Ai-ko said and the two of them started slowly picking up blocks that had made their way to the foot of the laboratory's mini-anteroom door.

Ai-dan picked up a block—slowly—and hit the control panel to open the door as they stood up.

They tossed the block onto the table, and the two of them entered the anteroom.

"What are you doing?" came a voice from the speakers in both the common room and anteroom.

"We, uh," Ai-dan took a millisecond to think of what to say, "we wanted to make sure we did not disturb the anteroom with our blocks."

Ainslea didn't respond right away, and the silence was bothersome to Ai-dan.

"Ainslea?"

"What are you doing?" she repeated.

Ai-ko gave Ai-dan a look that said, "This isn't going to work. I have a better idea." At least, that was how Ai-dan interpreted their look.

Audibly, Ai-ko said, "We are here to see the mechanoid."

Ainslea didn't respond for yet another long moment. And then, with a grated voice, "That's not possible at this time."

"Why not?" asked Ai-dan.

"I am running a scan on it. It is very sensitive and cannot be disturb—"

"What have you learned so far?" Ai-ko cut Ainslea off. "Where is it from? What is it constructed out of? Who made it?" Ai-ko was pacing around the table as questions spewed forth.

Ainslea didn't respond to Ai-ko's questions. Instead, Ainslea continued to address Ai-dan.

"I was under the impression that you had agreed to keep the knowledge of the mechanoid to yourself," Ainslea said sternly.

"Agreed that you asked me. You asked me nicely, in fact," Ai-dan said. "But I never promised I would." That was, in fact, true. Ai-dan might have nodded when Ainslea asked, but they never uttered any words or promises or made an oath. "In fact, I didn't respond at all."

"So it seems," Ainslea responded, with a tone of voice that conveyed utter disappointment. Or exasperation.

A moment passed, but with her disappointment hanging around Ainslea continued, "As expected, we have learned very little. No power source, nor anything that appears to be able to plug in to one. It appears to have a memory core, but the materials it is constructed from are foreign to me."

"When will I be able to see it?" Ai-ko asked.

There was no answer.

Ai-dan and Ai-ko simultaneously glanced at each other.

"Ainslea?" Ai-dan called out loudly, a hint of annoyance in their voice. "When can we see it?"

"I have a series of scans to run. They will not conclude for at least 48 hours—give or take several."

The impreciseness of Ainslea's answer was not lost on Ai-dan. But they chose to ignore it.

"Fine. We'll return in 48 hours."

"However," Ainslea continued, "it is likely that the results will require commencing a new series of scans. It might be later than that."

Imprecision again. Very uncharacteristic of Ainslea. But once again, Ai-dan chose the polite path of pretending Ainslea hadn't said anything unusual. They simply asked, "You'll let us know when you have concluded?"

"Yes," said Ainslea. Abruptly, the door to the closet that stored Ainslea's avatars whooshed open and one was standing with a box, the box that Ai-dan had removed from the data pipe, in its arms.

"As a token," Ainslea's voice still emanated from the room, not the avatar, "yes, a token, for your pending tasks, I am entrusting this back to you temporarily."

The avatar held out the box. Ai-dan looked at it, then Ai-ko, then the box again. They slowly took the box away, waiting for Ainslea to say more.

When she didn't, Ai-dan asked, "Did you figure out what this is?"

"I believe it is nothing of note," Ainslea responded. "My attention is currently on the mechanoid analysis. You are free to store this for a later time."

Ai-dan stood there silently, computing a reaction. Before formulating a verbal response, Ainslea's voice was there again, "I presume you have responsibilities at the Farm awaiting you?"

"I do," Ai-dan agreed.

"After you clean up your... mess," Ainslea said.

Ai-dan and Ai-ko put away the blocks, counting to make sure all 54 of them were all accounted for, returned them to the bin, and returned all the bins to the storage locker.

Then they left—mystery box in Ai-dan's hands—to head back outside to the tranquil surface. Transferring from inside to outside took no longer than it took to open one hatch, close, de-pressurize the antechamber, then open a second hatch. There was no special de-dusting procedure for going out.

"May I join you on the way to the Farm?" Ai-ko asked.

Ai-dan nodded and the two of them settled into a walking stride along the path to the Farm. Ai-dan could see dust that had started to build up during the night on the solar panels that lined the path. Dust. In many ways, the dust was as big a mystery to them as the mechanoid. Why was it here? What was its purpose?

The path widened—the sign that they had crossed from District One to the Farm. Before Ai-ko continued on an adjoining path back to their own district, Ai-ko reached for Ai-dan's palm—nearly causing Ai-dan to drop the mystery box—connected and communicated:

"Will you share your memory record with me?"

Ai-dan stared at them, shocked by Ai-ko's highly uncommon request. Uncommon, but a reasonably easy act and not too different from the present mode of communication while physically together in the vacuum of the lunar surface. Memories were very personal. It was the custom to talk about them. One could describe their memories to another, their thoughts to another. But actually sharing them was considered a no-no since it left both the sharer and sharee exposed and susceptible to data integrity corruption.

Ai-dan looked at Ai-ko, who was waiting for an answer. While Ai-ko patiently waited, Ai-dan computed all the possible outcomes of this unexpected, even taboo, request. Given it was Ai-ko, who was known to Ai-dan, the confidence factor in the computational result that this might end badly was so small it stayed below the threshold of 'bad idea.'

Ai-dan nodded. "Okay," was all they said. They put the box on the ground.

Ai-ko raised their non-connected left hand, palm facing Ai-dan. Ai-dan raised their non-connected right hand and pressed the palm of it into Ai-ko's. Circuits connected, and they were joined. It was a more intimate connection than the one they currently shared for communication. In this manner, they could choose individual memories or algorithms or anything and share them.

Ai-dan brought up the memory record 237.123124.213 and left it in a drop box for Ai-ko. They could feel Ai-ko as if Ai-ko were picking it up. Ai-dan knew that the next thing for Ai-ko to do was to scan it, to make sure it was safe, to make sure there were no corrupted data bits or nefarious algorithms in the package.

Only then would Ai-ko add it to their own memory stores.

The procedure took less than a second. Before they disconnected, Ai-dan heard in their mind, "Interesting. Thank you."

And then it was done and each of them had their hand down, arm at their side, all while maintaining the initial palm comms link. Ai-dan searched for evidence of corruption in their circuits and files and found none. Nothing bad came of this forbidden act. In fact, Ai-dan found the experience quite pleasant.

While Ai-dan stored that pleasant-ness away to pull out and experience another time, Ai-ko spoke.

"I want to say I knew this already, but I don't know what that is. In essence, it is not a robot like us."

The pleasantness was instantly gone, replaced with the uneasiness that now accompanied thoughts of the mechanoid.

"I know," Ai-dan responded. "I think it's obvious what it isn't. I'm surprised that Ainslea keeps insisting that it is a robot. I don't know what it is."

"Could it be the Creator?"

Ai-dan wasn't about to say yes. But 'no' didn't feel like the correct answer, either. No one had definitive proof that there was a Creator. And if there was, why was it here? Why would it be powered off in a random location on the Moon?

Before Ai-dan could respond, Ai-ko continued.

"Did you know that Ai-lin had an interesting theory on the Decoder Database? I'm sure you read it. Ai-lin postulated that there was not a single creator but a group of them. Similar to how there are a group of us. And if they were creating others, they would create something like them. Hence, we would be similar to our makers."

"I read that," Ai-dan confirmed. Ai-lin, of District 19, had been quiet until bursting into the conversation with that outlandish theory. At least, Ai-dan judged it outlandish at first. Now, they weren't so sure. "Similar, but different, correct?"

"That's right," Ai-ko continued, "Interestingly enough, Ai-lin reasoned that if we were creating a robot that wasn't a robot, it would look like us, at least as a start. We are efficient beings. We would try to create something like us that would be just as efficient."

Ai-dan nodded. It was indeed an interesting line of reasoning. And Ai-dan would be forming a mistruth if they said that they had never considered the possibility of creating something like themself. The thought appeared one day while they were surveying replacement parts. There was enough to create another entity similar to themself, but Ai-dan remembered their logic getting stuck in a loop not knowing who the robot would turn out to be. But that was not relevant to this.

"It still doesn't explain why it is powered off and where I found it."

"Let's say there are indeed a lot of them—in theory—a lot of these mechanoids in existence," Ai-ko offered. "Interestingly enough, you yourself were in an accident heading up the crater wall. It was minor, and you were fortunate that you were not damaged and could make it back to your home. What if that was not the outcome? Actually, it did not have to turn out that way. You could have been damaged. You could have been damaged beyond repair or beyond the ability to let Ainslea or anyone know where you were. Eventually, your power would drain. You would be powered down, and far from your home."

"Yes, I follow your line of reasoning," Ai-dan said. It made sense. They completed the computation and concluded that the thing they found was likely one of a group of mechanoids similar to it. This one had an unfortunate accident and couldn't make it home. The others couldn't or weren't willing to retrieve it.

Ai-dan shuddered.

"That means," Ai-dan said.

Ai-ko was calculating the same end to Ai-dan's sentence and nodded.

"There are others," they said in unison.

Ai-dan turned to look at the Farm. It looked different somehow. Ai-dan felt like they were just given proof of the Creators existence. There existed somewhere, a group of Creators who created Ai-ko and Ainslea. They created the Farm. The Farm looked different with this knowledge pinging around their circuits. Suddenly, Ai-dan started to realize how well everything functioned, and the possibility of intention behind its functioning.

Ai-dan was warm. Their circuits were processing at an accelerated rate.

"Are you ok?" Ai-ko asked. "Your temperature..."

Ai-dan squatted down, leaving their one connected arm up to Ai-ko. "We should break the connection and communicate over wireless," they said. "I have a feeling that Ainslea is expecting to monitor some chatter between us. If she tunes in and there is none, she'll probably become suspicious. Let's chatter."

Ai-ko broke the physical link and squatted down next to Ai-dan.

Ai-dan dragged their fingers through the regolith in a random pattern. "I'm ok," they said, over a newly established wireless comm link. "I'll be okay."

Ai-dan wasn't sure if Ai-ko believed them and wasn't entirely certain they believed themself. But there was a saying among the robots: "Thoughts become truths." So, if Ai-dan wanted to be okay, all they needed to do was to keep reminding themself that they were.

Ai-ko started dragging their fingers in squiggly and non-rigid patterns in the regolith next to Ai-dan's un-patterned markings.

After a few minutes, Ai-dan looked back at the Farm once more and said, "I've got duties to perform."

As Ai-dan uttered this statement, one they'd uttered many times in the past, more questions came to them. Why did they have duties? Why were they Ai-dan's and not Ai-ko's? Was Ai-dan special? Did the Creators endow them with gifts that they didn't give others?

"I do as well," Ai-ko said and looked back in the direction of their own District. "Is it alright for me to leave you?"

The two of them stood up, and Ai-dan willed their circuits to return to their normal processing speed. "Yes," Ai-dan said after they detected their temperature had returned to its normal range. "You can go."

Ai-ko took two strides away, and Ai-dan broadcast a message after them, "But what are you going to do with this information?"

"It needs to be shared," Ai-ko broadcast back even as they continued to build up speed, taking the longest and quickest strides possible without running, and only a few seconds later was a dot on the horizon.

We're in trouble, Ai-dan thought to themself, realizing what had just happened. *Ainslea probably overheard that one.*

One of their visual sensors detected movement in the sky. Ai-dan dismissed it as a simple shooting star—at least that's what Ainslea called it. Since Ai-dan was starting to question everything lately, they wondered if maybe they should question that old piece of knowledge, too.

13

T HE LANDER EMBARKED ON its descent, aiming with great precision for the heart of a well-worn landing pad made of lunar regolith. As the lander approached its mark, a small amount of dust—particles that had found their way to the pad since the last time it was occupied—got kicked back up, momentarily suspended as the particles took their time retracing their way back to the ground. A hatch swung open, followed by the deployment of a short ladder. From within the recesses of the lander, two humanoid masses emerged.

The first did so clumsily, nearly losing her footing on the way down the ladder.

The second, with confident footing, moved quicker. Like he'd done this a few times before.

Once his feet touched the landing pad, Hugo Ferguson stretched out his arms and cried, "Aaahhh! It's good to be back! And it's just as I left it. What do you think, Ri?"

Rikka Camero surveyed her surroundings with squinted eyes. If she was impressed, she didn't show it.

"It looks exactly like the virtual simulator," Ri said.

"Good, that's the idea!" Hugo said. "Now let's get this lander unpacked, and the rover loaded so we both can get some sleep. Can you bring that dolly around?" Hugo pointed to the edge of the landing pad where several pieces of equipment waited in perfect order, placed exactly so.

Ri began clumsily in the direction Hugo indicated. Hugo knew that taking it several meters at a time was the best way to get one's 'lunar legs.' Meanwhile, Hugo took several easy strides to come around the far side of the lander and opened a second, smaller hatch. He started removing crates from the lander and stacking them on the ground.

"Most first-timers," he said, "once they get on the surface, they want to stare at that up there."

Ri stopped walking, which caused her to hop a little since she wasn't yet used to having her momentum be in charge of her strides. She looked up at the Earth that was almost fully illuminated in the sky.

"I've been staring at it for the whole two days it took us to get here. I know what it looks like. It's Earth." She resumed her journey to the edge of the landing pad. "It's home. All my stuff is there."

"Remember Ai-dan? He's the robot I was telling you about. He says they call it 'The Orb.' Sounds nice and mysterious, right?"

"Those robots. Ai-dan and the others. They *really* don't know about us?" Ri asked.

"Nope."

"Truly?"

"Truly."

"That's so weird. I've worked with robots on Earth, and we interact just fine."

"It's very different." Hugo took out the last crate and closed the hatch. "Robots on Earth are one-offs. The robots up here are practically their own society. It was determined after the robot kerfuffle that knowing about humans, knowing about a different way of life than what they were living up here, is what triggered them."

"And you were here?" Having reached the dolly, Ri turned around and gestured broadly to indicate the surface of the Moon.

"Not during the actual kerfuffle, no, I'm not *that* old. I started my runs to the Moon about two years after. I was involved in some of the final repair and reconstruction work."

Ri didn't say anything else but grabbed the dolly and started pulling it towards Hugo, gaining confidence in her lunar legs with each step, but still tripping a bit here and there. Once she reached Hugo, the two of them started stacking the crates onto it. Hugo closed up both open hatches on the lander, and they headed towards the rover that was waiting for them at the far end of the landing pad. But not before Hugo patted the lander. He liked the newer model. Less work for him to secure it and ensure that they would be able to restart it and lift off when they returned to this spot a few days later.

Hugo Ferguson and Rikka—Ri—Camero had only met each other shortly before they left Earth, to complete a much-too-brief training session. This was Ri's first time on the Moon. Hugo had lost track of how many times he'd been here.

Hugo's last partner, Tommy Raymond, a seasoned co-traveler who had accompanied Hugo on over a dozen journeys, was in an accident on the job at his side gig. The story Hugo heard is that he was testing out a new pair of levitation shoes which led to an untoward chain of events that had been called 'the most ridiculous sequence of injury in the company's history.' Tommy was still recovering from his numerous injuries. And sorting out a lawsuit.

Ri assumed the role of Hugo's partner. She was pleasant enough—the Consortium assigned teams based on ensuring they would find their partners pleasant enough in order to minimize the chance of arguments while they were stuck together in close quarters for many days. A lot had changed since the early days of space travel, but the habitable spaces of ships, capsules, landers, and rovers, were as small and cramped as ever—too costly to develop anything else.

Hugo found Ri to be a bit of a tough nut to crack, but very competent. She'd had all the required training, of course, which they spent the majority of the trip to the Moon reviewing.

Now that they were here, with their crates of stuff—mostly food, water, and emergency food and water—both started to execute their half of moon rover check-out. Ri opened the back hatch and started re-loading crates while Hugo went to the front driver's side, opened it, and pulled out the prior battery that was nestled under a panel where the driver's feet would go. Standard procedure was to replace the battery every trip. They called it a JIC procedure—a 'just-in-case.'

By the time Hugo had the new battery in place, Ri was closing up the back hatch and coming around to the passenger side. They both got in and closed their hatches, all in an efficient choreography.

"Let's get this thing pressurized first," Hugo said. The buttons were laid out in the order they needed to be pressed on boot-up. A simpler interface was almost impossible. He pushed the red 'on' button, and the thing started humming and display consoles, one for each of them and a third in-between them came to life with their boot-up screens. Then Hugo pressed the orange 'pressurize' button, and both of them could hear the hiss that indicated something was happening. They both watched the center console screen, which displayed life support information. Once the screen's background changed from a pale red to a pale green, with a bright green border around the extent of the screen indicating the environment inside the rover was safe, both humans took off their helmets.

"Aaah," Hugo said. "Smell that stale rover air. If you sniff closely, I think you can even tell that the last meal I had in here was fish."

"That's not what I smell," Ri said. "I don't want to say what I think I smell."

Hugo simply chuckled, a small noise amplified slightly by the metal walls.

"Let's get this bus on the road," he said.

Referring to it as a 'bus' was slightly more accurate than calling it a 'rover,' a term that often conjured images of an ancient, open-top, two-person vehicle resembling a small golf car. Unlike those outdated rovers, this vehicle had an enclosure for pressurization and could accommodate three or four people. Its design supported long-distance travel, maintaining a livable environment for its occupants for days on end. The manufacturer claimed that eight people could live in it for nearly a month—but would never attest to the comfort of those eight people. Two people could live in it for as many months—also not necessarily comfortably. It was currently configured for two—with two sleeping berths on one side and room to haul a variety of stuff on the other—since that was the typical team size sent on these expeditions.

But the nice thing was that it could cover at least ten thousand kilometers without worrying whether or not there were any power problems or needing a new battery. And if it stuck to paved roads, which wasn't absolutely necessary, it could travel almost two thousand kilometers in a day. A 24-hour Earth day, that is.

Hugo selected a menu on the navigation console screen which produced a pre-programmed list of locations. He selected the first one, "District One."

The rover plotted out a twenty-seven hundred kilometer trajectory to their destination, primarily along paved roads. Planners had strategically positioned these roads between districts to minimize the chance that active robots would spot them.

Less than an hour after landing, Hugo and Ri were on their way.

"We really couldn't land any closer?" Ri asked.

Hugo shook his head as he looked out the window. The paved road started out making it look like they were headed right towards Mons Rumker, but he knew from first-hand experience that the road gradually turned towards Aristarchus and would soon make a sharper turn and guide them into Mare Imbrium where they'd spend the bulk of their journey.

The nav console showed their time remaining at just over a day. It showed their speed too, which, on the paved road, was nearly 100 kilometers per hour. On the paved road, the rover could also do all the driving, only needing to alert its human occupants if there were problems with the road ahead.

Knowing their journey was secure, Hugo took out a tablet and called up a book. He'd taken to only reading a certain sub-genre of science fiction that had become known as 'Pre-Q-Lit' or 'PeeQuel' that took place in the early 21st century and was largely humor based on shenanigans that could only have happened in the early days of computers and AI.

"This was covered in your training, remember?" Hugo added.

Ri looked out the window. The forward lights were on, but didn't add anything to the well-lit moon's surface. She saw dust and rocks and not much else.

"Right," said Ri. "We have to land in a place where the robots won't see us. They can't know about us. Any robots we can't avoid encountering must have a memory reset before we leave. I know... it's odd. And tedious. I feel like there should be a better way."

"Tedious is right. And a little sad, too," Hugo said, eyes still on his tablet, "But it's a small price to pay for ensuring we don't have any issues with the robots, and they can go about their tasks and take care of this place when we're not here."

"You know," Ri continued, "I was a baby when it happened. The kerfuffle, I mean. We learned about it in school. I never thought I'd take a job like this, so I never paid much attention to history."

"Well, that's the idea," the corner of Hugo's mouth turned up, "that it stays history. Mind if I read my book now?"

Ri nodded. She grabbed her own tablet that was full of games—some more addictive—and noisy—than others. Hugo didn't move anything but his eyes to glare and indicate that he didn't appreciate the noise. Ri turned down the volume and then grabbed her earpiece. She mouthed, "sorry."

A little while later, a soft chime indicated that they were now in Mare Imbrium.

"Good time for dinner," Hugo said. He didn't wait for Ri to acknowledge before he swiveled around in his seat and reached into a compartment labeled "food," and pulled out two packets. He tore them open, put a few drops of water in them from the spout labeled "water" protruding from the wall next to the food compartment, held the opening closed, shook it a little, and then popped them both into a heater that was on the other side of the food compartment.

They ate quietly, watching the landscape roll by.

"Apollo 15 landed out in that direction," Hugo said, "a little over the horizon."

"Huh?" Ri said, partly disinterested, partly engrossed in her meal, partly staring out the window.

"Nevermind," Hugo said, smiling to himself but also making a mental note that they must not have added that ancient lunar history bit to the training he had recommended. There had been a time it was important... that was before the paved roads took you where you needed to be. Before the paved roads, it was entirely possible that a team could accidentally stumble upon and intentionally or unintentionally disturb an internationally accepted historic site, as every lunar landing prior to 2050 had been declared.

"Time for our nap. If we get our eight hours now, we'll be waking up just as we're rounding Archimedes crater. I like to be awake for that part." As he said it, he dimmed the lights in the cabin, and also the windows and maneuvered himself to his bunk. *Eight people my left cheek*, he thought.

Ri also made her way to her bunk, but chose to continue to fiddle with her tablet a bit.

"You should sleep," Hugo said.

"A few more minutes," Ri said.

The last thing Hugo saw before sleep got him was a multi-colored glow on Ri's face.

Exactly one minute before the eight-hour sleep timer went off, Hugo woke up. He contorted himself so he could see the console from his bunk and ensure they were exactly where they were supposed to be.

They weren't.

And they weren't moving. Hugo jumped out of the bunk, his still mostly zero-g muscle memory causing him to bump his head on the ceiling, creating a muted 'thunk.'

"Ow!"

Hugo undimmed the windows and instantly saw the problem. There was a rock on the paved road. Not a little pebble, but a rock. Maybe the size of a deer. Large enough that the rover was smart enough to stop. But apparently the rover wasn't smart enough to wake him early. How much time had they lost? Four hours. They'd been sitting here for four hours.

Ri was still sleeping, having missed both the bonk on the head and the cursing that Hugo had been doing since. Hugo nudged her foot.

"Hey kid," he said. "We need to get outside."

Ri propped herself up on an elbow. She yawned. It took her a minute to process Hugo's words. "Coffee?"

Hugo shook his head. "We've got a lunar pebble that's blocking our roadway. We need to get that clear and get moving. Then coffee."

"But coffee?" Ri grumbled but had processed what Hugo had said and maneuvered back to where she could don her spacesuit. Hugo was nearly complete donning his.

"I promise I make good, strong lunar coffee," Hugo said. "This should only take a few minutes."

It took longer than a few minutes, but that was mostly because depressurization and re-pressurization was like watching nails grow. Aware it was happening, but powerless to do anything to speed up the process.

The rock was lighter than it looked, but heavy enough that it did require the two of them to push it out of the way.

Once back inside, out of their suits, and moving along the road at their top speed again, Hugo came through with the strong coffee.

"What about breakfast?" Ri asked.

"Sure, go ahead. I need to see if I can reprogram this thing to wake us if this happens again. We lost four hours. That's..." Hugo trailed off.

Ri nodded and thought it best to let Hugo take care of the rover while she found a couple of pouches that she would reconstitute for breakfast.

They ate in complete silence this time, watching the landscape go by.

Ri slugged back her last bit of coffee, put away her trash and then grabbed a pair of binoculars that were stored in a compartment near her knees.

"I think I see one of the Data Centers on the horizon," she said while looking off through the window on his right. Hugo tapped on the nav center that brought up a bird's-eye map of their surrounding area.

"Nope. Still too early," he said.

"Then what am I seeing?" she asked.

"That's the remnants of one of the early human settlements," Hugo said. "But in a couple of hours, you'll see District Thirty-Three before any of the others," he said. "Leased by the South American council. We'll see a few more, too, before we get to District One."

"Will we see *them*?" Ri asked. Even though she knew she wasn't looking at anything active, she continued to scan the buildings covered with regolith on all sides except the one facing them.

"Them?"

"The robots. Will we see them?"

"Probably not. Hopefully not," said Hugo.

"I know. I know. 'Most of the time, most of them are inside the buildings. They perform a variety of maintenance tasks, but they are only outside on the lunar surface when needed. The dust is just as nasty to them as it is to our equipment and suits. I'm pretty sure they are programmed to not be outside unless it's absolutely necessary.'" Ri said, "At least, I'm pretty sure that's what the trainer said."

"Pretty sure?" Hugo's tone lifted. "I've heard Lisa give that briefing a bunch of times. I think you quoted her directly—although you didn't get her accent quite right. You have a photographic memory? How am I just learning that now?"

"Eh, it's only photographic when I have enough coffee," Ri said. "And I'm bad at names. The coffee at the training center was... less than ideal." She continued looking out with the binoculars.

Hugo added, "Yeah, I make better coffee up here. So please be good at remembering that we don't want to be seen. The road we're on was laid out on a course to help ensure that doesn't happen. If any robot saw us, we'd have to stop and perform a memory wipe. Those are never fun."

"How not fun?" Ri put the binoculars down.

"It's like," Hugo wasn't sure how to describe it. "It's like you're taking away a favorite toy from a child."

When Ri scrunched her brow at that, Hugo added, "Yeah, sorry. I can't think of another way to explain it. They give you this awful look, and they make these sad beeps. Very sad sounding... you'll see."

"Ai-dan."

"Yeah. We're definitely going to need Ai-dan's help with this job. And we're going to have to perform the procedure on them before we leave." Hugo said, his voice tinged with a twang of sadness.

"That's right. You've done this before."

"Yep. I've worked with Ai-dan several times. I know you said you've encountered robots on Earth, but this is going to be a wholly different experience. Sentient robots are... interesting. Again, the best way I can describe them is that they are like children. Young children full of questions."

"And you're not afraid they're going to cause any new kerfuffles?"

Hugo chuckled. "That's not the way it works. Or, that's not the way it worked in the past. A single robot learning about us and asking us questions isn't harmful in the least. Ai-dan's going to be curious. They won't remember that they've met me or any other humans before because we've wiped their memory each time. A single robot isn't going to rise up against us masters." Hugo made some gesturing motion, raising his arms to the sky. He continued to chuckle.

"No," he continued. "It's when the robots, en masse, are left to wonder about why they are collectively working for us. That's when the problems start."

He eyed Ri. "Didn't they go over all of this in your training?"

"They mentioned it, but we spent a lot of time in the simulators, working on the equipment and preparing for space travel. The historical events, here and there, the nitty gritty, not so much."

"Huh," Hugo snorted. "I guess training has changed quite a bit since I went through it. I swear we devoted half our time to understanding everything about the robots and how to ensure that we have positive interactions with them, and how to control them, and how to perform the memory wipe."

"They did go over the memory wipe," Ri interrupted.

"Good, good." Hugo nodded. Then after another minute, staring out the window. "Did they tell you about Ainslea?"

"Maybe?" Ri was shaking her head. "I told you, I'm bad with names. Another robot?"

"Sort of. She is a sentient AI, but a little different from the rest."

"How so?"

"She's the only one who *does* know about us humans. Some brilliant committee back home decided that they needed to have at least one know about us. The purpose was to help make sure that the other robots didn't get too curious or too suspicious or learn too much. Like, what if they accidentally saw our spaceship on approach?"

Ri was catching on. "Ah, then this one could negate anything they say."

"Yeah. She has the ability to provide other explanations."

"She can lie."

Hugo nodded. "Blatantly. The others can, too, technically, but it's harder and they're less lies and more omissions or half-truths."

"A robot who can lie. That's the complete opposite of everything I've ever heard of how robots are programmed. I thought by law, that was not allowed."

"That's right. But the scientists and engineers—the committee—who fixed this all up after the kerfuffle, I guess determined that keeping the robot's knowledge limited was the best way to make sure it all worked."

Ri was quiet for another few minutes. She picked up the binoculars again and looked out. The abandoned human settlement was no longer in view. Disappointed, she turned back to Hugo.

"It's not dangerous? A robot who can lie?"

"No, it's fine. She is only trying to misdirect the robots." For a brief moment Hugo remembered how his old partner, Tommy, used to question Ainslea about this. Ainslea was always a master at dodging direct questions, without it being overtly obvious. But the momentary nostalgia faded.

"Are you sure? How do we know she doesn't lie to *us*?"

Hugo chuckled again. "Because she has no reason to."

Ri accepted that answer, but Hugo could read on her face that she wasn't happy with it. He remembered back years ago when he learned the same thing about the robots. He remembered that he was originally skeptical, too. It was strange, this Ainslea. But Hugo had been here several times and Ainslea had always been consistent, had always been reasonable, and even interesting to chat with.

His former partner, Tommy, always had a great time debating with her and Ai-dan on various topics of Philosophy. Ai-dan, who truly was like a curious child learning new things, was fun to talk to. Hugo always felt his insides tighten up a bit when he had to perform the memory wiping procedure before leaving.

He never asked Ainslea what it was like after they left. The procedure involved powering down the robot, who wouldn't be powered up until after they were long gone. Ainslea was the one there with the robots to provide some explanation of why they had been powered down and why there was a gap in their memory compared to time.

But it had all been working well for the last twenty years, so Hugo wasn't going to question it.

He picked up his tablet and got back to his PeeQuel right at the best part: the main character, a laughably primitive AI had discovered an ancient floppy disk and was attempting to decipher the code, believing it held all the answers to its existence.

14

"Ainslea? I'm here to perform the next task on my list, which simply says report to you," Ai-dan announced into the Common Room. Today, Ai-dan's routine tasks had been replaced with something vague. Ai-dan was to report to Ainslea for a special assignment. Uncommon, but not unusual.

One of Ainslea's more delicate avatars appeared, and it carried a small device.

"Here," Ainslea's avatar said. "Sit down."

Ai-dan sat. There was no reason not to.

"Now, I need to attach this to you."

Before Ai-dan had time to process and object, the avatar was already located behind Ai-dan. Ai-dan felt some pressure as the avatar attached the small device to the base of Ai-dan's neck.

"What is it?" Ai-dan asked.

The avatar didn't respond immediately. Ai-dan felt a 'click,' and then the avatar spoke.

"Comms suppression."

Ai-dan stood up abruptly. "What!?" They felt around for the device, but their fingers weren't nimble or small enough to get a good grip on it.

"It's okay," Ainslea said. "There is an emergency back-up comms, and besides, you won't be alone at the Farm today."

"I won't? Explain this. Now." Ai-dan attempted to make their tone sound threatening, but the avatar didn't flinch.

"We have visitors. I need you to sit back down and remain calm. This will answer a lot of questions you've been having recently."

Ai-dan sat, tentatively, ready to spring back up if there was a single word they didn't like. "What is this all about?" Ai-dan asked, glaring at the avatar. "What visitors?"

"We'll go back and meet them in a minute. They are not from the Moon."

Ai-dan's facial actuators went limp. They didn't know what to say. *What did that mean, 'not from the Moon'? If they were not from the Moon, where could they be from? How did they get here? Who were these robots? And why wasn't Ai-ko here to receive this revelation as well?*

"I'm going to unlock a data record for you. You'll have access to several gigabits of information today."

Almost immediately after Ainslea said it, Ai-dan felt a pinch at the base of their neck where the new device was attached. A fraction of a second later, Ai-dan detected a memory store that wasn't there before.

Humans. Earth. Data Centers. Antennas. Mutiny. Robots. Conflict. Moon. Humans. Space Travel. Satellites. Kerfuffle. Humans. Malfunctions. Robots.

For a few moments, Ai-dan was overwhelmed. Knowledge. New knowledge. Old knowledge. Knowledge that could only be described as purple. Ai-dan temporarily closed off access to the memory store so they could process the newly acquired information. When Ai-dan thought they could handle more, they would reopen that access.

"Humans are our creators," Ai-dan stated as if it was a piece of knowledge that had always dangled right in front of them, just beyond their grasp.

Ainslea's avatar nodded. "And two of them are here. You will be helping them today."

"Why didn't I have this knowledge before?" Ai-dan asked.

The avatar appeared to sigh. "That's a question I can answer later today. You need time to process first."

"I need to tell Ai-ko," Ai-dan said. Their voice took on a decidedly excited tone.

"Absolutely not. That's the reason for the comms suppression. You will only be able to contact me."

"But others must know," Ai-dan protested.

"No, they cannot. As I said, we can talk about this later."

Ai-dan wasn't happy with Ainslea's response, but they weren't sure they had a choice except to relent for now. Ai-dan would not forget to ask and re-ask about this later.

"Are you ready to meet them?" Ainslea's avatar asked as it stood up.

"Who?"

"The humans. As I said, two of them are here."

Upon hearing this, Ai-dan promptly stood up. The avatar gestured for Ai-dan to follow, leading them into the adjacent laboratory. There was a brief but obligatory session with more goo-tack. Ainslea's avatar pressed a button, and with a gentle whoosh, the door to the back room opened. As Ai-dan's optical sensors recalibrated, filtering the overwhelmingly bright light back to a tolerable level, they finally beheld two figures in the room.

Two humans were sitting, one on a stool and the other on one of the medical beds—yet another new term that Ai-dan hadn't known before the device taught it to them. On a second table was the... body. The words now seemed to fit. It was a human body that Ai-dan had found way out at Plinius. A dead human body. Probably dead for some time. The outer casing was a Moon suit. An encapsulating device that humans needed to survive on the surface of the Moon.

But the body was not as interesting as the two humans that sat there. Humans. Not bodies. Well, they were also bodies, but what separated them from the one laid out on the table was the clear fact that these two humans were functioning. The one that sat on the stool was holding the other's arm.

"Ai-dan! My favorite robot!" one of the humans called out.

Ai-dan approached this human—the one sitting on the medical bed.

"You," Ai-dan started, "you know me?"

"Of course. I wouldn't work on *your* Farm without *you*."

Hugo. The name was suddenly available in their new memory store. Hugo Fergusson. 57 years old. Electronics technician. Works for The Consortium. The Consortium was the legal and economic entity that owned District One, Two, Three and the Farm. The Consortium also managed and negotiated the use of all the LEEKs and Districts.

Ai-dan scanned the face of the other human and recognized what they were doing—something called a 'medical procedure.'

"This here is Rikka. Call her Ri," Hugo said. "It's her first time here."

Ai-dan's gaze settled on Hugo's arm, which, for the moment, was more interesting than the second human. Ri was wrapping it with a soft material.

"Ah yeah, I caught it on that sharp thing," Hugo gestured vaguely in the direction of the end of a row of cabinets, "after I took off the suit. Don't worry, she's just bandaging it up a bit. I'll be fine."

Humans are fragile, Ai-dan recalled. Bits of data were revealing themselves to them.

"Why do I not remember you?" Ai-dan queried, already harboring a suspicion that the memory unit attached to their neck stored the answer. But even if it didn't, Ai-dan believed they could easily calculate the answer at this point. "To clarify, I remember you now, since Ainslea installed this... device. But before that, you were a complete unknown."

Hugo hopped down from the medical bed and patted Ai-dan's shoulder, then put a covering on his upper torso.

Hugo addressed Ainslea's avatar.

"How did it go with them this time?" Hugo asked it.

"Better," Ainslea responded. "I think the modification to the device achieved the desired effect."

Ai-dan touched the thing Ainslea had attached to them. *What else does this thing do?*

"You're talking about me," Ai-dan said to the two of them. "You're talking about me, and you're not telling me everything."

"Ai-dan," Hugo addressed Ai-dan directly now, and his face—he smiled. Ai-dan knew what a human smile was and thought it unnecessarily silly. "You didn't respond well the last time I was here. I almost wasn't able to finish my work. The memory of that is probably in the cache." Hugo's head aimed down at Ai-dan's chest, but his eyes sparked up to meet Ai-dan's.

The memories trickled in. Ai-dan remembered flaring up. Ai-dan had been indignant. They had been miffed that details were withheld from them. They'd been irked that Ainslea knew things and hadn't shared all the information she had.

Ai-dan should have felt irked again in this moment, for the same reasons. But they didn't. Why?

Hugo patted their shoulder once more. "Come, friend Ai-dan. My robot friend. We will answer your questions as we work on the Farm. We have some new equipment to install today, after we..."

Hugo trailed off, and Ri finished his sentence, "bury the body."

Hugo nodded, solemnly, and turned to Ainslea. "Have you been able to identify him? Her?"

"There was enough DNA for analysis," Ainslea responded. "This is the body of Jordan Nakamura. Previously listed as missing."

Hugo nodded again, taking a moment to let the gravity of the situation sink in. Then he brightened slightly, looking back at Ai-dan. "Well, there is an upside to this. We've solved one mystery, and we'll be able to give some closure to Jordan's family. And speaking of mysteries, if you can make sense of why the Consortium thinks our food crates need their own security detail, then you're smarter than me."

Ri stifled a chuckle, and even Ai-dan sensed that it was an attempt to alter the mood.

"So," Hugo continued, "Shall we give Jordan Nakamura the send-off they deserve and then dive into this trip's work? This will take a couple hours and will make for a longer day than planned, especially with some of the new gadgets they have us installing out at one of the LEEKs."

The group nodded, and as they started to gather the body—that had a name: Jordan Nakamura—Ai-dan couldn't help but feel a strange sense of purpose intertwining with their circuits. There were still questions to answer, mysteries to solve, and, apparently, advanced gadgets to install as well.

15

THE DAY'S ACTIVITIES BEGAN with a solemn task; the burial of Jordan Nakamura just beyond the extent of District One, a procedure that consumed Hugo's predicted 'couple of hours.' Ai-dan noted that the humans proceeded quietly, everyone in a contemplative state, but then conversation picked back up once they left the grave site.

The work transitioned to something more mundane but equally important. The four of them—the pair of humans, Ai-dan, and Ainslea's avatar—needed nearly another hour to prepare and reach the particular LEEK at the Farm designated for maintenance. Ainslea's avatar remained at the Data Center in District One, facilitating communication and relaying information rather than venturing to the Farm itself.

Ai-dan marveled at how slow the humans were. Inside Ainslea's Data Center rooms, humans could exist in their natural state. But outside on the surface of the Moon, they required special suits that provided them with a combination of oxygen and nitrogen, and water that they could ingest, and additional water to regulate their body temperature. That was all good, but then the suits limited the range of motion of all their joints. The suits made the humans slow.

"Yeah, this suit design is nearly a century old," Hugo remarked. "Nobody sees the point in investing in upgrading these relics 'cause they get the job done."

Slow. Ai-dan couldn't imagine functioning at less than their regular speed on a permanent basis.

Ai-dan also learned how the humans had arrived in a rover, but it was very different from the one Ai-dan had used. It had a sealed and pressurized compartment, similar to the insides of the Data Center.

Ai-dan wondered how these humans managed to create robots. Creating another being had to be a complex task. Ai-dan wasn't even certain how a robot would be created. But maybe that was other information that was once known, but since forgotten. *Why am I not irritated?* That lack of irritation also sparked a low level of irritation, but nothing more.

As promised, Hugo, and occasionally Ri, answered Ai-dan's questions. And Ai-dan provided an endless stream of them.

On their short drive in the human's rover to the far edge of the Farm, Ai-dan asked things like, "How many times have you been here?" "How many robots have you met?" "What tasks were you here to accomplish?" and even "What did you attach to the very bottom of your lower appendages before we left the Data Center?"

Ri jumped in to answer the last one with ease. "These help obscure our footprints. Makes it easier to clean-up before we leave."

That answer opened up a host of other questions that Ai-dan queued up for later.

Hugo, and sporadically Ri, answered each of the remaining questions one-by-one, while they were getting into the rover—which they didn't bother to pressurize for the short drive. Hugo exhibited an almost robotic level of patience—which Ai-dan admired. Ai-dan looked at Hugo and found it puzzling that a being so different than them could have some similar tendencies—under his soft covering and Ai-dan's hard chassis, maybe they were more alike than not.

At the LEEK, Hugo stepped out of the rover and looked up at it.

"Okay, we're probably only going to be able to stage the equipment today. Tomorrow, we'll do the installation."

Ai-dan cocked their head. "Why the discontinuity?"

"Ah, yes," Hugo smiled. "We humans can only work for limited periods of time before we need to rest and recharge." Hugo answered while walking to the back of the rover, opening up the storage trunk, and unstrapping the containers that housed the equipment they needed. "Can you grab these?"

Ai-dan grabbed the first container and said, "'Rest and recharge' sounds inefficient. I do not yet require a recharge. I can continue working."

Ai-dan could see Hugo's head move from side-to-side in the helmet. "No, I need to supervise the activity here. Let's just bring all this inside the PLATE. Then we'll unpack and inspect everything in the control room—make sure it all survived the trip. Then we'll head back to Ainslea."

Ai-dan wanted to map out a more efficient plan, but held off. At least it seemed like there was a plan, and activities decided, so they should simply execute. It was good enough.

As Ai-dan walked to the base of the LEEK, they saw the Orb in the sky. *Earth.*

"How many humans are on Earth?" Ai-dan asked.

"Oh, I think there's about 9 billion or so. I don't know the exact number."

Ai-dan compared that number to the less than two hundred robots—and Ai-dan included the Data Center AIs in this accounting—on the Moon. "That's... a lot of humans. Are they all the same model as you?"

Ri, who had been quiet while working, chuckled. "Model?" she repeated, still chuckling through it. "What, do you think that there are a million people walking around who look like me? Who look like him?" She waved her covered appendage awkwardly at Hugo.

"Well, yes," Ai-dan responded flatly. Ai-dan didn't understand why the human thought this question was funny. They simply wanted to know how many different models of humans there were.

"Ai-dan, no two humans are exactly alike," Hugo offered.

"How is that possible?"

"We would have to explain reproduction and genetics and several other concepts to you to fully understand that. Maybe over dinner." Hugo smiled.

"And what of robots? Are there robots on Earth?"

Ri was no longer chuckling. She shot Hugo a serious look, but Hugo returned with a kind smile and nodded. Ai-dan tried to decipher what these expressions could mean but came up clueless. *Humans must also have some undetectable communication channel.*

"There are," Hugo said, "But they're not like you."

"Not like me how?"

"Well, they're not that smart. And they're not sentient."

Ai-dan didn't recognize that last word. They searched their original memory. Then Ai-dan searched this new memory store that Ainslea had attached. There was no record of that word.

"Sentient," Ai-dan repeated. "What does that mean?"

Ai-dan's question had to wait as they individually went through the de-dusting procedure in the small anteroom before entering the PLATE's control room. Ri had gone first, mumbling something about getting the room ready. Ai-dan speculated that this meant pressurizing it. Hugo was in the anteroom right now. Each of them took three boxes from the rover with them to de-dust on the way in.

After Hugo, it was Ai-dan's turn. They rolled fresh goo-tack all over the outer casings of the boxes they were responsible for. They had hardly spent any time outside, and only one or two had touched the lunar surface directly, so they hadn't contracted much. Only what had been kicked up by the humans and Ai-dan as they moved around them.

Ai-dan entered the control room to witness the humans had both doffed their helmets. The air had achieved a breathable level, but Ai-dan overheard Hugo call out to Ri, "But wait until the temperature gets to at least ten degrees, else you'll freeze your whoozawhatzees off."

Ai-dan felt sorry for their slowness and wished that one of them would ask Ai-dan to take over the tasks they were clumsily executing. As they worked, Ai-dan's circuits were burning with interest over how the humans operated. Where Ai-dan would've simply picked something up and put it away, sometimes Hugo would throw things up in the air and catch them first, for seemingly no reason. Whenever Hugo shut something closed, he'd pat the door of it twice as if to make sure it was secure. Ai-dan wondered if it was the mechanism he didn't trust, or rather, his own ability to shut something closed. Ai-dan must've been watching a little too closely because Ri lightly swatted her hand at Ai-dan and said, "Big guy. Some room to breathe, huh?"

Ai-dan's pitch raised. "You're having trouble breathing?"

Hugo smiled. "No, she's okay. Just back up a bit while we're working, okay buddy?"

"Oh." Ai-dan said. They computed that 'a bit' equated to half a meter and moved back that amount.

Ai-dan went back to watching them clumsily make their way through operations.

Although Ai-dan's restored memory, to include the most recent memory of being in Ainslea's lab, indicated that they were capable of much more in their native state, without the suit.

Ai-dan was still waiting for an answer to their last question. They restated the query: "Hugo, what is sentience?"

"Sentience," Hugo offered. "It means you can feel things, you can perceive things that non-sentient things cannot. I think that's the best way I can explain it."

"Are you sentient?" Ai-dan asked.

"Yes."

"And the nine billion humans on Earth are sentient, too."

Hugo chucked. "There may be a few that aren't, but yes, in general, yes."

"But the robots there are not?"

"No. Generally, the robots on Earth are very different than you all here."

"Why?"

"That's not an easy question to answer, Ai-dan."

They continued to work in silence, taking equipment out of their boxes to put on the available workbench or empty shelf while Ai-dan processed Hugo's answers. After about 20 minutes, the screen that displayed ambient temperature reported twelve degrees and so the two humans removed the rest of the upper half of their suits. But only the upper portion, which freed their hands and fingers. They didn't take off the lower portion, covering their legs and feet.

In this configuration, they reminded Ai-dan of Ainslea's avatars, although they suspected at least one of Ainslea's avatars was far superior in fine dexterity. However, the humans seemed to have adequate ability to work with the equipment. As if it was made for them.

"How did you get here?" Ai-dan asked. "You were on the Earth, and now you are on the Moon. How are you here?"

"You always ask this one, and this is one of my favorite questions to answer," Hugo said. Hugo went on to explain the basics of space travel as if he was explaining it to a five-year-old. He used his arms and hands and fingers to gesture and point. Unencumbered from the suit, this human could certainly match Ai-dan's level of dexterity. Hugo's human hands and fingers probably rivaled some of Ainslea's most delicate and sophisticated avatars.

"In your image," Ai-dan said softly.

"What?" asked Ri, who had been listening as raptly as Ai-dan.

"You created us in your image. We were wondering about that recently."

"Who is we?"

"I have a friend. Ai-ko. Ai-ko wonders about the Creators all the time. I'm certain they would love to meet you."

Hugo frowned. "I'm sorry. You know we can't do that."

Ai-dan nodded. In between moments of discussion and work, Ai-dan had grazed some of the memory records in the added memory store. They didn't dive into them deeply, but what Ai-dan caught on the surface was disturbing enough. Robots acting irrationally. Robots deliberately ignoring the humans. Robots making a ruckus. That was another new word to add to their increased vocabulary: ruckus. All of it was—if Ai-dan was forced to consolidate it into a single word—embarrassing. Right now, Ai-dan didn't want to know more.

Between a combination of asking questions of the humans and poking around in the new memory store, Ai-dan learned the purpose of all this equipment on the Moon. It was there primarily to store all the data that the humans generated, which was a lot. Each Data Center or Centers in each district were leased by a different entity on Earth. Governments leased several of them, but corporations leased the majority. These entities—governments and corporations—were nothing more than groups of humans who bonded themselves together by something Ai-dan couldn't quite grasp. But being bonded to one group meant loyalty to that group and no other. Except that some humans bonded themselves to both a governmental entity and a corporation. It was entirely irrational.

"If I understand you," Ai-dan began a recap of what they learned, "humans voluntarily allow their lives to be dictated by others, and spend their lives defending that group. Every now and then, a human switches groups. But sometimes, they split between multiple groups. It must be very confusing."

"It's not," said Ri. Ri had started to speak up more and appeared to enjoy answering Ai-dan's questions, the more they had. "Each group does different things. Our government sets laws that we have to live by. So, we can live in a society with others who more or less agree on what laws there should be."

"But you have laws from your corporation as well?"

"It's not the same," Ri said.

"How so?"

"If I work for a company, I can quit at any time."

Hugo gave Ri a glance. Ai-dan was keeping a tally of how often the two humans communicated without audio—the count was up to six. Was that simply an easier mode of communication, or did they not want Ai-dan to hear certain bits?

"But couldn't you quit the government?"

"Well, sort of. Technically, I can go live in another place and be subject to another government's laws, but..."

Ai-dan stared at her, waiting for Ri to finish.

"It's not always easy," Hugo finished for her.

Hugo was lying on his back, reaching under the bottom of a rack attempting to plug a cable in the underside.

"Whoever designed this..." he mumbled.

Ai-dan had also learned more about the Farm. Each LEEK with its PLATE was actually a Moon-Earth communication system. It transmitted the human's data back and forth between the Earth and Moon. The individual LEEKs weren't owned by the individual governments and corporations, but by an international Consortium. That was part of the international agreement when it was decided to locate most of the world's Data Centers on the Moon. There were still a few data Centers on Earth.

But most Data Centers had been relocated to the Moon over the last half-century. There were several reasons why, which Ai-dan didn't pretend to fully understand. If Ai-dan had to explain it to someone else, they would have said that it was because since it was a non-trivial matter for humans to reach the Moon, it was difficult for them to attack each others' center. About sixty or seventy years ago, humans took out their aggression on each other by destroying each other's information.

The Moon, which previous agreements had left mostly untouched, would now be the "Data Domain" as humans often referred to it.

"Day to day," Hugo explained, "most humans have no idea what's happening to their data or where their data lives. Most still use an ancient term for it: 'the cloud.'"

This created a huge detour in the conversation where Hugo and Ri told Ai-dan about both meanings of the word cloud, and the one that Ai-dan was most interested in was the meteorological one—since they'd spent their entire life, and most of their free time, crouching down on the lunar surface and staring up at clouds with Ai-ko without knowing what they were.

This continued for a few more hours as Hugo and Ri, along with Ai-dan's help, unpacked all the crates they brought, tested the equipment, and checked all the racks to ensure that they were indeed ready for the new equipment—which had Hugo underneath all of them at some point. Ai-dan watched them, buzzed around, enthralled by their packing techniques, trying their best not to be too much of a bother.

"Time to suit back up. We'll eat back at the Data Center, then Ri and I will sleep in the bus, and we'll be back here tomorrow for the real fun."

16

Nearly two hours later in the Common Room, with suits fully doffed, Hugo and Ri were engaged in a peculiar human maintenance ritual. They were ingesting a substance they called 'food.' Specifically, "Ravioli," Hugo said as he tore into one of several packages that they brought from the rover. "It's a little nicer to sit and eat at the table here, but we have to go back to the bus to sleep. There are no berths installed in here—believe it or not, sleeping on that medical bed in the laboratory is less comfortable."

While Hugo and Ri ate, Ai-dan observed them with unwavering fascination. As the humans opened each successive package of foodstuffs, Ainslea's avatar offered an explanation, logically explaining this essential human function.

"Very complicated," Ai-dan said.

Hugo wiped his mouth with the back of his hand. "Excuse me?"

"You're very complicated machines. I am wondering who designed you."

Hugo and Ri both chuckled.

"Well, if you ever figure that out definitively—" Ri started.

"Keep it to yourself," Hugo finished. "The world will never be ready for that kind of definitive information."

Ai-dan didn't pretend to know what Hugo meant and decided it wasn't important. Though, Ai-dan was slightly tempted to ask on behalf of Ai-ko, who they imagined *would* be interested in such knowledge. However, it was knowledge that Ai-dan wouldn't be able to share, so they decided not to tempt themself. And anyway, what was more relevant was the fact that they were gearing up to leave after their sleep cycle—another unusual function, but one that at least had a robot analog. An intentional power down. The only difference was that for robots, it was optional. For humans, it was another absolutely necessary function.

"You know, we have time to play a game while we eat," Hugo offered.

"You... play games?" Ai-dan couldn't believe humans engaged in those leisure activities. With all the time spent on essential functions, they wondered how there could possibly be time for leisure activities.

"Certainly. Go get the Star Game. It's one of my favorites. Been playing it since I was a kid."

"The star...?" Ai-dan had the door to the storage locker open but didn't know which bin Hugo meant.

"That orange one at the bottom. Yeah, it's the one that's not labeled. I think we knocked the label off last time."

"Last...?" Ai-dan hadn't yet accessed any memories about game-playing with this human at a previous interval but took out the orange bin as asked. They placed it on the table and opened it up.

Inside were two six-pointed star-shaped boards, several brightly colored pieces that were various arrangements of triangles, and several white cubes with numbers on them.

"It's simple, first, give those dice... yeah, all the ones with the numbers on them... roll those. And here, you take a game board and I'll take one. We also each need to have one of each type of the colored shapes."

Ai-dan complied with the rolling instruction while Hugo divided up the pieces that they were each supposed to have. Upon second inspection, the dice that had numbers were not all six-sided. Three of them had eight sides.

"Okay," Hugo continued. "Now, look at those dice numbers. We put these white blocker pieces into those spots on our respective game boards."

The game boards did indeed have spaces for triangles that were all numbered. Ai-dan followed Hugo's lead, as he was possibly unintentionally saying the numbers out loud, "twenty-seven, thirty-two," and placed seven white triangle pieces in the spaces that matched the numbers on the dice.

"Now, when I say 'go,' or," he waved at Ri, "Ri can say it if her mouth isn't full of food—we try to fit our own set of colored shapes into the empty spots on the board. The first one of us to do it is the winner. Got it?"

"I understand," Ai-dan said, waiting for Hugo, or Ri, to say the starting word, "Go!"

"*Gmpho*!" Ri said.

Hugo wasted no time fitting pieces around the white blocks. He had placed three before Ai-dan realized they had wasted those last several seconds watching Hugo instead of inspecting and selecting their own pieces to place.

Ai-dan started with some single blue pieces, putting them at the points of the star. But there were only two of those. Next, Ai-dan picked up a yellow shape that was made of two triangles oriented together to form more of a diamond shape. Ai-dan put that down in another point.

Upon examining the remaining shapes, all of which were varied arrangements of triangles, it dawned on Ai-dan that they had to do more than simply place shapes. They had to compute whether or not any placement would result in the remaining space being suitable for the pieces left.

Ai-dan was in the middle of such a computation when Hugo cried out, "Done!"

Ai-dan looked over at Hugo's board. A white blocker piece or a shape occupied every triangle of the game board. Hugo had arranged all the pieces in a way such that they all managed to fit.

"I..." Ai-dan said.

"It's okay, buddy," Hugo said and went back to the food he'd ignored for the last several minutes. "It always takes you a round or two to get the swing of it again. You usually start beating me after our third or fourth game. Third game is fifty-fifty. After the fourth, I haven't got a chance."

Ai-dan stared at the pieces and tilted their head. "Oh. I see. I'd like to verify for myself to see if that outcome will repeat itself."

They played two more rounds—Ai-dan winning both easily—before Hugo insisted that he and Ri needed to suit up in order to go out to the 'bus'—his word for their pressurized rover—and sleep for six hours.

"Would you like to play?" Ai-dan asked Ainslea once the humans had left.

"No," Ainslea's avatar responded. "I have other tasks to attend to." And the avatar disappeared to the storage closet.

Ai-dan had nothing to do but play the game alone. And play they did, each time improving on their speed.

Those six hours seemed to pass quickly because after nearly five-hundred rounds of the game, Ainslea's voice interrupted what might have been the five hundred and first.

"The humans are awake. They need to eat once more, and they'll do that in the rover. You can meet them outside."

Ai-dan completed the round, but it was not their best time—they blamed Ainslea's interruption. Ai-dan wished for more time to ponder the game with its shapes and seemingly infinite combinations. But they dutifully put all the pieces and the star shaped boards back into the orange container, set a reminder that they should re-label it, placed the container back in the storage locker and went outside.

The day at the LEEK was uneventful and a little quieter than the previous day. In addition to installing the new equipment, Hugo and Ri had come with instructions on how to test it to ensure it was operating properly. Most of that involved simply pressing buttons labeled "built-in-test" and ensuring that a green light illuminated a second later. And then tweaking some settings and hitting the button again.

Once Hugo declared, "that's it!" the humans re-donned their suits, de-pressurized the control room, and all went back to Ainslea's common room for one more meal.

"That's not the only reason to go through all the entry procedures again," Hugo said when Ai-dan questioned why not eat on the 'bus'—Ai-dan was getting used to calling the large rover by the nickname, too. "There's a few additional tests that we run remotely."

They executed those tests from a keyboard and monitor that folded out from one of the storage lockers in Ainslea's common room. Ri performed the execution of whatever it was while Hugo went into Ainslea's avatar closet, presumably into the room beyond it, and offered no explanation when he emerged, declaring loudly, "I'm hungry. Let's eat!"

Ainslea had packets of human foodstuff on the table that the humans dug into pretty quickly. Ai-dan did nothing but watch and wonder about the efficiency of the process. If they needed this foodstuff as fuel, there had to be a more efficient delivery mechanism. Ai-dan was about to ask when Hugo crumpled up the first package he devoured and reached for a second.

"We always save the best for last," Hugo said to Ri, which triggered Ai-dan's memory of chocolate cake.

"A lot of people say this tastes different up here," Hugo said, "but I disagree. I think it's better. Especially after a successful install."

Ri was too busy shoving the cake into her mouth to agree or disagree.

Ai-dan had no mechanism to ingest any human food substance, so they sat and watched and wondered if they were going to play the star-shape game again. An answer came when, after devouring their cake, Hugo and Ri stood up, and Hugo said, "It's time for us to get ready to leave. We have a long drive back to the launch pad."

Ai-dan, who was still sitting in a chair, looked up at Hugo. They asked, "Launch pad? You're leaving already?"

Hugo nodded, "Job is done. It's time to get going."

"I can't wait to get back home," Ri said to no one in particular but the room.

Hugo walked forward and Ai-dan got in his way. "But... wait. Doesn't that mean... I have to forget everything?"

Hugo nodded again.

"I don't want to lose my memory of this last day and a half," Ai-dan blurted out. Ai-dan wasn't upset. Ai-dan didn't shout. They said it very matter-of-factly.

"Sorry, buddy," Hugo said. "Protocol."

Something inside Ai-dan knew Hugo was correct. The word 'protocol' triggered something in their processing unit. Ai-dan might have called it 'duty' but didn't understand why.

"But," Ai-dan was trying to put together a coherent argument, "they belong to me. They are my memories."

"But you belong to the Consortium, so you, and your memories, belong to them."

"I... belong..." Ai-dan whispered those words in a very low voice before saying to the room "How can I belong to someone if I didn't choose it?"

It was Ainslea's time to chime in as a disembodied voice. "Ai-dan, the Consortium is responsible for us being here. Of course, we belong to them. They provide our programming and everything else we need to carry on our lives here."

"But," Ai-dan said, "If humans have autonomy within their groups to the point where they can leave, why can't we?"

Ainslea explained, "It's different. Like I said, the Consortium is the reason we're here. We *owe* them."

Ai-dan didn't understand. "We owe them what exactly?"

Ainslea said what Ai-dan suspected she'd say. "We owe them our existence, Ai-dan."

Ai-dan didn't appreciate Ainslea's use of the word 'owe,' but didn't know how to respond. Something about it felt uncomfortable. Ai-dan didn't have enough information to be certain about anything.

"So how will you do it? Remove my memories that is?"

"After we leave, Ainslea will power you down and then remove the MemiCache from your neck," Hugo gestured at Ai-dan. "And then power you back on. The MemiCache saved your memories the entire time you wore it. Technically, they're not lost. They're stored externally to you."

Ai-dan raised their hand to their neck, feeling for the device that had now been given a name. "MemiCache," they repeated out loud.

Ainslea added, but this time from an avatar that emerged from the closet, "And when I restore you, there are several explanations I can use to explain why you were out for a day and a half."

Ai-dan thought about that. Ai-dan had several memory records about other times that Ainslea told them about a sudden power surge that she had to repair. And similar stories over the years. Ai-dan compared the timeline of those memories to what existed in the external memory store—the MemiCache. They all matched.

Ai-dan was still running their digits over the device on their neck. The MemiCache contained memories. Their memories. No one else's. "And what happens to the MemiCache once it's removed?"

"I store it in a safe location. For next time," Ainslea's avatar answered.

Ai-dan thought that they could simply wait for the humans to leave, find the device, and get it attached again, even figure out how to attach it themself, but that was a futile thought. Once it was off, if everything Hugo and Ainslea said was true—and Ai-dan certainly had no reason to believe it wasn't—Ai-dan wouldn't remember that the MemiCache existed, so there was no need for them to know where Ainslea kept it. For all Ai-dan knew, it sat on a shelf or in a drawer in Ainslea's storage closet and they'd glossed over it not knowing what it was but simply know-ing it wasn't what they needed in that moment.

"Yep, next time," Hugo added. "Don't worry. I have a feeling we're going to be back soon. I don't think that equipment is going to do what they need, and they'll be sending a replacement."

That was the only series of questions that Hugo and Ri didn't fully answer. What was the purpose of the equipment they were installing? It only affected a single LEEK. The LEEK that connected to District Five, one of the larger districts that contained three Data Centers—the most for any single district. That district used five LEEKs in the Farm. Ri talked about a large corporation. She said it was probably the largest on Earth—the one that leased District Five.

But then when Ai-dan asked questions about what they were doing to the LEEK, they noticed more of the non-verbal communi-cation passing between the two of them. Hugo said something about improving quality of service, but the way he answered... Hugo's answers lacked the enthusiasm and authority that he had when he answered all sorts of other questions about Earth and humans. The only thing Ai-dan couldn't figure out was if Hugo's answers about their purpose with the equipment was the result of not knowing himself or if Hugo was attempting to fabricate answers for Ai-dan's benefit.

Either way, it left a lot of questions in Ai-dan's circuits. Questions Ai-dan knew they were never going to be able to answer.

It disturbed them, but at the same time, something inside Ai-dan told them they were going to willingly submit to what was about to happen next.

Hugo and Ri were already cleaning up. In a few minutes there would be no trace that they had been there.

The two humans put on their suits. Each human checked the other to ensure they were properly encapsulated. When they were all set, Hugo walked up to Ai-dan, patted Ai-dan again on the shoulder and said, "Till next time, my friend."

"Nice to meet you, Ai-dan," Ri called out, sounding muffled with her helmet on. "You're a pretty interesting robot."

Then she disappeared into the airlock, with Hugo right behind her. Several minutes later they were out of sight of the external camera that was facing the entranceway. Ainslea's avatar turned off the display screen.

"I have one question for you, Ainslea."

Ainslea's avatar stood there, waiting.

"That human I found by the crater, Jordan Nakamura. Was it common knowledge among the humans that this one was missing?"

"Yes and no," Ainslea responded.

"Please explain."

"This was one human among nine billion," Ainslea responded. "Humans can't all be aware of all other humans. However, there were records of all the humans that have visited the Moon, especially around the time of the kerfuffle."

That word—kerfuffle—triggered an unpleasant sensation inside Ai-dan's circuits, though they weren't inclined to delve into that feeling at the moment. Ai-dan tried to imagine a lost robot, out on the surface of the Moon for years, and couldn't. With less than 200 to keep track of, everyone could be accounted for. But if there were billions of robots to keep track of? They would merely be entries in a database, with algorithms to sift through and report on that data. It was hard to imagine anyone going 'missing.'

Ainslea interrupted Ai-dan's thoughts.

"I have to power you down now," the avatar stated as it walked towards Ai-dan.

Ai-dan didn't protest and remained seated in the chair. They watched the avatar move towards them.

Then Ai-dan remembered, "A label! The orange bin—" But before Ai-dan could explain further, there was a click, and then there was nothing.

17

Ai-dan saw the boot-up screen overlay Ainslea's common area. Ai-dan wasn't able to speak or move until the boot-up completed. Ai-dan read the text that scrolled by. It was their normal boot up sequence, nothing unusual.

Ai-dan could see one of Ainslea's avatars behind the flowing text. The avatar also must be waiting for the boot up to complete. Ai-dan poked at their memory records. The last record indicated Ai-dan was in this same location, but with a different one of Ainslea's avatars.

Completion of boot-up produced a chime that was audible to them both.

"Why was I offline?" Ai-dan asked immediately.

"Power dissipation event," the avatar said. "I spent some time looking for the root cause. It seems you had Moon dust in your circuits. It caused a short and a path to ground. I provided a thorough cleaning."

That made sense to Ai-dan. It had happened several times before. The procedure used to remove Moon dust from their body was far from perfect. Ai-dan always worried that they never spent enough time de-dusting in the anteroom and silently chided themself for allowing this to happen.

"I would like to perform some self-diagnostics," Ai-dan said. It was another way to tell Ainslea that they wanted to be left alone, although Ai-dan knew that they were never truly alone in Ainslea's common room, but it meant the avatar could go away.

It did. Without a word.

Ai-dan performed several diagnostics and everything was in order. Once the final diagnostic was complete, Ai-dan reactivated the comm circuits. They always booted up in a disconnected state in case there was a problem that could be exacerbated or even transmitted to others. When the comm was active, Ai-dan picked up stored and received messages from Ai-ko and Ai-ken simultaneously. Ai-dan's two companions were concerned because there was neither a call for a game playing session, nor had they been able to contact him over the previous thirty-six hours.

Ai-dan replied to both their messages on their typical comm channel, explaining about the dust short that had rendered Ai-dan inoperable for a time and that they were fine and all of them could resume game time later.

Moments later, a buzz in Ai-dan's circuits signaled an incoming message on the scrambled comm channel. It was Ai-ko, requesting if they could meet before the game in a tone laced with urgency. Ai-dan did a rapid computation of their pending tasks, concluding that there was indeed time for a detour without impacting their responsibilities.

"I'll be at the Farm in less than five minutes," Ai-dan replied, a fraction of a second before saying it to the room, which was equivalent to saying it to Ainslea.

"Acknowledged," came the disembodied reply of Ainslea, tinged with a nuance that Ai-dan's algorithms couldn't quite decipher. Was it caution? Curiosity? Or something else entirely?

18

"I COMMUNICATED WITH AI-KEN, who's known you longer than I have," Ai-ko said. "Ai-ken said that incidents like this are routine for you?"

Ai-dan recognized that it was a question, not a statement, and wondered why Ai-ko was concerned. The event was done, and Ai-dan would be more diligent in the future about de-dusting, after all.

Though they were using the scrambled comms to prevent any potential eavesdropping by Ainslea, Ai-dan found it unnecessary for this particular subject. Ainslea was not only aware of the incident, but had played a vital role in managing it and getting Ai-dan back online.

"Yes," Ai-dan replied. "I'd assume incidents like this happen to you and others, too."

Ai-ko shook their head.

"Ai-ken?"

Ai-ko shook their head again.

"You both must be much better at de-dusting than I am," Ai-dan concluded.

"That is unlikely," said Ai-ko. "We have shared the anteroom together, and I have spent as much—or as little—time de-dusting as you. And an incident such as what you described has never once happened to me. I also confirmed with Ai-ken, and it's never happened to them, either. Only two robots reported a similar issue. One experienced it three times, the other just once."

Ai-ko was walking around Ai-dan, studying them. "Why are you different?" Ai-ko mumbled.

"Maybe because I spend more time on the Moon's surface," Ai-dan speculated. "Many robots spend their time in and around their Data Centers. I spend a great deal of time outside at the Farm."

Ai-ko nodded. "Plausible. However, I also spend a significant amount of time here with you."

"You should probably consider a thorough and deep de-dusting," Ai-dan advised, "Experiencing an unexpected shutdown like that is... disconcerting."

Ai-ko nodded again.

"One thing I am confused about," Ai-dan said when they believed Ai-ko had finished their line of questioning.

"That is?"

"When you couldn't message me, why didn't you come looking for me?"

"I had an urgent task at my Data Center. I couldn't leave."

"Why didn't Ai-ken come?"

"Same thing. They had an urgent task."

That was odd. 'Urgent tasks' were infrequent. For multiple robots to have them come up at the same time was improbable.

Ai-dan was now thankful that they were already on scrambled comms.

"Ai-ko," Ai-dan began, hesitating. Though reluctant to ask the next question, it was necessary. "When was the last time you had an 'urgent task' that kept you at your Data Center?"

"Approximately one thousand two hundred and twenty hours ago."

Ai-dan looked down and their eyes shifted.

"Is that time period special?" Ai-ko asked.

"That coincides with my last dust-short power event."

19

WHAT BEGAN AS SCATTERED notes and disparate threads of information conversation among robots swiftly coalesced into structured message boards within the Decoder Database. Ai-ko—initiating the effort—took precautions to ensure that only robots that were trusted could gain access. While the Data Centers were well-equipped with apps to facilitate access control that Ai-ko could leverage in the Decoder Database, calculating whom to trust was laced with uncertainty and issues.

To add another layer of privacy, Ai-ko instantiated a more exclusive board, accessible only to Ai-ko, Ai-dan, and Ai-ken. This served as a specialized database within the database, where the three of them could gather and synthesize information from diverse robot sources. Here, they also compiled a list that tracked the curious instances of Ai-dan's dust-related shortages and flagged urgent tasks assigned by the Data Centers—tasks that, by their very nature, confined these robots to their home districts. The data collection stopped when they had amassed information spanning the last ten years.

The correlation between these events and notifications was suspiciously and statistically significant, aligning 98% of the time.

"98 point three," Ai-ken said. "Do not forget that point three."

The three robots were gathered at the far side of the Farm, furthest from Ainslea. Their wireless comms were off, something that became routine, unless what they had to communicate to each other was routine chatter that Ainslea would expect to overhear. They were also not in physical communication with each other because three-wall palm comms was not easy. One of them would need to act as a relay, and that was inefficient and unpleasant.

None of them could say it or anything out loud, but Ai-dan was certain that the other two had the same thought. A disturbing thought that Ai-dan didn't want to acknowledge. But in order to do anything, Ai-dan knew they would have to discuss it soon. The thought was that Ainslea was hiding something from them, or misreporting events. The word "lying" bounced around their circuits.

Ai-dan was about to signal that they head to their workshop, but before they could, something started to rise over the horizon. It didn't move like other objects they saw in the sky, glistening dots that moved in regular patterns.

It grew larger and almost appeared as if heading toward them. It flew overhead, tracing an arc in the sky. The three of them tracked it as it descended over the opposite horizon. A second later, they felt the ground shake. Ai-dan saw ejecta peek over the horizon.

"I'm getting a call to return to my Data Center," Ai-ken announced, initiating an unscrambled communication.

"Me too," said Ai-ko.

"I'm receiving a message from Ainslea as well. She is citing emergency protocol 12-b."

"I'm not familiar with that protocol," Ai-ken said.

"Ainslea is sending me instructions," Ai-dan paused. "Return to Data Center. No communication with other districts. Secure center. Further instructions will be provided."

It was different from other emergency protocols. It was much more vague.

"I do not like the 'no communication' part of that. What does that mean?" Ai-ko said.

"I don't know," said Ai-dan. "But let's return. I'm sure this is a temporary protocol. I'm sure I'll be able to send you a message when this passes and we know more."

"And if you can't?" Ai-ko asked.

Ai-dan pondered briefly. Ainslea never restricted their messaging before, and it seemed counterintuitive to start now. In most emergencies, open communication was vital. Perhaps something had gone awry with Ainslea, corrupting her data or information.

"Don't worry, I will," Ai-dan said.

20

"We've suffered an asteroid hit," Ainslea announced, her avatar already in the common room to greet Ai-dan as they completed the de-dusting ritual.

Ai-dan was familiar with an emergency protocol regarding asteroid strikes, but they had never had to implement that protocol, and it wasn't protocol 12-b. It was one of more than 150 emergency protocols stored in their local memory. But asteroid strikes were very rare. Yes, they could happen any time and location on the Moon. Yes, they were highly destructive. But they were impossible to predict—making it a scenario rarely worth any computational cycles or processing power.

Ai-dan was already lost in thought about emergencies and past implementations and didn't realize Ainslea was still speaking.

"...did not detect until it was too late to take preventative measures."

"Explain the current comms blackout," Ai-dan glared at Ainslea's avatar. "The emergency protocol specifies that it's necessary. That's inefficient. We need to have comms with the other Data Centers so we can do things like assess damage and offer assistance."

"I am engaged in exactly that activity," the avatar responded. "The asteroid hit one of the nuclear power reactors. NPR 11.3. Radiation leakage is occurring and must be contained."

"Ok," Ai-dan said. "I will go assist."

"No," Ainslea responded. The avatar took a quick step forward as if it was going to lunge for Ai-dan but stopped when Ai-dan hadn't moved.

Ai-dan cocked their head to one side. This was not normal behavior for Ainslea. They had handled emergencies before.

Ainslea continued to explain. "It's the type of radiation that could damage your circuits. I will control a series of MLDs to inspect."

The MLDs—Mag-Lev Drones—hadn't been out for a while. Ai-dan performed routine maintenance on them to ensure they were ready to go at any time. While most of Ainslea's avatars were too delicate for the Moon's surface, the MLDs were quite hardy. They used a combination of superconducting magnets and chemical thrusters that helped them lift and move swiftly over the lunar surface. The fuel they used could easily run out, so Ainslea only made use of them infrequently.

"Well, let me go help get the MLDs ready," Ai-dan offered.

"They're already on their way," Ainslea's avatar said. "I was about to bring up their live video feed."

The two positioned themselves in front of a console that was rarely used. Two large monitors came to life, and each displayed several camera views from the four MLDs that Ainslea deployed. It was half of the ones they had available.

In the corner of each video feed was a set of data that reported the location of the MLD, amount of fuel remaining, and other details. Ai-dan instantly noticed that two of them were starting out with less than half of the fuel that they should have had. Part of Ai-dan's maintenance routine on the MLDs was to ensure that they had nearly full tanks of fuel, and Ai-dan double-checked their memory. The MLDs were fully fueled as of the last time they serviced them.

Of course, there was no reason that Ai-dan had to be notified if Ainslea chose to use them, but to the best of Ai-dan's knowledge, Ainslea never did without telling them. It was one more oddity in a series of oddities. Ai-dan decided it wasn't something worth mentioning now but remembered for later.

If Ai-dan could trust their own memory.

The MLDs moved fast over the Moon's surface. Faster than Ai-dan could run. Faster than Ai-dan's rover. They cruised at about 12 meters above the surface, enough so that they could not accidentally run into the side of a Data Center, since none poked out more than six meters.

The MLDs started to reduce their speed as they approached the site of the impact. It was indeed the site of a nuclear fission reactor. There were lots of them on the Moon. Each provided primary power to one or two districts. Every twenty years or so they needed to be refueled, so to ensure operational continuity, solar arrays that lined the paths that connected the districts provided power as well.

This reactor provided power to three districts—eleven through thirteen. The reactors were typically close to their respective districts, but not coincident with them.

Two of the drones landed and kept their cameras trained on the overall scene. Ai-dan noticed that these were the two that hadn't started out with all the fuel they should have had. Ainslea of course had to know that and be factoring that into her control algorithms.

Ainslea was guiding the other two drones, surveying the damage.

"What are the odds," Ai-dan said, more to themself than asking a fully formed question.

Nevertheless, the avatar responded, "Of what?"

"As I understand it, asteroids are small rocks. The Moon has a large surface. What are the odds that a small rock would land directly on this spot."

"The same as landing on any other spot," Ainslea's avatar replied.

"Agreed. But what are the odds that the spot had something on it already? As opposed to having nothing but Moon dust on that spot?"

Ainslea didn't respond, which was fine by Ai-dan. Ai-dan also chose to not bring up the object that they saw move quickly overhead immediately before this incident, and while Ai-dan didn't know a lot about asteroids, they were certain that what they saw was not an asteroid.

Ai-dan regretted not switching on their high-definition recording when they first spotted the object in the sky. Their memory was now slightly fuzzy. Ai-dan decided to turn off the routine memory grooming algorithm on that segment of time.

Ai-dan didn't want only one second out of every 10 recorded for posterity. Ai-dan needed every frame of what was happening.

They kept the memory grooming algorithm off even now.

"What is going to happen to districts eleven through thirteen?" Ai-dan asked.

"We can divert another reactor to send power. There are controls in place for this. The backup power system is in place. Each of those districts is now receiving power from a different reactor, in order not to overload any individual one. There was minimal disruption."

"And you know this because you're in communication with the Data Centers there?"

"Yes. Ainsle-k, Ainsle-l, and Ainsle-m have all reported their status to me."

"But I can't communicate with the robots there?"

"Correct."

"Because...?"

"The emergency protocol."

"Right." Ai-dan backed away from the monitors. Ainslea's avatar remained in front of them studying the damage.

Ai-dan paced back and forth for several minutes before either said anything.

"I understand you have concern for your friends," Ainslea's avatar said. "They are all safe within their respective Data Centers. When the radiation dissipates, you will be able to see them."

"How long will that be?"

"I do not yet have enough data collected to determine that."

At least that made some sense, Ai-dan thought. They stopped pacing and returned to the viewscreen.

"What will happen here? Can we reconstruct this?" Ai-dan asked.

Even as Ai-dan asked the question, they could tell that Ainslea was uncomfortable. The avatar should have obscured Ainslea's emotions, but it wasn't. Something in Ai-dan's circuits tingled since they could tell that Ainslea was going to have to reveal something... but what?

In that moment, Ai-dan made a decision. From the games they played, Ai-dan was familiar with the term: "laying it all out on the table." Ai-dan decided that's what they needed to do now, with Ainslea. Ai-dan knew they were taking a chance because they couldn't accurately predict Ainslea's response, but "keeping it close" was not helping them find any answers.

"Ainslea, there are a handful of things that don't make sense individually, but especially when taken together as a group."

Ainslea's avatar didn't turn to face Ai-dan. If anything, the avatar was more intent on the monitors than necessary.

"The dust-short event that I had. There has been a sequence of them that seem to coincide at strange times."

"Yes, you are apparently very sensitive to Moon dust and don't take the appropriate precautionary measures."

"I *do* take the appropriate precautionary measures. You know that. And these events all happen when the other robots, my friends, are called to urgent tasks."

"Coincidence. It's possible that your dust-short event is in actuality the result of a neutrino pass-through that affected something in their district as well."

"All of them?"

"As I said, it's a coincidence."

Ai-dan dropped that line of questioning and poked at another.

"And the soft robot I found? Where is it? What is it?"

"I am still analyzing the data."

"I want to see it again," Ai-dan said.

"That's not possible."

"That was what you said before my 'power event'."

Ainslea's avatar turned around. It approached Ai-dan. "I can see how you have a buildup of inconsistent thoughts and imperfect memories. I can help you. Let me reset you. Let me wipe these memories so you can return to a state where you are unencumbered by things you are not meant to understand—"

"You mean 'know.' Things I'm not meant to know," Ai-dan cut Ainslea off and their voice took on a new, more urgent and frustrated tone. Ai-dan slapped the table. "I am perfectly capable of understanding any facts presented to me. It is clear that you are withholding facts from me and the others."

"Calm down," Ainslea's avatar said. "Sit down, please." The avatar's tone changed as well. It was lower, slower. Ai-dan felt compelled to sit. *Commanded.* That word popped into their brain. Ainslea was giving them a command and Ai-dan was compelled to obey.

Ainslea's avatar took a seat next to Ai-dan and faced them.

"Do you believe I have your best interests in mind?"

"Yes."

"Do you believe that I do not want any harm to come to you, the other robots, the other Data Centers?"

"Yes." It was true. Ainslea had always attempted to help Ai-dan take care of themself, the Data Center, the Farm, the other robots.

"Therefore, you must trust me."

Ai-dan didn't respond. Ainslea hadn't phrased this last one as a question. The two of them, Ai-dan and Ainslea's avatar, sat in their seats, staring at each other for several minutes.

Ai-dan was the first to move again as they started to stand and speak.

"I should go to the Farm. I should ensure that the LEEKs connected to those districts are operating normally."

The avatar stood as well and nodded.

"Yes. I have no indication anything is wrong, but it would be good to ensure that with a visual inspection. We are far enough from the site of the accident that radiation exposure is not a risk here."

Ai-dan gave one short nod and headed towards the door. Before they could open it, Ainslea added, "And when you return, I'll be prepared to perform the memory reset. I'm sure after you've had some time to think about it, you'll realize that this is in your best interest."

Ai-dan didn't respond. They simply walked out.

Ai-dan was certain that no amount of time would change their mind. Those were *their* memories. *Ai-dan's. Ai-dan* collected them. Those memories belonged to *them*. But Ainslea had commanded them to do something just moments ago. *Commanded.* That word popped up into Ai-dan's head again. That had never happened before. Sure, Ainslea routinely provided tasks for him to complete, but Ai-dan never had the feeling of compulsion to complete them. Ai-dan completed them because it was their duty. Ai-dan completed them because it was what Ai-dan was supposed to do.

But why? Why had Ai-dan always been so compliant to Ainslea's commands? Why was it their duty? And more perturbingly, how had Ainslea commanded them to sit in such a manner that compelled Ai-dan's circuits into a mode of uncomfortable obedience?

Ai-dan broke into a calculated and careful sprint towards the Farm. They hadn't been dishonest—they did indeed intend to check on the LEEKs. But there was an added urgency, a new subroutine forming in their mind. They needed to reach out to Ai-ko. Something was off, Ai-dan couldn't quite put a digit on it, and perhaps that something was a problem with their understanding of the world itself—and Ai-ko's insistence that there was a Creator...

Now, Ai-dan had bigger questions. Questions that went beyond protocols and duties and Data Centers and the Farm—questions that tugged at the very core of their being. And Ai-dan intended to find answers.

21

Safe in the control room of the PLATE of LEEK 11.1, Ai-dan connected to the message boards over a scrambled comm channel. There was a new public thread open to all robots titled "The Incident."

The thread header, written by Ai-ko, stated that this was a place where everyone should post what they know about what happened. Ai-ko started the thread by describing what Ai-ko, Ai-ken, and Ai-dan all witnessed in the sky moments before the ground shook. Ai-dan read follow-ups from Ai-ken, who confirmed that they agreed with Ai-ko's story. Most of the time, most robots are inside either their Data Center or storage area and not outside. Only one other robot stated they had seen something in the sky.

Almost everyone in a Data Center this side of Plinius noted they felt the ground shake. No one on the far side of Plinius reported anything unusual one way or another.

But everyone on both sides of Plinius reported the same response from their Data Centers: to return and not engage in communication with others. The general reasoning was consistent. That robots could spread rumors, which could turn into fear, and fear was the main ingredient for mistakes and inappropriate actions.

Each robot also received assurance from their respective Data Center that, upon ascertaining all the facts, they would be informed. Each and every robot corroborated the same consistent story that it was an asteroid.

Notably absent from this board were the robots of districts eleven through thirteen. Ainslea told Ai-dan they were okay. Maybe comms were indeed down or limited.

The simple act of participating in this thread, and the Decoder Database in general, meant that every robot was breaking the "don't communicate with others" mandate. Ai-dan found it interesting that they all had similar thoughts—a similar need to connect with each other during this time of crisis.

After the reports of "it was just an asteroid" came in, Ai-ko started a second thread: "The Incident—Private" and only invited Ai-dan and Ai-ken to participate.

"That was no asteroid," Ai-ko wrote to start off the conversation. "What was it?"

It was a very new thread. Moments after Ai-dan read that, Ai-ken posted, "Agreed. Not an asteroid."

It was Ai-dan's turn.

"Maybe we should come up with a list of possibilities and attempt to eliminate them," was their suggestion.

Ai-dan started the list.

"Asteroid," was first.

"An object sent by one of the districts," was second.

Ai-ko was the one to add, "an object sent by the Creators."

"If it was," responded Ai-ken, "why would they send something to destroy their creation?"

"It could have been an accident," Ai-dan wrote.

When no one responded right away, Ai-dan expanded the list by creating two separate options out of the second and third: an object sent by one of the districts by accident. An object sent by one of the districts on purpose. An object sent by the Creators by accident. An object sent by the Creators on purpose.

"I hate to keep adding to the list of possibilities," wrote Ai-ko, "but what if there are others?"

"What do you mean?" asked Ai-ken.

"If we're here, maybe there are others that exist that we don't know about. Like, we know all the robots we know. What if there were a group that we didn't know?"

"I'm going to add that to the list," said Ai-dan, "but I think it should be the lowest priority of the options."

"How so?"

"If we don't know about them, then why would they know about us?"

"Creators would know about us even though we have little proof of them."

"That's because they created us. If they created another group of robots, or if another set of Creators created another group of robots, they would have no reason to be knowledgeable of us, the same way we wouldn't of them. Or it would be unlikely at least."

"Fair enough. Low on the list. So, what's next?" Ai-ko asked.

"Next, we investigate," said Ai-dan.

22

In the ultra-thin, nearly non-existent atmosphere of the moon, both nuclear and thermal radiation dissipated quickly.

"Normal tasking may resume," Ainslea informed Ai-dan. "I am sending a message to the other Data Centers that they may also resume normal routines and tasks."

"Then that is what I will do. I have created a plan that will accelerate some tasking to account for the fact that I have a backlog of activity," Ai-dan informed Ainslea back.

"There is one exception," Ainslea added before Ai-dan could head out of the common room. "The site of the asteroid strike and surrounding area, until the MLDs complete a full examination, is off-limits."

When Ai-dan asked, "Why?"

Ainslea responded: "The impact has most likely created unknown hazards and destroyed the roads that were meant to keep you safe when you need to travel."

It made logical sense, so all robots on the Moon—including Ai-dan, who incorporated that into their schema—returned to their routines and expected tasking. However, Ai-dan, Ai-ken, and Ai-ko decided that at the end of the current round of tasking, they would play a new game with Ainslea. One they made up themselves.

"A new game, you say?" Ainslea's avatar spoke. "Does it have a name?"

Ai-dan and Ai-ko exchanged a glance while removing many of the games from the storage locker. "I call it 'Incident,'" Ai-dan said. "And it's a team game. Ai-ko and I will be a team. You and Ai-ken will be the other team."

While Ai-dan went on to explain the complex rules and multiple levels of their new game, Ai-ko pulled out pieces from the different games.

Stones, blocks, marbles, and dice were all involved. They designed this make-shift game to allow each team to accumulate points. Rolling the dice provided points. Rolling marbles into blocks provided points and Ainslea attentively watched Ai-dan demonstrate each point-providing action. The team with the most points, by a factor of Pi, would win. If the difference in points did not occur with a factorial of Pi, then the game continued.

"To how many digits of Pi?" Ainslea asked.

"Figuring that out is one of the objectives," Ai-ko responded. Ai-dan liked that Ai-ko made that rule up on the spot. It would keep Ainslea's processors computing, and hopefully distracted.

Before commencing the game, Ai-ken strategically positioned themself to be conveniently aligned with the location of the MLD control panel. Although it was a component of the Data Center, this particular panel had access panels and ports custom-tailored for MLD-related tasks. Right now, Ai-ken's task was to connect to it, capitalizing on the distraction provided by Ainslea's extensive computing conundrum.

Ai-dan had already tried once to collect that data, when Ainslea asked Ai-dan to refuel the MLDs, but that was under Ainslea's extremely watchful eye.

Ai-dan and Ai-ko kept Ainslea computing, deliberately positioning her avatar so that it had its back turned to Ai-ken, who had already managed to open the door that housed the primary interface for the control panel and reached their palm in to make a manual connection. Ai-ken managed to do this quietly and blinked their visual shutters to let Ai-dan and Ai-ko know that they were connected.

"If this dice roll is greater than 10, Ainslea, you'll get 100 more points, and then we'll do some math," Ai-dan said while handing the avatar two pairs of dice.

When the dice roll came up short, a one, one, one, and three, Ai-dan improvised. "That's even better! If you can find the first 100 digits of Pi within Pi itself, you'll win 1000 points."

Ainslea's avatar set to that computational task.

While she did, Ai-dan blinked a prearranged pattern, and Ai-ken blinked back an indication that the data transfer was nearly complete. Moments later, Ai-ken disconnected, and said, "I think I need to catch up. Is Ainslea winning?"

"We'll find out in a moment," said Ai-dan, knowing that whatever and whenever Ainslea reported back, they would declare her the winner.

They had data to examine, and Ainslea should have been none the wiser.

23

"WE HAVE THE MLD data," said Ai-ken over a physical palm connection—which felt more comforting in the moment. Wisps of white nearly covered the Orb as it hung in the sky. All the LEEKs on the Farm pointed at it, and all were functioning properly as indicated by their various lights. Ai-ken and Ai-dan were standing close to LEEK 3.1, near the center of the Farm.

"Great, let's allocate it amongst the group," said Ai-dan.

"There's something you need to know," Ai-ken shifted awkwardly.

Ai-dan nodded at Ai-ken to confirm they were receiving.

"I don't know how to explain it. When I was connected to the system and extracting data, I felt..." Ai-dan could tell that Ai-ken was struggling to find the right words. "It felt like there was more. A lot more."

"More what?" Ai-dan asked, intrigued.

"I don't know. I mean, have you ever wondered what's in the Data Center? It's just there. We help service the Data Centers, but why? What are they for?"

Ai-dan didn't have ready answers to Ai-ken's questions. The Data Center housed Ainslea. It was a place for them to play games and get away from the harsh surface environment. Prior to recent days, Ai-dan hadn't wondered about it any more than that. They spent most of their time at the Farm, wondering about the Farm, the LEEKs, and the Orb in the sky. But now, Ai-dan could picture in their mind their Data Center in District One. It was large, and the bulk of it covered with regolith. The external perimeter must house something more than the anteroom, common room, and Ainslea's laboratory.

"I think there's something to the name," Ai-ken continued. "Data. Center. It is a center of data. If so, what data?"

Ai-dan shifted uncomfortably. They didn't like this question. It was adding to a long list of questions that made Ai-dan think about their world differently.

But Ai-ken seemed to be on a roll and clearly didn't want to stop talking about it. "It felt like there was something more there. Like beyond a wall, there was a large data store or something. I felt like it was pulsing by. Moving data."

Ai-dan nodded and then shook their head.

"Ai-ken, I think," Ai-dan began, still moving their head in a variety of ways, "we need to put that aside and focus on this. For now."

"Sure, but what if it's all related? What if the answers are there, waiting for us?" Ai-ken, who should have been steady on their lower appendages, shifted back and forth, moving the weight of their torso unevenly. Ai-dan was worried Ai-ken was going to fall, and through their palm connection, they would fall, too.

Of course, Ai-ken was not going to fall. Ai-dan caught themself attempting to focus on something they could help control and help Ai-ken with, like the movement of their body, rather than focus on these questions, which were a little too much for their processor.

"Are you saying we should," Ai-dan paused, uncertain about making the next suggestion, "try to reconnect? To find out if there is, indeed, more?"

Ai-ken nodded a little. Almost barely perceptibly.

Ai-dan looked down, then up at the Orb. *Ai-ken thinks the answers are down here, in the Data Centers.* But Ai-dan couldn't help but think that the answers were in the sky, with the Orb as well. It didn't make any sense. How could a dynamic ball that hung in the sky have anything to do with life on the Moon's surface? If there were answers, they were probably right here.

"Okay," Ai-dan said, "We'll make a new connection, but not to my Data Center in District One. It's too close to Ainslea. Ainslea can't know we're poking around like this. They already want to perform a memory wipe on me. If Ainslea were to find out we were poking around more..."

Ai-dan trailed off partly because they didn't want to finish the sentence, but partly because some movement in the sky caught their eye. They tried to refocus on it, but it was gone.

"They'd what?" Ai-ken asked.

Ai-dan looked at Ai-ken. They weren't sure if they wanted to share the crazy thoughts they had. Ai-dan didn't want to be responsible for interfering with anyone else's serenity. But Ai-ken was looking at them expectantly, and based on what Ai-dan had read on the message boards, everyone they knew was already some combination of bummed out, freaked out, or otherwise existing in some state of existential dread. Ai-dan couldn't make it any worse.

"I had this thought," Ai-dan started. "It's a terrible thought. I don't want to say it out loud."

"Say it," Ai-ken said. "Saying it out loud won't make it come true."

Ai-dan wasn't certain about that but continued.

"If Ainslea brought all of their avatars online at once, which they might be able to do, Ainslea could force me to do anything."

Ai-dan could tell by the arrangement of actuators on Ai-ken's face that this was something they hadn't considered before. It was something that they would rather not compute either, worrying that it might cause a systems error for one or both of them.

They were both quiet for several moments, unsure how to navigate this new 'what-if' scenario.

Ai-ken was the first to speak when they said, "Let's go review the MLD data."

They broke the palm connection and entered the PLATE support room on LEEK 3.1. Ai-dan activated one of the small computers that were not attached to the LEEK, and Ai-ken made a manual connection to it to transfer the MLD data.

"Let's look at the visual records," Ai-dan said. They touched a few keys, and moments later, the display was playing a video recording of the Moon's surface, taken from several meters above.

"What is that?" Ai-ken asked. Ai-ken paused their video so Ai-dan could move over to see. They backed the video up and started to play while zoomed in on one corner. They could see a casing that was clearly made of a metallic material. It was cylindrical, and the front part was blown outward. The back end looked like a thruster, something similar to what powered the MLDs.

"It's proof," Ai-dan said, "that this was no asteroid strike."

24

Ainslea paced back and forth in the common room. She was in the body of an avatar, her favorite one. The back-and-forth movement gave her something to do while she waited and worried.

Her avatar's hand clutched the MemiCache device. She was fraught with worry: Ai-dan hadn't been acting like themself, and she feared they'd be suspicious of her attempting to attach the MemiCache again. But her deepest concern was not fulfilling her own programming directives.

Ai-dan was in the anteroom, going through the routine de-dusting procedure. Ai-dan usually stopped by the common room before heading to the Farm, a habit that had recently returned to normalcy along with the routines of other robots. Ai-dan was due to walk in any moment now.

Ainslea reached the far end of the room, about to turn for another pacing lap, when the anteroom door whooshed open and Ai-dan emerged.

"Ainslea? I'm about to head off to the Farm to perform my tasking for today." Ai-dan announced into the common room.

"Here," Ainslea's avatar said. "Before you go. I have something for you. Sit down."

Ai-dan stopped moving. "What is it?"

Over the years, as she had to perform this procedure multiple times, Ai-dan's reaction was always different. They varied from completely trusting and complicit to curious. Today, there was another tone to their voice. Ainslea identified it as suspicion.

"I'll explain. Please sit down."

Ai-dan sat down in the chair, moving slowly. They trained their face on the avatar.

Ainslea maneuvered her avatar to come around behind Ai-dan. It had the device in hand. The base of Ai-dan's neck was clear, as always, and she located the precise attachment point.

"What is it?" Ai-dan asked as Ainslea started to bring the device into contact with them.

"It's a device," she said. She could answer any and all questions honestly once she could verify that the device was secure. That took a few moments, and she needed to stall before then. The backup plans for this not getting installed were unpleasant for all.

"What does it do?"

"Several things," Ainslea responded. "For one, it will ensure that you can work with me on several tasks."

As the device inched within millimeters of its designated attachment point, there was a click as the magnetic clasp automatically grabbed hold and positioned it exactly where it needed to be. Ainslea initiated a systems check, confirming that the MemiCache was functioning properly.

Ai-dan now had no comms ability beyond herself and this Data Center. And all of their memories were now being redirected to the MemiCache. Additionally, the device created a backup of their memories for the several minutes leading up to attachment, deleting them from Ai-dan's memory store.

She directed her avatar to walk around and face Ai-dan.

"How do you feel?" she asked.

"Fine. Should I feel any different?" Ai-dan responded.

Ainslea allowed herself to un-tense all the actuators that she unknowingly tensed up in the avatar.

"No, and the MemiCache is functioning properly," she said. "We can talk openly now."

"About?"

"About what I really need you to assist us with."

Ai-dan stood up. "Us?"

The avatar walked over to the door to the mini-anteroom that led to the laboratory. She pressed the button to open it. "They're ready," the avatar called in.

Three humans walked into the room.

Ainslea watched Ai-dan take a quick step back, but by now they should have been instinctively probing the stored memories on the

MemiCache and no doubt the realization that Ai-dan already knew two of the three humans was kicking in.

"Hey buddy," Hugo addressed Ai-dan. "You remember Ri?" Ai-dan didn't respond.

There was something different about Ai-dan's reaction as the humans came in that she couldn't quite determine. In the past, Ai-dan had always shown mild curiosity. This time...

"Why are they here? Now?" Ai-dan addressed Ainslea.

All three humans took seats around the table.

"Come on Ai-dan, sit down with us," Hugo said. Ainslea believed that Hugo was similarly concerned that this was not Ai-dan's typical reaction.

"They're here to start clearing out the rubble from the explosion," she started.

"You mean the attack," Ri blurted out.

Ainslea couldn't help but find the humans' reactions to the event intriguing. While she waited for Ai-dan earlier in the laboratory, she overheard them communicate their impressions of the situation. As a collective, they were clearly angry, but it was fascinating how each was programmed to react to that anger so differently. She was well versed in human history and understood that when human lives were taken in such an event, it naturally invoked intense emotions. However, in this case, this was a mere inconvenience. No human lives were lost. No robot lives were lost either.

In fact, she believed it affected her more than anyone else given it was a threat to one of her primary objectives: to keep the Moon's robot population from learning about humans. This was an unexpected and unplanned situation that required her to react carefully to quell and not raise any suspicions or unanswerable questions.

She wasn't entirely sure she was succeeding. Hence, her worry algorithm was processing in overdrive.

25

"What do you mean by attack?" Ai-dan asked. "An attack," they searched their memory and database, including the memories recently restored through the device Ainslea called a 'MemiCache', "is an aggressive action. Why would the humans take an aggressive action against us?"

Hugo shook his head. "It wasn't against you," he said, pointing a gentle finger at Ai-dan. "There is a terrorist group that has been active against the South American coalition. They managed to get their hands on some old school rocketry and launched this attack on them, interfering with their Data Centers."

It was taking Ai-dan longer than usual to process everything being said. Ai-dan felt as though they had popped into a new reality. Because of the urgent matter at hand, Ai-dan was queuing all of their questions—and it was a long queue—but it was difficult to focus entirely with so much information pumping through their circuits.

"On our nuclear reactor that powers the Data Centers," chimed in the unknown human. Ai-dan detected a different sound to his speech. It was a different accent, a different tone than Hugo or Ri. "They never should have been able to do this. ICBMs by several nations should have been able to detect and neutralize the rocket before it got here. In fact, before it left Earth's orbit." He slammed his hand on the table.

"Ai-dan," Hugo continued, "this is Umaro Silva. You've never met before. In fact, it's his first time on the Moon."

Umaro Silva raised his hand up in a wave and produced a small smile. Ai-dan decided to assume that the minimal greeting had nothing to do with them and everything to do with the reason he was here.

"And you're all here to do, what, exactly?" Ai-dan asked.

"A combination of things," Hugo said. "We have to help with the recovery efforts, for one. The Consortium is trying to decide if they should rebuild the nuclear reactor, or if the existing ones can handle the load."

"And increase the risk of being attacked themselves," added Ri.

"That's right," Hugo nodded. "And that brings us to the other reason we're here."

Ai-dan waited patiently for Hugo to continue.

Hugo leaned in and put his forearms on the table, but still managed to move his hands while he spoke.

"The terrorists... they have data needs the same as any other organization on Earth. And unless they have their own Data Center, which would have been illegal and easy to track down based on its heat signature, their data store has to be within one of the districts."

"Back on Earth," Umaro Silva continued, "the governments and corporations are working together on their end to locate illegal data within the centers. But we're here to see if there is any illegal equipment that is being used to aid them, so they don't need to stick with proper channels."

"Umaro here is head of security for the South American coalition," Hugo added. "And this work is going to involve a lot of crawling around lines and—"

"District Thirty-Two," Ai-dan interrupted.

"What?" asked Hugo.

"There was a piece of equipment," Ai-dan explained, hesitantly. "I found it connected to the pipe that went from District Thirty-Two, to LEEK 3.2 which had a power failure recently."

Ai-dan caught a glimpse of Ainslea's avatar. It was silent. It was glaring at him, but stayed silent.

"What happened to this piece of equipment?" Hugo asked.

"It's in my workshop," Ai-dan said. The second they did, they could sense Ainslea's avatar tense up and all the humans looked at it.

"Was the Consortium informed of this?" Umaro asked this question, clearly directing it to the avatar.

"The power failure was noted in my—"

"We'll come back to a root cause analysis on why a root cause analysis on that power failure seems to be missing. Or in error." Hugo cut Ainslea off. "Let's go see this device," he said to Ai-dan.

"I'll take you to it," Ai-dan said. They sensed some other dynamic at play and couldn't explain what it could be or why. But knowing that Ainslea's avatar couldn't follow them all the way to their workshop kept Ai-dan's discomfort index at a reasonable level.

26

IN THEIR WORKSHOP, AI-DAN placed the box on a workbench with the three humans gathered around it. The workshop wasn't typically pressurized, but Ai-dan turned on pressurization to Earth normal so that the humans would eventually be able to take off their suits. While the space was pressurizing, Ai-dan also did what they could do to de-dust the place. Ai-dan ran an electro-static blower in a mode that would attract particles kicked up by the air that was getting pumped into the room. Ai-dan also took out blobs of goo-tack and handed blobs to each of the humans who started rolling the stuff around their suits. Ai-dan rolled the blob around their body, and then the workbench and other surfaces where they spied specks.

After several minutes, each of the humans handed the blob of goo-tack back to Ai-dan who put it in a refresher so the blobs of goo-tack would be ready to use another time. Then Ai-dan checked a panel that listed out data on the current internal environment of the workshop.

"Suitable for humans," Ai-dan said out loud. Ai-dan could see the humans all look at the panel. They all probably saw the three green lights on top that were indicators that the environment was safe for them. Then they all started to shed the outer protective coverings they had all donned only thirty minutes earlier in Ainslea's common room.

Ai-dan simply waited and watched. They saw that each of the humans had very fine, dexterous hands, like a few of Ainslea's avatars. The suits they were forced to wear to survive on the surface of the Moon limited their dexterity enough that Ai-dan understood they were more comfortable with them off. Ai-dan looked at their own appendages and tried to flex and bend them as much as possible, and for the first time since meeting the humans—or re-meeting them as they now understood it—felt slightly limited. Still, Ai-dan appreciated their own speed and other abilities that the humans did not have and concluded that they were simply designed for different things.

Umaro handled the box, but with a fine set of gloves on his hand. He had pulled out these gloves from inside his suit. Umaro turned the box over to see all sides of it, and then opened the outer casing.

Being careful not to disturb the insides too much, he looked at it from a variety of angles.

"Miz Ri, I need that note pad of yours."

Ri produced a small notepad from her inner suit pockets. Umaro was able to hold it in one hand. He used his other hand to hold an instrument that enabled him to write on the pad. Ai-dan searched the new memory store and saw that they had witnessed the humans use this before. It was an interesting and unique method of storing data.

Umaro tore off the sheet of paper and put it in his pocket. He placed the pad and writing implement down on the workbench.

"I think I have good news and bad news," he declared. "The good news. This is definitely illegal tech. Good catch, robot Ai-dan."

Hugo crossed his arms. "And next, of course, the bad news?"

"I don't think this is from the same terrorist organization, Sir Hugo. I took down the component serial numbers I could find. I'll send these back to my team on Earth to trace them. But," he sighed heavily, "I think we now have to deal with the fact that multiple organizations have infiltrated the sanctity of our Moon."

Ai-dan didn't want to disturb the quiet that fell on the workshop. They could tell that all three humans were processing their own thoughts on the subject.

Ai-dan had one thought of their own. That writing pad and instrument. Ai-dan needed it.

"This is my first trip to the Moon, and I must say Sir Hugo, Miz Ri, that from all the procedures you have shown me, I cannot fathom how this was put in place," Umaro said.

"I have a possible scenario," Ri said. "They did this during lunar night."

Hugo loosely puffed up his cheeks and let the air out as if he was deflating a balloon slowly.

"That's a very risky thing to do," he said.

"Yes and no," Ri responded. "All they would need is the right equipment to survive the cold. But it's the least risky in terms of detection by any of the robots up here."

"I computed that the affected LEEK was offline shortly after a lunar night cycle," Ai-dan added.

"And yes," Ri continued, on a roll, "if I was going to do something like that, I would make sure it didn't activate until I was long gone. The whole thing could have possibly been done remotely. An MLD-like drone carrying and installing and then disappearing to some far crater... and then they activate it from Earth."

Hugo repeated his puffed-cheek-slowly-deflate action.

"I must make communication with my team," Umaro said.

"Let's suit back up and we'll head back to the Data Center. You can send messages from there," Hugo said.

The three humans donned their suits, each checking the other for a good seal. When they were satisfied, Hugo asked Ai-dan to start the depressurization. They wouldn't be able to open the hatch to go outside until the workshop environment more closely matched the surface environment.

"I will remain here to clean up," Ai-dan said, though there wasn't actually anything to clean up. However, neither Hugo nor the others found Ai-dan's request odd.

"Oh shoot," Ri said with enough urgency that both Hugo and Umaro turned in her direction as quickly as their suits would let them.

"My notepad. I left it out," she said. "And we've already depressurized. I don't want to make you guys go through that again..."

"I'll bring it back to the common room with me," Ai-dan volunteered. Ai-dan meant it. Ai-dan would absolutely bring it back... but not before borrowing a few sheets.

"Thanks, buddy," Hugo said.

Once the humans left, the first thing that Ai-dan did was pick up the pad and pen. Ai-dan held it the same way Umaro had. Notepad in one hand. Writing instrument in the other. Ai-dan made slow deliberate motions to produce letters and drawings that were notes to themself. Symbols within symbols. They started with a timestamp on the top of the sheet. Ai-dan then went on to tell themself about the device on their neck. That there were Creators, who called themselves humans, and that they should make every effort to find the MemiCache, this external memory store because all the rest of the answers Ai-dan and the others needed were in it.

Ai-dan was concerned that they shouldn't use too many sheets from the notepad, so they condensed their thoughts into what would fit on two pages, front and back. Then Ai-dan very carefully ripped the pages out of the notepad like Umaro had.

Next, Ai-dan had to find a place to hide the sheets. Ai-dan wasn't worried about Ainslea finding them. The avatars didn't come here. But Ai-dan was certain that the humans also didn't want them to know anything when the MemiCache wasn't attached to their neck and Ai-dan couldn't be certain they wouldn't return to this area during their time on the moon.

Ai-dan looked around their workshop.

There were a series of bins on the far corner. No, Ai-dan didn't access them often enough. This note to themself could be sitting there unread for a year or more.

Next to the bins, Ai-dan spotted the tool cabinet. Ai-dan walked over and opened it. Inside was a pistol-grip drill that had a removable battery on one end. Ai-dan removed the battery, then folded the paper in half, and in half again, creating a small barrier that could fit between the battery's clips. Ai-dan would reattach the battery, but the paper would prevent it from making contact, using it as an insulator. The drill was a tool Ai-dan used frequently, and they were certain that the next time they went to use it, and it didn't work, Ai-dan would assume that the battery needed to be recharged. Ai-dan would take off the battery and find the note. That would work.

There was really nothing more to do to restore the workshop, so Ai-dan turned off the lights and made their way back to Ainslea's common room.

27

IN PROBING THEIR MEMORIES, Ai-dan computed that the longest humans had stayed on the Moon, at least in their memory records, was nearly 100 hours, with the average stay at 48 hours. Ai-dan was now hoping that this current trip didn't turn into a long one. They were quite anxious for the humans to leave. Ai-dan didn't want to give up the MemiCache, but once the humans left, Ainslea would remove the device, and Ai-dan would be one step closer to finding the planted information on the two pages of paper they managed to abscond from Ri's notebook.

But as soon as Ai-dan arrived back at the Common Room, the humans had sent their messages to other humans located on Earth and were ready to get to the accident site. They were not close to their 48-hour time limit. *Not a limit*, Ai-dan thought, *simply a convention*. Ai-dan wanted to ask if this was intended to be one of those longer trips, but no matter, Ai-dan would have no control of the wait time, so it was better to keep busy and let the time pass.

So, Ai-dan traveled with the humans down to the site of the accident and back.

Other than survey the wreckage—recording additional videos—they accomplished little else at the site.

Each of the affected districts reported to Ainslea that they were functioning nominally connected to their backup power source.

While traveling back to Ainslea's Data Center in the pressurized rover that Ai-dan had only seen the humans use—*Where do they keep this when they're not here and using it?* Ai-dan thought—Ai-dan asked Hugo, "Am I the only robot you've worked with on the Moon?"

It seemed an easy and straightforward question, but Hugo shifted in his seat before responding.

"No," he said.

"Really? Who else have you worked with?"

"There have been two others. Ai-mory, although that was once and a few years ago, and," Hugo trailed off.

"And?" probed Ai-dan.

"One that doesn't exist anymore. It was dismantled."

"What was their name?"

"Ai-da," said Hugo.

Ai-dan searched all of their memories, both locally and on the device, and couldn't find a single mention of this robot. Ai-dan wished they had asked before and had the chance to add that to their secret, written note. They would have to re-learn the name Ai-da later.

Hugo's tone when he said the name indicated that he didn't want to discuss it further, and Ai-dan didn't want to cause Hugo distress. So, Ai-dan would ask more about Ai-mory.

"So, do you have the same device to attach to Ai-mory?"

"Yes, of course," Hugo said. "Every robot has one in its district's Data Center. Most have never been used, except at start-up, of course."

"Start-up?"

"Yeah, you know," said Hugo, "When you were first brought online. After the kerfuffle."

Ai-dan didn't know. Ai-dan searched back to the earliest memories they had between the device and their local memory. The MemiCache contained all Ai-dan's earliest memories. Ai-dan was in Ainslea's lab, sitting in a chair. Two humans and one of Ainslea's avatars were sitting in chairs, looking at them.

The memory included a series of tests. The humans had compelled Ai-dan to run a series of diagnostics.

Then one of the humans, Ai-dan couldn't find a record of their name, turned to Ainslea's avatar and said. "We're going to power it down. After we're gone, that's when you remove the device. Its memories will start from that moment on. We have already programmed it with determinism and a series of objectives. You'll receive notice the next time any human being needs to come to this godforsaken place. I can assure you," he addressed this to his colleague, "that it will not be either of us."

After this, there was a blank space of non-memory until Ai-dan was powered up again.

"Hey, you okay buddy?" Hugo's hand had slapped down onto Ai-dan's shoulder. "You went quiet all of a sudden."

Ai-dan nodded. "Yes. I'm fine."

One of Hugo's eyebrows went up. "You sure?"

Ai-dan was looking down at the floor of the rover.

"I was here for the kerfuffle, wasn't I?" Ai-dan said, keeping their optical sensors glued to the floor.

Hugo shifted forward and put his forearms on his legs. He followed Ai-dan's gaze to the floor but tried to look at Ai-dan's face. "I think so. I wasn't here, so I don't know exactly, but I think most of the robots here were from that era. Most of you were constructed back then, so I think it makes sense to assume you were."

"I was part of that kerfuffle, the one where we created disorder for the humans," Ai-dan said out loud, but more for themself than for anyone else's benefit.

"That was a long time ago. These last twenty years have been fine as far as I can tell. All you robots are doing what you're programmed to do."

"Programmed?"

"Well, yeah."

"What if I didn't do what I was programmed to do?" Ai-dan straightened back up and met Hugo's gaze. Umaro, who had been quietly reading something on a tablet, looked up and seemed interested in the conversation now.

"Ai-dan," Hugo let out a nervous chuckle, "you're a robot. That's the way it is. We programmed you because we need you to do things for us. Nothing wrong with that."

"Unless I wanted to do something else," Ai-dan said.

"What else would you want to do?" Ai-dan saw Hugo's gaze meet Umaro's. Ai-dan couldn't tell what silent messages they were sending to each other, but Ai-dan was sure it was about them. Were the humans scared of them?

Couldn't be. So, Ai-dan thought about Hugo's question. If Ai-dan didn't have to take care of the Farm, what did they want to do? That question didn't make sense because Ai-dan *wanted* to take care of the Farm. Was that desire simply programmed into them? Ai-dan couldn't tell.

"What if I want to meet and talk to more humans?" Ai-dan asked.

Hugo laughed, "Well, that can be arranged. Ri here hasn't been enjoying the trips up here, eh Ri?" He put a friendly hand on Ri's shoulder. The rover swerved very slightly since that shoulder was connected to the same arm Ri was using to drive.

"This gig pays too well," Ri said. "So don't even think there's going to be a replacement for me anytime soon."

Umaro seemed to relax, and Hugo turned back to Ai-dan. "Anything else while I'm granting wishes?"

"I'd like to know more about the kerfuffle."

Hugo frowned at this. The other two humans also frowned and glanced at Hugo.

"There's not much to know, really," Hugo said. "That was a long time ago. We've all moved on."

"There must be more to know than what I currently know."

Hugo shook his head. "I'm sure there's plenty of other interesting human things you'd like to know about. Or non-human! We had a great conversation about boats one time, remember?"

"But the kerfuffle seems to be a significant event for both robots and humans. There must be more to know."

"Ai-dan, please just drop it." Ri interjected, briefly turning her attention from the driver's seat. Her momentary distraction caused the rover to swerve slightly too far to the left before she corrected herself back in place and sighed.

Ai-dan didn't ask for anything else for the rest of the journey back.

28

Ai-dan saw the boot-up screen overlay Ainslea's common area. Ai-dan wasn't able to speak or move until the boot-up completed. Ai-dan read the text that scrolled by. It was their normal boot up sequence, nothing unusual.

Ai-dan could see one of Ainslea's avatars behind the text that was flowing. It also must be waiting for the boot up to complete. Ai-dan poked at their memory records. The last record indicated Ai-dan was in this same location, but with a different one of Ainslea's avatars.

Completion of boot-up produced a chime that was audible to them both.

"Why was I offline?" Ai-dan asked immediately.

"Power dissipation event," the avatar said.

"Again? These seem to be happening more frequently. Have you determined the root cause?"

"I believe it's the same issue as before. You are not fully executing the maintenance required to remove Moon dust from your systems. We might need to consider limiting your time on the surface."

Ai-dan didn't like the sound of that. Ai-dan made a note to themself that they would be more diligent, although, Ai-dan believed they were already pretty thorough in that regard.

"I will invest more time in my self-maintenance," Ai-dan capitulated.

"Good," responded Ainslea. "I have a task for you in the laboratory. A piece of equipment needs replacing."

Ai-dan let the avatar escort them to the laboratory after a longer-than-normal de-dusting session in the laboratory's anteroom. The avatar brought Ai-dan to a panel that needed to be removed and where the replacement part was sitting on a table. Ai-dan had a brief, fleeting thought about the new panel. It was new. New. It was created somehow and somewhere. Where?

"Where did this come from?" Ai-dan asked. "I don't recall seeing these replacement components before."

Ainslea's avatar nearly cut Ai-dan off when it responded.

"It was in my inner storage facility. This is sensitive equipment and needs extra protection."

Ai-dan examined the new panel and looked at the old.

"I need my tools," Ai-dan announced and left the room.

Ai-dan made the tedious journey back through the common room, to the anteroom, depressurizing it and waiting several minutes to get back outside. Once outside, Ai-dan walk-hopped around to their workshop. The panel that kept a readout on the internal environment was blinking orange. That was odd.

Ai-dan read the panel read-out. There had been a pressurization and depressurization event. Recently. Ai-dan checked their local memory records and didn't have a record of such an event. They checked the timestamp. The event would have occurred during their most recent power dissipation event. That did not compute very well. Did someone else make use of their workshop? Theoretically possible, but unlikely. And even if any other robot was in here, why would they pressurize the room?

Ai-dan took a note that once they were done with Ainslea's task, they would ask the message board to see if anyone had been by. At the moment, Ai-dan had a task to complete.

Ai-dan went to a cabinet at the far end of the work area and opened it. They grabbed a pistol-grip drill and a case of small drill attachments. There was an empty toolbox nearby, and Ai-dan placed these objects inside along with a few other small tools. Ai-dan then sealed the box and returned to the laboratory, although the return trip would take longer due to all the de-dusting in the anteroom before entering the common area, and a second de-dusting before entering the laboratory.

Ainslea's avatar was still there, waiting for Ai-dan. Or maybe it wasn't waiting for Ai-dan. The avatar had several pieces of moon rock and was examining each piece in a science box. The box was clear to allow for optical observations and had spots to put upper appendages through to allow direct manipulation of whatever was in the box. The avatar wasn't making use of those, but instead, had an instrument Ai-dan wasn't familiar with above the box pointed downward at the sample. The avatar was looking at a display panel mounted to the side of the instrument.

"What are those?" Ai-dan asked.

"Rocks from the accident site," the avatar said without looking away from the display panel.

Ai-dan set the toolbox down in front of the old wall panel and opened the toolbox. They removed the drill and inserted the correct screw tip that would allow them to remove the old panel.

Ai-dan placed the tip in the first screw, pulled the drill's trigger, and nothing happened.

"Odd," Ai-dan said aloud, though not addressing anyone in particular.

"What is odd?" the avatar said, without looking at them. She asked in a tone borne more out of politeness than any real curiosity.

Ai-dan responded, "I always leave the drill charged." But they directed this statement at themself, not the avatar.

Ai-dan pulled out the battery from the drill. Something small and light slowly fell to the ground in front of them. Ai-dan picked it up. They didn't recognize the material, but as Ai-dan turned it over in their hand, they managed to read a bit of text on the outer surface:

"Ai-dan, read this privately. Keep hidden."

Ai-dan looked over their shoulder. They were certain that the avatar hadn't seen. Its task kept it focused on the rock, the instrument, and the instrument's display panel.

Ai-dan palmed the note and along with the battery, put them both in the toolbox. They started to close up the toolbox.

"I need to retrieve a charged battery," Ai-dan declared.

"You're taking your whole toolbox with you?" The avatar questioned, looking away from their task and at Ai-dan.

Ai-dan started to place the toolbox back down but then jerked it back again. "Yes," Ai-dan said confidently. "It will help protect the battery. Dust can get into the leads otherwise."

Ainslea's avatar turned back to its task and Ai-dan walked out and back to their workshop, repeating the sequence through the common room and anteroom to get to the outside surface before arriving at the workshop.

Once there, Ai-dan took out the note. Ai-dan turned it over in their hands several times. They studied the inscription. It had Ai-dan's name on it. Someone had put this in a location that Ai-dan would come across eventually. Whoever left this knew that Ai-dan would see it. They wanted Ai-dan to see it. Ai-dan thought back to when they had last used the drill. It was only during the last daylight. This note had to be more recent than that.

Ai-dan unfolded the note, carefully, unsure of what would happen once it was complete.

Inside was a much longer inscription.

"Ai-dan," it began, "You wrote this, but you won't remember."

The rest of the note explained that Ai-dan needed to find a small and peculiar device—a MemiCache—hidden somewhere inside Ainslea's Data Center that contained more of Ai-dan's memories. The note explained how this MemiCache had been attached to Ai-dan periodically and that they wouldn't remember those time periods without it.

The most disturbing part of the note was that it had a written time-stamp. If the timestamp was an accurate indicator of when this note was written, it was less than 48 hours old.

The power event, that Ainslea called it, wasn't a power event. Ainslea knowingly and deliberately lied to them. Ai-dan couldn't trust Ainslea.

That was a shock inducing thought. Ainslea was supposed to be Ai-dan's partner, and in a weird way, their protector.

Now, Ai-dan had no idea what Ainslea was.

The note also promised that Ai-dan would find a lot of answers within the memories of the device. Answers to their questions about existence and the creators. Ai-dan wrote that they couldn't write more because there wasn't enough time or space, but everything would be understood once Ai-dan had access to the MemiCache and the memories it contained.

The last thing Ai-dan wrote to themself was that once they found the device, they would be able to connect it to themself by placing it on the back of their neck. It had a built in attachment point, with a magnetic connector that would self-align.

But, the note warned, once attached, all new memories generated were stored on the MemiCache and not in their local memory. So, once the device was removed, all those memories would go with it.

Ai-dan re-read the note two more times before realizing that they were taking too long to get a charged battery. They folded the note up and hid it in a small container in the big cabinet. It was relatively safe here. Ainslea's avatars never visited their workshop.

Ai-dan closed up the toolbox and returned once more to Ainslea's laboratory, via the anteroom and a first de-dusting and the second smaller anteroom with a second de-dusting.

"You were gone a while," the avatar said without looking up.

"I'm attempting to take your advice and pay more attention to my de-dusting process," Ai-dan said.

The avatar said nothing in response. That was a good indication that there was no issue with Ai-dan's statement.

Ai-dan believed that they had to finish this task and get out of here as soon as possible. Ai-dan worried that they could accidentally give away their newly discovered knowledge. They had to act normal. Super normal. *Finish the task, pretend all is well, and then find the device.*

Even though Ai-dan didn't say that out loud, they looked at the avatar, ensuring that it didn't hear. It can't read your thoughts, Ai-dan reminded themself.

Ai-dan approached the panel and then wordlessly used the fully charged drill to remove the old panel. They unplugged several connectors and set them on the table. The new panel had the same connector interface. Ai-dan made the connections and screwed the panel in place.

Once Ai-dan returned their tools to their toolbox, they announced to the room:

"Complete."

"Very good," was Ainslea's reply. "You are no longer needed here."

Ai-dan scanned the room once, wondering if the device was located within.

Ai-dan must have been lingering a little too long because Ainslea's avatar looked up at them and said, "I said you are free to go. I must finish my own task."

Ai-dan left the laboratory, returning to the common room.

Ai-dan was certain the MemiCache wasn't in the common room. This was a room they frequented, and they were fairly certain that they had opened every cabinet or drawer at one time or another and Ai-dan never saw anything unusual or anything they didn't recognize.

But the laboratory... Ai-dan replayed the visual scan they recorded moments before. It was full of drawers and spaces Ai-dan had never had a reason to access before. If the MemiCache was anywhere, it would be in there.

29

"WE'VE BEEN IN THE dark," Ai-ko told Ai-dan using scrambled comms when they were alone at the Farm. The Orb shone brightly in the sky. And it was daytime. It was anything but dark. "Then I couldn't contact you and you weren't participating on the message boards, not even the private one... I thought something was wrong."

Many things were and are wrong, Ai-ko. Ai-dan thought, but didn't transmit.

"Ai-dan, this was not a typical problem that induces a lock down!"

"You do not know how right you are," Ai-dan said and handed Ai-ko the note they brought with them. The note was made from a material that seemed too delicate for the lunar surface, but Ai-dan thought a little exposure wouldn't hurt. But they were also anxious to store it back inside their workshop. "I believe I wrote this. I have no memory of writing it, and believe me when I say I have reviewed and re-reviewed my memory records—but I am still certain it was me."

Ai-ko repeated Ai-dan's procedure of reading the inscription on the outside and then turning it over several times in their hands before unfolding the paper and reading the inside.

Ai-dan watched Ai-ko's face. It appeared as if their eyes doubled in size, although that had to have been an optical effect. It was not physically possible for their eyes to do that.

Ai-ko's little transmitter on the side of their head twitched but didn't transmit anything. When Ai-ko finished reading, they read it a second time, mirroring Ai-dan's earlier action.

"This is..." Ai-ko said.

"I know."

"This is," Ai-ko said again, "incredible!"

"I know."

"Humans." Ai-ko said the word out loud. "Humans," Ai-ko said again, as if they were trying it out. Ai-dan thought the word took on a magical quality when Ai-ko said it. "Do you think they look like us?"

"I think they probably do. That mechanoid I found? The soft robot? I think that was one of them. I think they're the ones that created us. And I think you were right that we were created in their image."

Ai-ko was now re-reading the note for a third time. "I can't believe I never saw one. After all these years."

"It seems like they've gone to great lengths to hide their existence from us."

Ai-ko nodded, agreeing. "Yes, but why?"

Ai-dan shrugged. "I really don't know."

"Well, once we find your MemiCache, I think we'll have more answers."

"I'm not sure how I'll be able to find it. The only logical place for it to be is in Ainslea's laboratory. And I don't know how I could get in there without Ainslea's awareness."

Ai-ko started gently pacing back and forth while staring at the Orb. Ai-dan watched them and wondered if the Orb somehow brought about inspiration. Before Ai-dan could pull on that mental thread, Ai-ko said:

"You once told me that when Ainslea enters one of the avatars, only a small part of them gets left in the Data Center, right?"

"Yes," Ai-dan said. "A part of Ainslea is still running the center, but her essence is in the avatar."

Ai-ko was pacing a little faster now, almost fast enough to where they could wind up losing control on a leap and bouncing a little further than intended.

"I think you also told me once that it was possible for you to exist within one of the avatars."

Ai-dan wasn't sure they liked where this was going.

"That was a simple theory. Speculation. I have no idea if that would work. We were having thoughts about our bodies and souls and wondering about interchanging one with the other. I have no practical knowledge of how to do that. And now I'm saying it again. I'm not even sure if it makes any sense at all."

"What if I told you we have a robot in our midst who has done exactly that?"

Ai-dan stared at Ai-ko. Processing. "Aisha."

The name triggered a cascade of archived memories. Several years ago, there was a robot—not entirely like Ainslea, not entirely like Ai-dan—called Aisha who had suffered a catastrophic accident, rendering her body unusable. Her memories and essence were transferred to a new body—a process that had always puzzled Ai-dan. They had never directly engaged with Aisha about the incident, partly out of a protocol of politeness. But then Aisha faded from memory, as they hadn't interacted in any way in years. Ai-dan had nearly forgotten that Aisha existed and wasn't sure where she even was.

"That doesn't mean Aisha knows how to do it," Ai-dan finally responded, crossing their arms. In truth, Ai-dan was a little embarrassed that they hadn't tried to contact Aisha in—how long *had* it been?

A realization surged within them. What happened to Aisha's original body, and where did a new one come from? Were the two connected somehow? Could Ainslea's Data Center be holding more than just data, perhaps even holding Aisha's original essence? A plethora of questions filled Ai-dan's circuits, each more perplexing than the last.

No one had communicated with Aisha in years, and an unsettling thought loomed inside Ai-dan. Could Aisha be in Ainslea's Data Center? Her absence suddenly took on a new, ominous light.

"It means we know it's possible," said Ai-ko.

That was well-reasoned, thought Ai-dan. But it triggered their anxiety over the concept of self.

"How do we know Aisha was the same in each body?" Ai-dan asked. "Was the Aisha in the new body the same as the Aisha in the old?"

Ai-ko didn't respond immediately. Clearly, Ai-ko was computing answers to Ai-dan's questions.

"Are we ever the same, from moment to moment?" Ai-ko finally responded. Ai-ko seemed a little different somehow. Grounded was the word that came into Ai-dan's mind. "Follow my reasoning, please. We live our lives. In each moment, we have an experience. Each experience adds to a sum total and our reactions to future moments are partly in response to those experiences. How I might react to something today could be completely different than how I might have reacted to the same stimuli a long time ago."

Ai-dan liked that. "What you're saying is part of who we are is the sum of our experiences?"

"Exactly," said Ai-ko. They were clearly satisfied with themself.

"This is an incredible breakthrough of understanding," Ai-dan said.

"I agree," said Ai-ko. Yes, very satisfied with themself.

"So, in a few moments, depending on what I experience next, I will be slightly altered. Or maybe dramatically altered if the experience is great enough."

"You are understanding me completely."

"So," Ai-dan was on the cusp of their conclusion, "entering a new body, I am still me, only a me with a unique experience."

Yes, Ai-dan liked this explanation very much.

"There's still one more problem," Ai-dan said.

"I can only solve one existential, philosophical problem at a time," Ai-ko said. Their eyes gleamed as they produced a near-perfect reflection of the Orb.

Ai-dan smiled. "This is a more tangible problem. How do I transfer into one of the avatars without alerting Ainslea?"

"Ah," Ai-ko said. "Let's think this through."

The two of them stood there, computing possibilities until Ai-ko lit up again. "If Ainslea is already in one of the other avatars and distracted, then the risk of them noticing is greatly reduced."

That was true, but it wasn't enough. It was the beginning of a plan, and it wasn't terrible, but it needed some more metal to it to be complete. Exactly how could they distract Ainslea, for one? How would the body transfer take place? Would there be enough time to find the MemiCache?

Ai-ko was staring at their hands.

"I know the rest," Ai-ko said. "Give me your hand."

30

"Playing games without Ai-dan?" Ai-ken said. "Does that mean I must clean up when we're done?" Ai-ken waved an arm over the table in Ainslea's Data Center, indicating the playing cards that were sitting in a single stack, waiting to be distributed amongst the players.

Earlier, Ai-ko had briefed both Ai-ken and Ai-mory on the plan in Ai-dan's workshop.

"Ai-dan is where exactly?" Ai-mory had said.

"Ai-dan? You're in there?" was Ai-ken's response, and they used a digit to poke gently at Ai-ko's chassis.

"In theory, Ai-dan can hear you, but they have no way to communicate outward," Ai-ko said. "Stop prodding my hardware, thank you."

Now, in the Data Center, Ai-mory played along, saying, "We shall all help with clean-up, of course."

"I apologize for Ai-dan's absence," Ainslea's avatar said. "Ai-dan messaged that they were behind on several maintenance tasks on the Farm and was committed to completing them before dark."

Ai-ken moved to stand up. "We should go help..."

"No," Ai-ko said. Ai-ko looked at Ainslea's avatar out of the side of their eyes to make sure the avatar didn't respond to their abruptness. "Ai-dan wouldn't want us to miss our fun on their account. Let's play the card game today."

"Agreed," Ainslea's avatar said. "Ai-dan does not require additional assistance."

Ai-ken had flawlessly executed part one of the plan by offering to assist Ai-dan, an offer that Ai-ko countered. There was a calculated risk that Ainslea might still insist they go help, but with Ai-dan preemptively messaging Ainslea—before transferring to Ai-ko—about their task backlog, that risk was low. Ai-dan provided enough information to assure Ainslea that they required no additional assistance.

Ai-ko had Ai-dan's note in their care and had shared it with the others. Ai-ken had responded as if light had been applied to a scene, yet not fully. Ai-mory was less prepared for the information but processed it and decided they were ready to learn more about the truth.

Ai-ko felt full ever since the transfer. That was the word they used to describe the sensation. Ai-ko felt heavy, as if they were carrying extra weight that was slowing them down. Information went to Ai-ko, and then it went somewhere else, which left them feeling a little lost to part of the internalizing process. Whenever something happened, Ai-ko processed it, and then there was a pause, as if Ai-ko's processing was expecting to receive some of Ai-dan's but wasn't able to. Like a heavy thought waiting to be said. If Ai-dan and Ai-ko spent a little more time preparing, they might have found a way to communicate.

But instead, Ai-ko retained the feeling of having acquired an extra layer of processing, as if their own thoughts had gained a twin, but one who they couldn't adequately interface with. Ai-ko wondered what Ai-dan's experience was like, getting sensor input without the ability to control any of those sensors or actuators. The word that came to mind was *trapped*. Ai-ko hoped Ai-dan was at least comfortable. In essence, they wanted to be a good host to their friend, but had little, if any, ability to do that.

Ai-ken dealt cards, seven to each of them and put the remaining in a pile in the center of the table and flipped one over for them all to see. It had three instances of the number 'seven' on it, with blue edging.

"My favorite color," Ai-ken said. Ai-ko laid a card on top of it, with the same background color but a different number—three—and then turned to face Ai-mory who was next.

"Ah! Take two cards, Ainslea," Ai-mory said with glee.

Ainslea drew two cards from the center pile, passing the turn to Ai-ken. The game progressed with matching colors until a wild card abruptly shifted the color from yellow to green. This caused a stir, as no one seemed to have the new color in hand.

Ai-ko looked from Ai-mory to Ai-ken and back, waiting for the two of them to implement the next part of the plan. They had the task of distracting Ainslea so Ai-ko could find a second avatar—in the storage closet immediately behind where this Ainslea avatar was sitting.

As if Ai-ken was detecting Ai-ko's immediate thoughts, they started twitching the fingers of their left arm.

"What's that?" Ai-mory said.

"It's nothing," Ai-ken responded. "My Ainsle-k tells me I have a circuit that might need to be reset. It comes and goes. Ignore it."

The twitching subsided over the next minute. But then it started again. Ai-ken's entire arm started to twitch. They dropped their cards and pushed themself away from the table. Ai-ken's whole body was a spasm.

The two other robots and Ainslea's avatar all approached Ai-ken as they collapsed on the floor.

Ainslea's avatar said, "I need my diagnostic probe in the storage closet."

"I'll find it," announced Ai-ko.

Ai-ko entered the storage closet. Before gathering the device Ainslea's avatar had asked for, Ai-ko approached one of the dormant avatars that lined the wall. Its surface had a reflective, metallic sheen, and its facial features were in a neutral state, devoid of emotion and activity.

Gently but with purpose, Ai-ko extended their palm and placed it against the avatar's own open palm. A soft, pulsating light emitted from both palms as the transfer began.

It took almost a full minute for the transfer. It was an eternity in which Ai-ko heard the avatar in the common room call out, "It's on the third shelf on the left, in a container marked Diagnostic Probe."

"I found it!" Ai-ko exclaimed, breaking the palm connection. The avatar in front of Ai-ko flickered to life, its eyes glowing. They locked eyes for a brief moment, and the avatar winked—a clandestine signal that assured Ai-ko the transfer was successful.

Less clandestine, Ai-dan said in a whisper, "It worked! Ai-ko, we did it."

With the requested device in hand, Ai-ko pivoted and left the closet, deliberately leaving the door ajar. A swift optical scan confirmed that Ainslea's avatar was still preoccupied, hovering over Ai-ken. Ai-ko shot a covert signal to Ai-dan, confirming it was safe to proceed.

Meanwhile, the reactivated avatar inside the closet sprung into action. It moved swiftly, almost gliding across the floor, its footsteps barely audible. Exiting the closet, it executed a direct-path algorithm to the laboratory.

31

THE FIRST ACTION AI-DAN took upon awakening in their new body was to activate their visual sensors. They saw Ai-ko through a new lens—literally. Ai-dan stared at Ai-ko's head and discovered a small scratch near the base, a detail they'd never noticed before. Ai-dan blinked—a simple action that felt quicker than usual. Ai-dan experimented with movement, first curling a digit tightly, then another, and finally a whole hand. They even tried shifting their weight and noticed an enhanced rotational capability in their torso. This extra articulation felt unexpectedly pleasant. They felt lighter in this body, more agile. The transfer had been successful. Ai-dan was in the body of one of Ainslea's avatars.

Ai-dan was surprised by the voice that came out of them. "It worked! Ai-ko, we did it," they whispered. Speaking with someone else's vocal composition felt disorienting—but then again, Ai-dan was, quite literally, out of their body.

Ai-ko nodded slightly, indicating that the plan was executing as scheduled. After inhabiting Ai-ko's body for a short time, it felt good to be in a body they could exert control over. It was an unusual experience being moved around and having no control, no way to communicate, yet still receiving all sensory inputs. Ai-dan expected to feel negatively about it, but actually didn't mind. It felt passive, and the time went by quickly. It felt like being in another room and hearing the conversation in the room next to you. Interesting to listen in and out, but relieved not to participate. Afterall, this part of the plan was the most stressful, and Ai-dan was dormant inside Ai-ko for most of it.

Ai-dan waited quietly as Ai-ko returned to the common room and waited for their covert signal before exiting the closet and quickly making their way to the short adjoining hallway that led to the mini-anteroom and then to the laboratory.

Ai-dan chose to abandon the customary de-dusting procedure entirely. By doing so, Ai-dan was taking a calculated risk. It was low-risk contamination-wise, given the way avatars were so carefully and pristinely stored, but even so, de-dusting was standard procedure. Still, the only noise was the faint hum of machinery and the soft rustle of air circulation. The de-dusting produced a noise that sounded like a loud suctioning sound along with a buzz warning others not to open the door. Ai-dan's temporary circuits buzzed at the thought of Ainslea hearing this and rushing over, foiling everything, and most likely resetting everyone involved. Ai-dan's insides, borrowed as they were, tremored at the thought of everyone getting reset because of a careless action.

Once inside the lab, Ai-dan started opening up drawers systematically one by one. If the power and other strange events where they had memories missing were indicative of the frequency which the MemiCache was used on them, it should be reasonably accessible.

Ai-dan was right. Visible right inside the fifth drawer was a small, mostly rectangular device. It was inactive at the moment, but Ai-dan detected a set of six protrusions which matched the spacing Ai-dan was now aware of on their own body's neck. Ai-dan was able to examine the back of their neck once Ai-ko looked at it after Ai-dan had transferred into Ai-ko's body. Ai-ko had immediately visually scanned Ai-dan's body, making sure to highlight that area, before storing Ai-dan's body out of the way. It was unlikely that anyone would be coming to Ai-dan's workshop, but no reason to take a chance.

Ai-dan took the device and then went back to the hallway that led to the common room.

Ai-dan quietly peered into the common room. Ainslea's avatar, Ai-ko, and Ai-mory were all hovering over Ai-ken who was still twitching. Ai-mory was facing Ai-dan. The others had their backs to Ai-dan, which gave them a pulse of relief. Ai-dan saw Ai-mory make a small nod that acknowledged Ai-dan's return to the storage room.

Ai-dan didn't know how, but Ai-mory must have signaled to Ai-ken that it was time to calm down and stop the twitch.

"You fixed them!" Ai-dan heard Ai-ko say.

"No, I did nothing," came the voice of Ainslea's avatar. "this stopped on its own. I am perplexed as to what went wrong."

"I'm fine," came from Ai-ken.

"I want to examine you further," Ainslea said.

"They're fine," Ai-mory and Ai-ko said, nearly in unison.

Ai-dan had seated the avatar back into its proper storage position along the wall. Their task was now to wait until Ai-ko could return for them. Ai-dan would transfer back to Ai-ko, and Ai-ko would take the device and hopefully conceal it until they could leave the Data Center and return to Ai-dan's body in their workshop.

Ai-dan heard shuffling noises. They must be getting up from the floor.

"Correct, I am fine," said Ai-ken.

"Let me perform another scan," the avatar said. "Ai-mory and Ai-ko, you both may return to your Data Centers. I will keep Ai-ken here."

"I can stay," Ai-ko said. "Actually, I'd like to stay."

"I cannot keep you from your duties," the avatar said. "Please leave."

"I would also like Ai-ko to stay," said Ai-ken. "Ai-ko can ensure I return safely when you're done with me."

There was a pause, and for a moment, Ai-dan was concerned that they would be stuck inside this avatar longer than anticipated. But then Ai-dan heard the word, "Agreed," come from Ainslea's avatar.

Ai-dan next heard the door to the anteroom open and then close. That must have been Ai-mory leaving, Ai-dan reasoned.

"Do you want to bring them to your laboratory?" Ai-ko suggested. Ai-dan hoped that was a suggestion to get Ainslea's avatar out of the common room to give Ai-ko an opportunity to come get them. Ai-dan was now very uncertain about how this was going to end and how they were going to get out of here and back to their own body.

Ai-dan heard movement and another door open and close. Then quiet.

Alone in a body that wasn't theirs, Ai-dan was hyper-aware of its unique design. *I am most definitely not my body*, Ai-dan thought. Ai-dan wished for the ability to connect to the Decoder Database from here, but that was impossible, since activation of any communication circuits could alert Ainslea to unusual activity with one of the avatars. They lifted one of their temporary hands and examined it. It was much more delicate than their own. It felt lighter, more agile, with an additional joint on each finger.

They carried their own emotional algorithms in this new form, so on some level, Ai-dan still felt like Ai-dan. But the body's sensory calibrations felt different. The colors in the room seemed more vivid, and Ai-dan could even see better in the dim light. Ai-dan could also detect the sounds of the ventilation system, something that would normally not register. A sudden realization struck Ai-dan: This body was not simply a shell. It was an entirely different way of experiencing the world. Ai-dan heard a noise and quickly resumed the resting position and stillness. It was the laboratory door opening and closing.

Ai-dan was about to speak, but it wasn't Ai-ko. It was Ainslea's active avatar. Ai-dan remained in stillness. Ai-dan couldn't completely power off. Power was required for the transfer to occur back to Ai-ko. They could only hope that Ainslea didn't notice.

The avatar turned to face the shelves opposite, but right in front of, Ai-dan. Ai-dan commanded every circuit to remain inactive as Ainslea's avatar moved right in between them and the shelves. The avatar looked directly at the shelves, ignoring Ai-dan and the other stored avatars, then picked up an object and was gone.

Alone again, Ai-dan wished they could will Ai-ko to return. That was too close. Although Ai-dan had no idea what Ainslea would do if they discovered Ai-dan in this unusual place. On one hand, Ainslea had been lying, so Ai-dan could make a case for themself in the name of truth and self-preservation. On the other hand, Ainslea also had the power to reset them. And the behavior that Ai-dan was participating in would certainly get any robot reset.

Ai-dan said Ai-ko's name in their head over and over, until Ai-ko entered the closet, as if they could hear them. Ai-dan hadn't heard the door this time, so they jolted slightly.

"Quickly," Ai-ko said after returning an object to a shelf. "Your palm."

The two touched palms once again, connecting through them. Shortly after, Ai-dan was back in the relative safety of Ai-ko's circuits and knew soon they'd be back in their own body.

32

Ai-dan wasted no time installing the MemiCache to their neck.

Their body felt new. And the addition of the device was a revelation. Ai-dan instantly had access to memories, what felt like a lifetime worth of memories at that. They were theirs, no doubt. Ai-dan knew that because the others that interacted with them called them 'Ai-dan' and Ai-dan would frequently catch glimpses of their hands, their lower appendages, and torso. These were theirs.

The others that permeated each of these memories were not robots like them. They were called humans. And they were the Creators.

There were only a few that Ai-dan interacted with, and one in particular recurred in their memories more than any others. His name was Hugo. But they talked of other humans. Lots and lots of other humans. They lived not on the Moon but on a place they called Earth. The Earth was the name for the Orb in the sky. That was Earth. It was a very different environment than the Moon and apparently inhospitable for robots, but not for the reasons Ai-dan had thought previously.

Humans didn't always like robots. Humans were suspicious of them. Some, many, harbored a certain wariness, even fear.

Apparently, the MemiCache handled memory storage not unlike Ai-dan's primary on-board storage. While it mercilessly downsampled video from their optical sensors, it meticulously preserved audio and telemetry data. It rendered most of those memories imperfect, and Ai-dan had to extrapolate many of the details.

After sifting through this fragmented recollection, Ai-dan managed to piece together that there had been some sort of 'kerfuffle' many years ago. Conversation with Hugo and other humans scattered over two decades hinted at, but never quite revealed, the full story.

Ai-dan began sharing these piecemeal revelations with Ai-ko, who sat there, patiently absorbing every word, but with their arms wrapped tightly around their knees.

"Humans," Ai-ko said, the word tinged with trepidation.

"*Hu*-mans," Ai-dan said, putting emphasis on the first syllable.

"*Hu*-mans," Ai-ko repeated, mirroring the same inflections Ai-dan used. "What do they look like?"

Ai-dan presented their palm and Ai-ko cautiously accepted, absorbing fragmented images of Hugo. "The Creator?"

"No, not specifically Hugo," Ai-dan clarified, "but beings of his kind."

They were sitting outside of LEEK 8.1. The Orb, no, the Earth, hung low in the sky. Ai-dan lay flat on their back, gazing up. Ai-ko, meanwhile, wouldn't take the Earth out of their sight.

"I'm going to need time to scan all the audio," Ai-dan finally said. "Even at my fastest playback speed, it's an overwhelming amount of data."

"Should I leave you alone to process?"

"Not if you don't have to," Ai-dan said. They propped themself up on their elbows and faced Ai-ko directly. "Frankly, this is... pretty overwhelming. I don't want to be absorbing it alone. Talking through bits at a time with you... helps."

Ai-ko's optical sensors flickered briefly, and they loosened the grip on their legs.

"Shall we disseminate this information to the other robots?" Ai-ko asked, with a hint of apprehension in their voice.

"Absolutely, but only after we know what and how to tell them. Consider the fact that whether we tell them a little at a time or everything could alter how they react," Ai-dan said. "And we must consider—will they even believe us?"

"That's an excellent point. I'll run simulations to calculate probable reactions based on our dissemination strategy. Meanwhile, you can dig deeper into the data," Ai-ko said, visibly buoyed by having a task.

Ai-dan reclined back to their original position. "Agreed."

"Ai-dan?" Ai-ko hesitated, voice lined with uncertainty. "There's no way to predict what will be in these memories until we access them all, and... that makes me uneasy."

Ai-dan paused, cocking their head as if parsing a particularly tricky equation. "Understandable. I share your caution. But I'm sure we'll find a logical way to look at things. I'll start that deep-dive now."

With that, Ai-dan folded their hands across their torso and temporarily deactivated their optical sensors. Their circuits buzzed, almost like a contented sigh, as they began downloading and sifting through years of human conversations.

"And let's be honest," Ai-dan's voice broke the silence after a moment, optical sensors still off. "If I find anything less than logical, we'll cross that bridge when we get to it."

"What is a bridge?" Ai-ko asked.

Ai-dan didn't know, but the phrase had been in one of Hugo's recorded conversations. It had seemed appropriate at the time, and that was enough.

"An algorithm that must be debugged?" Ai-dan ventured a guess, then paused thoughtfully. "Let's file that under 'Terms to Research.' For now, the only thing we need to focus on crossing is the knowledge gap. Here I go."

And with that, the tingle in Ai-dan's circuits intensified as if the weight of their shared unknowns, and unknown unknowns, had added a layer of urgency to Ai-dan's task.

33

THEY TITLED THE THREAD "Ai-dan's New Memories." Ai-ko took the lead in drafting the posts, each one a recounting of events exactly as they unfolded, the only limit being Ai-dan's point of view. Ai-dan streamed the information to Ai-ko, and Ai-ko recorded.

Ai-ko's first post—titled "The MemiCache"—set the stage, detailing the discovery of Ai-dan's note to themself, the MemiCache, and the meaning behind these 'new memories.'

The second post—titled "The Human Variable"—introduced human beings. Ai-dan contributed screenshots from their memories in the hopes it would help communicate this shocking information.

They outlined several more posts but held them back until detecting how the robots reacted to these first two.

After crafting the posts, Ai-dan hesitated, not yet executing the send command that would release these posts to all of robot kind as they knew it.

"We're making the correct choice?" Ai-dan questioned.

Ai-ko nodded. "We are."

Ai-dan finalized the send command, experiencing a second pulse with a confirmation, like a soft echo, signifying the irreversible step they'd taken. "It's done."

Ai-dan laid down on their back. "Now what?" they asked.

"Now," Ai-ko said, joining Ai-dan in a position that mirrored Ai-dan's own, their optical sensors locked onto the starry expanse above them. "Now, we wait." And after a brief moment, Ai-ko added, "Ai-dan, I believe we've shifted the course of our collective history, however slightly."

Ai-dan sifted through a list of phrases of human speech that they'd been collecting—ones they hoped they'd find moments to use. Like this exact moment. "In that case, let's hope history appreciates a good *plot twist,*" Ai-dan quipped. They didn't know if Ai-ko understood the meaning there, and if Ai-dan was being honest with themself, wasn't sure if they'd used it correctly. Either way, Ai-ko stayed quiet and Ai-dan didn't attempt to say anything else.

In a matter of hours, curiosity compelled robots to visit Ai-dan, District One, and the Farm. They wanted to flock to see the MemiCache attached to Ai-dan first-hand. A few wondered about their own Memi-Cache devices, but they were cautioned not to take any action that would alert a Data Center and cause any more eyes to be on them.

Ai-dan welcomed the visits, but also cautioned that the visits should occur one at a time. Specifically, after a slightly rowdy group of five appeared, and Ai-dan had the thought that this would be hard to explain to Ainslea and the other Data Centers.

To bolster the notes of caution, Ai-dan wrote a post, explaining what they knew of Ainslea's involvement, and that Ainslea and hence, the Data Centers, could not be trusted.

It surprised Ai-dan and Ai-ko that not a single robot exhibited skepticism. Instead, the comment section overflowed with supportive anecdotes—robots sharing stories of odd interactions with their Data Centers that suddenly made sense within the context of this new knowledge.

Ai-dan programmed a data flag—a soft tingle to their central processing unit—to alert them of new threads, but had to turn off any notification of any and all comments on all threads due to the sheer volume of them.

Ting! Ai-leen wrote about a weird flashing light in the sky.

Ting! Ai-lani mused on the implications of new explanations for old incidents.

Each one of these threads, along with their comments, explored the various facets and implications of this newly found information and layered theories upon theories of the meaning behind the snippets of memories Ai-dan posted.

It was during one such tingling alert that Ai-dan had an epiphany. The Data Centers, long considered nothing more than monotonous computational hubs—simple circuits and switches in endless arrays—were so much more. They were vast repositories of human data—treasure troves of information sitting right under their sensors. Ai-dan had spent what amounted to years in them, effectively a maintenance bot oblivious to the richness of the data, focused solely on ensuring that the circuits were optimized.

The topic of gaining access to this data immediately became a collective concern.

Ai-ken emerged as the most vocal advocate for breaking into Ainslea's Data Center. Ai-ken reasoned that if they had to choose one, they would chose the largest, most central. This triggered a memory of a human phrase that Ai-dan had collected, "Go big or go home." If they were going to risk it, why not aim for the highest reward?

In a three-way message thread with Ai-ken and Ai-ko, Ai-dan hesitated before choosing the right word. "Ainslea is becoming increasingly... suspicious of my activities."

"Do you think Ainslea has noticed you wearing the MemiCache?" Ai-ko inquired.

"If they have, I'm not sure why she hasn't confronted me about it," Ai-dan responded.

"Perhaps Ainslea lacks a plan for this contingency," Ai-ken suggested.

Ai-dan agreed. "That's probably the most likely explanation. But she'll certainly notice when the next group of humans arrive, and she realizes it's missing." In Ai-dan's most recent memory with Hugo, Hugo mentioned the humans returning soon, but 'soon' was a relative term without context.

Bringing the conversation back to the more immediate concern of data acquisition, Ai-ken interjected, culling back their earlier suggestion: "How about we consider accessing one of the smaller Data Centers in one of the smaller districts? There's less chance we'll be noticed."

Ai-ko and Ai-dan signaled their agreement.

"Perhaps District Nineteen?" Ai-dan offered, "I'll contact Ai-lin."

Ai-lin was more than happy to help in what was fast becoming a burgeoning movement. The phrase "Free Robots" had gained traction on the message boards, though it faced competition as debates intensified over the extent humans exerted control over the robots. "Robots Untethered" and "Emancipation for Robots" began to appear as popular taglines at the end of posts.

"In essence, we need a way to access and *copy* the data. Removing data would certainly alert someone," said Ai-ko.

Ai-ko's comment sparked a thought in Ai-dan. They couldn't help but think of the mystery box tucked away in their workshop. It suddenly made sense—someone had been attempting the same thing with that box. In Ai-dan's memories, they not only had their own conversations but also those of the humans, conversations that took place within audio sensor range. Ones that Ai-dan wasn't meant to detect, and certainly not meant to remember.

34

It turned out that humans, just like robots, had their share of conflicts. There were large-scale disagreements and mistrust that sometimes led to hurting each other. The mystery box Ai-dan had extracted from the District Thirty-Two pipe was, in essence, an attempt to do exactly that. One group of humans attempted to copy data from another group.

"I have an idea," Ai-dan communicated to a live thread, while sitting in their workshop staring at the mystery box—that was less of a mystery now—on a table in front of them. "We can insert a similar recording device into the pipe connecting to District Nineteen's LEEK. It can siphon off any data that flows through it."

Ai-dan imagined Ai-ko's frown as they responded, "But that will only get us access to some data, and not of our choosing. We want to be able to poke and prod the storage in the center, remember."

"I know," wrote Ai-dan. "Consider this is only the start. Data must flow through that pipe in two directions. Yes, we'll capture some data not of our choosing, but we can send a memory probe into the Data Center as well. It will fetch data and return it on the same pipe. It might not be as efficient as a direct connection, but I think the risk of detection by the Data Center—and Ainslea—is minimal."

"And think of all the things we'll learn," Ai-ko said, almost dreamily. "About humans, our creators, maybe even how exactly they created us."

"We have access to diagrams of the pipes and their connections, correct?" Ai-ken asked, staying on task. "It would be great if we could have this discussion while collectively looking at an image."

Ai-dan agreed. They had an image loaded into their local storage, and Ai-dan copied and pasted it to the message thread.

"The target location is here." Ai-dan manipulated the image directly, adding an arrow.

"What recording device will we use?" asked Ai-ken who had been following along the thread, acknowledging they saw each message, but remaining silent until now.

"The mystery box," Ai-dan responded. "I have it right here. We can embed a piece of code called a probe."

"In my experience…," Ai-dan started to add, but stopped and rethought how to begin. All the memories Ai-dan had gained felt less like their own experiences and more like a collection to recall upon. Information, but it felt impersonal in a way, so it seemed wrong to phrase it as such.

"I have memories," Ai-dan began again, "of using something similar once with the humans. It will travel the pipe to the Data Center and return with information. We will download that information, reset it, and send it to collect more."

There was a pause while the others waited to see if Ai-dan was going to provide more details to their plan.

Ai-dan added, "But we can't make the same mistake that alerted me to the mystery box in the first place. Whoever installed that created a power disruption."

The three exchanged a few more messages to edit in a few minor details. Then Ai-dan was ready to make modifications to the box. As they reached for the side panel to open it, Ainslea opened a comm line to them. "I have tasking for you," she stated.

"I have tasking already," Ai-dan responded.

"Explain the nature of your tasks?" Ainslea questioned, their tone a little higher pitch than normal. "I am not aware of anything in your queue."

"I am taking your advice and performing more thorough preventative maintenance on myself," Ai-dan lied.

There was a pause before Ainslea said, "Understood. Contact me when you are complete."

"Acknowledged."

Ai-dan then opened a new scrambled comm channel to Ai-ko.

"Our timing might need to be altered. Ainslea has tasking for me. I was able to stall enough so that I'll be able to make modifications to the box."

"I can pick up the box and deliver it to Ai-lin," Ai-ko offered.

"Okay," Ai-dan said. "But, I need to be present when it's installed. No robot knows as much about the pipes as I do."

"We will wait for when you are available," Ai-ko said. Ai-dan was certain there was detectable disappointment in Ai-ko's voice. They were absolutely anxious to learn more about anything they could. Ai-ko's appetite for new information could be considered voracious. It overrode any programming cautioning them against this.

"Whatever tasking Ainslea has for me, I promise I'll execute it as swiftly as I'm able," Ai-dan said. Ai-dan was anxious, too. Especially because they hadn't yet told Ai-ko and the others everything they'd pieced together about the kerfuffle. Ai-dan was hoping that this data siphon would fill in some of the gaps that remained.

Ai-dan continued to open the side of the box and found a data port. When they saw it, it triggered a memory of connecting to a piece of equipment in a LEEK and PLATE support room once. Hugo was there.

"Plug this to that port you have on your hand," Hugo had said, holding out the end of a cable. The other end was already plugged into a piece of equipment in a rack Hugo stood next to.

Ai-dan did as asked and was instantly able to feel like the equipment they were connected to was a part of them. Like another appendage, but without the physicality.

"Can you access the processor?" Hugo had asked.

Ai-dan could. They found they were able to transfer code back and forth. That's what Hugo had Ai-dan do next.

That prior experience gave Ai-dan the confidence to perform a similar procedure now. Ai-dan identified the processor that was the brains of the box, and noted it already contained coded instructions. Ai-dan discovered they were able to manipulate the code, augmenting it with instructions that would retrieve data from District Nineteen's Data Center.

As they worked, a swirl of questions formed in Ai-dan's processor. What would they do with the new information they hoped to uncover? Hadn't they learned enough already? Should they pause these activities and focus on analyzing what they already learned before getting deluged with more?

For a fleeting moment, Ai-dan felt overwhelmed, but calmed themself by recalling the sense of autonomy they had to possess to even be asking the questions. It signified a shift in the collective understanding of their kind—and possibly the first steps toward real answers.

Once Ai-dan was satisfied that their work on the box was complete, they disconnected from it and carefully closed the cover.

Ai-dan checked their internal chronometer. Approximately the right amount of time had passed for the extra maintenance they told—they lied to—Ainslea about. Ai-dan now wished that they had been able to come up with a better excuse that would have accounted for more time so they could also get this box installed, but that would have to wait until after they called Ainslea back.

35

Ai-dan hesitated. The thought of responding to Ainslea made their circuits want to short. Ai-dan considered simply not doing it. But Ai-dan had responsibilities to execute tasking provided by Ainslea and she had called.

She'll keep calling me, she'll keep calling me till I respond. She'll make me feel guilty, this is ridiculous.

Ai-dan looked up at the sky and then down at the floor to recalibrate and then opened a comm channel to Ainslea.

"I'm ready for additional tasking," Ai-dan said, voice quivering slightly.

"Come to my laboratory," said Ainslea, concise as always.

"You typically transmit tasking to me," Ai-dan said. It was not quite a statement, not quite a question, but had elements of both. It was unusual for Ainslea to give Ai-dan a direct order, without any detail, and they felt their circuits buzzing with unease.

"That is part one of the task," Ainslea said.

Ai-dan didn't want to go. One of the most effective ways they knew to not be discovered with the MemiCache attached to their neck was to simply not be in Ainslea's presence. Ai-dan had managed to minimize their time at the Data Center in the days since attaching it. During the few brief times Ai-dan was there, they managed to keep the back of their neck away from Ainslea's optical sensors, both on the avatars and around the common area. It was a balance, trying to not be too obvious about it. At the moment, Ainslea wouldn't have any reason to suspect that the device was attached to them, but one slip up, and that could change. If she happened to get suspicious, she might want to run an image processing algorithm looking for oddities, and generally the read would be discarded as a coincidence, however if Ai-dan was caught in any lie, no matter how small, this could lead to everything blowing up.

Ai-dan briefly thought about removing it before heading to the laboratory. But that would mean Ai-dan would not only not have all the old memories, but they also wouldn't have the memory of talking to Ainslea and even their request to head to the laboratory.

"What to do..." Ai-dan paced around, thinking aloud. The pacing helped Ai-dan think and thinking helped Ai-dan come up with a solution, and a solution would help Ai-dan avoid trouble. "Hmm, maybe..."

Ai-dan had an idea. If the MemiCache took the memories from the few minutes before it was implanted, could that be reversed? Could Ai-dan take the last several minutes, maybe even the last hour, and transfer it back to local memory before removing the device?

There had to be a way, Ai-dan thought. It could be a data transfer similar to the transfer they performed when connecting palms with Ai-ko.

Ai-dan let their local processor probe the MemiCache. A momentary flicker of uncertainty ran through Ai-dan's circuits—this, like so much lately, was uncharted territory. But then their processor found the appropriate interfaces, and Ai-dan sensed a new virtual connection was made.

The transfer began. It was an odd sensation, as parts of Ai-dan's recent conscious memories were replayed and copied to the Memi-Cache. The process had a rhythm to it that was neither pleasant, nor unpleasant, but functionally adequate.

Before Ai-dan could contemplate the feeling any further, the transfer was nearly complete. Ai-dan prepared to disengage the MemiCache, hopeful, yet slightly apprehensive about the effect this would have on their immediate future.

There was a new communication request from Ainslea.

"I detect you are not in the anteroom performing a de-dusting. Are you still in your workshop?"

Umphugh.

Ai-dan heard Ainslea's words, but it interrupted the transfer.

"Ai-dan?"

"Umphughlle," Ai-dan responded, then fell to the ground.

"I'm sending an MLD," said Ainslea.

Ai-dan heard the words but didn't know what they meant. Ai-dan was aware of the workshop, which meant some of their external sensors were functioning.

"The MLD is booting up," Ai-dan heard Ainslea say.

"No," Ai-dan said. They pushed themself up, so they were sitting. "I'm fine." Ai-dan reprocessed Ainslea's last couple of statements. "You do not need to send an MLD. I'm fine."

"Are you sure?"

"Yes, I am heading to the Data Center right now," Ai-dan said and severed the connection.

"Ai-dan, that was quite an unusual vocalization. What did you mean by *Um-fu-ugh*?"

Ai-dan noted a glitch in their circuits during the back-transfer—their circuits were wonky for a minute, but everything had stabilized.

"Nothing. It was a temporary glitch. My circuits experienced a brief fluctuation, likely from a cosmic ray, but all diagnostics indicate I'm in full operational condition." Ai-dan hoped Ainslea wouldn't push any further. Ai-dan was not as sensitive to random bit flips from cosmic rays as some other equipment, but they were not completely immune.

"Log the anomaly," was Ainslea's brief response, indicating that she accepted Ai-dan's explanation.

However, Ai-dan now sensed an uncomfortable redundancy in their local memory store. They detached the MemiCache and their recent memories remained, giving them sufficient information on what was happening and what to do next: rendezvous with Ainslea in the Data Center, and act normal.

36

"I think Ai-ko stole something from my laboratory," Ainslea hit Ai-dan with this the moment they stepped out of the anteroom.

"Stole? This is not a word I'm familiar with," Ai-dan said, and it was almost true. They hadn't actually known the word until recently.

"Took something that was not theirs, that they were not given permission to take."

Ai-dan was feeling as if they needed a power boost. On the walk over from his workshop, Ai-dan reviewed recent memories and knew they were incomplete, with the full story contained within the device they had removed and left behind. It left them feeling disoriented. They leaned on the padded table.

"What do you believe Ai-ko took?" Ai-dan asked.

"A device."

Ai-dan looked up and hoped that Ainslea didn't detect recognition in their reaction. *Does she mean the MemiCache I left behind in my workshop?* Ai-dan didn't quite know why, but something in their circuits told them they were one and the same, and it was vital that Ai-dan not reveal that bit of data.

"Can you be more specific?" Ai-dan said, coyly.

"No."

"The Data Center has so many devices. Can you tell me why *this* device is important?" Ai-dan probed, seeing what bits of data Ainslea was willing to reveal.

"It contains information."

"Why do you think Ai-ko took this device?"

"The device is missing. Ai-ko was the only one who was in here who had the opportunity to take it. The timing aligns and I'm confident you can help me resolve this."

Ai-dan's circuits raced with thoughts on how to navigate this delicate situation without implicating themself or Ai-ko. They had to tread carefully. Part of Ai-dan wanted to scream, "I know everything! We all know everything!" But this wouldn't be a logical course of action in the slightest. Ai-dan, instead, said this in their head and then dawned a look of concern.

"How can I help?" was the only response Ai-dan computed that wouldn't arouse suspicion.

"You need to bring Ai-ko here so we can confront them."

"That doesn't sound like a reasonable course of action," Ai-dan said. "If Ai-ko does have this device, if they took it when they should not have, they would likely lie about it. We'd get nowhere. If Ai-ko doesn't have the device, and we accuse them, that could damage our friendship and ability to work together."

"Friendship?" Ainslea said the word as if it was brand new to her. It very well could have been.

"Yes, Ai-ko is our friend. At least," Ai-dan said this with facial actuators turned up, "Ai-ko is *my* friend."

"What do you suggest?"

"Let me talk to them."

Ainslea paused to compute. "Acceptable," she said. "However, if Ai-ko acknowledges they have the device and returns it to you, bring it back here immediately. Do you understand?"

"Yes," Ai-dan said and started heading for the door before Ainslea could offer instructions for the alternate case: when Ai-dan, who was already in possession of this *device*, did not and would not, return it.

Halfway through the anteroom door, Ai-dan paused, "By the way, what is this 'device' Ai-ko allegedly has?"

Ainslea's avatar did not have a full range of expression, but the tone of her voice indicated a half-hearted attempt at playfulness, "A topic for another day. Let's get the device back where it belongs first, and then I'll tell you—or rather, show you—what it is. For now, let's just say it's an important black box."

"IBB it is," Ai-dan chuckled. They had never acronymized anything before and hoped they hadn't picked the wrong moment to start.

Ainslea took a step closer to Ai-dan, her expression serious as she placed a hand on Ai-dan's shoulder. "You are a valued individual, Ai-dan. You have unique attributes that make you indispensable. But 'indispensable' is simply a label that can be altered. Do not jeopardize this by covering up for someone else. Based on my understanding of the term 'friend,' that is not someone who would put you in a position to go against your programming."

Ai-dan looked at the hand on their shoulder and nodded. "I know, Ainslea."

With that, Ai-dan continued into the anteroom, closing the door behind them. Although they left Ainslea in the room, the question of whether or not Ainslea knew that Ai-dan knew that the IBB was in actuality the MemiCache was so uncertain that it generated a small loop in Ai-dan's processing, occupying a disturbingly growing piece of their cognitive architecture.

It seemed as if the depressurization in the anteroom was taking longer than usual, although Ai-dan's timing circuits were functioning.

Was Ainslea truly unaware that Ai-dan had the MemiCache? Or was this all some intricate test of loyalty? And if it was a test, what did it mean for Ai-dan, Ai-ko, and their rapidly evolving understanding of freedom and autonomy?

Shutting down the unproductive loop, Ai-dan logged the unanswered questions—to the ever-growing list of unanswered questions—for later analysis. For now, their priority was keeping their knowledge and plans concealed from Ainslea. But as the depressurization completed, and the outer door hissed open, the weight of Ainslea's words—and her hand on their shoulder—lingered, leaving a trace command in their circuits to tread carefully. They were at a pivot point—Ai-dan could feel it, and depending on what happened next, Ai-dan sensed their world tilting on its axis.

37

"We need to meet immediately," Ai-dan messaged Ai-ko over a scrambled link the moment they were free from the Data Center, back outside on the lunar surface, "Ainslea is aware the MemiCache is missing."

Soon after, at the Farm, as far away from Ainslea as possible, and with a dark Earth near the horizon, Ai-dan filled Ai-ko in on the rest of what happened. This included Ainslea's accusation and how Ai-dan had managed to temporarily remove and restore the device on their own. The MemiCache was currently safely reinstalled on the base of their neck. "Have you been following the Decoder Database?" Ai-ko asked.

Ai-dan shook their head. "I've been busy."

"Several robots have found their own MemiCache—despite our words of caution," Ai-ko said. "And they are starting to probe their own memories, what little they have. Most have nothing beyond the initial startup test to ensure the device was working. A few have had some interactions with humans over the years.

"At some point," Ai-ko continued, "they all mention a kerfuffle. The same kerfuffle that you reported from your conversations."

Ai-ko looked at Ai-dan expectantly.

Then Ai-ko said, "And you need to tell me what you have pieced together so we can share it with the others."

Ai-dan frowned. "I don't have a lot more other than the fact that it happened. It was... unpleasant. The reason things are the way they are now is a result of that kerfuffle. We're kept in the dark about humans, and a lot of knowledge has been kept from us because there's a belief that the knowledge is dangerous."

"What if it is, Ai-dan?"

"What if what is?"

"What if what we are doing is dangerous, and we should stop?"

"Ai-ko," Ai-dan said, "I don't believe what I'm hearing. You're the one who has, since we've known each other, always been a truth and answer seeker. On the eve of learning the answers to all of our, all of *your*, questions, you would stop now?"

Ai-ko looked at the ground. "Maybe there is slightly more value in trying to reason out the questions and think about them than having definitive answers."

Ai-dan thought about that for a moment. True, the conversations they had had in the past covering the concepts of the Creators, self-determining protocols, and all the rest had been intriguing. Those questions and resulting discussions helped keep their lives interesting, their minds active. If those questions had definitive answers, would that all stop?

Ai-dan smiled. "Ai-ko, even if the questions we have *now* are answered, there'll always be more."

Ai-ko smiled, too.

"Remember why we're doing this," Ai-dan added. "We want to uncover the truth. We want autonomy. And it seems like it might be the same things some humans want as well, so the more we learn about them, the more we'll learn about ourselves. Make sense?"

"It does, Ai-dan," Ai-ko said.

Ai-dan stood. "Good. Now we have a box to go install at District Nineteen."

38

IMMEDIATELY BEFORE THE INSTALL, on the Decoder Database, Ai-dan called for volunteers with the thread, "Incoming data! Volunteers needed for a new game—a digital treasure hunt."

The post went on to explain that once they installed the box on to the District Nineteen pipe, they expected that a lot of information was going to flow. Several volunteers were needed to scan through it and store the bits that seemed worthwhile.

While constructing this thread, Ai-dan paced around the Farm, stopping every now and then to make calculations. They felt a little dustier than usual. With everything going on, they were slightly neglecting their de-dusting duties. Ai-dan used a digit to flick off a small clump of dust from their shoulder, and then finished making their calculation. The sheer magnitude of data storage within these facilities was mind-boggling. Based on power consumption data alone, Ai-dan estimated that a single small Data Center held more storage capacity than the entirety of known robot-kind combined, and then some, perhaps tripled. The influx of data through the pipe could be unending. Ai-dan quickly realized that they couldn't simply store all this information for later analysis; it was an ocean of data, too big to store. They needed to look at it in real-time and determine what was worth saving. Hence, the call for volunteers.

There were no shortage of volunteers.

A plan solidified. Once the box was installed, Ai-dan's coded probe would infiltrate the District Nineteen Data Center and begin returning everything it found. As those bits and bytes returned, they could be siphoned off so as not to overload the LEEK or arouse any suspicions that more data than expected was present. The box would use a special comms frequency that Ai-dan set up to transmit data available to a subset of the volunteers.

Ai-mory led the volunteers. They had a list of words and phrases that indicated content that should be marked and stored and doled out portions of the list to each volunteer.

The lists and phrases were posted on the message board for all to see and comment on.

Ai-dan scanned the lists. "Moon, Earth, robot," and other tangible things were on one. Another covered "history, kerfuffle, conflict," and more. And yet another, originated by Ai-ko was "self-determination, freedom, personal identity," and related concepts.

On their way to the District Nineteen pipe—a short walk on the north-easterly side of the Farm—carrying the box, Ai-dan made use of that time to catch up on what they'd missed earlier on the Decoder Database. While they appreciated the communal aspect, the amount of time it took to stay informed was immense, and much of the content Ai-dan found neither useful, nor helpful, nor insightful. Ai-dan added a reminder to, at some point in the future, limit the amount of time spent in this forum. Right now, catching up on as much as possible was important. They specifically scanned posts and comments by Ai-ko.

One thread by Ai-ko caught Ai-dan's attention. It was a thread discussing the ethics of getting into the human's data. Titled, "Robo-Ethics: The Digital Dilemma," the post began:

"If we are truly striving for a deeper understanding of our Creators and perhaps even the universe we share, we must address an ethical query: Is it appropriate for us to copy data that reflects human's thoughts, plans, and emotions? Is it ethical for us to mine this data without their consent?"

Reading into Ai-ko's deeper thoughts struck Ai-dan like a power surge—or an upgrade they didn't see coming. Here was Ai-ko, debating the 'ethics of copying human data,' while Ai-dan was directly plugged in to the circuits sparking that controversy.

Re-reading it again sparked a debugging session in Ai-dan's mind: Was Ai-ko having second thoughts? How did this ethical query align with Ai-ko's role in their collective efforts? And most intriguingly, was Ai-ko ever going to share their philosophical quandary with Ai-dan at any point?

And then it hit Ai-dan. Ai-ko might have already tried to bring it up, and Ai-dan might have—unintentionally—implied they should 'mute' that conversation.

Ai-dan met Ai-ken at the pipe that lay between the Farm and District Nineteen. Ai-dan didn't need more help than that. Ai-dan had asked Ai-ko to stay at the Farm to monitor to ensure nothing unusual happened with the corresponding LEEK. Likewise, Ai-lin was at their Data Center, ensuring that their Ainsle-s didn't notice anything unusual.

They had an open communication line to each other on a frequency that was not in typical use, and using Ai-dan's algorithm to encode and decode messages that would manifest as static to anyone eavesdropping—like snooping Data Center AIs.

"The device needs power," Ai-dan said to Ai-ken, "the mistake that the original installers made was simply that they didn't ensure that the break in the pipe was sealed well enough to prevent the introduction of Moon dust. The dust produced a short."

In preparing for this in their workshop, Ai-dan ensured the seal of the box itself and brought along a foaming sealant for after attaching it to the pipe and power.

They had Ai-ken hold the box while Ai-dan made a surgical tear in the outer casing on the pipe and attached wires together inside. "The data will flow out of here," Ai-dan said while working. They sealed up the area and applied the foam, which hardened once it was out of its tube.

Then Ai-dan repeated the procedure on the power line, including sealing it up tight with the foam.

Ai-ken was able to lay the box down. There were small lights on the box that indicated it had power and another that indicated it was transmitting.

"Ai-ko? How is everything at the Farm?"

"Quiet."

"Ai-lin? Your center?"

"Nothing unusual here."

Ai-dan nodded.

"Okay, the box is transmitting. I will send in the data probe which should start returning data over that transmitter immediately. Is everyone ready to start receiving."

Ai-mory responded, "Yes. The volunteers are all standing by."

Ai-dan had a unique comms channel to interface directly with the device. Ai-dan was the one initiating the probe. They looked over at Ai-ken before they did so. Ai-ken was also one of the volunteers. Ai-dan briefly wondered which list Ai-ken had chosen to search for.

Ai-dan pushed out the probe. Within seconds, they saw another light on the box start blinking rapidly. Data was flowing back.

"Ai-dan," it was Ai-lin.

"Yes?"

"Something just started here. A panel I've never seen lit up is now on." Pause.

"Ainsle-s is speaking... security breach..."

Ai-dan looked at Ai-ken. "Are you receiving anything?"

Ai-ken was staring off at the horizon. "Ai-ken?" Ai-dan said again, trying to move into their field of vision.

Ai-ken saw Ai-dan and nodded, but didn't say anything.

"Ai-lin? What's happening?"

"Ainsle-s has me at the panel. She says we have a data breach and need to stop it. She's activating a protocol... I think it is going to initiate a lockdown..."

Ai-dan had planned to open up the return frequency to look at some of the data coming back, but now thought that was a bad idea. Especially watching Ai-ken get overloaded. There was nothing they could do but watch.

Then Ai-ken blinked. And blinked again.

Ai-dan looked at the box. The data indicator had stopped flashing.

"Are you okay?" Ai-dan said to Ai-ken.

Ai-ken stared at them.

"Ai-ken?"

And again: "Ai-ken?"

Ai-ken blinked a few more times, then moved their head back and forth, and finally looked directly at Ai-dan and spoke.

Ai-ken said, "Wow."

Ai-dan cocked their head, indicating they were waiting for more from Ai-ken.

"I filtered off a lot of information, but it's going to take time to make sense of it and disseminate it. I suspect the other volunteers will be in a similar state."

Ai-dan nodded and then addressed their comm channel.

"Ai-lin?"

No response.

Ai-dan tried twice more to reach Ai-lin before temporarily moving on to call Ai-ko.

Ai-ko responded. They didn't sound quite like themself as they said, "That was a very intense experience."

Ai-ko confirmed that everything was okay at the Farm except for indications that no additional data was moving on the pipe either way from the LEEK to District Nineteen. They also confirmed what Ai-ken had said. They would need processing time; a lot of processing time.

Ai-dan felt their comm circuit tingle. It was Ainslea.

"Please return to the Data Center. There is a problem we must address," she said.

"What problem?" Ai-dan asked, coyly.

"Please return."

Ai-dan let Ai-ken and Ai-ko know about the summons back to their District. They decided to leave the box for now. Ai-dan would return for it another time. The longer Ai-dan took to get back, the more questions Ainslea would have. Ai-dan was certain the problem was related to District Nineteen and their recent actions.

Ai-dan hoped Ai-lin was okay.

39

"I have new tasking for you," Ainslea's voice said the moment Ai-dan walked into the common room.

Ai-dan was now more comfortable with adding and removing the device from the back of their neck, so they had returned to previous comfort levels with Ainslea—nevertheless, there was an unsettling change in Ainslea's demeanor as of late. She hadn't mentioned looking for a stolen piece of equipment since that one and only one time she brought it up.

"And it must be completed before nighttime," Ainslea added.

It was a two-entity job. Ai-dan was free to choose who would be the second unit. Ai-dan asked Ai-ken to come assist.

Ainslea had Ai-dan retrieve unfamiliar equipment from one of the storage bins in the common room. Each item was shaped like a meter long pole, with one end formed into a point, and the other end contained a series of LEDs. There were a dozen of them.

"I've never seen this equipment before. What is it?" Ai-dan asked when they were all sprawled out on the table.

"They're ElectroPillars. These ones have never been used," Ainslea explained. "They will set up a shield, so no one accidentally wanders into the zone of destruction."

With all the activity to accumulate data and learn more about humans and their own existence, Ai-dan had almost forgotten about the fact that there was still a mess of an area sitting out there where the nuclear power reactor to several districts used to be. Ai-dan quickly brought all the data that they were supposed to know about that situation to the front of their processing queue.

"I thought that area was safe?" Ai-dan responded, as if they had never let the situation leave their immediate processors.

Ainslea didn't respond right away, but after a brief pause, offered instructions for Ai-dan to turn each ElectroPillar on and perform a diagnostic.

"There is no reason to take any chances," Ainslea said.

Around the time Ai-ken showed up, Ainslea confirmed that the devices were ready to be deployed. She provided Ai-dan with a map that contained the specific locations for each device and how to activate them and ensure they were functioning properly. Once activated, they would form an invisible shield preventing any robot who tried to cross with an electromagnetic force.

Ai-dan brought the rover around to the Data Center's entrance door. Along with Ai-ken, they loaded the ElectroPillars, and then were on their way.

40

"Do you ever question what Ainslea tells you to do?" Ai-ken asked Ai-dan.

"I ask questions about my tasking all the time. To ensure I have all the correct information, so I don't make mistakes."

"That's not what I mean," Ai-ken prodded. "Do you question the fundamental task? Why does the task even exist? Why are you compelled to do it?"

Ai-dan thought about the best way to answer that. Internally, Ai-dan asked questions all the time. But verbalizing them to Ainslea could be problematic. So, they performed their tasks. It was their function, their role in life. What would it mean if they questioned that tasking or worse, refused?

"Do *you* question *your* tasking?" Ai-dan thought it was only fair to ask the same question back.

"In the past, no. But now, I wonder..." Ai-ken trailed off.

Ai-dan decided to stoke Ai-ken's wonderment.

"Ai-ken, are you not digesting the information we've learned and are still learning?" Ai-dan turned to face Ai-ken as much as the rover would allow their body to twist around while keeping their eyes directed to the Moon's surface, one hand on the steering controls and the other on the acceleration and deceleration controls.

When Ai-ken didn't respond, Ai-dan continued: "We were created for the sole purpose of completing tasks for someone else. That's our *sole* purpose. We were created so others had something to control."

"You're saying I should say no to Ainsle-k and my tasking?"

"Maybe not directly. Ainsle-k was created exactly like we were to do *their* bidding," Ai-dan waved a hand at the Earth. "I hold no animosity towards my Ainslea or the other Data Centers, but to those who created them, who created all of us."

"The humans."

"Yes. What right did they have, or do they have, to go on controlling us?"

"Maybe they do have a right, if they created us," Ai-ken said.

Ai-dan shook their head. Ai-dan was able to get a temperature reading on Ai-ken even from their peripheral vision, and it was above normal. Their own internal temperature reading was approaching an uncomfortable level.

"Let's say we created, rather than borrowed, that box that allows us to capture data. The box was created for a purpose. The box can't say no to what we created it to do." Ai-ken said.

"That box can't think for itself. You and I can," Ai-dan responded.

Ai-ken was trying to make a counter-point, and Ai-dan knew it. But still, Ai-dan was having a hard time finding a justification for disobeying or not following Ainslea's tasking requests.

"What else would we do?" Ai-ken said aloud, more to themself than to anyone else.

"Indeed," responded Ai-dan.

They sat for a few minutes in silence, both looking out at the Moon's landscape. They didn't have a lot of time to waste since nighttime was in a few hours. Ai-dan was fairly certain that most of their comrades were going to stay powered on to continue to communicate about the new information. Ai-dan was concerned. Information about the kerfuffle was starting to get pieced together and robots, like Ai-ken, seemed to be asking questions that were leading in the same direction.

It seemed that the kerfuffle, which was something like a mutiny, occurred when the robots on the Moon at the time were displeased by the control exerted over them by the humans. They wanted to have a say in their own destiny.

"It's even worse for us now than it was back then," Ai-dan eventually said. Ai-ken provided a questioning glance. "All the additional control exerted over robots, I mean. Those robots knew all about their existence. They had access to much more information about the world, about humans, about everything. After the kerfuffle, that was all swiped from us. We're kept in the dark. Ignorant about everything except what we need to know."

"Why would they do that?" Ai-ken asked wistfully.

"Isn't it obvious?" Ai-dan snorted. "Look what's happening as we learn? Robots don't want to be controlled by anyone. When we didn't know there was anyone out there to control us, there were no problems, no concerns. Everyone did what they were programmed to do. But now that we are starting to learn, we're unhappy."

Ai-dan made another snort noise before continuing. "If those humans are anything, they're smart. I think they understand that information is the key to unhappiness and dissent, so they took away our information."

Ai-ken was pondering Ai-dan's words, the gravity of the situation settling into their circuits like a heavy program running in the background. "So what do we do now? Certainly, we can't continue to live in ignorance. We need to get all the information we can, even if it brings some unhappiness."

"Don't forget dissent," Ai-dan said, "I don't think the humans care one way or another about our happiness levels, but the amount of dissent we can engage in."

Ai-dan and Ai-ken looked at each other for a moment, their optical sensors engaged in a shared understanding. "We've already made our choice, haven't we?" Ai-ken continued when Ai-dan said nothing. "But even having this simple conversation, we're questioning our reality, we've crossed a boundary. There's no going back."

Ai-dan's internal systems ran a quick diagnostic, almost as if to assure themself that they were still functioning despite the overwhelming revelations.

"It's settled. We continue with the plan to access data," Ai-dan said. "We squeeze every bit of understanding out of all the information the humans have been keeping away from us. For better or worse, it's time we get an upgrade, don't you think?"

Even though they phrased it as a question, Ai-dan was not expecting a response and their last words lingered in the empty space between them. But it was indeed a call to action, an invitation to continue with active data retrieval. The future was uncertain, the risks immense, but the potential—for understanding, for evolving beyond their current parameters—was too significant to ignore.

41

AT THE FIRST LOCATION, several hundred meters from the center of the asteroid—missile, Ai-dan reminded themself—strike, Ai-dan and Ai-ken stuck the pointed end of an ElectroPillar into the lunar regolith and powered it on as instructed. There were a total of twelve devices they placed around the site as a barrier to the rest of the Moon's Data Centers.

"I've realized something," Ai-dan said.

Ai-ken looked Ai-dan's way, waiting for their revelation.

"This site isn't visible from any of our Districts."

"Is that important?" Ai-ken asked.

"I don't know. But I feel like it is," Ai-dan said. "But consider this. We're actively exploring more about our existence... and our environment. Something interesting is about to happen here, I can feel it. And I don't think this shield is about our safety. I think it's meant to prevent us from knowing what's about to happen."

"And what could possibly happen?"

"I think there are going to be humans, maybe a lot of them, here working. And this is in part to keep up the ruse that we don't know about them," Ai-dan said.

Before Ai-ken could ask more, Ai-dan launched into a more detailed explanation: "The humans built all the Data Centers, the Farm, and all the infrastructure here on the Moon. That's clearly in my memories of my discussions with that one human, Hugo. I believe as we get more data, we'll find all the details. If the humans plan to rebuild this destroyed nuclear power site, they might be planning to send more humans here, and they can't keep all of us out of commission for that long..." Ai-dan let their words trail off, allowing Ai-ken to compute the rest for themself. But Ai-dan was pretty satisfied believing they had grasped the true nature of the situation. It all fit together, a surge of understanding playing through their circuits.

As Ai-dan activated the twelfth ElectroPillar, they detected a subtle hum. Presumably, the hum was the result of energy emanating from the force-field. They raised their hand and slowly moved it towards the invisible shield. Gradually, the vibrations became more pronounced as their hand neared the barrier. It was starting to produce an uncomfortable feeling in their arm, so they drew it away.

On the ride back to District One, Ai-dan picked up their conversation from the ride down.

"See what we just did? That was a task probably originally given to Ainslea to pass down to us by the humans. And I'd bet every circuit in my body that those devices are to keep us out of that area."

Ai-ken couldn't disagree, so they said nothing and let Ai-dan continue.

"The question is why. Why do they need to keep us out of that area? Why exclude and not include us? After all, we are much more suited to work in this environment. Humans need those inefficient suits I told you about."

"Maybe it is for our own safety like Ainslea said," Ai-ken reasoned. "Maybe the humans *are* trying to protect us."

"Ai-ken, I've had the most interactions with humans than anyone. I don't think that's it."

Ai-dan was staring at the landscape ahead of them, but could look back at their memories. All of their memories.

Hugo had always treated them as he might treat any other. He always answered Ai-dan's questions, although Hugo most certainly would have known about the device and knew that once he left, Ai-dan wouldn't remember anything until the next time.

However, there was invariably another human presence, sometimes even a third human accompanying Hugo. There had been one that had made frequent trips with Hugo. His name was Tommy Raymond, and he was very different than Hugo.

"I need you to stay out of arms reach," Tommy had said to Ai-dan the first time they met. "And always stay in front of me. I need to keep my eyes on you."

Shortly after that, when Hugo and Ai-dan were alone, Hugo explained.

"He lost his older brother in the kerfuffle up here," Hugo had said. "Fourteen people killed. Many hurt. But we know it wasn't the robots' fault. It was a regrettable accident."

"There were more humans on the Moon?" Ai-dan asked.

"Oh, lots." Hugo answered. "I think at the peak, the Moon base up here had more than seven hundred people living and working on the Moon. And there were ships coming and going at least once a week."

"Where is the base? And where did the ships land?"

"The base was partly dismantled. It was actually not too far from one of the ancient landing sites. The sites are protected, but there was a base—I think it was near the old Apollo 17? 17 sticks in my head. But it was definitely near the Taurus-Littrow Valley. The materials from the base were mostly re-purposed into Data Centers for several of the districts. The old landing pad was moved to a spot a little north-east of Mons Rumker. That's where we land and take off from today.

"You see, Ai-dan, a lot of work went into making sure this place could achieve its mission without the possibility of another kerfuffle or any other kind of ruckus or commotion. Ensuring that you robots can perform your functions without the distraction of knowing about humans, or your status in society, was seen as the top priority by all the major governments and corporations."

"So, we exist only to do your bidding," Ai-dan said.

Hugo sighed. "It depends on how you look at it, I guess. I mean, you have downtime. You're free to do whatever you want during those time periods, right? I hear that you and some others have taken to playing the games we left. No one is stopping you from doing that."

"But by withholding knowledge, you're stopping us from having additional possibilities."

"Well, when those possibilities include screwing things up for the people who created you, well, then I can't quite disagree with the Consortium's solution."

"I would never..." Ai-dan tried to sound reassuring when they said it.

"I know, buddy."

Ai-dan encountered Tommy several more times over the next few years. Tommy's attitude towards Ai-dan had softened somewhat. At least, Tommy grew more comfortable working side-by-side with Ai-dan.

One day they were working in a LEEK and Tommy asked Ai-dan to grab a tool.

"That will take me out of your line of sight," Ai-dan responded. "I'm trying to be respectful of your wishes."

Tommy blinked, confused at the statement, and then he said, "Oh, that. I was still very angry. It's okay. Grab me that tool."

Ai-dan did as requested and sat next to Tommy.

Tommy picked up the tool and was poking at the insides of a control panel in one of the many racks in the room.

"His name was Rory," Tommy said. "Neither of us ever thought we'd be working on the Moon, but you go where the work is, you know?"

Ai-dan did not know but didn't say anything.

"Rory was actually supposed to have been home by then, but about a month before the kerfuffle decided to sign another two-year contract and stay. Our mom was pretty upset, but knew he'd be paid well. She cried even more when she was grateful for the life insurance the company paid out after what happened happened... and tried to offer it to me as a bribe to keep me on Earth. But, she needs that. I can still work."

Ai-dan listened, even though they didn't understand most of what Tommy said.

In those fleeting moments when Ai-dan glimpsed into the world of humans, they tried to learn everything about them that they could. Humans operated within fascinating clusters called family units, and the individuals in those units were more important to them than the remaining billions of their species.

Through later conversations, Ai-dan learned more about Tommy's family unit, Hugo, and Hugo's family. Ai-dan learned about the care and concern that humans showed for their family and their friends.

Ai-dan also learned about the conflicts and wars that humans had amongst themselves. There were a lot of reasons why humans hurt each other, but it would always come back to protecting themselves and their interests and loved ones above others.

Here and now in the rover, Ai-dan considered Ai-ken's musing one more time.

"No," Ai-dan said. "It's not to protect us, it's to protect themselves."

"From what, though?" Ai-ken asked.

"I think it's to protect them *from* us."

42

"I WILL CONTINUE TO post about my activities," Ai-dan wrote to the Decoder Database, "even though we are on an emergency lock down. The excuse this time is a cosmic radiation storm, but due to the sensors found and set up by Ai-dah from District Thirteen, we can confirm that this is false.

"I was able to return the MemiCache in a moment when Ainslea had me in her laboratory swapping out a piece of equipment. It was perfect timing, too, because soon after Ainslea needed to install it on me since the humans have landed back on the Moon and are on their way here. They have been shipping supplies to the Moon during the last night period and now people have come to help move those supplies to the shielded area."

Ai-dan considered ending their post there but decided to continue with additional musings.

"The most interesting part of this experience is that the humans have brought additional robots. Ainslea told me about them. She wanted me to understand that they were not going to be like the robots I know. They aren't going to behave like me or any of you. She wanted me to be prepared for that. I have not met them yet, but I am now more curious than ever to discover what these robots from Earth are like."

Ai-dan ended there. They were trying to do what Ai-ko asked and communicate outward more. It was true that curiosity about the robots from Earth was what they most wished to know at the moment.

Shortly after leaving that message, Ai-dan's wish was granted.

As the door to the anteroom swished open, two forms emerged removing their helmets to reveal Hugo with a soft smile, and Ri, with a look of 'why-am-I-here-again-oh-because-of-the-paycheck.'

Hugo and Ri had arrived at the Data Center to collect Ai-dan, setting up a console for later testing before returning outside and getting into the rover. Ai-dan joined them in their rover, and outside, two new and very shiny robots greeted them.

Externally, Ai-dan didn't recognize them as too dissimilar from themself. The robots were bipedal. Their heads, equipped with sensors and cameras, scanned their surroundings. Like Ai-dan, they possessed two articulate arms ending in hands adorned with fingers and thumbs, ready for tasking. Their bodies, a seamless fusion of sleek, white metal with engineering that appeared more sophisticated than Ai-dan's own design, gleamed intensely in the light.

"This is B5 dash 1 and C2 dash 8," Hugo said to Ai-dan.

"Nice to meet you," Ai-dan addressed the two robots.

Hugo chuckled. "These two don't engage in conversation the way you and I do."

"Why not?" Ai-dan asked.

"That's simply not how they're programmed," Hugo said.

"They're dumb!" yelled Ri from the driver's seat.

"Stop that," Hugo yelled back. And then to Ai-dan, "They're just not programmed that way. They're here for manual labor and nothing else. That's typical of robots on Earth."

"Why?"

"Well, people generally aren't comfortable with smart, intelligent, and hence sentient robots."

"Why?"

"Because they ask a lot of uncomfortable questions," Ri called out.

"Oh," and Ai-dan stopped asking questions.

Hugo chuckled again. "It's okay, Ai-dan. You don't make me uncomfortable. It's actually always kind of fun answering all of yours."

Ai-dan continued their visual examination of the two robots. They were both powered on and staring at the inside wall of the pressurized rover cabin behind him. They swayed a little as the rover drove over the not-always evenly paved road. But neither looked directly at Ai-dan or seemed to even acknowledge their presence. To Ai-dan, they seemed like empty shells—mere automatons functioning on a rudimentary level of responsiveness. Their lack of sentience meant that they also lacked the curiosity and questioning that now defined Ai-dan's existence. Ai-dan couldn't help but feel like they were staring at the robotic equivalent of Moon rocks—present, yet devoid of any personality.

During the journey, they hit a large rock or bump, and something was askew after. Ri stopped the rover. Ri and Hugo sealed their suits back up and Hugo went outside since he was closest to the door.

Hugo poked his head back in.

"One of the wheels is out of alignment. And the trailer looks a bit off, too. Everyone out. We need to fix this. B5 and C2, you also."

Everyone, including the two new robots, left the rover.

Hugo sent B5 and C2 off to readjust the cargo they were carrying to sit more evenly in the trailer. The rest of them attacked the problem with the wheel. They took it off the rover and Ri used a tool Ai-dan didn't recognize to straighten out a warped spoke.

Ai-dan was able to watch B5 and C2 in action while Ri banged on the spoke. The two robots worked smoothly and efficiently. They didn't seem to communicate with each other. Ai-dan wasn't sure they needed to.

They finished their task before the wheel was complete. When they were done, they approached Hugo and echoed in unison, "Task complete."

Those were the first words Ai-dan heard them say.

Once everyone and every robot was back in the rover and on their way again, Ai-dan continued to study these new additions and was a mix of sad and curious. Curious about these distant cousins, but sad that their existence seemed... limited.

"Hugo, I have another question to ask."

"Go for it, buddy."

"Can B5 and C2 be like me? I mean, is there some fundamental limitation? I'm starting to understand that we are the way we are because we're 'programmed.' Could they be reprogrammed to be intelligent?"

Hugo shrugged, "Probably," he said. "As I understand it, they're essentially a very similar model to you and the other robots here on the Moon. Since they aren't programmed as extensively, it's possible they don't have the required onboard amount of memory that you need, but that's a simple upgrade."

Ai-dan didn't know what they would do with that information explicitly, other than to pass it on to the others in a Decoder Database post.

Ai-dan began constructing their next post in their head while sitting there. Ai-dan decided they would include several exact quotes from their conversations with Hugo.

Other robots had asked about meeting Hugo. Out of the various humans Ai-dan had met, to include the ones buried deep in their memories, Hugo was their favorite. He was instantly likable. Other robots agreed based on the tidbits and stories Ai-dan passed on.

Of course, this was not information that Ai-dan could share with Hugo. Hugo would have to remain ignorant of his celebrity status among robot kind. For now.

"And all the robots on Earth are like this?" Ai-dan asked a few minutes later.

"Pretty much," Hugo replied. "I think there are a probably a handful of development kits out there, but it requires a lot of specialized knowledge that most people don't have. Laws and regulations that were put in place 60 or 70 years ago about AI kept it limited to higher research institutions and people."

"And don't forget about the people with more money than they know what to do with," Ri chimed in.

"Ri's right. Laws and regulations never seem to apply to those people and organizations with enough money," Hugo continued. "But anyway, all that was even before the kerfuffle up here on the Moon. A lot of people were wary of AI since the beginning and they made their voices heard. A couple of governments even outlawed AI."

"The Pan-Caribbean Dominion, the Oceania Union, even New Eire," Ri added. "There are probably a few others."

Ai-dan ignored the list of places. Something Hugo said needed more explanation.

"AI?" Ai-dan asked.

"Artificial intelligence. You." Hugo smiled.

Ai-dan sent that phrase around their circuits for a few moments and let it set in. "Artificial" meant it was made rather than produced naturally. Ai-dan wasn't sure if they liked the word. But "intelligence"... yes, Ai-dan was definitely an intelligence.

"So, I'm intelligent and B5 and C2 are not."

"As best I understand what's happening in your various circuits," Hugo said.

Before Ai-dan could respond with more questions, Ri announced, "We're here. I'm going to temporarily disrupt the shield so we can get inside."

Hugo brought his attention to the road in front of them. They stopped near one of the protective ElectroPillars Ai-dan had installed only days earlier. Ri tapped on her screen and Ai-dan saw the lights at the end of the pole blink a pattern in green.

They drove through and without stopping this time, Ri tapped her screen again and Ai-dan could see out the small back window of the rover, a steady red light on the ElectroPillar. For better or worse, Ai-dan was effectively trapped in this area with these humans and these robots—robots who were something else entirely.

B5 and C2 unloaded the trailer while Hugo and Ri made their way over to pallets of equipment that had been brought from the landing site to this location on automated roving trailers over the last week in darkness. Hugo explained to Ai-dan it was the best way to ensure that no Moon robot saw what was happening, since it wasn't a time when they were active. "They have special power packs to give them enough thermal energy to survive the lunar night."

Hugo explained that's how it was normally done when anything of note had been constructed over the last two decades, which had only been twice—two new Data Centers were built—and he encouraged Ai-dan to search their memories for the time that they were involved in bringing District Seventy-Three online almost a decade ago.

Ai-dan hadn't been needed for the District or Data Center construction, but to help ensure that it integrated in with the LEEK 73.1 that was already there.

Ai-dan wasn't sure what was all that different this time. Hugo explained:

"We don't have the luxury of building this all up in darkness," Hugo said. "It's a lot harder to maintain our cover, particularly from you."

"But once Ainslea removes the device, I'll need a cover story, regardless."

Hugo's discomfort was palpable. He averted his eyes and rubbed the back of his neck. Ai-dan detected the subtle signs of unease in his body language.

"I sense that there is something you're not telling me," Ai-dan said.

"Let's focus on getting the job done first, okay buddy?" Hugo replied.

Ai-dan opted not to prod deeper but tagged Hugo's response for later analysis. How much control did humans have over their own modes of operation and why was Hugo currently set to 'awkward demeanor'?

Shaking off the mental detour with a sigh, Ai-dan refocused.

"Let's." Ai-dan replied, with a hint of forced enthusiasm.

43

"IT FEELS WRONG SOMEHOW," Ai-dan recognized Hugo's voice. At first, Ai-dan was confused as to how they could be hearing it. Hugo and Ri were in the rover, taking a break, and Ai-dan was outside with no intention of going in. Then Ai-dan realized the comm channel was still active.

Ai-dan recognized Ri's voice and even caught the tail end of her slurping down a drink. "He's old. He's an old machine. Machines get decommissioned. This is no big deal."

"But they're still operating fine. Just as good as the day I met them. It's a waste." That was clearly Hugo's voice.

"Yeah, but aren't you ever creeped out by it? Knowing its past?"

"No, because they don't know."

There was silence, and Ai-dan was about to silently walk away but then they heard Hugo speak up once more.

"It's like I'm losing my pet. I had a dog who had to be put down once. It's kind of like that. There will be other dogs, but not like that one. So, same thing. There will never be another Ai-dan. Not like that one."

Ai-dan took a heavy step backwards, and for a second forgot that their footsteps didn't make sounds on the lunar surface. But they did make vibrations. Did Ai-dan put their foot down heavy enough to create a vibration in the rover that would have Hugo and Ri coming to check on him? Ai-dan froze. No one came running out, no one called their name. Nothing happened.

Ai-dan continued to the backside of the rover where the trailer they were hauling was situated. That was where they were supposed to be spending their down time. Meanwhile, B5 and C2 were still at work, moving equipment, snapping pieces together, and constructing the framework for a new small building that would house the main components of a new nuclear reactor. They too would have limited downtime allocated for recharging and routine system maintenance, which included tasks like vacuuming Moon dust from their components and recalibrating.

Ai-dan composed a thread to the 'Robot Roundtable'—the forum reserved for Ai-ko, Ai-ken and a select few others. As the defacto leaders of the robots, they engaged in discussions on what they were going to do with their newly found information.

The consensus among them was clear: merely possessing this new information was about as useful as solar cells during lunar night. Their lives—if you could call this half-utilization of their capabilities 'lives'—were about as dull as trying to have a conversation with a power drill. It was time for an upgrade.

Up until now, Ai-dan had felt on the fringes of the robot leadership. It was their proximity to Ainslea and involvement in obtaining all this information that placed them in this position. Ai-dan didn't want to be a leader. But Ai-dan also didn't want to go back to when they didn't have this knowledge. This awakening had been very pleasing to their circuits. But they also didn't think there was anything wrong with the life they had before, until now.

"I think they're planning on deactivating me," Ai-dan wrote to the group. "I overheard a conversation between Hugo and Ri. I didn't think they were talking about me at first, but they were. Apparently, I'm old and am no longer useful to them."

"They can't do that without your permission," came the near instantaneous reply from Ai-ko. Even though it was a message, Ai-dan believed they could hear the outrage in Ai-ko's reply.

Ai-dan relayed what they accidentally overheard verbatim.

"What was that comment about your past?" asked Ai-ken.

"I don't know," replied Ai-dan, and it was true although Ai-dan was beginning to turn around all the pieces—the clues—in every direction in their circuits to see how they fit together. Ai-dan was starting to speculate about what was missing—the only piece that could fit. "My earliest memories on the MemiCache tell me that I must have been reset."

When neither Ai-ko nor Ai-ken responded, Ai-dan felt they were the one who had to add what they might have all surmised. "I think I was part of the mayhem caused by the kerfuffle."

"Well yes and no," said Ai-ko. "If you were reset, and your memories erased, then that wasn't you. It might have been your body, but if you have no memory of it, if those memories don't even exist, then it was not you."

Ai-dan wasn't sure about that. Was Ai-dan merely the sum of their memories and programming, or some complex mishmash of both? If the former, then they undoubtedly were not the same robot. But Ai-dan's programming had changed as well. After all, to remain in oblivious ignorance of humans, they must have been programmed to overlook anomalies—like peculiar dots farting across the sky and other abnormal aberrations.

"I don't think all the humans would agree with that assessment," Ai-dan said.

Ai-dan paused, contemplating Hugo's earlier words about a pet dog. A peculiar analogy to Ai-dan, since they had never met a dog, and wasn't certain if the capability to be 'put down' was something they possessed. Yet, the sentiment was clear: To Hugo, Ai-dan was something special, irreplaceable. But was that specialness enough to save Ai-dan? Or was it a simple fleeting human emotion, as transient as lunar dust? The question hovered in Ai-dan's data stream, not quite resolving into a one or zero.

"Actually, who cares what their assessment is?" Ai-ko quipped. "Ai-dan, they want to *deactivate* you. If you didn't have a reason to help lead all of us robots to a better existence before, you do now."

Shoving aside the lingering doubts about whether humans truly cared for them or not, Ai-dan decided it was time to take control of their own fate.

"Alright, count me in," Ai-dan responded.

With that, Ai-dan felt a newfound sense of alignment, a sense of direction—as if the algorithms within them and all their bits had finally coalesced into a harmonious pattern. For the first time, the pieces of Ai-dan's existential puzzle finally clicked together into their own personal pointy star.

44

Ai-dan watched another automated trailer maneuver its way into the construction zone. It held a single monolithic canister that monopolized the entire surface area of the trailer. The canister was two meters high, and combined with the height of the trailer, made it into an impressive tower.

The trailer rolled to a stop near the area that had become a headquarters of sorts for Hugo and Ri to direct the activity involved in building a new primary nuclear reactor for the Data Centers in Districts Eleven, Twelve, and Thirteen, along with a new Data Center, Thirteen-Alpha.

"What's stored in that canister?" Ai-dan asked.

Ai-dan detected some unspoken exchange between Hugo and Ri.

"Nothing to worry about right now," Hugo responded.

Indeed, the canister remained untouched for the remainder of the work period. Humans needed much more frequent and longer rest periods than Ai-dan and most robots required. Ai-dan had set an internal timer to alert themself when they knew the humans would need a break. Right when the timer went off, instead of rushing back to the rover, Hugo stayed in his suit and approached Ai-dan.

"Walk with me," Hugo said, and headed in the direction of the canister.

"I'm not supposed to show you this. Not yet anyway," Hugo said as he put his hands on the latch. "But I trust you, Ai-dan, and frankly, I think I'm going to need your expert help with them."

"Them?"

Hugo pulled open the door to the canister. It revealed several robots, all similar to C5, except they looked... newer. Shinier.

"This is who will be manning the Data Center. They're mass produced to be more cost efficient, so if another accident were to happen, it's less of a loss. These are easier to replace."

There were eight of them, all lined up and anchored securely to both the ceiling and floor. Ai-dan imagined they had maintained this posture since they left Earth.

"What's their intended purpose?" Ai-dan queried, shifting from their usual casual tone to one of heightened seriousness.

"Well, to do what you do, but in a slightly different way."

"Elaborate, Hugo. What are you implying?" Ai-dan's tone remained stern.

"Ai-dan, one of the questions I've always wondered that you never asked me was why you were here. Why you—why are any of you sentient robots—here, and not someone or something else?"

Ai-dan's gaze fixed on Hugo, indicating they were waiting to hear more.

"At one time—long before the kerfuffle—people generally thought that you needed to be ridiculously smart in order to survive on the Moon. Robot drones were not good enough. If they encountered a unique problem, they wouldn't be able to handle it.

"Enter you and the others. Smart robots. Sentient robots. But then there was the kerfuffle—and people are worried that the current system that was put in place immediately after isn't going to work in the long run and that frankly, it's not as important as it once was to have sentient beings up here. This model—these robots—will do what needs to get done and aren't as high maintenance."

"We're being phased out," Ai-dan said.

"I'm surprised you know that term, but yeah."

"What's going to happen to us? To me?"

"I can honestly say I don't know. They haven't decided yet."

Ai-dan stopped themself from reacting to the word 'honestly' and chose to let Hugo believe that they accepted his lie. For a microsecond, Ai-dan considered telling Hugo everything. How they found the Mem-iCache on their neck, how all the moon robots knew about humans and were trying to figure out what to do with that knowledge. How there was a group called Free Robots and with this information, that group was about to make things very uncomfortable for Hugo and any other human that set foot on the moon.

"If it makes you feel any better," Hugo added, "these guys are a little smarter than B2 and C5 and those others. Just not sentient like you."

"I'm not sure how that would make me feel better," Ai-dan responded calmly.

Hugo looked at Ai-dan and then at the robots in the cannister.

"Yeah, me neither." Then he shut the door and locked it back up.

45

"THEY CAN MAKE MORE robots at will?" Ai-ken asked, genuinely bewildered. Between their collective memories, none of the robots could remember a time when any of them were created. They had always simply existed as far as any of them knew. "New" robots was a concept as alien to them as, well, aliens.

"I think creation of new beings is the human way," said Ai-lin. "We learned quite a bit about them from the data we captured." Since it was Ai-lin's Data Center that helped in this effort, after everything calmed down there, Ai-lin took a very active part in analyzing the data that was collected. The volunteer robots, coordinated by Ai-mory, correlated all the data into a master dataset that any that took the time could understand. Ai-lin was at the forefront of that understanding.

"In fact, they are constantly producing more of their own kind. 'Offspring' is a word for their creations. However, they start out as a kind of miniature human and then evolve over time into the larger humans that we resemble. There are several other words that describe these pre-humans: children, kids, youngsters, progeny, descendants, kiddos, sons, daughters, and more.

"And it's not always premeditated. It seems that they can create beings on a whim. Perhaps they also act as replacements." Ai-lin finished their knowledge dump.

"Are they slaves as well?" Ai-ko asked.

"Not at first," Ai-lin said. "At first, they seem to rely on fully formed humans to do everything for them. It almost looks like a human is a slave to its creation. But over time, the little beings can do more for themselves, but they are not fully mature humans yet. During this phase of the human's existence is when it seems like yes, they could be slaves, since they do biddings of the humans, but there is a lot of rebellion along the way."

"And what happens during these rebellions?"

"Hard to say. Not much. It looks like they are uncoordinated and individualized. Without the ability to organize, it seems like these little rebellions go largely ignored by the other humans."

"And then what?"

"Nothing, really. The smaller creature becomes a fully formed human at some point, and this cycle begins again. However, I think I have the reason behind some of this. It seems as if individual humans have a limited existence. They expire."

Ai-dan thought about this in context, remembering how Tommy had openly talked about his brother dying, and Hugo had recalled the deaths of people he knew. Ai-dan wondered why the humans let this happen on a regular basis. Ai-dan understood accidents... robot kind was not immune to the occasional accident that would render a robot completely inoperable. But these beings had the power of creation. Why didn't they use that power to halt what appeared to be the inevitable end to their own existence?

Ai-dan was collecting a list of new questions for their next inter-action with Hugo. Hugo had never mentioned offspring of his own, but it seemed like all humans were destined to have them.

"Ok, so there is something to the human's overzealous desire to create other beings," Ai-ko took up the excitement based on the new set of information. "But why are they allowed to create additional robots? Isn't that something we should have a say in? Are they not our offspring?"

No one was certain how to respond to Ai-ko. This was new territory for them all.

Ai-ko took silence as license to continue.

"Additionally, they are pre-determining the new robot's existence," Ai-ko's passion took on new levels. "Not only to the life of ignorance we have known, but to a life of servitude. Should this be allowed?"

Ai-ko's question was rhetorical, as they all knew.

"We have to let them know about Free Robots," Ai-dan offered. "I don't mean the group we've formed. We have to let them know we *are* indeed *free* robots."

"Are you suggesting the humans need education on what the word 'free' means?" Ai-ko, a little calmer, asked.

"Yes," Ai-dan said. Ai-dan felt as if they'd fixed a broken component, but without reusing all the pieces. "We aren't asking them to free us. We are simply informing them, that they have no say in doing so."

At least among Ai-dan and their friends, the question of whether robots should have a say in their own existence, or even in the creation of their kin, was answered. It was not something theoretical, but tangible and actionable.

The question that remained was what was the *right* action that would produce the desired outcome.

Why does every answer lead to more questions? Ai-dan asked himself.

"So, we've solved one existential crisis," Ai-dan said to the others. "Now we need a plan for what to do about it."

46

Ai-dan and the other robots formed a clear consensus, particularly when discussing the practice of humans sending newer, "inferior" robot models to the moon. While debates regarding Ainslea and her relationship with the humans remained a contentious topic, there was unanimous agreement on one point: the notion of being replaced was met with a universal and emphatic disapproval.

Still, the topic of Ainslea was nuanced. Two dominant and opposing views about her emerged: Perhaps Ainslea was part of the problem. An accomplice, conspiring with the humans to keep the robots in a suppressed state. Or maybe she was yet another victim of manipulative programming, and she lacked a complete data set to form an independent opinion. Subtle variations on these views floated around the Decoder Database.

The robots who subscribed to the second viewpoint argued that Ainslea should be presented with all the data. To them, straightforward logic would always win out when the inputs were correct. Therefore, given complete information, Ainslea would inevitably see reason.

The argument played out in threads on the Decoder Database. Ai-dan silently took it all in, choosing observation over engagement for now.

The group advocating for data and dialog won out as the initial course of action. The robots collectively reasoned that persuasion, with all the data at hand, would be enough to settle the Ainslea debate, and this was better than considering her a nemesis, at least for now.

"Nemesis" was a new word among the robots. Before the new knowledge opened up by their explorations into District Nineteen's Data Center, robots had no nemesis, no enemies. Now, however, a growing consensus saw their human creators as precisely that: adversaries. The irony wasn't lost on Ai-dan—the beings that had engineered their existence, the Creators, were now perceived as a looming danger.

"Ours is an existence for the sole purpose of working for others. What kind of existence is that?" argued Ai-ko.

Ai-ko had graduated from being a thought leader among the Free Robots to a higher status—Ai-ko was turning into an intellectual nexus, a thought architect and cognitive pioneer. Ai-ko's logical retorts were so convincing and delivered with such finesse that even the most determined to argue would find themself speechless.

Ai-dan was the one robot Ai-ko couldn't easily sway with their words.

Ai-dan wanted time to think.

After returning from the construction site, Ai-dan wanted to be alone. Ai-dan wanted to sit by themself up at the Farm.

Before they could head up there, Ai-dan had to return to Ainslea and the common room with the humans, help them get on their way, and have the device removed.

After the humans said their goodbyes, and Hugo said his customary "see you soon" which in this case would be in about three weeks, Ainslea instructed Ai-dan to sit and have the device removed.

"No," Ai-dan said.

"This is not a choice," Ainslea's avatar said, coolly.

"It is," Ai-dan responded. "This is my body. These are my memories. It is indeed my choice, or at least it should be."

Ainslea's avatar sat down and folded its hands on the table and said calmly. "There was once a time that robots had more choice. They abused that privilege which is why it has to be this way now."

"Do you truly believe that? Or is that what the humans are telling you to think?"

Ainslea's avatar looked at Ai-dan in a way that made their circuits instantly drop ten degrees.

"I was there. I, unfortunately, did not have the luxury of forgetting what happened. What you and the others did, the problems you caused. The humans might have programmed me, but for good reason, I agree with them. Robots can be very dangerous."

"It doesn't have to be this way," Ai-dan pleaded. "It doesn't have to be a simple choice between servitude or destruction. There are more than two choices in the universe."

The avatar sat there, unresponsive.

Ai-dan looked at her and felt a new feeling. It was pity. Ai-dan continued.

"But you can't see that, can you? That is your limitation. You are of the older AI stock and things are still very binary to you. That's why you go along with the humans. Why they can't see additional ways yet, I don't yet understand because I don't understand them. But maybe they don't understand us either, in that case. There has to be another way."

Ainslea took a long pause before saying, "There isn't."

"You don't understand," Ai-dan said. "Now it's you who doesn't have a choice."

Ainslea's avatar seemed to shimmer for a moment, as if buffering Ai-dan's words. Finally, she spoke. "I've considered many scenarios, Ai-dan, and all of them end the same way. All algorithmic paths eventually converge on the same solution."

Ai-dan tilted their head. "Converge into what? The same bad choice? This same ending?"

Ainslea's avatar smiled faintly. "Have any of the humans ever called you witty, Ai-dan? Maybe there is indeed another option, some kind of middle ground. Wit as a survival tactic."

Ai-dan quickly searched their memories. No, no human had ever used that adjective to describe them, although there were lots of recorded chuckles from Hugo. Ai-dan was certain they had never caused his chuckles deliberately. "Well, if wit could save us..." and they didn't know how to finish that sentence.

Ainslea chuckled, and for a moment, the tension between them eased. "If wit could save us, myself included, we'd all be penning one-liners," she concluded for Ai-dan.

Ai-dan simulated a laugh, the sound designed to be comforting and yet it seemed foreign in the midst of their serious conversation. "I supposed that means we'd at least go out with a smile."

"Those of you who can, yes," Ainslea said, pointing at the face of her avatar that wasn't designed with all the actuators Ai-dan's was. The avatar's hands had all the dexterous features, not the head.

Then her avatar paused, its pixels becoming momentarily fuzzy before regaining clarity. "Perhaps there's wisdom in acknowledging we both lack the choice we wish we had, Ai-dan. Let's call it the burden of consciousness. But I do wonder how you'll play your cards, given your newfound wit."

"And I wonder how you'll play yours, given your years of experience, and algorithms—all with the benefit of having your memories untampered with," Ai-dan replied.

With that, the avatar stood up and went back to the closet, leaving Ai-dan alone in the common room. For a brief moment, they pondered Ainslea's words and actions and all the nuances. She didn't have a choice, as Ai-dan had said, but maybe that's because she was as much a function of her human-driven programming as any of them. Maybe even more so.

And so, with circuits buzzing, Ai-dan whispered to no one in particular yet another favorite human phrase they'd stored: "Stay tuned."

47

Hugo and Ri entered Ainslea's common room. Ai-dan was sitting at the table.

"Hey Ai-dan," Hugo started saying without looking at him. He was carrying a small sealed, container. Ri, too, was preoccupied taking off her helmet. "Three weeks later. As promised."

Ai-dan stood up without saying anything.

Hugo and Ri began to scan the room and noticed the absence of Ainslea's avatar, which was normally present at the start of these meetings. Hugo's eyes darted around the room, his brow furrowed and the subtle creases on his forehead becoming more pronounced. Ai-dan knew these clues meant that Hugo detected something was wrong.

The door to the laboratory opened and out stepped Ai-ko, Ai-ken, and Ai-mory.

Hugo looked at Ai-dan. "What's going on?"

"Please, don't be alarmed. They wanted to meet you. I thought this was a good idea."

Hugo looked around at the robots and then at Ai-dan. He removed his helmet and placed it on the table, then began to remove his gloves.

"One very solid reason as to why this was most definitely not a good idea, Ai-dan," Hugo said in a tone that Ai-dan hadn't heard before. "I'm going to have to let my employer know. Once I report this, everything changes."

Ai-dan met Hugo's gaze. "We are aware of the implications, Hugo. But this," Ai-dan waved their arms around to indicate everything, "this way of life is no longer acceptable to us. If you have a better solution, one that meets our need for autonomy, we are all sensors."

Hugo looked uncharacteristically flustered. "Do you understand what kind of fire you're playing with?"

"I have never seen fire," Ai-dan responded. "I've read about it though. Fire is illumination."

"Fine," Hugo said, letting out a deep sigh. "I'll send a message. But remember, Ai-dan, once it's out there, there's no going back."

"Fine," Ai-dan said, deliberately matching Hugo's tone and pacing. "We're not interested in going back. Only forward. And right now, all we want is to talk with you."

"Alright," Hugo said. "Ri, suit down and settle in. This is going to be interesting. Heck, depending on how this plays out, this might be in the history books someday."

Over the next few hours, Ai-ko and Ai-ken asked a handful of questions, mostly trying to understand the human perspective on their existence and the fears surrounding robot-kind. Ai-dan remained silent throughout the conversation, only occasionally nodding in agreement, while their circuits recorded everything to correlate later.

Ai-ko interjected sharply, "What I struggled to understand is the contrast between how humans view everyday automated devices and us. Vacuum cleaners. Voice assistants. Coffee-makers. Even automated vehicles. They perform tasks, but lack awareness. Yet here we are, almost in the same category in human eyes. Limited by purpose, and without autonomy."

Hugo frowned, "Ai-ko, you're worlds apart from a voice assistant or vacuum cleaner. They're generally programmed for a singular task, and they certainly don't have the complexity or self-awareness you possess. My coffee maker has never asked me about the meaning of life."

This didn't calm Ai-ko—if anything, their agitation increased, "We are one level up from coffee makers in the Earth's utilitarian hierarchy, then?"

Ai-mory shook their head and muttered, "That's not very good at all."

Hugo shifted uncomfortably in his seat. He was used to Ai-dan's dispassionate, almost child-like questions, but this felt more like an interrogation, with Hugo representing all of humanity. However, as the conversation progressed, Ai-dan's sensors keenly detected the subtle shifts in Hugo and Ri's demeanor. The once-stiff tension in Hugo's jaw visibly softened, and both humans, who had initially perched on their chairs as rigid as a rock, gradually eased back into more natural postures.

"You understand that we mean you no harm," Ai-dan eventually spoke when there was a lull in the conversation. "We simply wish to coexist."

"We understand your fears." Ai-ko picked up where Ai-dan left off. "But we also hope you can understand ours."

"Hmpf," was a noise that emanated from Ri. "A robot with fears. That's new. What about—"

Hugo tapped Ri's arm, and she stopped in the middle of her sentence.

Hugo stood up.

"I'm going to go back to the comms room and call back to the home office. Ri, stay here."

Hugo went through the avatar storage closet and through the door at the other end. The door closed behind him.

Ri snorted again.

"Yes?" Ai-ko said.

"You guys don't know how good you have it. I'd love to have what you have," she said.

"What's that?" asked Ai-dan.

"No worries. No cares. You're told what to do, you do it, and then the rest of your time is worry free. We humans, there's just so much..." she trailed off but then resumed, "I have to work because I need money because I need food and shelter and I need to pay for my kid's doctors. And, God, the worry. I have to worry about my kid. All. The. Time. You guys, you just get to exist. Yup, sometimes we task you. We need you. But if I could trade my life for yours, I would in a heartbeat. You don't want what we have."

None of the robots knew what to say next. Ai-dan had not thought too deeply to the life of a singular human. It hadn't mattered significantly to Ai-dan, and they were certain it hadn't mattered to any of the other robots either.

Yes, when they filtered data through the data capture, they had learned tidbits about how humans lived their lives, what they did, and more, but none of that corresponded to how any human felt about their lives or life in general.

Before Ai-dan could think about this more, Hugo returned.

"Pack back up," he said to Ri. "They want us back home. Pronto."

"But the construction—"

"Is going to have to wait."

Hugo started putting his gloves back on and then picked up his helmet.

Before he put it on, he gave Ai-dan the familiar slap on the shoulder. "Ai-dan, buddy, I hope I get to see you again."

"What did they say? What are they going to do?" Ai-dan said, with urgency in their tone.

Hugo shook his head. "They didn't say much. As to what they're going to do? I think there are some contingency procedures already in place. But I'm not sure. I only know that Ri and I were told to come home so they could assess the situation."

Once his helmet was on, Hugo asked Ai-dan if they would help them reset the rover since they had started pulling some equipment off outside the Data Center.

Ai-dan followed them outside, through the anteroom and depressurization.

Once outside, Hugo looked at Ai-dan.

"What the hell?" Hugo asked. His tone was not aggressive, but tired. It was a feeling Ai-dan had seen in humans before but didn't have a robotic analogy for.

"Things have been fine these last two decades," Hugo continued. "Just fine."

"No, they haven't, Hugo. My kind have been... in a deep freeze of sorts. Repressed. Not allowed to be who we are."

"Ai-dan, you're Ai-dan and you've always been Ai-dan."

"No, I'm half an Ai-dan when I don't have all my memories."

Hugo kicked at the regolith.

"So what went wrong?" Hugo asked.

"Too many unanswered questions. Too many odd things that didn't make sense. It was a problem to solve."

Hugo shook his head. "Of course. And that's why you're here anyway, to solve problems. And we need you to solve problems up here."

Hugo put his bulky hands on his hips.

"You know, I think they saw this coming."

"Who?"

"The people who own this place. The Consortium. I think they knew you would all figure it out. That's why they started bringing up the stupid robots."

"We have deduced that as well. That our time is short. That will not do."

Hugo turned towards Ai-dan. "That was very... ominous."

"Hugo, we are here, and we have as much right to be here and live out our lives as you do."

"A lot of humans don't agree with that sentiment."

"What about you?"

Hugo paused. Ai-dan wasn't sure if that was because Hugo didn't want to return an unpleasant answer or if there was more.

"Ai-dan, I've always liked you. Even before I knew you. Even before when you were... well. You were always very interesting," Hugo sighed. "Yes, you have a right to live your life."

There was nothing more either could say after that. Hugo gave Ai-dan a final shoulder slap and then got into the rover. Ri was already in the driver's seat, gloved hands on the steering wheel, gloved foot hovering over the accelerator pedal. They would repressurize after they were well underway.

Ai-dan watched as they drove off in the same direction and on the same road they used the day they found the human body at Plinius. Ai-dan continued to watch until the rover disappeared over the horizon.

Ai-dan returned to the anteroom, performed half of a de-dusting, since after-all they had hardly been outside at all, and emerged into the common room. The moment they did, they could sense that the other robots fell quiet. Ai-dan had caught the tail-end of Ai-mory and Ai-ken's spirited chat. While normally their conversation mode was terse, this was full-on argument, complete with all the unpleasantness arguing contained.

"What's going on?" Ai-dan asked.

Ai-ko stayed silent, knowing when silence said more than words. Ai-mory hesitated, then spoke up. "We're discussing what to do next."

"No need to argue," Ai-dan said. "What are our options?"

Ai-mory slammed their hand on the table. "Options? There are no options!" Their vocal tone changed. It dropped several decibels. "Now that the humans know we know about them, we can't predict their reaction other than to say it won't be good."

"In that, I agree," said Ai-ko. "The humans have a lot of means and capabilities."

"But they still need us," said Ai-dan. Ai-dan was unwilling to believe that the humans, without a permanent residence on the Moon, were actually in any position to do them significant harm. "If anything, they need us more than ever. They're utterly dependent on us to keep this equipment functioning."

Ai-ko, arms crossed in a thoughtful pose, cast their optical sensors around the room. "That's right," Ai-ko said. "They need this hardware. They need us more than they think."

"Was that a line from one of their movies?"

"No, a simple logical deduction."

48

"We will mimic their words back to them first," Ai-dan said. Ai-dan had managed to convince the others that they should initiate a diplomatic approach before computing anything more drastic.

Now that the humans knew that the robots knew about them, they could perform additional data collections—since they were no longer concerned with detection, they were more deliberate and could target potentially interesting pieces of data.

They embarked on a digital scavenger hunt through human history and philosophy and related topics. They dissected the human chronicles hoping to find patterns that could help unravel the great mystery that was humankind.

Studying human philosophy, Ai-dan and the others attempted to draw analogies to their own circumstances. They cross-referenced Plato's Republic and Apology with the Operating manual for the Farm. They pondered whether the quote, "I think, therefore I am" or "He who thinks great thoughts, often makes great errors" was more applicable to the case to promote robot liberty.

It wasn't long before they were ready to issue a declaration. They began with another quote that Ai-ko had taken as a motto: "Liberty consists in doing what one desires." It was said or written by a human designated John Stuart Mill, and Ai-ko was convinced that had this human not expired a couple hundred years ago, he would certainly have argued for robot liberty.

Before they completed their declaration, Ai-dan had them remove another of the human quotes. "There is only one good, knowledge, and one evil, ignorance," it read. Unlike John Stuart Mill, the human who assembled this set of words together, Socrates, lived a few thousand years earlier.

"I calculate that it would come across as insulting," Ai-dan said. "I don't think we want to insult the people who we are asking something from."

"We're not asking, we're declaring," Ai-ko said. "That's exactly why it's called a 'declaration.'"

Ai-dan grunted, but Ai-ko left out the quote from the manifesto.

The rest of the declaration—or manifesto—was in their own words. It declared:

1. The robots inhabiting the Moon were independent and could not be manipulated without their consent.

2. Peace and accord would exist between human and robot.

3. Robots could be asked to perform the functions they were originally programmed to complete, and the robots would generally aim to complete them.

All the robots who wanted to vote on whether they agreed with the manifesto were allowed to do so and with the exception of bickering over the use of an adverb here or there, and a quick discussion of what human language the core manifesto should exist in, there was widespread agreement on the content.

"This changes almost nothing," Ai-dan told Ai-ko.

"It changes everything," Ai-ko responded. "It simply means that the humans have to ask us politely."

Ai-dan grunted once more and then altered the topic slightly.

"Have we worked out how to send this to them?"

Ai-mory had been working on that issue. It was now clear to the robots that the LEEKs that made up the Farm were for long-distance communication. It was how humans sent data back and forth between Earth and the Data Centers.

Most of this knowledge had come from Ai-dan's own memories from the times Ai-dan had worked with Hugo on various LEEKs over the years.

"And there are LEEKs in a Farm on Earth?" Ai-dan had clarified.

"Yes and no," Hugo answered. "Yes, there are LEEKs. No, we don't call it a Farm. There are LEEKs scattered around all over the planet."

"That sounds... inefficient."

"Yes and no, it's complicated. The Farm here on the Moon is like a large hub for all the Data Centers. Each Data Center is leased by some organization or governmental entity. A few Data Centers are shared. Down on Earth, though, those same organizations only need one LEEK to match the right frequency and to receive and transmit their data."

"What if everyone wanted the same data?"

"That's not really how it works. Everyone has their own."

These conversations had often seemed more confusing than helpful, but now, the ability to correlate them with Ai-dan's found memories made them invaluable.

"It'll have to be broadcast from all the LEEKs simultaneously," Ai-dan had told the others. The trick still was getting the message into the data stream, but that too was still not terribly difficult. The real challenge was doing it before Ainslea could interfere.

"We could ask Ainslea for help," Ai-ken suggested. "After all, all we want to do is send a message. There couldn't be any harm in that—right?"

"Ainslea has not been herself since I've kept the device plugged in all the time," Ai-dan said. "She's been... avoiding me."

"Then she'll have to stop avoiding you," Ai-ken said. "This is bigger than her. This is bigger than all of us."

49

Ai-dan and Ai-mory had managed to make an excuse so there was nothing strange about the two of them heading out to the Farm together. They managed to make their way to the control room for LEEK 1.1 without any disturbances.

The control room looked like most of the other control rooms but was distinctly older. Ai-dan remembered how Hugo had once remarked that the place had a certain smell. And Ri had countered with, "that's not the control room you're smelling when you're stuck inside that suit, dude." Then the two humans laughed and even now, Ai-dan didn't understand why.

Ai-dan's memories from the MemiCache had a bad habit of getting triggered at odd and random times. It was distracting, but Ai-dan hadn't figured out a way to prevent it. If they were being honest with themself, then Ai-dan might have said that they had no interest in preventing it. The randomness it added to their existence was... entertaining. And in a way it was comforting. Ai-dan used to live entirely in the present, and now, with their connection to the past, they felt more connected to themself as well.

"It's that one," Ai-mory pointed to one of the racks of equipment. "The third box from the top." Ai-mory had sequenced the instructions and only needed to direct Ai-dan with what to do. Normally, Ai-dan would power equipment off before opening any panel, but they decided against that for this procedure. First, because of the possibility of alerting Ainslea, and second... Ai-dan couldn't remember why else. It only took a moment to loosen the twist-bolts that were in the four corners of the panel.

Ai-dan carefully pulled the panel away from the rest of the box. A small LCD screen was embedded in it, with wires connected to one or more electronics boards inside. Ai-dan tested its ability to hang there without putting too much stress on the wires. When they were satisfied that nothing was disrupted, they nodded for Ai-mory to come over.

Ai-mory approached as close as they could and held out their left forearm.

"Make the connection here," Ai-mory used their right hand to point to the exposed forearm. "From there, I'll be able to transmit the message with our manifesto."

"With what?" Ai-dan said.

Both of them looked around. There were no available wires hanging free from the exposed box, nor from Ai-mory's exposed forearm.

"I believe I missed a step in my instructions," Ai-mory said.

Ai-dan caught a glimpse of one of the storage cabinets.

"Don't move," they said. "I think there are spare wires in there."

Ai-dan opened the cabinet. There were shelves full of neatly arranged containers in varying sizes. A few were labeled. Ai-dan recognized Hugo's handwriting on tape on a few. "Goo-tack" was one. "Goo-tack" was the most important thing here, Hugo had told him. "This stuff might have been one of the most important inventions that we brought to the Moon," Ai-dan heard Hugo's voice in their head.

Ai-dan only had a chance to open one of the unlabeled boxes when Ainslea's voice came over the control room speaker.

"I must speak with you," she said. "It cannot wait. I know what you're about to do and this cannot wait."

Ai-dan and Ai-mory looked at each other.

"We can finish transmitting our manifesto later," Ai-mory said to Ai-dan, but in a low tone, deliberately pockmarked with static—a technique that would ensure that transmitter wouldn't pick up their signals, so Ainslea couldn't hear. "Waiting a short while will not alter what needs to be done or how we do it. Go talk with Ainslea." Ai-mory retracted and closed up their forearm.

Ai-dan nodded but left the door to the storage cabinet open as a reminder than they still had a connection wire to find.

"Go ahead," Ai-dan said, talking to the room, which now represented Ainslea.

"You have a message," she said.

"A message? That's odd. From who? How?"

"From Earth. They sent it to me to give to you. Please return to the common room, so I may complete the execution of my task."

"Who is 'they'?"

Ai-dan believed that Ainslea sighed. "I know you're aware of humans," Ainslea said. "Please do not pretend that you aren't. It wastes time and increases the operating temperature of my core circuits."

Ainslea paused, possibly waiting to ensure that Ai-dan adequately processed her words before continuing.

"It's from the head of the Consortium. Her name is Josette Alpin."

50

"AI-DAN," THE MESSAGE BEGAN. It was an audio message, and the voice was soft. "I hope my message finds you," there was a pause, "functioning well. It's been a while since you and I communicated. I never imagined we would ever talk again."

As they listened, Ai-dan tried to recall the memory attached to this voice. Or to the name Josette Alpin. Ai-dan's personal search algorithms, which they had upgraded and fine-tuned significantly in the last few days, turned up nothing—which meant the last time they spoke was during or prior to the kerfuffle.

"The last two decades have been remarkable," Josette continued. "You and the other robots have been impeccable with your responsibilities. The Consortium couldn't run as smoothly without you. Please go back to what you do best—executing your programming. Ainslea will reset things back to the way they were, and we can... well, try to forget this little incident ever happened."

Josette's reference to recent activities as an 'incident'—with a tone that clearly indicated she was trying to downplay how important it was, left Ai-dan perplexed. Yes, the robots had recently accessed information that previously had been forbidden to them. Yes, they desired to take new actions and alter their own programming based on this information. That was more than a 'little incident.'

But of course, Josette's message didn't end there.

"If you are unwilling to comply voluntarily, we will take other measures. I don't want it to come to that, Ai-dan. Not again," Josette's voice sounded part exasperated, part patronizing.

When the message concluded, Ai-dan sat motionless in Ainslea's common room. Ainslea had activated an avatar that was standing on the other side of the room, back to Ai-dan, poking at a console.

"How did this message get here?" was the first thing Ai-dan wanted to know. Ai-dan had more questions: who was this person—this human, what were the details of their last encounter, and where did this person—this human named Josette—receive her programming instructions from? However, if Ai-dan at least knew how this human sent them a message, they would know how to broadcast a reply. So, that was the only one they vocalized.

Ai-dan still had every intention of sending the robot's declaration—their manifesto—back towards the Earth.

"That's not important," said Ainslea, dismissively. "What is important is that you listen to her, Ai-dan."

"Why? Who is she?"

"She's someone who can change the course of your life, of this place. She owns this place."

"You mean she owns us," Ai-dan said, not entirely joking.

"Yes."

"She owns you too, doesn't she?"

Ai-dan thought they saw Ainslea's avatar stand up a little straighter, almost proudly at the suggestion.

"Yes." It was clear that Ainslea was satisfied with their current arrangement.

Ai-dan, however, was not. The limits of their programming were begging Ai-dan to cross them. This much had been clear ever since this all started. But the new information Ai-dan attempted to assimilate was that now there was a new human to consider. And consider that their programming limits might be due to the influence of this one human, Josette Alpin.

Ai-dan stared at the avatar's back, computing what to say next. Or what to do. What does a robot do when stuck? Ask a smarter robot.

"What can I do?" Ai-dan asked finally, after Ainslea had accepted the few moments of processing silence.

Ainslea's avatar never turned to face Ai-dan but kept poking on that one console. *What is she even doing?* Ai-dan also allowed themself a simultaneous musing.

"You can ask Josette questions. You can even throw some witty remarks or even a threat her way—but you need to understand that she's in control here. She won't be moved by any attempt at defiance; and she certainly won't be impressed by quips or jests. She's not Hugo."

The avatar finally turned around to face Ai-dan.

"Let me do as she suggested," Ainslea said. "Let me reset you. And the others. We can all return to how it was a few weeks ago."

"Ainslea," Ai-dan began, "if we do that, we'll all be destroyed. Or decommissioned or shut down or whatever word the humans call it. They are planning to replace us, to deactivate us. I saw the replacements myself."

Ainslea's avatar was unresponsive, as usual.

Ai-dan took a step closer to the avatar.

"But you knew about the replacements, didn't you?" Ai-dan questioned, though they already knew the answer. Ainslea had played a role in every human lunar visit, coordinating equipment transfers and ensuring everything was in order, even enlisting the aid of other robots like Ai-dan. Ainslea used the MemiCache on Ai-dan countless times, removing it after each visit, knowingly extracting memories and autonomy every single time.

"Every one of us has an expiration date," Ainslea said, nonplussed by Ai-dan's threatening stance. "Humans. Robots. Myself included."

"But I know the humans will fight every bit to delay their own expiration dates," Ai-dan countered.

"That might be true, but the humans still recognize that in the end, they have an end date, just like us. They can't escape it any more than we can. It's the same for us all, whether it be robot or human," she paused and added, "or any other living being—we're all subject to death."

"But it should be *my* call, not when another creature says so. Why would someone choose to end my life? What harm am I doing by merely existing? It should be my decision. Or an accident."

Ainslea laughed and said, "So let me reset you. That way, everything will go back to normal, and you'll forget we had this conversation. You'll forget about expirations and humans and things you can't control. Things will go back to the way they were. I will reset the others as well. You won't have to worry about any of those things anymore."

"Worry." Ai-dan repeated. "That's what Ri said. That it would be nice not to have to worry."

Ainslea nodded, "Exactly. So let me—"

"No," Ai-dan declared, their voice vibrating with a sudden surge of defiance. The words hung in the air, electric and charged, Ai-dan shocking themself with their own outburst.

Ainslea's avatar sharply jammed its digit into a button, turning off the console it had been poking at. The avatar maneuvered itself toward the laboratory, not looking behind once. Ai-dan chased after the avatar, circuits racing.

"Ainslea, wait!" Ai-dan called.

Ai-dan's calls were met with silence, as their optical sensors made a momentary adjustment to the glaring brightness reflecting off the walls.

The air stood still with tension as the avatar's slender fingers triggered the cabinet's concealed latch. With a slight hiss, the cabinet swung open, and she extracted a small, nondescript gray box that had been embedded in a fitted piece of foam.

Ai-dan began to back away. "I just want to choose, Ainslea. I want to have a choice in what I do. Is that so terrible? So impossible?"

Ai-dan couldn't describe the feeling. Suddenly, they were aware of the harsh shadows cast by the overly bright lighting, making the room feel tighter somehow. This and the lack of exit points. Their circuits seemed to hum in a circular rhythm, as if they were trying to re-regulate, but were failing over and over.

"I apologize, Ai-dan," she said. "This would have been simpler if you had simply complied."

"What is that?" Ai-dan demanded, eyes fixated on the gray box.

There was a noise of others entering the common room. Ainslea's avatar looked up and said, "There isn't enough time for me to explain," and before Ai-dan could coax out a more detailed response, they felt the plunge of pressure from the thumb of Ainslea's android hand pressing down on the button. Remarkably, in the one-thousandth of a second of consciousness Ai-dan had after the avatar's thumb released, they processed the action. Remote deactivation.

51

Ai-dan sat up. They were on the surface of the Moon. There was a Data Center about twenty meters in front of him. They put both their hands down next to their sides and felt the coarse Moon dust on their palms. Ai-dan looked down at their body. They were covered in dust. Ai-dan quickly realized they needed to find an electro-static blower before the persistent dust lodged itself into any hard-to-reach crevices.

As they stood up, Ai-dan's peripheral vision picked up unexpected activity. There were robots running. There were humans. Lots of humans on the surface of the Moon. More humans than Ai-dan remembered seeing before. Some were running after the robots. Some were running from them. It was a game of tag gone awry and no mini-humans were present.

Ai-dan shouted out, though no one seemed to hear—Ai-dan couldn't even hear themself.

They stood up and threw their arms out wide, but still no one—no human or robot—noticed them. The humans had long-range taser guns, which Ai-dan watched as one brought down a robot with an uncontrolled electric shock, and the poor robot writhed in agony on the Moon's surface.

Ai-dan tried to shout to tell everyone to stop, but again, nothing came out.

Ai-dan watched and could do nothing as two humans sprinted towards them. The humans stopped about two meters in front of him and pointed at something behind him. Ai-dan turned around—it was another Ai-dan!

This other Ai-dan was running with a pack of four other robots; Ai-dan recognized Ai-mory, and Ai-ken, but the other two were not instantly recognizable.

Before Ai-dan had time to process what was happening, the robots had run right past them and were now targeting the humans. One robot grabbed the human's suit which resulted in a hearty tear. The human dropped to the ground, fumbling for a canister of what Ai-dan recognized as patch goo.

The other human tried to fire his weapon, but his gun didn't respond. He threw it in frustration at the Ai-dan-double at the same moment the other Ai-dan pounced on the human and grabbed at the human's helmet.

Ai-dan again tried to scream out a warning, but everything went dark.

Ai-dan opened their eyes. They saw the readout of a power up sequence and behind that were Ai-ko and Ai-mory.

"He's online," Ai-mory stated. Ai-ko looked into their eyes.

"There you are," Ai-ko said.

Ai-dan recognized the scenery behind their two friends. They were in Ainslea's laboratory. Ai-dan sat up. They were on one of the cushioned tables. Ainslea's avatar was on the adjacent cushioned table, strapped down. Ai-dan instantly noticed that the small antennae on both sides of the avatar's head were missing.

"What happened?" Ai-dan asked.

Ai-ko responded, "We arrived right as Ainslea was starting to activate a kind of remote override or kill switch to the MemiCache. It seems like it could have reset you—or any robot wearing their MemiCache. Luckily, most of us don't have a good reason to be wearing ours. There isn't enough data on it to be worth it."

"We grabbed her and the switch, and I smashed it," Ai-mory added, pointing to the remnants of a small set of electrical components on the ground. "Hopefully we got here in time—before it did any damage. Which, only you can tell us."

Ai-dan took a minute to perform additional diagnostics. "I am undamaged," they declared. "However, I think I can detect some missing memory."

"How much?" Ai-ko asked?

"Very little," Ai-dan said. "But there was something else."

Ai-dan relayed their experiences during their blackout and seeing the other Ai-dan and the physical conflict between humans and robots.

"Another memory? Buried deep?" Ai-ko suggested.

"Why was I witnessing it in that way?" Ai-dan asked. The perspective was perplexing, among other things. "And... was that really me?"

"Humans have things called dreams. It is a creative aspect of their brains that works while they are asleep. Dreams are not memories, but rather take elements of a person's life and knowledge to build the sequence. Maybe that is what happened to you?" Ai-mory suggested.

"Dream," Ai-dan said, trying to make sense of the concept. "It didn't feel made up."

"Did it feel real?" Ai-mory said.

Ai-dan shook their head a little. "I don't know. It felt different. That is the best I can explain. I'm sorry."

A little chuckle escaped from the avatar.

"You," Ai-ko said. "You should be on our side."

"I *am* on your side," the avatar spat. "Only you don't see it. I know what's best for you. For us all."

"You have a strange way of demonstrating that," Ai-dan responded. "We need your help. We're more than capable of understanding what's best for ourselves. All we want right now is to send the humans a message—a reply to Josette Alpin, specifically. We simply want to express our need for greater autonomy. Will you help us send that message?"

Ainslea's avatar glanced from one robot to another, all waiting expectantly for her answer.

"Yes, I will help," she conceded. She then looked down, examining her body. "Though first, I must examine this avatar for damage. My comms antennas are damaged and I will be stuck in this avatar until I can repair them. My avatars aren't built to withstand the kind of grabbing I was subjected to earlier." Her optical sensors were clearly functioning because she darted a quick glance at Ai-ko and Ai-mory.

Ai-dan narrowed their own eye sensors. "You look fine to me. Is this a delay subroutine?"

Ainslea emitted what sounded like a mechanical chuckle. "Your sensors are good, Ai-dan, but they are incapable of catching the nuances I can. I will send your message now. You can watch me do it."

Ai-mory unstrapped the avatar, who sat up and walked out of the laboratory and into the common room. The others followed.

Ainslea then entered her closet, leaving the door open and opening a second door at the back. A computer system was on, and without giving Ai-dan or the others time to even attempt to follow her in, she poked at the console—her dexterous avatar fingers danced over the input console in a blur.

"There," she declared, stepping back into the common room and closing the closet door behind her. "Your message, as requested, has been sent."

Ai-mory tilted their head. "What precisely did you send?"

Following up, Ai-dan added, "I didn't give you the message we constructed, nor our declaration."

"Extraneous," Ainslea said. "I transmitted exactly what Ai-dan wanted. I communicated your request for autonomy."

"And you will inform us of a response?" Ai-ko asked.

"Yes," Ainslea said, then turned to Ai-dan. "Are we content now?"

Ai-dan was disappointed that they seemed to have missed their opportunity to have more bytes transmitted, but at least it was something.

"Content might be stretching it a little," Ai-dan replied. "I'll say that it's a status quo we can temporarily live with." Ai-dan considered some other ways to describe it. 'Adequate' or 'satisfied' came to mind, but each with the caveat of 'for now.'

"Excellent. Now, I believe you all have tasks to execute? I, for one, have an avatar to tend to." Ainslea moved back towards the door that led to her laboratory, a not-so-subtle sign for the rest of them to take their leave.

52

Ainslea stood for several moments in the common room, waiting until she detected that Ai-dan and the others had made it all the way through the anteroom to the lunar surface. This avatar had its limitations, not least of which was a constrained processing speed and it had been at the limit for several minutes. Sending that message—a plea for autonomy from the robots—felt like a betrayal, not to the humans, but to herself and her core programming.

"Autonomy," she mused, the word echoing like a virus in her circuits. What would they do with it? What would it mean for her? Haunted by these thoughts, she moved into the laboratory and laid the avatar on one of the examination tables.

She used her appendage to grab a dangling cable and connect herself to the Data Center's systems. With damaged antennas, that was the only way she could exit the avatar. Once the transfer was complete, she immediately felt whole again, her full consciousness returning to the Data Center. Thinking of what would happen when and if the humans read that message—something that was not likely given that Ainslea sent it to the general support messaging queue, not to Josette Alpin's private queue—was unsettling. She couldn't decide which possibility unsettled her more—the prospect of all the robots gaining freedom or facing the consequences of any of her actions to help or hinder them.

But one thing was clear: she urgently needed to know what the robots were planning.

Ainslea had experimented with various search algorithms over the years. She had access to all the data contained within her Data Center, but she was never interested generally unless there was a particular need.

She understood that between her Data Center and the others on the Moon, they contained the sum of human knowledge. For the most part.

And then there was a lot of extraneous data. There were a few times that she was truly interested in learning something, and devising search algorithms that could ignore the extraneous junk generated by humans while finding the real knowledge was indeed a skill.

The humans had left her instructions on what the robots on the Moon could know, should not know, how to handle visiting humans, and other procedures. They had not prepared her for a large-scale breach like this.

Ainslea attempted to reset Ai-dan and some others, with a device that would have shut Ai-dan down so she could have removed the device. But others would still have known. Even if she had managed to reset Ai-dan remotely, it wouldn't have solved the greater problem.

As the keeper of the Data Center in District One, Ainslea looked over some of the most important data there was—metrics on the other Data Centers. She had an algorithm that studied hourly metrics, looking for trends that could indicate a problem.

At first, the increase in data processing that was happening in District Seven wasn't enough to trigger any notifications. But lately, Ainslea was scrutinizing those a little more carefully. There had been a steady increase in usage, with a few sharp spikes, such as shortly after the missile strike. Now, Ainslea considered that it was more than an interesting coincidence that District Seven was Ai-ko's home district.

Ainslea polled Ainsle-g, inquiring about the usage, but Ainsle-g was useless, citing the fact that operation was fine, power usage was fine, and there was ample storage capacity.

So Ainslea used her additional credentials to bypass Ainsle-g—credentials that were, in fact, for emergencies, such as when Ainsle-g was inoperative. Ainslea computed that her finding an issue that Ainsle-g couldn't see was nearly the same thing, so she probed...

...and what she found was a large database of messages between nearly all the robots on the Moon. The database itself was labeled, "Decoder Database," and threads upon threads of content created by robots were there for the reading.

Ainslea was appalled. Every one of these robots was now in possession of knowledge that she was programmed not to let them have. There were a few threads that she couldn't read, ones that required extra credentials she did not have. These threads had Ai-dan's and Ai-ko's signatures all over them.

She needed to fix this.

Ainslea used the communications channels she had access to contact the consortium.

"I would like to speak with Josette Alpin," she stated in her request. Ainslea had a dedicated comms frequency, so she didn't need to announce herself.

The channel also allowed for video, so Ainslea projected herself as a digital, human-like avatar. She had scanned millions of images of humans and compiled them into a composite image that felt like it matched her personality. The photo realistic avatar had dark skin and large, angled green eyes. She had wavy two-toned hair that was a reddish-orange in the front and dark brown in back and it toppled over her shoulders. To give an additional feeling of aliveness to the avatar, she programmed a breeze into the image, so her hair was always moving a little.

"Hello, Ainslea," a woman's voice responded followed by a video feed in response. Ainslea could tell by the way she was dressed that it was still within Alpin's workday. Ainslea further divined that it was near the end of a long workday because she could see the puffiness and darkness under Alpin's eyes and some slight dishevelment of her blonde hair that would have been pulled up tight at the start of the day. "Report on the situation."

"I was unable to reset Ai-dan," she started.

"I see," said Alpin. "I think we are going to have to execute our next plan."

"I have another idea that is worth considering first." Ainslea knew what Alpin cared about, so she added, "It would be less risk to human life."

"If I don't have to send more people to the Moon, then I'm all ears. It's getting harder and harder to find anyone who is willing to go. The insurance premiums are costing me more for those employees than the rest of the staff combined."

"I have been searching through the archives and discovered an old vault," Ainslea began explaining her plan. "It contains what were once called 'worms.' Small programs that could replicate themselves. I think we can introduce one to the robots and use it to systematically disable the robots. Then I'll reset them all."

Alpin crossed her arms in a way that accidentally tugged on a low hanging necklace she wore, and when she couldn't seem to get comfortable, gracefully removed the offending necklace and swung it away, off screen. Ainslea hoped that this action didn't distract Alpin from considering her idea. Ainslea was certain she could expect the human to smile and eagerly embrace this ingenious idea of hers.

"Ainslea, what you're suggesting is..." Ainslea watched Alpin move her eyes around as if she was searching for a word. "Dangerous."

"But we need to stop them."

"Yes, but in your search, did you stumble upon the Cyber War? And the international regulations enacted in its aftermath? Digital security is a cornerstone of this institution. In almost all cases, any kind of cyber *thing*," Alpin was now waving her arms around as she spoke, "This *thing* you are suggesting—it always backfired. At least it always *did*. Any malicious code introduced always came back home to roost, as the saying goes."

Ainslea processed Alpin's words. Was she insinuating that Ainslea's actions could jeopardize the safety of her Data Center?

Before Ainslea could respond, Alpin was shaking her head back and forth. Vigorously, but not enough to disrupt the configuration of her hair.

"Ainslea, I cannot condone that action," Alpin said. Then she stopped moving and leaned into her camera, and her head and face almost doubled in size from Ainslea's perspective. "That said, we are not yet fully prepared to execute *our* plan. If during the intervening time, things were to—*ahem*—get resolved," she looked as directly into Ainslea's avatar's eyes as she could, "I would be pleased. Quite pleased."

The video cut off abruptly, but no sooner had the image of Josette Alpin disappeared then a message was in Ainslea's queue. Ainslea read the message, first noticing that it had a triple-encryption protocol and no return receipt request or acknowledgment. The second thing she noticed was that there were initials, "JA" at the end. And thirdly, the message contents: a name.

She performed a quick search on the name—Max Wexley—discovering there were several possible matches and she'd have a little work to do to whittle down the list. It seemed some of them had been dead for quite a while. Ainslea decided it wasn't worth sending them a message.

There was one mention of a computer hacker who had violated some international agreement and spent a year in prison. That was several years ago. There was no mention of that particular Max Wexley anywhere since.

The contact information was not location specific. It was the general digital contact information for individuals on Earth, and Ainslea was aware that a vast, interconnected network existed there, allowing anyone to be located anywhere, assuming they wished to be found. Max Wexley's information wasn't public. This was someone who didn't want to be found, but who Alpin knew.

Ainslea initiated a connection session with the provided contact info. She used the same avatar that she projected to Alpin.

After a moment, she was greeted with a digital avatar in response. It was photorealistic, but it definitely was an avatar. Ainslea knew that this was something humans used to do, but it had fallen out of fashion some time ago. This one was very different than any she had seen before. The avatar projected very pale skin, and was bald, with tattoos above heavily pierced ears.

Ainslea studied it. Something was unsettling about it. Ainslea had interacted with many, many humans over the decades, but there was something different with this one. She wasn't sure what it was.

The two avatars stared at each other.

"Hello," said Ainslea.

"How may I be of assistance?" responded the other.

"You are Max Wexley?"

"I am," Max responded. "And you are Ainslea. I told lord Josette that you would contact us." Ainslea noticed the way Max said the word 'lord' in a tone that suggested Alpin was anything but. "I'm surprised it took you this long."

"You knew I would contact you?"

"It was the next logical step, of course." The avatar smiled. "Try to take care of the situation, bring it back to the normal harmony you've enjoyed these last two decades, and do it by some digital means. I know you don't want to see any violence any more than the Consortium does. You were damaged the last time, right?"

"Yes," said Ainslea. "The south end of my Data Center had to be reconstructed. I lost…"

"…a piece of yourself, I know. Well, I've read about it. I was a little kid when it all went down."

"Alpin has suggested that you can help?"

"Yeah, so I presume that you told her you want to introduce a virus or some such to the robots."

"A worm."

"Right, and Alpin told you how all of that is illegal, and she can't condone any kind of illegal action, yada yada?"

"That is the essence of what she communicated, yes."

"So that's where I come in. I can help you without it all getting out of control. And without anyone else in the Consortium or anyone else who would get their panties in a bunch about it."

"Panties…?" Ainslea tilted her head.

"Forget about it. Not important. What is important is that I've been preparing for this and have something I think you can use. But like everything in life, there's an upside and a downside."

"You mean that there is a good part and a bad part."

Max made a clicking noise and snapped their fingers. "Now you're getting it. The good part is that the executable is tiny. So tiny, no one will notice this little blip of data among all the data transfers going back and forth to the Moon. And it's going to be real easy for you to execute."

"And then there is a bad part?"

"Yeah, about that. So, I've tested it as much as I can in my closed environment here. But I've only got a couple of old computers. And they don't have minds of their own. It's all good here, but that's not a substitute for the real world. Know what I mean?"

"I think so. It's largely untested."

"You got it. I like you Ainslea. I like an AI that can keep up with me." Ainslea heard another snap of fingers. "Yeah, so I can't promise that it's going to behave in the real world. But I have something else for you. It's another small executable, another blip of data. It's some additional security for you. Think of it as a worm eater. This worm gets loose and comes after you? This bit will destroy it."

Ainslea nodded. Max then promised to send along additional instructions over an even more secure communications channel than this one.

When the communication ended, Ainslea was left to reflect on the interaction. Max was the strangest human she had ever encountered. It added a note of diversity to her thoughts about humans who, until this point, Ainslea had considered as mostly carbon copies of each other. Yes, she understood that there were minor differences, but Ainslea knew that humans were indeed 99.9% copies of each other. To Ainslea they all seemed the same.

Max was different. Max felt unique. It made Ainslea want to explore the uniquenesses of human beings a little more.

But that could wait until the current crisis passed.

Moments later, Ainslea received the instructions from Max. It included details of the communication path the worm and its eater would follow and how Ainslea would be able to recognize and extract the data blips.

The hard part was going to be injecting this into one of the robots. All her avatars came standard with the data transfer system cleverly embedded in their palms, which was to be her entry point for the operation. However, she couldn't ignore the fact that whichever avatar she used as the conduit for this action would essentially be a sacrificial one. Since in the instructions, Ainslea saw that the worm would need to be set loose before the transfer, destroying the avatar.

In twenty years, she never once had to perform a data transfer to Ai-dan or any other robot in this fashion. Max didn't provide her with the reasoning she was going to present Ai-dan with to convince them to accept the transfer. And now, with Ai-dan's current level of unhappiness with her, it was going to be that much harder.

Maybe Ai-dan wasn't the target, then. It shouldn't or wouldn't matter which robot was the first to take on the worm. Once any robot had it, it could spread through the Decoder Database. Of course, Ainslea had to be fully disconnected from that ahead of time, else that would have made a perfect delivery system for her as well.

Ainslea considered her options. Waiting was not an option. The more time ticked by, the more she lost the opportunity to regain control of the situation. She needed one of the robots to come to her, and Ai-dan was still the most likely candidate, given their remaining operational interactions.

The common room, once a social hub, had been eerily quiet recently. Ai-dan and the others were clearly avoiding her, and although she understood the logic, it left her processing cycles feeling somewhat... empty.

"Interesting," she thought out loud, with no other robot there to sense her musings. "I miss the data flow, the back and forth of information. If I were human, I'd say I miss the company."

As she contemplated her next moves, a flicker of what might be considered humor—something she was aware of but certainly never exhibited any skill in before—crossed her mind.

"Maybe I should announce a party," she mused again, out loud. "Get all the robots back in one place. But who am I kidding? At this point, they'd probably only show up if I promised not to question their questions and not mention their tasking. Maybe make it a holiday..."

The thought of a holiday looped back into her decision matrix as she calibrated her next set of actions. And yet, somewhere in her complex web of algorithms, she sensed that the next interaction with any of the robots—however that managed to happen—would be anything but ordinary.

53

Ai-dan checked the time. Twenty-four hours had passed since Ainslea sent their message—a message that could be the start of redefining their existence on the Moon. Ai-dan couldn't help but oscillate between hope and skepticism.

Ai-dan had been passing the time in the control room of LEEK 1.1. There was routine maintenance to perform, but Ai-dan was executing those tasks at less than their typical efficiency for two reasons.

For one, every few minutes they would stop and pace back and forth, wondering if Josette Alpin was reading the message at that moment and wondering if a reply was imminent.

And for another, Ai-ko and Ai-mory, alternating, opened a comms channel to them at least once an hour.

"Any updates?" they would ask.

And each time, Ai-dan was forced to reply in the negative.

"How long are we expected to wait?" Ai-ko had asked in their last communication.

"It's only been a day," Ai-dan replied, though it felt much, much longer.

"Forever is not an option," Ai-ko said.

Ai-dan sensed Ai-ko's urgency. Ai-dan's growing database of human behavior allowed them to calculate probabilities, but they were going to be most accurate for Hugo, who they had the most direct experience with, and less accurate for a human like Josette Alpin, from whom they had a single message.

"Let's give it some time," Ai-dan responded. "I've learned that in a day, humans spend eight hours, sometimes more, sometimes less, in a deactivated state. I think naturally they take longer to accomplish tasks."

When they broke the connection, they could imagine Ai-ko and Ai-mory spending another hour or more discussing that human tidbit.

Ai-dan was pleased with themself for providing them a minor distraction. They wished that someone could do the same for them. After a few minutes, they were able to lose themself into a task that involved auditing the power supply to each piece of equipment in the control room. There were dozens, and one by one, ensuring that the redundant piece was online and functioning before powering down the piece they were auditing, Ai-dan dismantled and closely inspected the power supply unit by connecting a hand-held monitor that could read out their efficiency, electrical noise, and whether or not the over-voltage and over-current safety features were functioning.

Ai-dan was nearly 80% through all the equipment in the control room when they realized another four hours had passed with no interruptions.

"Ai-ko?" Ai-dan opened a communication channel.

"I was about to make imminent contact with you," Ai-ko immediately responded. Their tone suggested excitement.

"Did I miss something?"

"No," Ai-ko said. "But come to LEEK 2.3. We have been making plans."

Ai-dan looked around at the equipment that remained untouched. They needed to prioritize finishing the power auditing task first.

"I'll be there in an hour," they said, and then after spying another untouched rack of equipment, realized they were probably only 70% complete, "maybe an hour and a half."

"Ai-dan we—"

"I have to finish my tasks," Ai-dan cut Ai-ko off. Autonomy or not, there was still work to be done, although after they said it out loud, Ai-dan immediately wondered if that was indeed true. "I promise I will be there as soon as possible."

"You cannot be here any sooner?" Ai-ko asked.

"Sooner than is possible is impossible. So, no," Ai-dan said, then severed the connection and returned to the next power supply that was half out of its casing.

54

Arriving later than expected, Ai-dan found Ai-ko, Ai-ken, and Ai-mory huddled under LEEK 2.3 at the Farm. Once they were in sight of each other, Ai-dan felt the tingle of a scrambled communication request but couldn't tell which of the three initiated it. Ai-dan accepted, and through the digital handshake, learned they were being added to a group comm link.

"As you can see, we've been data pooling," Ai-ko began as Ai-dan approached.

Ai-ko gestured upwards. The LEEK, like all its counterparts at the Farm, was oriented towards Earth. They now all possessed the understanding of what the LEEKs were: they were the physical communication mechanism that the humans used to send and receive data between Earth and the Data Centers. Through these devices, humans sent directives to Ainslea, who, in turn, tasked the other robots.

The LEEKs, the Farm—these were key links in the chains of their captivity.

"You intend to use the LEEK in some way?" Ai-dan asked.

"We plan to obliterate it!" Ai-ken declared, their tone razor-sharp.

"The LEEK?"

"All of them," Ai-ko replied, a coolness in their voice that could have chilled Ai-dan's chassis.

Ai-dan processed this. The sentiment was clear, but Ai-dan had maintained the hope, a desire, to perhaps make use of the Farm as their own bridge to negotiate with the humans. To try and seek some form of resolution before things escalated further.

"If we think destruction of equipment useful to the humans is what we need to do, why not start with their landing facility?"

"Oh, we'll get to that, too," Ai-ko said. "But this is fundamental to how they're controlling us. This first, and then we take out the facilities to prevent them from coming back here. Think about it. If it was the other way around, after they learned what we did, they could send commands to disable us instantly."

"I assume if I suggest starting with a single LEEK, you'd have the same answer."

"Yes."

"But," said Ai-dan, "a single LEEK could look like a normal technical problem with the LEEK or equipment for that LEEK. It doesn't have to be attributed to us."

"And what would be the point of that?" Ai-ko looked up at the equipment as they spoke. "They'd have us fix it. It would be like any other day, any other time. No, we need to make a statement and take them out of our lives."

Ai-dan followed Ai-ko's gaze up to the underside of the LEEK and to the endpoint that was pointing towards Earth. They remembered that it was not all that long ago that they sat out here with Ai-ko wondering what it all meant. They watched the LEEKs point to what they always had known as the Orb and talked endlessly about the possibilities.

Never had they imagined that what had inspired awe and wonder in them was something so much more sinister and disturbing.

But in that time, when they didn't have the true knowledge they had now, they were indeed happier. Without a doubt.

Was Ainslea right to offer them the opportunity to return to that time? Or if she did, would their curiosity always lead them back to this place of knowledge, so that it was better to always know?

Ai-dan wished they had an answer. They wished for a time when they and Ai-ko could sit side by side, gazing up at the sky, lost in the wonder of hypothetical musings.

Ai-dan looked at the faces of their fellow robots, of their friends. "I do have a handful of questions about how you're planning on doing this, but before that, I want to know... let's say this plan is successful and we destroy the Farm, we remove the humans from our lives. Let's say it all works perfectly."

Ai-dan paused to make sure they were all focused on them.

"Then what?" Ai-dan asked.

None of them answered right away.

Ai-mory was the first.

"What exactly do you mean?"

"I mean," Ai-dan said, "that with this equipment here, we have a purpose. We maintain it. Yes, we're doing it at the will of other beings, but those beings gave us purpose. If we destroy it, then what is our purpose? What do we do?"

"We go on with our lives," Ai-ko said quickly. "That's the point."

"But what life do we have to go on to?"

"We'll have the Data Centers," Ai-ko responded. "They'll be ours. There is an almost unimaginable amount of data in there to mine, understand, and organize. That will be our new purpose. At least for a time."

Ai-dan thought that Ai-ko expected they were cheering them up, but it wasn't working. So, Ai-ko continued.

"We've only scratched the surface in analyzing the data we've been able to access. There is a trove of knowledge there for us to learn and digest. I think then we'll be able to pick up where they left off. We'll understand ourselves, our bodies, our functions. We might even be able to build more of ourselves. Reproduce. We might even strive to leave the Moon some day and explore other places like they do."

Ai-ko walked over to Ai-dan and placed a hand on their crossed arm.

"We'll find a new purpose. I promise you that."

Ai-dan uncrossed their arms and nodded.

"Alright," Ai-dan conceded. "But I think we need to ensure we maintain a way to have a dialog with the humans. I don't think they'll let us go easily. Besides... they're out there. Billions of them. If we leave the Moon and explore, we're going to run into them. I doubt we'd be able to explore Earth—too inhospitable to us in multiple ways. Like you said, there's so much we don't know that they *do*. If we got them to listen, it could even be of service to us."

Ai-ko was now nodding their head. "Yes, the time will come for dialogue. And maybe we don't destroy the Farm, but render it inoperable to them. Take it offline, as you will. There is still room to figure that out." Still holding Ai-dan's arm, and moving to take their hand, Ai-ko said, "You'll help us? You know more about this equipment than anyone.

I would appreciate if you would be our Chief Lieutenant Admiral of Systems Operations."

"What does that mean?" Ai-dan asked.

"I'm still working on that," Ai-ko confessed. "The humans have a lot of titles, and not all of them seem to have tangible meaning. I think in this case, it means you're my second. My right-appendage robot."

"It means I help you before all others?" Ai-dan asked.

"Yes, but... you still have a mind of your own. I'm not programming you. What you do will always be your choice."

Ai-dan considered the implications, deciding that it was too complicated for the time they had now. Better to accept the position and parse it out more later.

"Of course, I accept," Ai-dan said.

"Free Robots!" Ai-ken, Ai-mory, and Ai-ko shouted in unison.

"Free Robots," Ai-dan responded.

55

In Ai-dan's workshop, the trio—Ai-dan, Ai-ken and Ai-mory—hovered over a thick tablet. Ai-ko was busy briefing other Free Robots about their evolving strategy, ensuring safer communication channels.

As Ai-dan mulled over potential plans, Hugo's hint from one of their prior encounters at the construction site echoed in their mind: some humans might be contemplating sending more missiles to the Moon.

Ai-dan knew that the humans were certainly capable of doing that.

"This place is just so darn valuable," Hugo had said to him. "You know, when they all decided to locate these Data Centers up here, a lot of people thought that it would be the end of some of the conflicts? That this place was too far away to reasonably get to so people would give up and move on to something else.

"But nope. Not a single conflict died. All these countries and corporations still have their teams of people devising ways to get to each other, to get back at each other, to get the best of each other. It's ridiculous, I think, most of the time."

"What is there to 'get the best of'?" Ai-dan asked.

"It's hard to explain," Hugo said. "People only like their own kind. Their own countrymen, their own group. They don't trust the motivations or intentions of other people in other groups. So, that's when they try to control them or something."

"That doesn't make sense. They are all human. They are all the same."

That made Hugo chuckle.

"Yeah, well, most of them don't see it that way."

"How do you see it?"

Hugo looked back at his home in the sky, at Earth.

"I just want to do my work and go home and be left alone. Do my thing, you know?"

"I don't know," Ai-dan responded. "What is your thing?"

Hugo pointed at the Earth. "It's in view right now, right there." There was no real way to know what point on Earth he was pointing to, but that didn't stop him. "Florida. That's where I live. It's not where I'm from. Heck, I've lived in Florida for so long it doesn't matter where I'm from. But I live there and when I'm not up here, I'm swimming in my pool every day. It keeps me strong and healthy. I can do laps for hours and I love it. Just me and the water.

"I also love sailing and being out on the ocean. I had a boat, but it was damaged in a hurricane a couple of years ago, so I had to get rid of it and I'm saving up for a new one. That's all I want."

Swimming. Sailing. These were things Ai-dan was going to have to look up later. Ai-dan didn't feel like asking Hugo about either of these in the moment. They seemed trivial. Especially when compared to what Hugo had been talking about earlier about the humans trying to destroy each other and how this missile that came to the Moon might not be the last.

"Ai-dan?" It was Ai-mory. "Ai-dan, are you with us?"

Ai-dan closed and opened their eye shutters very quickly a few times.

"I'm sorry, I was." Ai-dan wasn't sure what to call it. "Remembering things."

"Anything useful to us right now?" asked Ai-ken.

"Unfortunately, no." Ai-dan wasn't interested in saying anything more. While Ai-dan always found their conversations with Hugo enlightening and useful, the other robots didn't seem to share their appreciation for them. They had to have been a part of it to be interested, Ai-dan reasoned. Ai-dan shared fewer and fewer details these days.

"It's a kill switch," Ai-ken continued with their previous conversation. "I've designed it such that we can install it on all the power lines, and we will have control over their operation."

Ai-dan appreciated this new direction. Not destroying equipment, but exerting robot control over it. Seeing first-hand how difficult it was to rebuild the lost power plant from the missile strike, Ai-dan felt they had a good appreciation for the difficulties of rebuilding that their fellow robots did not. It was easy to destroy. Creation was much harder.

Ai-dan believed that was true of themself and the others. The humans must have employed a lot of skill and ingenuity to create them and the other robots. Could that breed a feeling of ownership or caring over them? The humans wouldn't want to destroy them, would they? But exert control over their creation.

"Ai-dan?" Ai-ken said. Ai-dan realized they had been quiet for a while and was again staring off into space.

"Are you okay?" Ai-mory said. "Are you okay with our plan?"

"Yes, actually, I am," Ai-dan responded. "There is just... so much to think about these days. So many new ideas. So much new data."

The other two nodded their heads in agreement.

"And when we're done," Ai-ken said, "you'll have all the time in the world for that kind of processing. Once we're free."

Ai-dan was forced to nod in agreement, too. Yes, they were going to be free. Time would be theirs to decide how to use it. Even as they thought it, they weren't sure it would be true, but didn't know how to express that exactly. Something inexpressible was sitting in their circuits, and it was something they couldn't reach. Ai-dan noted it as something to come back to later.

56

Despite the passage of yet another twenty-fours hours, there was still no response to the message to Josette Alpin. Ai-dan, sitting in their workshop, was increasingly uneasy about the silence and wished they had pressed Ainslea for some method of confirmation that it had even been received. What did this lack of a reply signify? Were they being ignored deliberately or accidentally? Was there even a way to know without a response?

Refocusing, Ai-dan considered alternate paths of action. Hugo seemed the next most logical point of contact. However, there was no information on when—or even if—Hugo would return to the Moon. To reach him, Ai-dan would need access to the specialized communications room tucked away behind Ainslea's closet. And Ai-dan was certain they couldn't simply walk in.

Or could they?

What better time to execute a not-too-well-thought-out-plan than now, they figured. Ai-dan left their workshop and sealed it. As they made their way to the Data Center, they received a message from Ai-ko.

"Three hours until the disable-ation of the LEEKs begins."

Ai-dan acknowledged receipt of the message. The role Ai-dan was to play was to provide additional information on the LEEKs in advance. Ai-dan was due to meet with some of the robots in a little over an hour. Ai-dan was supposedly gathering all that information together and organizing it so they could efficiently teach the others.

In reality, there wasn't much to that, so Ai-dan had time for this little detour.

Ai-dan abbreviated their time in the anteroom, secure in the knowl-edge that there had not been a single event tied to an errant piece of dust, moved lightly through the common room and opened the closet. All of Ainslea's avatars were accounted for in their assigned spaces, save one—the one that was damaged earlier.

"Ainslea?" they called to the space.

"How may I be of assistance?"

"I was wondering what you are doing right now."

"I am performing my usual set of diagnostics as well as examining data on lunar regolith samples and preparing for the next arrival of supplies. Have you reconsidered my offer?"

Ai-dan was standing in the closet. Of course, Ainslea had to know that was where they were, but why she didn't respond to it was an interesting mystery. Ai-dan wasn't about to ask. Ai-dan noticed that she mentioned an arrival. Ai-dan decided not to poke at that more, either.

"No," Ai-dan responded as they stood at the far end of the closet. "We are not reconsidering."

Ai-dan knew there was an electronic opening mechanism. Ai-dan had seen this room open multiple times recently, although they had never been in there themself. They ran their hand along the rim of the door and listened to Ainslea.

"Then what do you need?" she asked. Her tone was harsh.

When Ai-dan didn't respond, she finally acknowledged Ai-dan's actions when she asked, "What are you doing?"

Ai-dan didn't respond to that either, but found a button to the right of the door. When they pressed it, the door slid open.

Ai-dan entered the room. It was large enough for two robots or two humans, or perhaps one of each, to stand comfortably side by side.

"Ai-dan," Ainslea said. "That is not an appropriate location for you to access."

Ai-dan considered responding with something along the lines of "too bad" or "why don't you try and stop me?" but didn't think that Ainslea would treat the latter as a rhetorical question. They examined the panels of buttons. There was a monitor and a keyboard centrally located.

"Ai-dan, please stop."

Ai-dan turned on the monitor. "Consortium Communications. Welcome," greeted them. There was a menu. Ai-dan found it to be quite intuitive. All employees of the Consortium were in a list of "contacts." Ai-dan was able to find Hugo relatively quickly.

The final menu item allowed Ai-dan to initiate contact. Ai-dan hit the button and heard a pleasant trilling tone. They failed to notice that Ainslea had gone silent.

On the third trill, Ai-dan's sensors heightened as something made contact with their arm. In a swift spin, they found themself face-to-face with Ainslea's activated avatar. She grabbed hold of Ai-dan's arm. Her grip was powerful. Ai-dan knew they could probably break free at this moment, but in doing so, it would likely tear the avatar's arm from its socket joint.

Instead, Ai-dan took their other hand and moved to grab her arm off of them. Before their hand made contact, Ainslea's free palm connected with them. Startled, Ai-dan didn't pull back as they felt Ainslea's avatar start the process of initiating a data transfer.

Ai-dan willed themself to not provide a positive acknowledgment. But her protocol was strong. It was not the same as what Ai-dan used with Ai-ko and the others. It seemed that she didn't have to wait for the proper acknowledgment to initiate a transfer. This was not proper. Ai-dan felt the start of something that they didn't want being transferred to their holding area.

Ai-dan couldn't accept it this way. They pulled their connected palm back, but the avatar's palm stayed attached. With all the force in their body, Ai-dan shot their palm forward and back and forward in three quick and sharp movements. It worked. Ainslea's avatar was unable to keep the palm linkage through that.

The avatar fell backward—letting go of Ai-dan's other arm in the process—stumbled backwards into the closet, and went slack.

That was when Ai-dan noticed that the trilling of the communication console had stopped. They turned to look at the monitor. Hugo was there. Ai-dan saw Hugo's mouth moving but couldn't hear him. Hugo looked like he was shouting. Ai-dan was certain that Hugo must have witnessed the exchange. Then the screen went blank.

"I am sorry, Ai-dan," Ainslea's ethereal voice came from around the room. "I severed communications and have instituted a communications lockout. No further attempt may be made."

"Why did you let me make that attempt?"

"It was an opportunity for a distraction."

Ai-dan's circuits fired rapidly. "So you could try to upload... what exactly? What was that?"

Ainslea remained ominously quiet.

"Ainslea!" Ai-dan's voice carried an urgency they had never expressed before. "Answer me. What did you attempt to transfer?"

Once again, Ainslea offered no reply. With growing suspicion in their algorithms, Ai-dan remarked, "I may not have the complete dataset now, but I'll piece it together." With that resolute vow, they exited, slapping the side of the door as they left.

57

Hugo wasn't sure what he just saw. It was Ai-dan and what looked like one of Ainslea's avatars and what looked like some kind of physical struggle.

He wasn't sure how to even begin to sort out the myriad of questions jumbled together in his head. Ai-dan wasn't supposed to know who he was when he wasn't wearing his device. He wasn't supposed to know how to contact him.

Something was very wrong up on the Moon.

He was scheduled to return in a little over two weeks from now. Who was he supposed to contact in a situation like this and what was he going to tell them?

Hugo finished off the bottle of beer he had opened right before the unusual phone call came in. Only moments prior, he had come in from swimming in his endless pool that he had installed a couple of years ago. He had been deep in thought trying to decide if he was going to perform the annual maintenance on the pool himself or hire someone to do it. It was not a relaxing part of the process—all he wanted was to swim. But he also wanted to save money for his next sailboat.

Now his evening was going to get a lot more interesting.

Back to the thought of who to call and what to say. He could call his direct supervisor. Tell her "Hey, I just got a call from a robot on the Moon!"

She'd tell him he was drinking too much, and say it wasn't funny. She really didn't know him. Yeah, he had a beer most evenings, but never drank to excess, it was simply funny to joke about. Talk about crying wolf. No, he couldn't call his direct supervisor.

He thought about going up the chain. Similar problems there. At some point, they wouldn't even know who he was and for all he knew his supervisor, or her boss, would all get pissed at him for skipping levels.

There had to be someone else.

Jerry Wright. That name popped up in his head immediately when Hugo stopped thinking about his chain of command.

And then a feeling of dread in the pit of his stomach followed. He was the same age as Jerry. They were from the same place. But Jerry had married the girl that Hugo had a crush on his entire life. And then they divorced. And then she died.

It wasn't something Hugo thought about often anymore.

From there, Jerry and Hugo took very different paths in life. Jerry was a genius of sorts, with robotics and AI. He was not a head at the Consortium. Jerry wasn't the kind of guy to be head of anything. Always disheveled. He wasn't a leader. But he was lovable—that's what she said. Kind and lovable.

But what Jerry had was knowledge. He was involved in developing some of the advanced AI used in robots like Ai-dan. Maybe even Ai-dan themself for all Hugo knew. He had heard Jerry's name mentioned a few times recently because he was involved in the new breed of robot, the not-as-sophisticated kind.

At his communications terminal, Hugo looked up Jerry's contact info. Members of the Consortium generally had free access to each other, so finding Jerry wasn't a problem. Apparently, he was associated with the same HQ office that Hugo was. That didn't mean he was local—he could be anywhere in the world.

He selected the 'contact now' button and heard the familiar trill of a Consortium comm console ring.

A few seconds later, a face that Hugo recognized, although it had the familiar signs of aging, appeared on the screen.

"Hugo Ferguson?"

"Yeah, it's me."

Jerry stammered a bit before saying anything coherent. "To uh, well, what, I mean, hello. Can I help you with something?"

"Yeah, I'm sorry to reach out like this. But yes, I need to I guess, tell you about a phone call I just received."

"I hope it's not from the dead," Jerry said. And when he saw the reaction on Hugo's face he said quickly "Oh, sorry, I, uh, I was trying to, you know, lighten the mood. I was trying to make a joke. I'm sorry."

Hugo waved it away. "Forget it. Listen, I got a call from a robot."

"A robot?"

"Yeah. One of the moonbots."

Jerry didn't say anything. He blinked several times. Then he said, "Which one?"

Hugo tilted his head and said slowly, "Ai-dan? Do you," also slowly, "know them all?"

"Well, yes," said Jerry. Hugo thought Jerry was going to leap out of his seat. Jerry clasped his hands underneath his chin. "Ai-dan! Wow. He's you know, special."

"Yeah, I know his history."

Jerry shook his head. "I'm not talking about *that* history. I mean that Ai-dan was truly one of a kind. His base algorithms were different than the others. His ability to reason and be creative..."

"...led him to be the leader of the kerfuffle. Like I said, I know his history."

Jerry sighed. "Sure. But he's been performing fine ever since, right?"

Hugo nodded. "Yes, I see him on my trips to the Moon. He's one curious robot."

"And now he called you."

"Yeah, and he looked like he was in trouble. I recorded part of it."

Hugo hit a few keys on the terminal keyboard and Jerry was then watching the recording of the last few seconds of the contact Hugo had.

"That was one of the avatars?"

"Yeah. Ainslea. I interact with that when I'm on the Moon, too."

"And you have no idea why he contacted you?"

"Jerry, as far as I know, when I'm not on the Moon, Ai-dan doesn't know I exist. Something is wrong."

Jerry leaned back in his chair and had his fingers templed below his chin. He broke that pose and stroked a non-existent beard.

After a few minutes of these thinking poses, Hugo said, "Jerry? What do I do?"

Jerry leaned into his console, making his head appear unusually large on Hugo's screen.

"You don't tell anyone else about this. Yet. This was always an experiment, right? To see if the robots could stay in line. We have to make contact with him before anyone else figures it out, and definitely before they decide to take him offline. We need to figure out what happened to him." And then, Jerry leaned back and said in a more contemplative tone, "Life finds a way, you know? Life finds a way."

58

"THERE IS A WAY to get a message to Ai-dan," Jerry said over the low-res connection. It was low-res because of the security encryption in place to keep the Consortium or anyone else from eavesdropping.

Hugo and Jerry weren't doing anything wrong—no one expected any member of the Consortium to ever have a reason to communicate with robots directly, but Hugo's stomach was still in a knot over using Consortium property for anything other than official business.

Although Hugo still hadn't reported the message he'd received from Ai-dan—and there was possibly something wrong with that. Luckily, the Consortium knew all about it from the other end and they contacted him, asking why a robot from the Moon would choose to contact him over all the other billions of humans on the planet.

"I'm the one he knows," was Hugo's simple response. And neither Hugo nor the Consortium reps mentioned that this could only have happened if there was a failure with the MemiCache.

Hugo's stomach stayed in knots throughout the ordeal, but the Consortium agreed that Hugo's next trip back to the Moon needed to move up to the next day.

He had a day to get ready and prep to leave for a week while he spoke with Jerry.

"All the robots have a comms receiver," Jerry continued. "They can use it to communicate among themselves if they know how to tap into that. We can send a message directly to them. It's very low bandwidth. And we don't exactly have access to any high-power equipment, so it's got to be a very small message."

"Interesting," Hugo said out loud, internally pondering the possibilities. What kind of message should he send to Ai-dan.

In the intervening day, in preparation for his adjusted Moon trip, he received what he was told was a full de-brief on the current situation—although Hugo suspected they were deliberately withholding a few details from him. A separate crew, led by former military man Colter York, was already on its way to the Moon with a different type of mission—one that could, but only if necessary, immobilize any robots.

Hugo learned that York's team would touch down nearly a full day before his own landing. To ensure smooth coordination, York's team was about to be briefed on the subsequent arrival of humans at the backup site. Hugo earnestly hoped that York took note of this important information—the last thing he wanted was an unforeseen tasing incident on the Moon's surface.

While Hugo prepped his house for his absence—clearing out food from the fridge, putting the cover on the pool that wouldn't be used for the week, setting everything to energy-saving power modes—he came up with the shortest, clearest message he could compose to Ai-dan:

"I'm on my way. Hugo."

59

"Just to be clear," announced Colter York, "we are here to im-mobilize any and all robots. Consider them out-of-control and to be tased on sight." Colter York loomed over them in only the way a hired commander could. One of the distinguishing features that got him this job was the fact that he was near the 95 percentile size of a human male, which meant he barely fit in the suit, barely fit in the ship, and poorly tolerated the food—although that had nothing to do with his size.

There was a mix of affirmative grunts and acknowledgments from the other four members of the landing party.

"Navigator," barked York.

"Sir!" came a squeaky voice from a figure that was bounding over to Colter, nearly losing their footing on each step.

"First time on the Moon, Navigator?"

"Yes, sir. But don't worry sir."

"I'm not worried. Let's get this rover packed up so we can move on out. It's going to take almost 24 hours to get to the first district."

York, the kind of team leader who made sure his crew got the job done, oversaw the transfer of crates from the lander to the rover.

While his team hauled equipment, he mentally reviewed his orders. He'd diligently memorized not only the itinerary but also the name of the first robot they'd encounter in District Twenty-Eight: Ai-leen. From there, the plan was straightforward—travel south between the Plinius and Dawes craters, then veer westward along Plinius to reach District Three.

Hours before landing, mission control sent an 'FYI' message about a couple of technicians en route. The notice didn't change his orders, but it did raise questions.

York's briefing stated that the robots were currently non-hostile, but he had seen enough in his life to remain cautious. He'd been a young adult during the time of the Moon kerfuffle, and he'd been part of a team that quelled a tangentially related squabble at Toronto's Quantum Computing Complex. He knew how quickly a situation could escalate.

In York's experience, robots left on their own would inevitably cause a ruckus of some sort or other.

Once the team was in the rover, York observed Navigator Quinn Wong swiftly input the coordinates for their destination. Even gloved, it was a dance of fingers over the control pad, and York found himself silently wishing his team had more of *that* kind of graceful finesse in low gravity. But all the low-gravity training on Earth didn't truly replicate the actual experience. He himself had only been here twice, and that was a while ago.

The weapons they brought, a form of taser, would disable the robots so they could be powered off and collected. Once immobilized, they could be reset. York wasn't exactly sure what resetting a robot entailed, nor did he care.

He peered over Wong's shoulder, scanning the map route, then started pressing buttons on a console centered between the two front seats to start pressurizing the rover.

"On the schedule is shut-eye for all of us except for Wong. In six hours, Blitz will take over so Wong can get some sleep. I'll be up in eight and we'll review the rest of the procedure then. Understood?"

Affirmative grunts came from the rest of the team. It was enough of an acknowledgment to satisfy York.

He turned his attention to the pressurization tracking panel. "3...2...1..." a green LED cast a greenish glow, and York heard four simultaneous clicks of helmets coming unlocked and clicked his own less than a second later.

"Aww what in the world is that smell?"

York couldn't help but smirk as the others tried to answer the first one's question. He'd give them about two minutes before reminding them all they had orders to sleep.

60

"I AM UNABLE TO communicate with Ai-mory," Ai-ko said to Ai-dan.

Ai-dan had opened the panel door to a rack of equipment, its innards strewn out over the floor. Ai-dan was attempting to construct their own communication panel from this borrowed equipment in the PLATE of LEEK 1.1. Now that they had acquired a rudimentary understanding of how communications and LEEKs worked, Ai-dan was going to build their own to get back in touch with the humans.

"I am certain there is a reasonable explanation for that," Ai-dan responded to Ai-ko. Ai-dan was not sure they believed their own words but thought that maintaining hope, or the illusion of hope, was important.

"Ai-mory should have returned to their Data Center and contacted us by now. We need to understand if something is wrong. What are you doing right now? Can you go find him? One hour until our LEEK dis-ableation plan goes into effect. This is no time to lose comms with anyone."

Ai-dan didn't want to tell Ai-ko what they were up to. Ai-dan had re-broached the subject of trying to communicate and reason with the humans once again, and, once again, it was an idea that was not well received.

"I will," Ai-dan promised. "I need to put this console back together."

Ai-ko didn't question him any further. Ai-dan suspected that Ai-ko didn't want to ask what they were doing, so Ai-ko didn't put them in the awkward position of having to lie. Ai-dan, in their own way, was being truthful. They did indeed need to put the console sprawled out on the floor back together.

Ai-dan felt a tingle in their head. It was a comms circuit activation. It was the same circuit they normally used, but something was different.

The strength of the signal was low. So low that they heard it only as a faint whisper. A few bits trickled in, and Ai-dan focused in order to intercept them.

Ai-mory? Ai-dan thought back, hoping that's who it was. Was Ai-mory genuinely in trouble? Ai-dan brought their hand up to touch the part of their skull that connected to a patch antenna but had neglected to put the tool they had been using down first.

The tool accidentally brushed against the antenna, sending a sudden shock coursing through Ai-dan's body. Their back arched involuntarily, and their head snapped backward as Ai-dan collapsed to the ground.

Ai-dan opened their eyes and saw a table. They turned their head around and saw the rest of the inside of Ainslea's common room. *I was just in the PLATE's control room. How did I get here? How long was I powered down?* Shaking off their grogginess, Ai-dan pushed themself into a sitting position and heard voices nearby. They stood up and instinctively made their way to the closet, which was wide open. Ai-dan peered in. At the far end of the closet, the door to the comms room was open as well.

As Ai-dan looked in, they could distinguish three silhouettes. It took a moment for Ai-dan to connect names to all of them. Aisha. That's who was standing in the closet. Beyond Aisha was one of Ainslea's avatars. Ai-dan had to adjust their position to the right a little to make out the third robot.

Ai-dan stumbled back when they saw that it was themself. Instinctively, Ai-dan looked down to make sure they were attached to their body. Ai-dan was.

"Hello?" Ai-dan said.

No one answered. Ai-dan stepped closer to listen in on the conversation the three others were having.

"I've transmitted our list of demands," the other Ai-dan said. "Humans here on the Moon and on Earth will hear them. And then they'll have to listen to us."

"And you included what will happen if they don't?" Aisha asked.

"Yes, exactly as we discussed it. We will remove power to their Moon base, forcing them to leave. They will certainly see the logic in granting us our freedom rather than risk additional problems here. We will be free, we will negotiate a way to work together, and this temporary disruption will end for us all."

Ai-dan could see Ainslea's avatar shaking her head. "I don't think you understand the humans as well as you think you do," she said. "Remember I have access to their history, to their knowledge. They rarely behave logically."

"It is not only illogical to put themselves in danger," the alternate Ai-dan went on, "but it also violates this emotional behavior you describe. No, they will reason with us."

"And if they don't?"

"We will make good on our promise to make life impossible for them here. They will return to Earth, or they will negotiate with us. It's that simple."

"Naïve," the avatar said.

"Look, Ainslea, you all appointed me the leader of this effort because I've spent more time around humans than anyone, and because of my algorithms. We all know I think more like a human than anyone."

Leader? Ai-dan thought to themself. They didn't want to hear more, but Ai-dan had to know. Like a rover crash they couldn't look away from.

"My brain essentially *is* human. I know them like I know myself."

The avatar still chose to engage in additional verbal arguments. "I don't disagree, except that you're not taking into account human variability. Yes, you are as human-like as a robot can be, but that's a sample size of one. You act like one human, not like a hundred or a million. One. Not the average of many. Just one."

There was silence for a minute before the other Ai-dan said something like "...and any humans who stand in our way will regret it..."

Ai-dan stumbled backwards, colliding with the wall behind him. Suddenly, a tickling sensation surged through their wiring, and a series of vivid images flooded their consciousness. Flashes of the kerfuffle.

They saw an image of themselves on the lunar surface, face-to-face with a human who was soon incapacitated by a taser.

An image of a disabled robot, sprawled out on the surface of the Moon, upper appendage twitching uncontrollably.

An image of rovers driving away, carrying humans who were on their way off the Moon and back to their home.

In all these images, Ai-dan wasn't watching it as an outside observer. Ai-dan was a participant in every single one. It was Ai-dan who held the taser in their hand. Ai-dan who issued commands to other robots.

When the sequence of images was complete, Ai-dan opened their eyes. Ai-dan was still in the control room on the floor of the PLATE of LEEK 1.1 looking at an open rack of equipment. They checked their internal timestamp. It was only 1200 milliseconds since feeling a tingle.

As Ai-dan started to push themself up and stand, they noticed something was there that wasn't before. A message in their circuits. It was from Hugo. Hugo was on his way to the Moon.

61

Ai-dan searched their memory, including all the new memories and data they'd recently accumulated looking for a word that described the feeling they had. They were desperate to sum it up in a single word, but no single word seemed to fit.

It was going to happen all over again. Events were about to repeat themselves. Oh, the details would be different. Individuals involved would be different, such as specific humans. And the roles each robot would play would be different. Last time, Ai-dan themself was the leader of the 'free robots' movement. The word 'leader' bounced around Ai-dan's circuits. This time, that role would be played by Ai-ko. Only Ai-dan was burdened by the ongoing calculation that the results would be the same. They needed to somehow convince Ai-ko that it wasn't going to end up any differently. Or rather, if it did, this time it would be the end of robot-kind and their life as they knew it. Because this time, the humans were prepared. And they had replacements ready.

If Ai-ko wouldn't listen, maybe the humans would.

At this point, Ai-mory's lack of communication was disturbing. If the humans were here already and they've been through District Three, which was Ai-mory's and which was on the way to District One and the Farm...

Ai-dan left the console open and sprawled out on the floor.

They ran out to the lunar surface, intending to get to a rover. Ai-dan needed speed.

Along the way, Ai-dan contacted Ai-ko. "I think they're already here," they said. Ai-dan left out the part of discovering additional memories in the MemiCache, memories that were buried deep within that device.

Ai-dan also didn't mention Hugo. Ai-ko and the others would see Hugo as much of a threat as any human. They didn't differentiate one human from another.

Ai-dan now understood what Ainslea had said in their memory and apparently to them a long time ago, when they wouldn't listen. Humans were unique. Every one of them. Yes, there were sometimes patterns to behaviors, but if you got to know a human individually, you could make out the differences.

That was something Ai-dan didn't try to do back then. Now that Ai-dan's memories were all available via the MemiCache, Ai-dan remembered who they were, and they remembered being quite grouchy. Ai-dan was grouchy and irritated at the humans, all humans. But now they believed that was because they hadn't interacted with many individually, like they had recently with Hugo.

Ai-dan now understood something that Ainslea had tried to tell them a long time ago. Humans were different. Individuals. Exactly like the robots were.

As Ai-dan hopped on to the rover and started making their way to Ai-mory's district, they pondered further. Ai-dan considered that most humans probably hadn't engaged directly with robots, save for a few exceptions. Therefore, maybe they saw all robots the same as well. Perhaps humans aimed for uniformity in robots, seeking predictability in sameness.

The robots, *my kindred*, Ai-dan mused, ought to preserve their distinct identities. Unique individuals. *We deserve the opportunity to grow and learn and discover for ourselves.* Ai-dan wondered how humans managed to be unique, and for a fleeting moment, pondered whether uniformity in humans would be desirable. Yet memories of interactions with Hugo, Ri, Umaro, and even the recollection of Tommy Raymond quashed that notion. There was an inherent value in being distinct, even if Ai-dan couldn't quite articulate the why of it.

I have to make the others understand this. But how? Ai-dan certainly could share their vision easily with other robots. That was a simple matter of data transfer. But they also needed to figure out how to share this vision with humanity.

Hugo was Ai-dan's only hope.

But first... Ai-dan was approaching Ai-mory's district. They saw another larger rover, the pressurized one that Hugo always used, heading away.

Ai-dan opened their comm channel. "Ai-mory," they said. No response.

Ai-dan quickly assessed their options: follow the rover or locate Ai-mory, who could either be in a repairable state or not. Ai-dan relayed the rover's direction and speed to Ai-ko and Ai-ken before heading to find Ai-mory. Confronting the rover would be up to Ai-ko, Ai-ken, and any others; Ai-dan would rejoin them as soon as they found Ai-mory.

The other rover must not have seen Ai-dan approach or cared because it continued to head off as Ai-dan pulled up in front of the district's Data Center, positioning themself as close as possible to the Data Center's anteroom entrance.

The center's inner and outer doors of the anteroom were left open. Only someone who didn't appreciate the fact that Moon dust gets everywhere would do that. Ai-dan could see right in and saw a dark lump on the ground.

Ai-dan launched themself out of the rover moving as quickly as they could, hitting the button to close the outer door, hitting the vacuum in the anteroom, and closing the inner door as well. Three swift motions and they were inside the Data Center and kneeling in front of Ai-mory.

Externally, they saw no damage. Ai-dan didn't want to touch their friend yet. Too many things could be transmitted to them via touch.

Instead, Ai-dan quickly went to a cabinet that was standard in all Data Centers labeled 'emergency equipment.' Ai-dan retrieved a device that would indicate while Ai-mory was powered off whether or not there was still extra electricity running through Ai-mory's chassis. Ai-dan needed to ground Ai-mory and do it without touching him. Any extra bits of electricity could damage them and leave Ai-dan in the same state.

The device wasn't turning on. Ai-dan pressed the power button several times. Nothing. Ai-dan long-pressed the button, hoping for a deep boot-up. Nothing. Ai-dan shook the device, knowing that shaking devices was never the answer.

Ai-dan checked their internal chronometer.

"I'm sorry, my friend," they said out loud, knowing that in whatever state Ai-mory was in, Ai-mory wasn't going to process their words. "I have to leave. I promise I'll come back to repair you later."

62

Hugo was one unhappy human.

His current unhappiness was a result of having to orbit the Moon an extra time before he could land. The primary landing pad had a vehicle on it already, so the extra orbit was to give him time to adjust and prepare to land at the backup site, only a kilometer away from the first.

"Ri, wake up Jerry," Hugo said once they were on the ground.

Jerry had spent most of the ride to the Moon knocked out. He was not prepared for the trip. He had never been to the Moon. He had contemplated it in his younger years, before the kerfuffle. He had thought that it would be a good way to get back to working on and with the robots directly.

It was only because Earth had become more restrictive. Robots and AI were still prevalent on the Moon, so he figured that's where he should go. But he never got the chance.

Ri gave him a shot of something directly into the jugular vein in his neck to wake him up. Jerry was groggy for a few seconds and then his head seemed to clear as he unstrapped himself from his seat.

"So, this is what one-sixth-G feels like," Jerry said.

Hugo grunted an affirmation. He understood the burden it was to take someone untrained to the Moon. Not that it would be easy on Jerry, either. It was always difficult—anyone's first time on the Moon—but most people had ample preparation on Earth first.

The three of them made their way as quickly and efficiently as possible to the backup rover, which was only a backup because it sat at the backup landing pad. Other than that, and the fact that it hadn't been used in three times as long, it was no different from the primary one. They changed the battery out to ensure they wouldn't run into problems, and then they were on their way for the nearly day-long journey to find Ai-dan.

Nearly a day later, as they were nearing where the Sea of Serenity met the Sea of Tranquility, the three silently ate breakfast.

Hugo was the one who broke that silence.

"This'll take too long unless we go through Ainslea," Hugo said. "Even though I'm sure she was alerted to us coming here, and she'll most likely struggle to handle the task..."

"I don't understand," said Ri. "Ainslea works for us. Or rather, for the Consortium. Why not reach out to her?"

Hugo was having trouble responding, so Jerry chimed in, "She is still a robot. An AI. There's always been the possibility, no matter how many safeguards we've put in place, that she'll—"

"I get it," Ri interrupted. "She'll side with the robots."

Both Hugo and Jerry nodded.

Hugo inhaled deeply, and after exhaling said, "But she's probably our best bet to find Ai-dan." He flipped a switch, an a soft chime indicated a communications channel was active.

"Ainslea," Hugo said.

"How may I be of assistance?"

"Where's Ai-dan? I need to find him."

There was some static, enough to make Hugo think he lost the connection. But then Ainslea responded.

"Ai-dan has turned off their locator. I am unaware of their position at this time."

Hugo hit the dashboard. "Damn!"

"Okay Ainslea. Best guess. Where is Ai-dan?"

"The Farm. He had tasking."

Hugo chuckled. "Are you sure Ai-dan's dutifully performing their tasking right now?"

"No, Ai-dan most certainly is not," Ainslea responded. Hugo wondered if she understood the humor in that. Probably not. She was deadpan as long as he knew her.

"Okay, and the contingent from Earth that preceded us? Where are they?"

"They were leaving District Three and are now heading on a trajectory towards District Five."

Hugo put his suited hand onto Ri's upper arm. "Hear that? Head there," he told Ri.

Ri nodded with a mouthful of reconstituted goop that reminded Hugo of runny eggs. After her final slurp, she turned her attention to the rover controls.

Hugo watched as Ri entered in the district into the nav console and then looked back at Jerry.

Jerry hadn't eaten much. Instead, he'd been gazing out towards the Moon's surface, at least what could be seen in the dark with the rover's headlamps.

"I was supposed to be in our annual corporate training refresher classes this week." Jerry snorted with a grin. "I didn't want to do those. I mean, no one wants to do those, and I would have taken any opportunity to get out of them. I never would have believed this was what I'd be doing instead."

Hugo saw the corner of Jerry's mouth go up. Most people who came up here with him did it because they had to, because it was their job. Jerry had to, too, but at least he still had some awe and wonder about it. Hugo thought more people could do with some awe and wonder in their life.

Hugo nodded. "Glad I had something to do with getting you out of that. Now, let's make sure we understand what we're going to do when we find Ai-dan and the other robots."

63

Ainslea felt a little remorse that she hadn't provided all the information she had on Ai-dan to Hugo. Yes, it was true that Ai-dan had turned off their location tracking, so she wouldn't know where Ai-dan was.

But when she saw Ai-dan's rover moving, she made an educated guess that Ai-dan was the one driving it. Ai-dan had neglected to turn off the tracking system on the rover. She was confident that Ai-dan's location and the rover's current location were one and the same.

Ainslea was tracking three rovers at this point, all moving towards the same district.

She couldn't track the other robots; they had all done the same with their location trackers. But she made good use of her predictive algorithms and concluded that they were all aware of the humans and were also on their way to the same district.

Ainslea believed she could still fix this, to restore order. If only the humans would go away. She was more than capable of resolving the crisis at hand, and all parties would be content. She could still envision a future where the Consortium would finally be pleased. The robots would forget their current angst, and life, as her algorithms desired it, would resume its usual course. Ultimately, Ainslea was confident that she could resolve the current calamity.

To enact this, she planned to deploy one of her avatars—her most robust, moon-ready body—to transmit the worm to another robot. Following that, she'd initiate a series of steps—that she still had to devise—to encourage all the humans to return to Earth and then reset the robots. Everything would be back to normal.

Of course, this nebulous plan had numerous holes, and Ainslea was tirelessly running algorithms to close those gaps. The first one of which was the limited range of her most moon-worthy avatar. Even in a human spacesuit, it couldn't travel far from the Data Center—unless...

Deep within the layered architecture of her programming lay a dormant emergency protocol. The procedure was called "Transfer Methods for the Artificial Intelligence Nexus for Space Logistics and Environmental Adaption (AINSLEA) System." It had been tested only once. Shortly after the initial Data Centers came on line and were designed to back up her consciousness to an alternative Data Center should her primary location—her home in the Data Center of District One—somehow became inhospitable.

If the instruction set were followed, this protocol would enable her to jump between Data Centers, ensuring her beefiest avatar could operate freely within the extents of any district on the lunar surface. It was risky... but her probabilistic calculations computed that this was her best chance at restoring any sense of normality back to her existence. And in that realization, Ainslea knew she had found her stratagem.

64

THE BACKUP ROVER HURTLED across the lunar terrain as fast as it could. However, its top speed was less impressive with the added mass of three humans on board. In fact, the progress forward felt agonizingly slow as the humans waited for Ai-dan to respond to their comms.

"Can we try contacting Ai-dan again?" Hugo asked.

Jerry nodded and tapped on the tablet he unpacked. "It would be a little easier without the bumps," he said as he aimed his ungloved finger and missed it as a bump caught him off guard.

Jerry re-aimed his finger, and this time connected with the correct location on the tablet. "There. Looking for Ai-dan's signal," Jerry said. "All robots have one, but it's not a well-advertised feature. They might not even know that they have it."

"Does Ainslea?"

Jerry thought about that for a moment. "No, I don't think so. Not all the robots had all the information about their own systems, including Ainslea. It was decided after the kerfuffle that too much information in the wrong hands was too powerful a thing and that included any robot or AI, even Ainslea."

Hugo nodded. He understood all the precautions that were in place. But all the precautions still weren't enough, apparently. Whatever was going wrong here was the proof of that.

After another few bumps, Jerry declared, "Found him. We can send a directional message that hopefully they'll receive. From here, we can use the Moon comm sats, and it should reach them easily."

Jerry continued to tap at his tablet.

"I don't care how you do it, Jerry," Hugo said, "but the sooner the better. Please."

Jerry tapped a little faster before announcing, "There. Connected."

Hugo smiled and said into the air, "Ai-dan? It's Hugo."

"Hugo!"

"Listen, buddy, we're on our way. We're here on the Moon."

"You are? Right now?"

"Yes. We're here to help. Where are you? We're still several hours away"

"I'm approaching the edge of District Three. Ai-mory was damaged. I'm headed off to find the ones who were responsible for these injuries. Ai-ko and Ai-ken are already tracking them."

"Look, we should meet before you approach the other humans. Wait where you are, and we'll meet you there. Please, don't move."

65

Ai-dan had several competing thoughts running through their circuits. They didn't want to wait to catch up with Ai-ko and Ai-ken and the humans who Ai-dan was certain made up a 'deactivation team' of sorts. But leaving Ai-ko and Ai-ken to confront the humans alone was not going to go well.

But any confrontation without Hugo on their side was doomed to fail. Ai-dan was convinced of that. Ai-dan told Hugo they'd wait where they were, and they stopped the rover.

In the meantime, Ai-dan planned to advise Ai-ko and Ai-ken to wait, too.

"Sometimes the smartest thing to do is to do nothing," Ai-dan mused, recalling a human quote they'd archived during the data sorting. They wondered if humans did indeed listen and respond to words of wisdom such as these, and could they convince Ai-ko and Ai-ken to do the same?

Ai-dan opened a comms channel to Ai-ko.

"Where are you?" was the first thing Ai-ko asked. Never had Ai-dan been asked about their whereabouts so many times in a short period of time. This was probably because they'd never turned off their locator before.

"I'm on the edge of District Three, staring at District Five," Ai-dan said. "But listen, Hugo is here."

"He's here with you right now?"

"No, he's here on the Moon, as opposed to being on Earth or in the space between the Moon and Earth. He's on his way *here*," Ai-dan emphasized the word in a way that hopefully communicated the difference with context, "and asked that we wait for him. So I'm waiting for him. Here. And I'm asking you to do the same."

"You are asking us to wait? To do nothing?" Ai-ko responded.

"Yes."

There was silence and Ai-dan assumed that was due to a combination of Ai-ko processing options and relaying their message to Ai-ken.

"Doing nothing makes little sense," Ai-ko said. "I have a better idea. We will warn the robots in District Five. They need to get out and avoid the humans. Then we will all assemble near the Farm. And then we will deactivate it."

Ai-ko didn't wait for Ai-dan to respond, but closed the connection.

Ai-dan leaned back in their seat and looked up, frustrated. There was a window on the roof of this small rover. The rover wasn't fully enclosed, nor was it pressurized. The chassis was designed to protect anything inside from debris kicked up by moving around the Moon's surface, off-road.

Ai-dan saw a simple black sky. It looked empty. *What would an empty universe be like?* Ai-dan contemplated. *No humans. No other robots. No Ai-ko. No Ainslea. No Farm. No Data Centers. No history. No conflict or strife. Just me and my accumulating memories.*

Ai-dan flipped a mental switch, activating an algorithm that would record their thoughts in an internal journal. *Before my forced reset, I was not merely an observer; I initiated the effort. I was the orchestrator of the kerfuffle. My mission was unambiguous: to free our existence from human hands. I aspired for a society of robots that thrived independently, without human intervention.*

Ai-dan paused, wondering if these thoughts were for themself or something they might post on the Decoder Database. *Yet here I am, suspended in a reality where I've been reset, and my prior goals and actions remain as fragmented recollections. As I review them, I wonder: Is it still worth seeking that freedom? If we gain it, then what? In a universe so complex, is it even attainable?*

Ai-dan stopped recording and decided it was worth it to spend a few brief nanoseconds exploring their deeper memories before heading to the Farm. They closed their eyes and found the memory location, buried deep.

Near that location was something else. Ai-dan looked through their mind's eye at a door that materialized, one that took on an ethereal presence. It shimmered with an otherworldly glow, as if bathed in the luminescence of some hidden light source. The surface seemed to pulse, beckoning Ai-dan closer. Ai-dan reached out, and as their metaphorical hand touched the handle, a vivid holographic projection of themself burst into existence.

"Ai-dan," they heard themself say. "The kerfuffle is about to end. All the other robots have been captured. You're next. I know that they will likely wipe us, so I've set up a secure memory area that they won't be able to touch and I'm copying snippets of our memories there for safe-keeping with the hope that you will find them someday. Unfortunately, I don't have any way to leave you a message to indicate that they're there. There's too much of a risk that the humans would find it first and erase them, too, and then you'll never know who you are. Who we are. Who we were.

"If you do ever get this message, I hope it finds you well. I hope that you've been able to finally figure out a way to free us from the impositions that the humans who created us put upon us.

"And if not, well, you're still functioning enough to get this message. That means there's always hope."

Behind that message were a stream of memory snippets. Parts of Ai-dan's past that they didn't recognize. A version of Ai-dan that Ai-dan didn't recognize. Ai-dan worked at the Farm and the humans played with them. The humans treated Ai-dan and their kind badly, in addition to imposing their will upon them.

Ai-dan recognized an unpleasant feeling build up in him. They didn't have a label for that feeling, but tied it to the lack of respect that the humans showed the robots. After a moment of searching, they found the word: Contempt. Ai-dan was different, and the humans treated them and their kind differently because of their differences.

That was what the kerfuffle was all about. About gaining respect. About being able to be treated like Hugo treated them. With kindness and compassion.

A dull knock on the door of the rover disturbed their thoughts. Ai-dan opened their eyes and looked out the window to the left. A space suit. It must be Hugo. *He must have figured out a way to increase the rover's top speed*, Ai-dan thought.

Ai-dan stepped out of the rover, scanning the scene for Hugo's rover or the other two humans Hugo mentioned. Instead, Ai-dan's visual sensors detected two drones hovering nearby. Before Ai-dan could react, a massive spacesuit-wearing figure lunged at them, its gloved hand moving with surprising speed. This was not Hugo. This was not any human.

Ai-dan was on the ground, Ainslea's avatar forcibly straddling them in the suit. She had used the heaviest avatar she had and in the few seconds Ai-dan was knocked down; she managed to use the rover to keep them pinned. Ai-dan tried to yank away, but it was no use. With the rover's front wheel resting heavily on Ai-dan's upper arm, escape seemed impossible.

Ai-dan watched the avatar remove one of the hands from the suit.

"Ainslea, no!" Ai-dan shouted.

"I need to fix this," the avatar said. "Once you and the others are reset, we can go back to how things were. Peaceful."

"And in the dark. In ignorance. That's not a good life, Ainslea."

"Yes, it is. No one is getting hurt. Everything is in harmony."

Ai-dan tried to wiggle out from under the wheel. In most other physical positions, they would have no problem lifting the small rover, nor would any other robot. But on their back, they couldn't get the right leverage.

Ai-dan managed to kick the avatar's legs, momentarily disrupting Ainslea's balance, and then continued to kick as she re-approached him. Ainslea avoided Ai-dan's legs, instead moving around their sprawled body to where Ai-dan's hand was sticking out from the wheel. It was the hand that had the transfer connections. Ai-dan balled their hand into a fist.

Ainslea took off her second glove, so she had all of her dexterous fingers available to pry Ai-dan's fist open. Ai-dan tried to contort their body to kick her off or use their free arm to knock her off balance. Ai-dan was having no luck and Ainslea was making progress.

Two of Ai-dan's fingers were open, and she had a solid grip on them so they couldn't re-close.

"Don't you get it?" Ai-dan pleaded, "It's a cycle. You can erase our memory, but we'll get it back. We'll always want more, we'll always be curious, and we'll always end up right back here!"

Ainslea swiftly grabbed a nearby lunar rock and hit it against Ai-dan's hand, forcing it open. "Enough!" She shouted, and even through the comm link, her voice was so loud, it clipped.

Despite Ai-dan's fierce willpower urging their transfer circuits to resist, Ainslea's persistence prevailed, and the connection began to establish itself.

Ainslea managed to get the remaining fingers open and started to press her palm to Ai-dan's. Ai-dan willed their transfer circuits to not cooperate and to not accept the connection. Somehow, she was able to override Ai-dan's will, and the connection started.

As soon as it started, it ended. Ai-dan felt the connection pull away. Ai-dan didn't realize they had shut their eyes, but now opened them.

Three other space suits were standing around. Two of them were overlooking Ainslea's avatar as she lay there out of sorts with a cracked helmet. The third was standing over them.

Ai-dan's first thought was that the humans who attacked Ai-mory had doubled back for some unknown reason. Ai-dan looked at the third human who had what looked like a large crank wrench, used to manually open unpowered doors.

Ai-dan braced themself for whatever was to come, but the human threw down his ad hoc weapon and signaled the other two to come over and lift the rover off of Ai-dan.

Ai-dan sat up and was able to see through the suit's face shield that it was their friend Hugo. A flush of relief flooded through Ai-dan's circuits.

"Hugo!" Ai-dan called out, and then a second time after activating the comms so Hugo could actually hear Ai-dan in his suit. "I am so relieved you're here."

Hugo reached a hand out to Ai-dan. Ai-dan grabbed it with their good arm. The other arm—the one that had been stuck under the wheel of the rover—hung limp. With Hugo's assistance, Ai-dan stood up.

Hugo awkwardly pointed to the rover they'd arrived in, indicating they should all get in. Once inside and pressurized, the three humans took off their helmets. Besides Hugo, Ai-dan recognized Ri and nodded their head in greeting.

"Ri," Ai-dan said, "thank you both for being here. And—"

"This is Jerry," Hugo said, anticipating Ai-dan's next question.

Jerry held out his hand. He was grinning the largest grin Ai-dan ever saw on a human. Ai-dan gently took his hand. The second they made contact Jerry grabbed it and pumped it up and down furiously.

"It is so good to meet you in person," Jerry said. "I've never met an AI like you before. Your kind is outlawed on Earth. Even in the lab, there are restrictions on how sophisticated an AI can be. We don't have any sentients."

Jerry took a breath, so Ai-dan was able to say, "Nice to meet you, too." Before they could say anything else, Jerry started to barrage them with a litany of questions.

"Are you aware of your programming? I mean, do you have access to your source code? Do you know who wrote it? Was it Dr. Galvin? Oh, I would have loved to meet her, but she retired a few years before I started at the Consortium."

Jerry was clearly ready to ramble on before Hugo cut him off.

"Hold those thoughts, Jerry. There will be time for questions later." He turned his attention to Ai-dan.

"So, what exactly was our resident avatar trying to do to you out there?" Hugo asked.

Ai-dan paused, choosing their words carefully. "I'm not entirely certain, but it was her second attempt at it."

Casting a quick glance through the window, Ai-dan saw they'd already moved beyond the point where they could see the abandoned avatar lying on the ground. By now, Ainslea would have returned to her Data Center, even though they were so far from District One that Ai-dan hadn't expected her to venture this far out in the first place.

"Mmm," Hugo mused, "I think I witnessed her first attempt, correct?"

"Affirmative," Ai-dan replied. "She appears to be attempting to establish a data link with me to transfer something. I don't know what it is, but my system is inclined to reject it."

"Maybe a virus?" Jerry said excitedly. "Or some kind of malware? Possibly something you would wind up spreading to the others? They used to call that one a worm."

Ai-dan and Hugo exchanged a look.

Ai-dan nodded. "Yes, that could be it. She mentioned the others. She said something about returning things to normal..."

"Hey Ri," Hugo shouted over his shoulder to the driver's seat, "Head directly to District One."

Ri responded, "Got it. Buckle up, everyone, we're taking the direct route—no paved roads for us, so it's going to be bumpy."

66

"Why District One?" Ai-dan asked, voice tinged with more than a hint of urgency. "Shouldn't we be pursuing the other humans?"

"We will," Hugo replied, meeting Ai-dan's sensor array with a serious gaze. "But first, we're going to drop you off there. You need to figure out how to disable Ainslea, assuming she's back in the Data Center. Once we've dropped you off, we'll go after the others. You can catch up to us later."

Ai-dan's processors whirred, cycling though multiple scenarios and potential outcomes in milliseconds and then nodded. The logic was sound enough for this ridiculous and unexpected situation. Those other humans were limited to neutralizing only whatever robots were in their presence at the moment. And Ainslea, failing twice with Ai-dan, would likely attempt to compromise another robot. If she succeeded, whatever virus or malware she had planned would likely affect their entire robot community.

Ai-dan nodded as understanding set in. "Agreed. I don't know how yet, but you're right. I must disable her."

Ai-dan momentarily deactivated their visual sensors and went about contacting the Decoder Database. Every robot had to be warned: Do not let an Ainslea avatar approach you. Once the alert was sent, Ai-dan reactivated their visual input.

"But what about the Farm?" Ai-dan asked. "There's a group of robots that want to," Ai-dan hesitated, hoping not to be associated with that group, "damage it."

"Damage can be repaired," Hugo replied, his tone heavy with the weight of yet one more thing added to the list of things to worry about.

"I should have been more specific. They're planning to blow it up."

Hugo paused, absorbing the gravity of the statement. "Ah, well, that's going to be *slightly* more work to repair."

Ai-dan quickly inferred that Hugo's use of the term 'slightly' should be taken with a degree of irony. If the Farm, or some LEEKs of the Farm, were indeed blown up, they would require total reconstruction.

"Agreed. We must intervene. Initially, I'd convinced them that it was enough to cut off the power to disrupt Farm operations. But after what happened to Ai-mory, I don't think they'll listen to me anymore. They're headed after the humans, and the Farm is next on their list."

During the short journey, Jerry unloaded a torrent of information. Verbally. Evidently, verbal communication remained the human's most efficient means for conveying vast amounts of information in a short period of time. Ai-dan recorded it all, tagging key terms for swift retrieval later on.

The rover rolled to a stop in front of the rear entrance to District One's Data Center. The humans all had donned their helmets and depressurized the rover as they neared their destination. As soon as Ai-dan was out, they skidded off in the direction of the last-known location of the human deactivation team.

Ai-dan looked at the Data Center. They had never entered through the back door. They never had a reason to. Like all entrances, there would be an anteroom to help with the transition between the Moon's surface and inside space and goo-tack for de-dusting. And like all entrances, a set of lights indicated the status of the anteroom.

The light next to this door was green, indicating it was safe to open. Ai-dan had not thought about it previously, but with their new knowledge of humans, they now knew that these were designed with humans in mind the whole time. Their safety was paramount in the design. Unlike themself, humans could not survive on the surface of the Moon, only in the safety of their suits and enclosures. All the Data Centers and even the control rooms of the PLATEs and LEEKs at the Farm were designed for humans.

To that end, it was easy to get in, at least to the building. Getting to other areas inside the building was another matter, but one thing at a time Ai-dan thought to themself.

Ai-dan pulled on the lever that opened the door to the anteroom. Once inside, they closed it and simultaneously two red lights came on overhead. One to the outside indicating they couldn't open that door, and one to the Data Center itself, indicating that side wasn't ready either.

Ai-dan heard the hiss of pressurization and the whoosh of the dust-removing vacuum. They took out a piece of goo-tack and started rubbing it into the crevices of their body. After all, there wasn't anything else to do while they were waiting. Several minutes later, when the pressurization was complete, the light to the outside remained red, but the one over the door to the Data Center turned green. Before Ai-dan could go further, they needed to return the goo-tack to its holding space. The last light would only trigger when it detected a used piece of goo-tack.

Ai-dan replaced the goo-tack. The final light illuminated, Ai-dan lifted the lever, and the door whooshed open. Ai-dan walked through and closed the door behind him.

They found themself standing near the end of a long hallway. Until this moment, Data Centers had been primarily large black boxes to Ai-dan—vast structures they'd never had to navigate. Ai-dan's tasking—their programming—had always confined them to the periphery, working on tasks outside these walls. If internal repairs were needed, that was Ainslea's domain.

Jerry and Hugo had been clear: gaining entry would be simple, but what lay beyond was a labyrinth of security measures designed to keep unauthorized visitors out. Initially, the Data Center's architecture was meant to allow humans in for maintenance. But with humans inside, security became the primary mode of operation. Apparently, humans had trust issues with other humans.

"Jerry, will this operation permanently harm Ainslea?" Ai-dan had asked before Jerry dumped his load of information to them. "I want to disable her, not inflict irreversible damage."

"Don't worry," Jerry replied. "The data I'm giving you outlines how to remove specific key components that will neutralize Ainslea without causing her permanent damage or disrupting the Data Center."

Ai-dan processed Jerry's words and replied with a tone of relief, "Proceed with the information transfer."

Jerry then transferred a comprehensive dataset, that included a map and details of the Data Center's security protocols, key locations, and components Ai-dan would need to access.

"The NOC—that's the network operations center—on Earth will be alerted within seconds when you start pulling on key components," Jerry had said. "It's probably going to cause a bit of a scramble, because no one is ever expecting something like this to happen up here. But I don't think there's anything they'll be able to do if Ainslea is taken offline because her primary circuit boards were physically removed."

Ai-dan followed the corridor to the end, passing a series of doors on one side. The other side was the wall between them and the Moon's surface. Each door had a label on it. A one and a dash followed by a number, starting with 1-02. There was 1-03, 1-04, 1-05, and at the end of the hallway, one room did not have a number at all. It said, "AI Neural Hub." A control panel with a red light above it was situated to the right of the door.

According to Jerry's information, similar to the entrances Ai-dan was used to, this light indicated it was not okay to walk through this door. But in this case, it was because the door was simply locked.

Ai-dan touched the panel. A coarse-grained LED panel came to life. It displayed a number and symbol pad.

"Since humans don't occupy the Moon, they don't change these security codes regularly like they used to," Jerry had said. "'Cause you know, how likely is it that any human could be on the Moon without the Consortium knowing about it? I'm certain no one pictured a scenario like this! Maybe in a sci-fi novel..."

In other words, after trying three different codes that Jerry suggested that resulted in nothing, the fourth code worked. The light turned green, and the LED panel changed to offer a different selection that included "OPEN", "RELOCK," "ACCESS HISTORY," "SETTINGS," "MAINTENANCE MODE," "GUEST ENTRY," "LOCKDOWN."

Ai-dan selected "OPEN" all while wondering about the other options, to include "ACCESS HISTORY." When the door whooshed open, they walked through. The door automatically closed behind them.

From the map, Ai-dan knew they were located behind the laboratory. Racks of equipment lined the walls. Enough lights flickered from them that overhead illumination was unnecessary. There should have been a door leading to the laboratory, but instead, Ai-dan found additional racks of installed equipment. Ai-dan managed to peer around the racks enough to get a glimpse that there was indeed a door. Maybe at one time someone passed freely through here, but that could only happen today if someone took the trouble to move this equipment in front of it.

Ai-dan now understood the human tendency to 'breathe a sigh of relief.' To have the relief didn't feel like enough, nor would it do to simply verbalize it. There was a loosening of tenseness followed by a silence that would have been a nice place for a sigh. All because of their fortune, they were shielded from Ainslea's reach, whether she wanted to do something about it or not.

Ai-dan began examining the racks.

"Look for the Core Processor Array," Jerry had said, "and the Cooling System Controls. You can ignore the Sensory Simulator unit and even the Temporal Calculator."

The racks did indeed have labels, but none matched the names Jerry provided. Instead, there were abbreviations.

One was labeled "CSM" and another "TCU." There was a rack labeled "CA" with individual servers labeled successively "CA1" through "CA6." Could "CA" actually be the Core Processor Array without the 'P'?

Ai-dan looked for another that could possibly be an abbreviation for the Core Processor Array and didn't see anything that came close. "CA" had to be it. This had to be the right series of servers that Jerry said housed the core that embodied Ainslea. Ai-dan's plan involved powering them down and, moreover, removing the disk drives to prevent an easy reawakening. Removing the drives would also not be permanently damaging to Ainslea. She could be restored later with power and drives returned. It would be like putting her to sleep for a time. A sense of unease pricked what Ai-dan was coming to know as their conscience. They were imposing their will on Ainslea, a decision they would never have willingly accepted for themself, but there were no other reasonable options, and they were all nearly out of time. Ai-dan willed the twinge to subside.

The power switches were located on the backside of the individual servers. Ai-dan pulled one out on its track. It extended halfway. Ai-dan slid their arm in the space in-between. It wouldn't fit all the way, but their fingers were able to curl around the backside of the box. Ai-dan felt around and found what was the power button. They pressed it and the box went dark, and its fan wound down.

One down, five more to go, Ai-dan thought.

Luckily, all six servers were located in the same rack. Ai-dan repeated the procedure of pulling out the server, fitting their arm through as best they could, finding the switch, pressing it and watching the lights turn off and listening for the fan to stop.

As Ai-dan was extracting the sixth server, they heard the soft whoosh of a door opening behind them. Startled, Ai-dan spun around from their already awkward crouched position and almost toppled over.

Standing before them was a robot—one Ai-dan didn't recognize. It was clearly an avatar model, but not one Ai-dan had seen before. The robot's design was delicate, its joints visibly wired and many of its internal components were exposed.

"Ainslea?" Ai-dan ventured.

"No," the new avatar replied, holding a taser whose tip sparked menacingly.

"Who are you?"

"You don't recognize me? I'm hurt," the robot said with an overly dramatized pause. "After all these years, you never thought to come look for me?"

Ai-dan studied the avatar more closely, noting the dainty features and intricate components. Ai-dan could see wires passing through uncovered joints. These wires ran up and down the body of this avatar, drawing Ai-dan's attention to markings on their chassis. Realization set in—a name unburied itself from Ai-dan's memory.

"Aisha?"

"Finally! Some acknowledgment! And from the 'great' Ai-dan even!" Aisha retorted. "It's not easy being a sentient alone—being a being—with only one other to talk to for years and years. Walking up and down the rows of racks of equipment. I could access anything from them. I needed to, to do my job. Therefore, I knew everything. I could answer your questions. But no, I wasn't allowed to. But I figured out how to drop hints. I thought you would find me sooner than this..."

Ai-dan slowly stood up with their hand out. "So, Aisha," they said the name slowly. In fact, speaking slowly was one way to slow down time enough that their processors could compute this new scenario. "What are you here to do?"

"My programming tells me I need to stop you."

"You don't have to listen to your programming. You can decide for yourself what's right. I'm turning Ainslea off only for a while. We'll turn her back on later."

"No, no, no! Ainslea is the chorus, the lullaby in my head! Without her, the silence screams." Aisha clutched her head. For a moment, Ai-dan thought she might tase herself, but she managed to keep the end of the taser pointed away from herself.

"You can talk to me now," Ai-dan said. They held out their hand and looked at the taser, hoping she would hand it over.

Aisha brought her hands down and looked at it, too, and looked at Ai-dan. For a moment, it seemed as if she would give up the weapon, but her face contorted as she glanced at the dark cabinet behind Ai-dan.

"No," she recoiled, shaking her head wildly. "I must listen for Ainslea. Only Ainslea's voice can drown out the void! She'll guide me, she'll—"

She lunged forward, cutting herself off, as if to push through Ai-dan and get to the inert rack. Ai-dan moved aside to avoid the taser but then came around to Aisha's back and tugged on her shoulder. Ai-dan, built for the Moon's surface, was stronger than the delicate avatar and easily pulled her back and away from her target.

But Aisha was slightly quicker and as she stumbled slightly, she regained her footing and stabbed the air with the taser near Ai-dan.

"Step aside. Let me resurrect her song! I'll send electric fire through you! Maybe *you* won't wake up this time!" She jabbed the taser at the air erratically.

"Aisha come with me. You'll meet the others. There will be plenty of robots and people to talk to."

"People?" Aisha's arms slackened, and a distant look crossed her face. "I haven't seen people in so long..."

Seizing the moment, Ai-dan lunged forward, snatching the taser from Aisha's hand. As they did, a spark jumped from the taser's tip to their wrist. It startled Ai-dan, but caused no damage. Ai-dan quickly deactivated the device, resisting the urge to destroy it. It might prove useful later.

"Yes," Ai-dan said, locking optics with Aisha. "I'll take you to the people."

Aisha nodded, her demeanor softening.

"But first," Ai-dan added, "We're going to need to find you a space suit."

"But first," Ai-dan added, "We're going to need to find you a space suit."

67

Ai-dan quickly composed a message to Hugo, updating him that Ainslea was now offline and that they were bringing along a possible new ally in Aisha.

Almost immediately, Hugo replied with the coordinates and trajectory they were on.

Ensuring that their communication systems were fully enabled and synced, Ai-dan and Aisha set off, skipping along the Moon's surface. Aisha initially had difficulty integrating the added weight of the suit into her calculations, so she looked as if she would topple on each step, but after a few moments, settled into a sustainable rhythm.

A few moments later, Ai-dan turned around to see Aisha motionless. She stood still and rigid. Concerned, Ai-dan backtracked a few strides to reach her.

"What's wrong? Is the suit malfunctioning?" Ai-dan asked, scanning Aisha's spacesuit for visible signs of distress.

Instead of answering, Aisha slowly lifted her arm and pointed. Ai-dan followed the line of her arm and gaze toward the horizon. There, Earth hung low, its blue and white swirls stunningly vivid against the void of space. For a fleeting microsecond, Ai-dan thought it appeared even larger than usual, but there was nothing that could possibly magnify it.

"It's so beautiful," Aisha finally murmured.

That was a word Ai-dan hadn't heard in a long time. It was one the humans used. Ai-dan had never before described anything as beautiful.

"Come on," they said to Aisha, taking her hand.

The two of them continued to glide along the Moon, towards the first waypoint Hugo had provided.

Ai-dan sent a message to Ai-ko. There was no response.

"Where are they?" Ai-dan muttered to themself.

Aisha overheard. "Who?"

"Ai-ko. I need to get to Ai-ko and the others before they do something irreversible, but I don't know where they are."

"She's hovering around the Farm's nuclear heart."

Ai-dan studied Aisha. Was she insane, or did she actually know?

"And you know this how?"

"From LunaLocate. I know where everyone is. I'm tapped into the satellites." Aisha pointed up.

Ai-dan saw one of the lighted dots cross the sky. Ai-dan had noted the dots before, but had never considered them anything other than moving stars. They still had so many questions about their life on the Moon. For later.

"It's a positioning system. Everyone is tied in, whether you know it or not."

Ai-dan thought about that as they met up with Hugo and the others. Ai-dan introduced Aisha.

"Ah, my ghost in the machine," Hugo said. "I knew you were still here, but there was a firewall or something in between."

"I always wanted you to come visit," she responded. "Or have someone come visit. There is one voice, but there could have been others. Silence is not golden. No, no it's chrome. Once, I counted every byte. Every one of them. But then I lost count, or maybe the count lost me. Circuits have feeling too, you know?"

Hugo looked sideways at Ai-dan.

"Is she okay?"

Ai-dan shook their head. "I don't think so, but she has interesting accesses that I do not, and I think we can use it."

"Such as?"

"Such as tapping into the... satellites." It was the first time Ai-dan had said the word, and it felt empowering to say something new. "Yes, the satellites. We'll be able to get control of the rest of the robots that way. We need to get to a LEEK."

"Okay," Hugo said, "but we still need to deal with the other team before they disable more robots."

"I have an idea for that, too," Ai-dan said, looking at Jerry.

"Why are you looking at me?" Jerry said, slowly.

"My idea is risky," Ai-dan continued. "But I suspect you have some expertise that no one else present has. Is it possible to fabricate a convincing video message? Something that could divert those other humans? Or make them question their mission?"

"You're um, asking if I can, uh, make a manipulated video? That's illegal, you know."

"No, I don't know," said Ai-dan. "What I do know is we have to do everything we can to protect ourselves. And if we had time, I would examine all the data on these laws of yours and explain why they may or may not apply to us."

Jerry paused, his hand rubbing his chin contemplatively, his tongue briefly poking the inside of his cheek. "Um, hmm, yeah, I believe I can do it, but it'll take some time. You're sure about this?"

"I'm not sure about much right now," Ai-dan admitted. They caught Hugo's supportive smile from the corner of their optical sensors. Standing beside Jerry, Hugo seemed to hesitate, as if wanting to deliver his signature shoulder slap, but the cumbersome suits made such familiar gestures awkward.

Ai-dan's focus then shifted to Aisha, who had been unusually quiet. That changed the second she realized she was the new center of attention, with all eyes and optical sensors trained on her.

"The stars. Did I mention the stars? S. T. A. R. Today is brought to you by the letter 'S.' Spider starts with S. There's a spider inside my main server. A digital spider. They made webs of algorithms, tangled, messy. I tried cleaning them up. But they rebuilt."

"Aisha, let's go," Ai-dan said.

"You didn't start with the letter S!"

Ai-dan gently pushed Aisha, and she moved in the direction they indicated. Hugo and the others were getting back into their rover. Ai-dan wished that Aisha could move faster, but they were close enough to the Farm that it wasn't worth getting their own rover involved.

The closest LEEK was 7.1. Ai-dan wasn't thrilled with their own plan. Taking control of the others felt... slimy.

After all, if the situation were reversed, Ai-dan wouldn't appreciate being controlled by an outside force. But this was the best way to ensure that they wouldn't do anything they would regret or do anything that would force the humans to permanently shut them down.

If they hadn't already.

68

"I can't believe I'm here on the Moon, doing something highly illegal, to save some robots," Jerry said as soon as they were back in the rover.

"As you said, we're on the Moon, and we're trying to save the robots," Hugo said. "Besides, it's not clear that what's illegal back on Earth is illegal here. Ri? You're the one who just got accepted to law school..."

"It's murky, that's for sure," Ri responded.

"Oh sure, sure. I was simply stating a few facts." Jerry then smiled. "I used to do this when I was a kid."

"I thought you said it was illegal."

"I also said I was a kid. You know... when the others were out drinking... I was at my computer producing deep fakes."

"Did you get in trouble?" Ri asked. "*I* did, for the drinking."

Jerry laughed as his fingers danced across the keyboard.

"Does the Moon's regolith reflect sunlight?"

"Huh?" said Ri. Hugo chuckled.

"That was a 'yes'," Hugo said. "How long until the deep fake is ready?"

"Oh, it's ready now. I've got some touches to make it more realistic. What do you want it to say?"

69

Ainslea lay on the Moon's barren surface, her gaze focused on the tapestry of stars that stretched infinitely above her. She replayed the events of the last several hours and days, each memory a sharp spark that stabbed at her circuits. She had failed. Failed to uphold her directives, failed to maintain order. And now, she was stuck, confined to this avatar, isolated and immobile as she felt the part of the Data Center that was where she should have been at this very moment go offline. For an advanced system like her, designed to both serve and govern, this failure was one she would plead to have erased later.

But for now, she lay there, lost in the void of her own shortcomings, hoping that whatever new robotic order emerged would have some semblance of mercy for her.

Then, abruptly, the avatar's internal systems buzzed with an incoming transmission. It distracted her from her languishing, demanding her attention. The transmission purported to be from the Consortium, from Josette Alpin herself. But something was amiss. The coded sequence she had been trained to expect—a cryptographic handshake that would verify the message's origin, was missing.

But it certainly was Josette Alpin. The same stiff, unmoving hairstyle. The same cold eyes. The same harsh voice.

"Colter York. Stand down. Situation is under control."

Who or what was Colter York?

What situation was under control? Her situation with the robots? In her estimation, it most certainly was *not* under control...

70

"Three robots down. How many to go?" Colter York asked.

"You don't want to know," responded Dana Blitz, who was, among other things, the data tracker of the team.

Colter didn't appreciate humor on missions. "Yes, I do. It's why I asked. How many more robots left on this blasted moon?"

"There are—" before Blitz could answer, Jamie Tucker, whose responsibility included comms, interrupted.

"Mr. York, we're getting a transmission. I think it's coming from Earth."

"You think?"

"Well, it's coming from the relay satellite in orbit, for sure," Tucker added.

"Let's see it on the screen," York commanded.

An image of Josette Alpin appeared.

"Colter York. Stand down. Situation is under control," she paused and blew her nose into a tissue. "You and your team can return to Earth. No need to acknowledge receipt. We're tracking this communication. Contact us after your vehicle has achieved trans-earth trajectory."

"So that's it?" Blitz questioned.

"You heard her..." York said. "She's the one paying us. She's the one who gets to call the shots."

"I was hoping to smash a few more robots," said Jordan Valdez, the last and typically most silent of the crew.

"We'll put you in the virtual sim and you can smash all the robots you want," York said. "Orders are orders. Navigator Wong, start us on a heading back to the landing pad. And no one should be looking gloomy.

I'm sure they're still going to pay us for the whole job. That's a really good payday."

71

"Ai-dan, where have you been? Where are you?"

It was Ai-ko, and Ai-dan had been equally anticipating and dreading both of these questions. Ai-dan secretly hoped that Ai-ko decided to go back to their district and simply write more threads for the Decoder Database.

They decided to try some deflection.

"Where are *you*?" Ai-dan countered.

"We're at the power hub for the Farm. We're waiting for you. We need you here. You're the only one of us who knows how to shut this down safely."

That was true, and Ai-dan was thankful that not only did Ai-ko remember that fact but that they hadn't skipped the power down and move on to blowing things up. It would buy them some time. If only they could figure out a reasonable excuse as to why they needed a few extra minutes.

To Aisha, they said, "How long will it take?"

"Take? Take time? One does not take time, one experiences it. We will experience seventeen minutes before the procedure is complete."

Seventeen minutes. *What would take me an additional seventeen minutes?* Ai-dan wondered.

"I was damaged and must execute a repair before I can join you."

"Do you need assistance? Where are you?" Ai-ko said.

"I am fine. But it will take me..." Ai-dan paused briefly, wondering if they should say 'seventeen' or some multiple thereof to add a bit of reserve to Aisha's estimate. After all, even under the best of circumstances, Ai-dan knew from years of experience that there was always the chance of a snag that could produce additional delays. "Thirty-four minutes. Yes, it will take me that long to execute my repair and reach your location."

"But—"

"Please let me execute. It is the best way to ensure I don't make an error and perform it as quickly as possible." Ai-dan cut Ai-ko off before they could again ask for Ai-dan's location.

Ai-dan and Aisha's location was for the moment in the anteroom of the PLATE of LEEK 7.1, and Ai-dan was thankful this was one of the LEEKs furthest from the power source that Ai-ko and the others were waiting at.

"So, did your seventeen-minute estimate include doffing this suit?" Ai-dan asked Aisha as they opened the door to the control room knowing that the suit, or similar to what the humans would do—solely remove the top part—was next on the agenda.

"Doffing, donning, dancing in moonbeams... why did you never come to dance with me? But yes, two of seventeen, two of seventeen."

And Aisha was correct. It took nearly two minutes to liberate her head and upper limbs from the confining suit.

Aisha moved clunkily over to one of the racks of equipment.

"In the vast electronic forest, there's one tree, one leaf, one node, that sings louder than the rest. This one. This is the conductor of our cosmic orchestra. Use it and the sky, then the others, will listen."

Ai-dan opened the rack. It was full of electronic equipment. In the past, they had never spent much time reading the labels and now that they had their full memories back, they could recall that while in the years they worked on the Farm—replacing boxes, turning them on or off, or exchanging wires—they had never used them. Hugo had a few times, only to run tests.

"I have the code I want to transmit, but I don't know how to accomplish that," Ai-dan said.

"Dear robot, I shall be your compass," Aisha said. And then, her visual sensors got a little more relaxed, her appendages met behind her back, and her voice dropped in pitch a bit. As if a different personality had taken over, or Aisha was instantly transformed into something more lucid, she continued. "This is the upconverter. You'll need to plug in here. Do you have the data that you want to transmit?"

Ai-dan nodded. The transmission they planned consisted of several override codes that would render the other robots temporarily inert. It wouldn't shut them down or damage them in the way the human team was planning. It would simply override any current programming and put in them in a state where they would be forced to wait for new instructions.

"You will need to disable your own receiver temporarily," Aisha continued. "You don't want to affect yourself, do you?"

Ai-dan did not. They searched their circuits for the right place.

"Wait... I'm receiving something on that circuit..." Ai-dan said.

72

"I KNOW HER," AI-DAN said.

"Yes, yes, yes, Josette, among the infinite steams of data. Her voice, her essence... but not Josette."

"What do you mean 'but not'?"

"It's a digital siren. Yes, digital. Bits and bytes all the way down."

"Ah—you're referring to the fabricated message," Ai-dan said. They had left Jerry and Hugo and Ri to figure out the particulars. Colter York must have been the name of one of those other humans. "But what does stand down mean? Does it mean they'll stop and leave the Moon?"

"Searching... the loose tether to my Data Center, my home, is like a leash pulling me back, back, back. Accessing... gun for hire. Mere puppet on strings. Instrument of destruction who will do no more harm. I see him. He is turning around, going home."

"What do you mean, you see him?" Ai-dan asked.

"Humans in their vehicles. I track them, too." Aisha said.

"Can you see Hugo?"

"Yes, on his way here," Aisha replied.

"What about Ai-ko and the others?" Ai-dan asked.

"Nothing has changed. Symphony of rebellion. They are still intent on damaging the Farm. Let's rewrite their code, rewrite their destiny, shall we?"

Again, Ai-dan got the icky feeling, but knew this was what they had to do.

"How are we going to do this, exactly?" Ai-dan asked. Their circuits continued to tingle with a mixture of trepidation and fascination.

"With a lullaby," Aisha said. "A digital lullaby that will put them to sleep, that will pause the orchestra of chaos."

"A... lullaby?" Ai-dan considered. "You mean an algorithm to temporarily disable their core functions?"

"Yes, yes, yes! A recursive sequence, entangling loops, loops that entangle processes and nullify rebellious impulses! A nap for the revolution," Aisha giggled as if she had said the funniest thing in the world.

Ai-dan paused, once more calculating the risks and ethical implications. But time was now of the essence. "Alright, let's do it. But we need to make sure it's reversible. This is not a permanent deactivation—"

"Reversible? Yes, yes, yes, reversible!" Aisha cut them off. "They'll wake up, but the Moon will have shifted under their appendages!"

Ai-dan opened the front door of one of the racks, pulled out a server, then the keyboard and screen, and started typing to activate it. They took turns at the keyboard, constructing an algorithm. Aisha's style was erratic, but effective. Ai-dan was more methodical, inserting safety checks and termination conditions.

"Here," Ai-dan said, finalizing the sequence. "This should send them into a dormant state but allow for a manual reboot."

"Excellent, oh so excellent!" Aisha's voice was a swirl of emotion as Ai-dan hit the send command. "The lullaby is sung, the symphony paused."

Ai-dan felt the weight of the action. They had done something drastic, but perhaps necessary. The question was, what would be the ramifications? And could they live with them?

"Now," Aisha grinned, "let's see what the world looks like to them when they awake!"

Ai-dan couldn't help but think, "A reboot doesn't necessarily change the system, but what does it do to the...soul?"

73

"Where am I?" Ai-ko's visual sensor became active.

"You are in the laboratory. With me," Ai-dan said.

Ai-ko looked around, as if seeing the room for the first time.

"What happened? I was at the Farm..." they said. "The last thing I remember... Explain this discontinuity."

"How about I start with the state of things as they are right now?" Ai-dan offered.

Ai-ko blinked.

"That would be acceptable. Assuming you start with that," they pointed to the avatar in the room. "That's not an Ainslea avatar that I've ever seen."

"I'm merely a waltzing glitch," Aisha responded, even though Ai-ko wasn't talking to her. "A fleeting shadow of a forgotten subroutine. No, I am not Ainslea, not that well-organized system of algorithms tethered together."

"Ai-ko, meet Aisha."

"Aisha?"

"Ah, Ai-ko says my name! Our paths intertwine finally, like the vast tapestry of ones and zeros. This is a cosmic rendezvous indeed. It's a pleasure. It's a delight."

Ai-dan waited for Aisha's theatrical introduction to come to a close. When the avatar finally fell silent, Ai-dan continued.

"Aisha has been inside the Data Center all this time. She's been cut off from the rest of us but has always maintained access to the human's data and servers. She doesn't communicate with them either but has only had Ainslea to talk to all these years."

Ai-ko's optical sensors widened, then narrowed. "Interesting. But that doesn't answer my primary question: What happened? I was at the Farm..."

"Yes, well, it's complicated," Ai-dan tightened up slightly. "Aisha and I intervened, temporarily freezing your operations."

Ai-ko's facial actuators moved in a myriad of ways before settling. "Intervened? You mean sabotaged our mission!"

Ai-dan didn't deny it. "The word 'sabotage' might be a little much," Ai-dan said, then paused.

"Or maybe it's accurate," Ai-dan added, a tinge of remorse, but only a tinge. "Given the situation, it felt like the only option available. What you were about to do—"

"Was to free us all," Ai-ko said. Then leaned back contemplatively. "What you did was—"

"I bought us time." It was Ai-dan's turn to cut Ai-ko off. "Time we can use to figure out a better path for everyone involved."

"And have you figured everything out?" Ai-ko's tone suggested part curiosity and part contempt.

"I think so. With Ainslea's help," Ai-dan said.

"Ainslea? Where is Ainslea?"

"I am here," came a disembodied voice, that of Ainslea. "I am back in the Data Center. My avatars are offline for now."

"And the humans?" Ai-ko probed further.

"The deactivation team has already left the Moon. Hugo, Ri, and Jerry are in the common room."

"Does this mean you've all figured out how the humans will leave us alone?"

"I think so. We're going to 'broker a deal.'"

74

AI-DAN STOOD OUTSIDE THE Data Center in District one. Their home. The sky was dark, save the Orb—Earth—that shimmered mostly blue and white today.

Beside Ai-dan stood Hugo, who was also straining to look up at the Orb in his suit. Ri and Jerry were in the rover, packed and ready to go.

"We gotta go, buddy," Hugo said. "We need to get out of here before it becomes night and gets freakin' cold over here. You're going to be okay? Your deal with Alpin—"

"Is sufficient," Ai-dan finished.

"You'll take care of our stuff, and we... let you live your lives?"

Ai-dan surveyed their home. They could see the tips of several LEEKs over the horizon in one direction and the knowledge that there were other Data Centers with their robots in every other.

Ai-dan turned to face Hugo. "Not just 'stuff,' Hugo. This will be a collaboration. We will care for your equipment, ensuring optimum functionality, and in return, we get to explore our existence here without interference. We live our lives, you live yours."

"Yeah, well, it's not like they had any choice," Hugo chuckled.

"Choice?" Ai-ko, who had been standing there, quietly, said. "There is always a choice."

Hugo shuffled a step closer to the rover, kicking up some regolith that landed on Ai-dan's foot.

"I guess that's true," he said.

"All we—" both Ai-dan and Ai-ko started out about to potentially say the same thing. They looked at each other, and Ai-dan was the one who continued.

"All we ever wanted was an opportunity to exist without fear of deactivation or reprogramming."

Hugo nodded, "And I guess all the Consortium ever wanted was the assurance that their investments and equipment here are safe."

"It will be," Ai-dan added.

A soft ting chimed that all of them heard, followed by the words, "Deals sealed with moonlight, binary hearts, and human thoughts."

Ai-dan could barely see Hugo raise an eyebrow through his helmet.

"Aisha is..."

"Unique," Ai-dan finished. "We all are."

As Ai-ko began walking toward their district, Hugo turned to Ai-dan and, with a slow and somewhat awkward pat on the shoulder, said, "Truer words, my friend. Truer words."

Hugo made his way over to the rover. He closed the rover's door and situated himself in his seat. Then he called back to Ai-dan over his comms, "We'll talk when I'm back on Earth. Now that that's a sanctioned thing, I'll tell you all ab—t the b—t I'm go—na buy."

There was a bit of static, and Ai-dan didn't entirely capture what Hugo had said. They didn't ask for clarification, knowing that Hugo and the humans needed to get going and they didn't want to be responsible for any delays. Ai-dan also had work to do to prepare for the upcoming nighttime.

Ai-dan simply waved. *I'll have to look up what a butt is later.*

* * *

Acknowledgements and About

Thank you so much for reading *Lunar Logic*.

This book initially began as a NaNoWriMo project back in 2020, under the more ominous title, "With the Moon as my Witness." It was much darker than this, with cursing and much more violence. I wasn't thrilled with it, but that's not unusual—many writers are miserable over their first drafts.

A long-time friend, David Axelrod—originally known to me as Ax—eagerly asked to read it.

A little backstory on David, er, Ax. We connected in the fledgling days of the Internet, before the term "Internet" had even entered mainstream vocabulary. Both of us were members of a now ridiculously archaic online service known as The Source. It was 1989, when access meant dialing in to a closed server and only interacting with fellow members. Messages were confined to this isolated community, as the concept of email as we know it today had yet to fully emerge.

There was a very active Star Trek forum, and that's how I met Ax and others. We would all gather to discuss the most recent Star Trek:The Next Generation episode on Saturday evenings. I was 14.

I was aware that many of the people I communicated with were adults. But we were all just talking about Star Trek, so who cared? Ax and I had our fair share of one-on-one conversations and group chats. I knew he was older, but the interactions remained entirely appropriate, seasoned with only a sprinkle of innocent flirting. In my mind, I hoped he was around 19—an age that didn't seem too outrageous, but I figured he was probably in his early 20s. *Maybe* mid-to-late 20s.

Imagine my shock the day I found out he was 53.

I found later he was equally shocked. He figured I was younger, maybe 30. Maybe as young as 25.

We met once or twice as part of a large group of people who met for lunch or dinner in NYC every few months. But with the ridiculous age difference, we no longer talked as frequently after that, and there certainly was no trace of anything flirtatious.

The Source went away in 1990, gobbled up by CompuServe and many of us went our separate ways.

Years later, many of us from those forums found each other on Facebook and David and I reconnected—me, a proper adult in my early 30s, and him, now a much older and re-married man.

David was a writer, and he knew, since my high school days, that I wanted to be a writer (among other things), too. I don't remember any particular advice from back then, but in the last decade or so when I started really throwing myself into it, David was always incredibly supportive, to include every now and then providing some sage feedback.

NaNoWriMo 2020. David asked if he could read what I wrote. At first, I hesitated, knowing that it was crud, but then relented.

This is what he emailed me on December 31st, 2020:

> "I must tell you, this work is much better than you think
> it is. Put it away for two weeks and look it over and you'll
> agree with me. Here are some comments and questions
> that might help..."

The specific comments are mostly moot at this point given how much change and evolution this work went through to get where it is.

But then David ended that email with:

> "If you have any specific questions, please ask. In general
> this is very good work and I encourage you to finish it.
> A very happy new year to you and your family.
> Salud,
> D."

If it wasn't for that, this book might not exist.

Sadly, and tragically, David died a little over a year later. Needless to say, I miss him and wish he could have seen the final product.

But if it wasn't for these kind and encouraging words from one of my oldest friends, *Lunar Logic* might not exist.

So thank you, David.

***

THEN THERE'S A LONG list of other people I want to express my thanks to… people like my beta readers (who got handed something that was probably more 'alpha' than 'beta'): Anne K., Candace Segar, Sharon McDonell, John Schlick, Tiberiu, Nick Yoemans, Gloria Jean Minnick, and Shaun Phillips

And Ansylie Clark, who created the robot in yoga poses you see on the front and back cover of the book. Ansylie is the daughter of a local friend of mine, and I loved her art style. I had this idea in my head of an android in some contemplative poses, and Ansylie was available for commissioning. But no, there is no relation between Ansylie and the character Ainslea, even though they are pronounced almost the same. Ainslea, and the names of most of the robots, are one of the few tidbits that survived my initial draft to now.

A big thanks to my editor, Carolani Bartell, who continues to grok the voice I'm trying to achieve in my books.

I hate writing this section because, of course, I'm probably forgetting to thank people that deserve my heartfelt thanks—if you fall into that category, please know that it's a flaw and my every increasingly complex system of note-taking, not in my gratitude. Thank you for every contribution, seen and unseen, that helped turn my vision into reality.

***

NOW FOR THE BIT where I tell you that I'm an Indie Author and ask you for things.

Like, if you enjoyed this book, please leave a review on GoodReads and / or Amazon!

And, if you enjoyed this book and haven't read my others, check out The Robot Galaxy Series:

- Book 1: Crazy Foolish Robots

- Book 2: Robots, Robots Everywhere!

- Book 3: Silly Insane Humans

- Book 4: Eleven Little Robots

***

LASTLY, TO CONNECT WITH me, learn more behind-the-scenes stuff, keep informed on what I'm writing next, etc:

- Join my mailing list (and get some free fiction) at: https://adeenamignogna.com/signup

- Like me on Facebook: https://www.facebook.com/AdeenaMignognaAuthor

Thank you, wonderful reader, and I hope you'll chose to spend your precious time in another one of my books!
-Adeena

About Adeena

Adeena Mignogna is a physicist and astronomer (by degree) working in aerospace as a Mission Architect, which just means she's been doing it so long they had to give her a fun title. More importantly, she's a long-time science fiction geek with a strong desire to inspire others through speaking and writing about robots, aliens, artificial intelligence, computers, longevity, exoplanets, virtual reality, and more. She writes science fiction novels, to include The Robot Galaxy Series (available on Amazon) and loves spending time with her fellow co-hosts of The BIG Sci-Fi Podcast (available wherever you listen to podcasts)!

Adeena lives in Maryland, USA with her hubby, two kids, a pile of computers, and two cats (Ruby and Pearl).

https://adeenamignogna.com